A RAW MIX OF CARELESSNESS AND LONGING

Cecelia Frey

BRINDLE & GLASS

LIBRARY AND ARCHIVES CANADA CATALOGUING IN PUBLICATION
Library and Archives Canada Cataloguing in Publication
 Frey, Cecelia
A raw mix of carelessness and longing / Cecelia Frey.
ISBN 978-1-897142-36-3
    I. Title.
PS8561.R48R39 2009 C813'.54 C2008-907718-0

LIBRARY OF CONGRESS NUMBER: 2009920290

Editor: Lee Shedden
Cover image: Zoe Chan, istockphoto.com

 Canada Council Conseil des Arts
for the Arts du Canada

 Canadian   Patrimoine
Heritage   canadien

Brindle & Glass is pleased acknowledges the financial support to its publishing program from the Government of Canada through the Book Publishing Industry Development Program (BPIDP) and the Canada Council for the Arts.

Brindle & Glass is committed to protecting the environment and to the responsible use of natural resources. This book is printed on 100% post-consumer recycled and ancient-forest-friendly paper. For more information, please visit www.oldgrowthfree.com.

Brindle & Glass Publishing
www.brindleandglass.com

1 2 3 4 5 12 11 10 09
PRINTED AND BOUND IN CANADA

for Doug, Christopher and Brendan

PART
ONE

BREAKING BREAD

Terrabain Street goes around and around in my head like a song I can't get rid of. It's driving me crazy, I said to Zeke. It's like a stuck CD.

Write it down, Zeke said. Get it out of your head and down on paper.

I don't know how, I said.

Write it like a song, he said. You've written a hundred songs.

A song has verses and a chorus and a bridge in the middle, I said. Life's all over the place.

A song's all over the place, too, he said. Until you put it in order.

I wouldn't know where to begin, I said.

Just write it as it comes, he said. Whatever pops into your head.

What pops into my head is a picture of Paquette appearing in the Popilowski doorway holding up a huge black iron pot full of fish soup as though he was going to pull a rabbit out of a silk hat. I hear him pronounce in his uplifted voice, "One big happy family!"

And music, always music, that summer *The Unforgettable Fire*, which Jamey was still listening to like a fiend even though it had been out a couple of years. Against that background, Beth and me would make faces at each other and giggle. We'd be standing at the kitchen counter slathering soda crackers with peanut butter, while our moms, who'd just come home from work, hers from Rosa's Beauty Salon,

1

mine from Guiseppe's Pasta, both on their feet all day, were sprawled at the kitchen table with their shoes kicked off, smoking up a blue haze and looking grateful.

"Jeez, Romeo, you're a lifesaver," Rita would breathe out with her smoke. She was the only one in the house who called Paquette by his first name. "You're a romeo, all right, you old lover, you," she'd tease him and her brown eyes would fire up.

My mom Tree, short for Teresa, Tree Turner née Cellini, would shoot him one of her baleful looks, which didn't necessarily mean she was displeased, just that she was Italian.

Although he must've been past sixty and had just carried that heavy pot up a steep flight of stairs, Paquette would bounce into the room as though he had springs on his legs. Pouf! He appeared, rosy cheeks, curly grey hair, bushy moustache dancing above his wide smile. When I close my eyes, Paquette and the rooming house are one, his face superimposed on the two-storey white clapboard with its wonky verandah, high sloped roof and two windows on top like lopsided eyes.

He was the caretaker watching the furnace in winter, cutting the grass in summer, raising his granddaughter, Marie, or trying to—but the Corset Lady was the anchor. She'd been there forever, at the back across the hall from Paquette, her room cluttered with corset makings. I still feel her big lap, her mound of flesh that kept me safe. I still hear her croaky voice telling me stories about my father being a great man who really loved me even though he took off when I was a baby. He had to, according to her. He got an important call from Cape Canaveral, and between that and being a movie star he never had time to come back for a visit. "What d'y' expect then, love?" she'd say in her English accent. "He can't get away from where he's orbiting the moon."

Upstairs at the front in three cramped rooms under the sharp angle of the roof lived us: the widow Tree and her daughter Lilah, as we were known. At the back, on the other side of the stairs, in a similar space, lived the four Popilowskis: Rita and Popi and Beth and Jamey. It was a rabbit warren, all right, but it wasn't as bad as it sounds because, in effect, we all lived together, always in each other's rooms, so familiar we didn't even stop to knock, just hollered in, "Are you home?" or "Hi, whatcha doin?"

It must have been a Friday, the picture in my mind, because Paquette always made fish soup on Fridays. With a flourish, he'd set the pot in the middle of the table, straighten and look around at us all in wide-eyed amazement at the wonder of life.

Then Rita's eyes would snap us to attention. "Hey, you girls," she'd say, "get some dishes on the table. Me, I've had the biscuit." Rita with the biscuit still crackled with more energy than most people fully charged. Maybe it was her red hair. Maybe it was her three-inch heels and her thin legs tensed for takeoff.

Then Popi would come out from the back shadows, lurching on his stump and his one good foot, folding himself down onto his wooden chair and reaching for a pack of cigarettes, yelling at us to turn down that goddamned noise.

I never did know Beth and Jamey's dad by any other name except Popi, short for Popilowski, and when I think of him, I think of Beckett, as in Samuel, *Waiting for Godot* and all that, which we hit on in grade 12. I couldn't understand a word of it at the time, but now, having been in the music business for fifteen years, I can see how you might wait for a call all your life, sit by the phone waiting for a call that never comes. But which you think is coming any minute. That's the pitiful thing, the way you imagine your little demo tape out in the world with somebody listening to it, when in reality it hasn't even made its way out from the bottom of the in-basket.

"How do you stand your dad?" I said to Beth once. I never would've said that to Jamey. Jamey was very sensitive about that subject.

"How about your mom?" Beth answered.

Right on, I thought, but no way was I going to admit it.

"At least my mom isn't writing The Great Epic," I said.

That was the worst, when I'd go across the hall to the Popilowski apartment looking for Beth or Jamey and Popi would be sitting at the kitchen table silhouetted by the window light. Day after day, he hunched over his word processor, his thin nicotine-stained fingers curved above the keys, his green visor clamped to his forehead, so still he might have been a corpse, except if I'd go close, he'd look up at me with two deep pools of black water.

Rita would sometimes roll her eyes at him and mutter, "crazy old coot," but mostly she was like Tammy Wynette, the way she stood by her man.

The thing was, writing his epic was what had kept Popi going ever since he had come home from Viet Nam sixteen years before. First, he got Rita pregnant with Jamey, then he started right in on it, and Rita was so glad to have him back even minus a foot, she didn't give him much of a hard time about anything.

Although sometimes she'd say, "whyn't you act like any normal human being, for Chrissake!" But she meant the writing. "Like a damned brooding hen," she'd say. But on those one-big-happy-family nights, he would swing himself over to the fridge and the beer caps would fly and once again it was Friday night and the beginning of freedom, the best of times, like the start of summer. Beth and me would get busy with the table and, after they got their second wind, Rita and Tree would hustle up some bread and cheese and salami and Jamey would swagger in wafting smells of crank grease and motor oil because of his new job at PetroCan and my heart would skip a beat the way it always did right from the first time I saw him swinging on the creaky front gate of the rooming house and me and Tree standing on the dusty sidewalk, having got off at the wrong bus stop and walking six blocks in the scorching heat of a prairie July sun, me with my cracked-head doll, Tree with her shopping bag in one hand and the suites for rent page in the other, looking up with her worried face at the windows that we would be looking out of for all the years to come, and me looking at Jamey, with all his freckles standing out across his nose and his tongue licking up a white ice cream cone that would have tasted so cool on my tongue and in my parched throat, and his blue blue eyes piercing right into me even then.

That first love, the most important one. How it defines love for you for the rest of your life. How it determines all your other loves and so your life. How it can make all your other loves happy, or can make them sad. How it can stand between you and other people who might try and love you. How it can stand between you and other people you might try and love.

I can't remember ever not being in love with Jamey. Even when we'd play aggies kneeling in the dirt and he'd tell me we were playing for funsies and then, after winning all my marbles, changing it to keeps, I didn't hate him. And I was so stupid or maybe gullible that I fell for it more than once. "Come on," he'd say, "this time it really will be for funsies. Honest." And I'd look into those blue eyes that seemed so true and say yes. Maybe it was the music inside him even then that so appealed to me, music calling to music. Maybe it was the lightness of his body moving to a rhythm he heard in his head even before he always had a Walkman plugged into his ears. Rita said he came into the world rocking, arms and legs twisting and jerking. From the moment he could stand, pulling himself up on the rail, he rocked his crib clean across the room. And before he could stand, he would sit and whack his back against the end board and move it like that, so desperate he was for rhythm she said.

The Popilowskis' table overlooked the back where, the other side of the gravel lane, a hill rose up. When I looked straight across, my eye came against a wall of brush. In winter it was grey like Paquette's bush of hair and moustache, but in summer green. As my eye travelled down, there was Wong next door, as usual on a warm evening out working in his garden. There was a ramshackle garage and Jamey's Sunbeam up on blocks. When he was sixteen, cars were even more important to Jamey than his guitar, maybe because he was always leaving home and a car gave him something to do it in. And that little white Sunbeam, bucket seats and four on the floor, takes prime spot because it was the first, the beginning of a long string of cars, each one his pride and joy at the start. He was always so excited, each time he made a trade he always had such high hopes. Strip her down. Set her up. Motor, transmission, body. "Howja like that baby, eh?" he'd beam like a proud new father, while I sat on an abandoned tire, nothing but admiration shining my eyes.

In summer, the green lace of Paquette's trees, suckering crabs that he called an orchard, only partially covered the sight of a disassembled chassis and engine innards strewn on the ground,

"What an eyesore to look at all day." Popi's twitchety voice comes in on the soundtrack of the film that runs in my head. "When're you gonna get that scrap heap going? And get that goddamn thing out of your ear when I'm talking to you."

I remember when we used to fight/just about every night . . . the first Gun Wylde single to make it onto the charts had its start right there those nights in the Popilowski kitchen.

"After supper. I plan to work on it after supper." Jamey's voice was quick and he looked down at his plate.

"Yeah, like every other night lately. Off with those tattooed yahoos playing that guitar."

. . . *I remember always being wrong/cause right never seemed to be my song* . . .

And Rita's loud defence of her boy, "Jamey's doin real good with that music."

And Tree's relentless gloom, "Lilah's always playing that loud music. That music gives me a headache."

And Beth's silence, so important, so necessary, her role in the family like sizing, that stuff you put between raw wallboard and paint, to balance the moisture, so one material doesn't draw too much from the other.

"It needs money," said Jamey. "I gotta put some money into it, that's all. I gotta get some money." He was drumming his thumbs on the table and jerking his head to a rhythm inside himself. . . . *Well, I say I'm gonna be, gonna be, gonna be* . . . His mop of curly hair would have been bouncing except he'd cut it off and had spikes.

"Throwing good money after bad." Popi pecked at a crust of bread, caught a nibble between his teeth, stared straight ahead at nobody. "Sell it for parts. That's all it's good for."

. . . *screaming/i wanna be, wanna be, wanna be/i wanna be/a contender!*

I didn't have to look at Jamey to see the hurt look in his eyes. To attack Jamey's car was to attack him. But it was only Popi who could truly wound him, and his reaction to that hurt was defiance. "It's my money," he'd mumble. "I guess I'll do what I want with it."

"Do you two have to start?" said Rita. "Can't we have one meal in peace?"

"I feel perfectly peaceful." Popi's twitchy chittering ran on. "What's the problem? Can't I talk to my own son? You call talking arguing? Cars are a waste of money, that's all I'm saying."

"That's the trouble with Lilah," said Tree. "All she does is listen to that music. That's why she's so fat, she eats all the time and listens to that music. That's why she's got those heavy legs."

"All I'm saying," said Popi. "They saw you coming with that one all right."

"Who's got heavy legs?" I said.

"You have heavy legs."

"I don't have heavy legs."

"Whaddayou call them things there?"

"I need a vehicle," said Jamey. "For my equipment."

"You call that a vehicle?" said Popi. "A vehicle goes someplace. That's what the word means, something that goes someplace."

"Lookit that." Paquette shoved his leg out in front of Tree and pulled up his pant leg. That's a heavy leg."

"That's not heavy," said Tree. "For a man."

"I'll have some money soon," Jamey's drumming intensifying . . . *my head got so full of rage/frustration pounding at its cage* . . . "Next month, when school's out. I'll get more hours."

"I don't know where you get such heavy legs," said Tree. "Italians are supposed to have thin legs."

"How about you, you got heavy legs."

"They are now, but when I was young I had thin legs."

"Money spent on cars," said Popi. "May as well flush it down the toilet."

"You never had thin legs."

"I did have thin legs."

"It's my money," Jamey said.

"Do we have to have this kind of talk when we eat?" said Rita. "This kind of talk gives me a stomach ache."

"What's with you?" said Popi. "We're just talking, we're just having a family discussion. What's your problem?"

"You didn't know me then," Tree said. "How do you know what kind of legs I had?"

"My feet hurt, that's my problem. How would you like to stand on your feet all day up to your elbows in hair."

"I saw pictures, " I said. "You have those old pictures."

"Jamey's doing okay. He don't need no hassling."

"He'd do a helluva lot better if he'd quit wasting his time on cars and that music."

"Italians have thin legs," said Tree. "I don't know what happened to you."

"No way I'll ever quit music," said Jamey. "Forget it."

"All that caterwauling on the verandah, sound like a buncha cats in heat."

"That's the style nowadays," Rita inserted. "Maybe I don't like the way someone wants her hair cut but I don't argue with her."

"I'm only half Italian," I said. "Thank God." The big problem was I didn't know what the other half of me was.

Tree's thin lips crooked down at the outer edges. She gave me her black Italian scowl. "Every other way you look like me, except for the legs."

"You gotta keep up with the trends." Rita picked up her beer.

"I don't look like you. Name one thing where I look like you."

"What you mean? The hair, the eyes, the nose, the mouth." As Tree went through the list, she gestured with taut open fingers at each item, finishing with splayed hand palm up and flat out across the table. "Name one thing where you *don't* look like me."

I opened my mouth even though I didn't know what to answer, but then I didn't have to because Jamey dropped his bombshell. "What I'm gonna quit is school," he said. "No way I'm going back in September."

Wow, did that stop the conversation. All we could hear in the silence was Jamey's drumming, now incorporating fingers as well as thumbs. . . . *i'm practising my right hook/working on my dirty look/'cause i remember/things i wanted to say to you* . . . "I'm gonna get a job that pays real money," he said.

"You don't always get what you want in this life," Popi said. "And stop that goddamned racket."

Jamey's fingers stopped in midair, as though they'd suddenly been chopped off. For an instant there was total silence. Jamey, needing to fill it and needing something to do with his hands, reached for the cheese and salami. "Something that pays better than that garage."

"You better be careful. You'll end up with no job at all."

"Don't quit one job until you have another. That's my advice," said Paquette, who'd been through the Great Depression.

"No sweat," said Jamey. "I'll get another job easy."

"You kids nowadays with your up-yours attitude," said Popi. "You got a lot to learn."

"At least he has a job," said Rita.

"What sort of crack is that?" Popi was looking at the salt and pepper in the middle of the table. "You think writing an epic isn't a job, try it sometime. An epic is sweating blood, that's what an epic is. Isn't that right, Paquette?"

"Right," said Paquette and would have added to it, but Popi rushed on.

"There. Y'see. Paquette knows. He's around when I'm sweatin it."

"Watching them bottles go past all day at the brewery," said Paquette, ladling more soup into his bowl. "Man that was a job and a half. I nearly went to sleep there, my head in a bottle, going along the belt there."

"Same with the tortellini," said Tree. "All those plastic containers. My eyes want to close."

"I make more with my pension than you do at Rosa's," said Popi to Rita. "What kind of money can you make?"

Paquette cleared his throat as if he was going to interrupt but he didn't.

"I earned my money in Nam," said Popi. "I paid my dues. I earned every bit of that pension. You think it's fun hopping around on one foot? You think it's fun, try it sometime."

"You don't hafta hop around," said Rita. "If you'd wear that foot they gave you."

"I'm not wearing no goddamned false foot," said Popi. "If I can't have my own foot, to hell with it." He reached for another slice of bread and his hand twitched in a spasm against the empty plate. "Is there any more bread around this place?" he darted a look at Beth.

Jamey couldn't stand it when Popi started coming apart like that. I'd even seen it where he turned on Rita after she'd sprung to his side against Popi. So many times, he'd try to soft-pedal it. "Writing an epic must be like writing music," he said. "Music's hard."

So many times he was met with another rejection.

9

"Isn't anything like music," said Popi. "An epic's serious. Not a bunch of weirdos sitting around smoking pot."

"What pot?"

"Think I don't know? Whaddaya take me for?"

Rita's antennae shot up. "I don't want you smoking that pot. I read where pot isn't good for your brain."

"Pot's not gonna hurt nothing," said Jamey. "It's no worse than tobacco."

"How about Brian?" said Beth and I thought, oh, no, but what can you expect from someone who likes the Beach Boys?

Rita's head switched direction to where she was looking straight at Beth. She was holding her fork like a spear in her small fist. "What about Brian?"

"They had to take him to emergency," said Beth. "After Rudy's party last Saturday. They called his mother to the hospital."

"It was nothing," said Jamey, shooting Beth a killer glare. In Beth's defence, I happened to know that she was sincerely worried about her brother.

"What you mean nothing?" Rita said. "If they had to take him to the emergency."

"It wasn't pot," said Jamey. "Somebody at the party gave him something else."

"What?"

"I dunno what. Some pills or something."

"That's even worse!" Rita dropped her fork and lit a cigarette.

"Well they're not gonna give it to me. Don't worry, I'm smarter than Brian."

"Yeah," said Popi. "They can slip you somethin and you don't even know it. You stay away from that bunch."

"You need some different friends," said Beth.

"You need a brain," said Jamey. "And how about you and Gord? Parking on the front street with your feet sticking out the window. In broad daylight."

"What's this?" said Popi, turning on Beth.

"I just had my head on Gord's lap," said Beth. "We were listening to his new tape."

10

Popi's head turned to Rita. "Ain't you watching these kids?"

"How can I watch them when I'm at work all day? You're the one who's home."

"How am I supposed to know what's happening at the front? I watch the back, you watch the front."

"So now it's my fault. How come everything around here always turns out to be my fault? That's what I'd like to know."

"You're the mother. Mothers are supposed to know what their daughters are doing."

"Yeah? How about fathers and sons? Your son's gonna end up in emergency and what do you do about it?"

"Look, young lady," Popi said to Beth. "No more parking with your feet out the window, that's all I gotta say."

"No more parking, period." Cigarette in left hand, Rita picked up her fork with her right and jabbed it into a sausage. She looked around on the table. "Beth, go get the ketchup, will you?"

"Get us a cold beer while you're up," said Popi.

"Jeez," said Rita. "I did three perms today. It must've been a hundred in that place. And no air. It's a wonder I didn't pass out from that setting solution. God knows what it's doing to my lungs. And then you have to pick something to bitch about the minute I get in the door . . ."

"That's the trouble with young people nowadays," said Paquette, putting his elbows on the table and puffing himself up for his regular after-dinner speech of fatherly advice. "What they don't know, you're more free when you got something to do than when you don't got something to do. You're more free when you got somebody than when you got nobody. When you got nothing to do and nobody to do it for then you got nothing to live for so you might as well kick the bucket right then and there."

"I can't understand how come you look like me every other way," said Tree.

"What's wrong with this ketchup?" screeched Rita, holding the ketchup bottle in her hand and looking down at a piddle of watery red in her bowl. "Who's been watering the ketchup again? It's pure water! If there's one thing I can't stand it's watery ketchup. Somebody around this house has been putting water in the ketchup and I would like to know who!"

She smashed her cigarette into an overflowing ashtray. Just then a big bruiser of a fly nose-dived its way in through the open window, cutting a swath clean across the table. Popi half raised himself on his one good foot, at the same time picking up a folded newspaper and swatting the air. "Will someone get that goddamn fly?" he shouted.

Ketchup in hand, Rita scraped back her chair, leaped past everybody to get to the window, open wide to try and catch a trickle of air in the summer heat. With all the strength of her hundred and five pounds, she flung the bottle high and wide. Then she marched back to her place at the table, flumped herself into her chair, and picked up her fork. Popi sank back into his chair. The fly droned off into the apartment.

Nobody said a word. Nobody looked at anybody else. From where I sat I could see Wong shuffling from garden shed to plot where the rows were straight as ruled lines in a notebook, the little green shoots precise squiggles like Chinese script. As I watched, his slow hands picked up a knife from a bench and slit a peat pot clean down, from top to bottom, without disturbing even a tendril of root. I was so struck by his skill and the quiet order of his life, I think now that part of me, even then, must've been longing for such order. I wondered if he'd seen that bottle arc high, high into the air. I wondered what he might have thought. Whatever, he just kept on, so patient and methodical, like the regular beat of practising music scales, which I felt myself responding to, even then.

NIGHTS IN PARADISE

I remember a soft evening freshness coming through the windows, wide open to chase away the hot stuffiness of a prairie midsummer day. Unlike where I live now, it always cooled off there at night. Jamey would be bent over his guitar, and after a while we'd say, "C'mon Jamey. C'mon, we wanta dance," and he'd play us a slow one, and he'd sing, too, his voice wobbling all over the register, "Straight From the Heart." Beth and me were learning to dance the waltz and the tango in phys ed. We'd try to put in those pauses where you balance on one foot and dangle the other in the air, but we'd unbalance each other and topple.

Saturday nights, Beth and me spent a lot of time doing our nails and hair and pretending that's what we wanted to do more than anything else in the world. Like if Bryan Adams knocked at the door, forget it. No thanks Bryan, we'd rather stick around here with our blow dryers and curling irons and Dippity-do and white freckles of pimple cream all over our faces, preening and bogeying around, singing *la te da* like in Van Morrison and waving our cigarettes in the air, pretending we had long holders, which we'd seen in old movies and thought looked oh so cool. We'd let down the tops of our robes and twitch our bare shoulders, Beth's pale and delicate, mine brown and deep-fleshed. We'd pull our robes tight and swing our hips at Jamey who had his ear to the tape deck trying to pick out a chord progression and ignoring us. We'd turn all his dials and flip all his switches, then fall on the couch and laugh until our sides ached. We'd leap on him and tickle him until he threatened us with no smokes.

"C'mon Jamey, teach us some chords," we'd whine and he actually condescended to do so. But since there was only one guitar and that was Jamey's, we mostly did the vocals. We got pretty good, too. We could sing pretty good harmony, the three of us together, as long as it wasn't one of Jamey's compositions. He was the only one who could sing them—to do them justice, that is. He was the only one who could play them, too, which was a problem when he got a band, because each performance was different depending on how he was feeling, and no one, including him, could predict what he was going to do. He was always improvising. That was his genius: his intuition and spontaneity, which was what I lacked. When he wasn't using his guitar—which would only be when he was at work or school—he let me practise on it, which I did, methodically, one chord over and over again until I got it right. But Jamey was all spontaneity, nothing but. If his fingers hit an extra string on a D chord, so what, he more or less got it right and he always had the rhythm to back it up. But as Zeke explained years later, his natural talent was also his flaw, because it kept him from developing. So then Zeke had his work cut out for him.

But I'm getting ahead of myself, putting the middle where the beginning should be.

From the earliest I can remember, Jamey was always making up songs in his head. Anything was an excuse for a song, for a chance to beat out rhythm and rhyme. *Rag picker rag picker rag picker rock, gunnysack gunnysack gunnysack back.* Popi'd yell at him to for God's sake take out the garbage and Jamey'd pick up the brown paper bag and boogie his way to the door, tossing the bag from one arm to the other, spilling chewed chicken bones and soggy potato peelings all over Rita's clean floor, singing *Oh those mean old trash can blues.* Or, *sizzle me baby*, he'd screech, frying himself up a hamburger and sliding the toes of his Reeboks across the linoleum, jerking his neat bum up tight, playing his pancake flipper like it was an España.

Music was running through his head always, like to drive him crazy, or maybe sane, because it was like rhythm gave him some grounding, like if he shook the world to jelly he could keep himself together, and it must've got into me from him, because when I was doing ordinary things like walking home from school or washing dishes, I'd be counting a beat in my head and I'd wake up in the morning with a song in my head that'd stay there the whole day.

In those days, Jamey never wrote anything down. That would have been too organized. But at some point, I started to make notes, and the first song that got down on paper, he made up for me.

I have to admit that Tree was right about me in my early teens. Fat and shapeless pretty well described it. And I was always scowling, Tree said because I watched too much TV, but I think it was a genetic thing because she was always scowling too, especially when she'd come home from work and I'd have my music blasting and be singing along. Once, she ripped my tape, actually Jamey's tape, out of the deck and stomped it with the heel of her shoe. I didn't know how to tell Jamey, but when I did he said I couldn't help my mother. But to get back to TV, one thing I watched were those morning talk shows, and as I said to Tree when she found out I was skipping school and raised holy hell, you can actually learn more by not going to school. Like, I learned if you tossed a hundred toothpicks on the floor every night then picked each one up separately without bending your knees, you could reduce your waistline about a hundred inches in a week, which was the amount mine needed reducing because of Tree's Italian descent.

I got Beth to do it with me. I could always talk her into anything. Beth was small like Rita and her waistline would've been reduced to a minus if it'd worked, so luckily it didn't—maybe because we only did it three nights. It wasn't hard to find more interesting things to do, like cleaning the toilet. Anyways, there we were, bending and groaning, when Jamey slouched into our apartment, his guitar swinging like a giant claw from his right arm. "What're you guys doing?" he said in that soft quick way of his, slurring all the words together. So we told him and right on the spot he struck a chord. I can still hear the way his voice cracked between boy and man when he went into his performance: *try picking up toothpicks, it's the thing to do/try picking up toothpicks, lose a pound or two.*

Those were the words I wrote on a little scrap of paper so I wouldn't forget, maybe not the greatest lyrics but it was the performance that counted. The song went more like: *hey then baba you wanna pick up a toothpick or two ordoo/ well now that's just the thing to do/ well now Lilah baba you can lose a pound well I said abound or two/ or maybe four, or more/ or maybe a hundred and ten/ well then I'll getcha in these ever lovin arms again/ yeah my sweeta little cuddle bun* . . . And he'd toss his long curly hair and squeeze tight his eyes and rock his body forward and back on his heels then forward again and swung his guitar around on his hip.

When he started putting songs down on paper, I collected as much as I could, some torn off penny match folders or crumpled inside paper napkins. I put them in brown envelopes, all the bits and pieces I picked up over the years. He never kept anything and I never threw anything away, anything of Jamey that is. But I couldn't save what he threw away or what he wrote on the back of his hand. Or his performances. Which was a shame, because that was the real Jamey—sliding, strutting, moving to the music.

That was his magic. Even his first guitar, which cost all of fifty bucks, which he bought with money he got delivering flyers, he made sound like something. He put so much energy into it, like he was strangling somebody at crotch level. He kept snapping strings, ping zing this way and that. He played that thing until his fingers bled and every time he got some money ahead he traded up.

He never took any lessons because where was the money? Anyway, nobody ever took him seriously. "All that hollering," Popi said. "Do something useful for a change. Get out here and help your mother," he'd yell into the bedroom where Jamey sat on the edge of his bed with his guitar. "Don't you have any homework?" he'd yell.

Rita liked it, though. "What's that one called?" she'd shout, dancing around on her spiked heels when she came home from work at Rosa's, high stepping over to the fridge door, leaning into the fridge and wagging her bottom, her short skirt hiking up shorter. How I wished I had those Tina Turner legs instead of my Italian ones.

The Corset Lady was another of a select audience who liked our music. Or said she did. She was old even before Tree and I arrived on

Terrabain Street, and ten years later she couldn't make it up the stairs any more. So we'd put on a performance for her down in her room in winter or out in the backyard in summer, harmonizing and Beth and me dancing. "How do you do that?" she'd say, wonder in her voice, shaking her tangle of unbelievable black hair, jiggling the soft pouches of her cheeks, their cracks filled with red rouge. "That's lovely," she'd say. "Yous are great kids, entertaining an old fogey like me."

But Jamey longed for an audience bigger than me and Beth and Rita and the Corset Lady. That happened when he got a chance to play at a school dance at St. Helena's Junior High, his old stomping grounds, where I was still in grade nine. He was the entertainment between disc jockey sets. It was his first real gig—they even paid him a little something. By then he'd gone electric with money he'd made from his gas jockey job.

When he walked out onto that stage, I stopped breathing, I was so afraid for him. I'd seen him a few minutes before, backstage with the sports equipment, tapping his feet, jumping up to pace up and down, biting his fingernails, his fingers twitching, almost in spasms.

"What are you worried about?" I had said to him. "You know you're good."

"Being good alone by yourself in your room in front of the mirror is different from being good up there on a stage," he mumbled.

He walked out quick, as though he didn't want to think too much about it. He started in on a slow ballad. Again, I held my breath. Slow songs revealed more weaknesses in Jamey's voice, more unsteadiness about where it was going. Then he switched to some fast stuff. Loosened up and relaxed, he felt his power, I could tell, first in his music, then over his audience. Cool and slick as they come, he became. Within two minutes all those kids at that dance were on their feet just a rocking right along with him. It was just like in the movies. When the disc jockey came back with his tapes, some of them even booed.

After that kind of attention, Jamey was hooked. There was no turning back. Still, it went in fits and starts. Getting up in front of the kids at a hick junior high is different from singing in bars and clubs and Klondike Days and even gas station promotions and shopping centre openings. He still had to go to endless tryouts and auditions. He still had to be told a hundred times, thanks but no thanks, go back to school kid, take my advice learn a trade. And I can see his answer, his lips curling into a grin that tried to hide his hurt and came out as a superior smirk, superior with the knowledge of his secret strength, his secret power.

It was like Batman, which Jamey played all the time when he was about twelve. He used to shimmy up and down the drainpipe and swing around in trees. He'd leap over fences and the verandah railing and jump off the verandah roof and try to climb up the side of the house. But what he liked best of all was how, in his ordinary life, no one knew he was Batman. Like Adam West, he had a secret power, which was his music. But if you're a performer, keeping your power secret isn't going to do you much good. If you're a performer, you have to reveal your power. You have to want to show it to the world.

Jamey wanted to be a star, and if he was going to be a star, he had to convince other people of his power. He had to sell himself, which meant talking somebody into giving him a chance. The way most people were willing to give him that chance was if he'd perform for free, or almost free. So then he still had his gas pump job as well as music and school, which latter he had just quit before the junior high job. Which turned out to be, among other things, a running battle between him and Popi.

But the time I still like to think about in bed at night just before sleep, the memory that lulls me to sleep, is the one about when we were kids together, before our eyes were opened to the world, before we were exposed to the opinions of other people, before things got complicated, those summer nights on Terrabain Street, when Jamey was still Jamey Popilowski, before he started running around town with his guitar slung across his back trying to get heard by anyone who'd listen.

I like to think that when we passed by Jamey, his music snagged onto the fuzz of our robes and we floated it to the open window where it wafted out across the verandah roof to the leaves of the big poplar in the front yard and down the trunk to the sidewalk where old man Hobbes was walking his dog and it latched onto the sleeve of his sweater and he carried it home to his son who was here on holidays from London, England. His son carried it way way across the Atlantic Ocean. There it was, flying like Jamey wanted to, in one of those jet airliners. In another country, someone else heard it and couldn't get it out of his head and started whistling it and somebody else picked it up and took it to yet another country.

Or so I imagined. In reality, of course, it's more a matter of marketing and distribution. But when we were kids, I thought of Jamey's song out there someplace, that brave little song doing its stuff, loud in my mind, finding a home out there, caught in a throat, curled into the tip of a tongue, while we remained on Terrabain Street, so old and shabby and yet we thought wonderful as children. We didn't know that we were impossibly different, impossibly poor and gawky. We hadn't yet heard the buzz word, dysfunctional. We didn't know that some of the other kids at school made fun of us for our strange ways and clothes, even our strange speech. We had each other and, left to ourselves like that, not yet comparing ourselves on the outside, we thought we were shit-hot. Although we were impatient, viewing our life as running on a gerbil wheel, only waiting for it to start.

"Oooeee," Jamey would laugh his infectious laugh as Beth and me drifted past, waving our arms and tripping on our trailing robes. "Whadda coupla birds," he'd say, a mixture of derision and love in his voice.

"We're birds . . . we're birds . . . we're birds of paradise," we'd trill back in the lifting air.

SOFT SHELL

Sometimes, it seems to me, life is the scenes you can't get out of your head, the scenes you keep replaying. All the rest is filler.

One of those scenes for me is Jamey and me kneeling in the bright moonlight on the bank of the North Saskatchewan letting go these two little turtles onto the river mud, then, holding hands, running, running across the golf course and up the one hundred and thirty-seven steps home.

I must have been twelve and Jamey fourteen because that was when Beth and me were listening endlessly to *Cuts Like a Knife*, which had been out a year. And it was before Jamey got so deep into his music, even before he got his first car. It's out of context, I guess you'd say. But I want to put it in for Carmen who thought I was a babe in the woods away from home and was afraid Jamey was going to do me wrong, which was her experience with musicians. "Just don't put up with shit," she told me more than once those Vancouver nights when we'd sit around sharing a joint, me waiting for Jamey to come home from somewhere, she not having a date for the evening, paying or otherwise. I told her that Jamey took good care of me. I told her about when we were kids, crouching in the potato patch picking potato beetles, which the Corset Lady gave us a penny each for, and I couldn't stand to touch them to flick them into my tin can, and Jamey flicked all mine in for me but let me take the money. "We go back a long ways together," I told her. "He's very sensitive."

Like it was me who had to dump Henri and Henrietta, two of those looney-sized turtles that all the kids had then and that Jamey had got at Dollar Daze and after a while they got soft shell. Soft shell is definitely icky. It maims but it does not kill, as the Corset Lady said. I had it figured that she spoke strange words like that because she'd been saved during *Back to the Bible Hour*. The way she told it, when they called out oh sinner come home, she heard this voice from on high about the same time she felt this huge hand grab her up by the shabby coat collar and set her in the aisle. So down she went to the stage where she emptied herself of her sins and the Lord filled her and from that moment on she had a vocation to spread the word.

"Well that was a long time ago," she'd sigh, mounded on her stool, her skirts like a globe around her, and Paquette, rising up out of his cellar of furnace dust, would say something like, "It must've been some big Jesus hand."

What he meant was it would've taken a powerful force to lift that two hundred plus pounds of wobbly flesh and set it on the straight and narrow. But, "Don't talk so daft," she'd answer back. "The spirit can lift any weight, not always pleasant for the weight but sometimes necessary for it to travel the pathway to God."

Or, "You don't know nothing," she'd sometimes say for variety. "I was slim and trim as a new willow once. I was as young as anybody once."

I didn't believe it. The Corset Lady had always been and forever would be the way she was then. My mind couldn't think how she might have been different, the same way I couldn't imagine life without her. So when she up and died the summer I turned sixteen, it was a terrible shock. Gone was her lap and her wobbly old knees and her stories that had kept me from being lonely for so many years, leaving me with my mother who made me feel more lonely, as if where love should be was a total blank. Marie getting married that same summer added to my world being tossed into a spin. Marie, like everyone else in the house, had always been there, and I had to learn how things you've always counted on can change, and I was left like a wet and shivering newborn pup until Jamey took me in and snuggled me to him. And I'm saying to Carmen wherever she is now after all these years, I guess I could put up with some shit from someone who did that for me.

But to get back to the Corset Lady being saved, she said that's what gave her power, that's what let her know about things. "The truth will set you free," she said and made up the story of my astronaut father. "The truth is with the dying," was another one of her sayings. Apparently, the dying are the only ones who can give to the living the right message. So you depend on them to do that and if they don't do it, well then they're not doing their job. Not that she always practised what she preached either. Like, when I had to help my mom and Rita clear out her room, I heard her voice eerie and rising from a mountain of junk including some unfinished corsets. "Throw out your own stuff," it said clear as clear. "You can't expect someone else to do it for you."

Which is what Popi said to Jamey. "They're your soft shells, you get ridda them."

We were all over at the Popilowskis'. The Corset Lady had made it up the stairs and Marie the glamourpuss was in the improbable situation of not having a date. At the sight of those turtles, she flung up her head as though sniffing bad air, the same snooty way she sniffed a way out of Terrabain Street and away from us, which way turned out to be Rick, but that was later. At the time of the turtles, she was safe in Paquette's care on the main floor, smoking and reading *True Romance* in the toilet, spraying herself with eau de cologne and practising her pout in the mirror, while on the floor above, I wanted to be like her, because then Jamey would notice me in a different way. Dream on, Lilah, I told myself. To make matters worse, everybody kept telling me I was the spitting image of my mom. No way I wanted her dumpiness, her straight black hair, her black-rimmed raccoon eyes, her sad Italian face. Her resignation as to why she had stayed so long on Terrabain Street and at Giuseppe's Pasta Factory. Her, "That's life, so whaddaya gonna do?"

"That's life," she said, looking down into that glass bowl half-filled with water, looking down at that little turtle sitting still as a lab specimen mounted on a rock. Henrietta it was, because the soft shell was more on the left, while Henri's was more on the right.

But the thing is, Jamey looked after those turtles real good. "Lilah," he'd call from his room, "fill this bowl with clean water willya? Get me summa that raw hamburger that's in the fridge, willya?" And I'd jump to answer, because Jamey had told me how hamburger was better for them than the regular turtle food that comes in a box. He had explained to me how their bowl had to be clean of scum. But, maybe I didn't polish that glass to a high enough sparkle or relay Jamey the right amount of hamburger, because in spite of everything, those turtles got soft shell, which, in turn, made Jamey feel bad but he didn't know what to do.

The situation might have gone on like that forever because it didn't appear that those little guys were going to die on their own, but Popi was having a fit because he was home all the time working on his epic. Rita said if he'd get up off his ass and put on his foot and go out and get a job he'd have worse problems than soft shell and he'd forget about it. She said that by the time she got home from eight hours on her feet at Rosa's, she couldn't care less if they had green cheese with purple polka dot shell. But Popi said he wasn't sharing no damned three-room flat with no rotting turtles and that Jamey had to get rid of them.

The thing was, Jamey wanted to get rid of them. The question was, how do you get rid of a turtle that isn't dead, but how do you keep one that isn't really alive either? And this could go on for years. It had already gone on for months.

"Easy as falling off a log," Popi said from his chair in front of the window, his footless leg resting on top of the other, his teeth braced for four hundred blows, his skinny jowls settling into pasty folds. "Just flush them down the toilet."

"Eeeee!" said Rita, turning from the stove, flinging up her Rampage Red nails, her hair flaming out like a bush around her narrow face. "I'd never be able to sit on that toilet again."

"I'm going to puke," said Beth, who always did have a delicate system.

"We should be thinking about the turtles, not ourselves," said the Corset Lady from her stool pulled into the middle of the floor because she tended to spread herself and needed a lot of room. "We should be thinking about their immortal souls. Maybe they're meant to have soft shell."

Immortal souls was a very large subject with the Corset Lady. "Our main job on earth is to save our immortal soul," she'd say, catching a thread in her brown stumps for teeth. She'd quote from the Bible: "What have I to do with thee woman. I must go about my Father's business."

Since you couldn't argue with the Bible, that shut everybody up, except Paquette, who said how immortal souls had nothing to do with it and how when he was growing up on the farm, when a thing was old and useless, like a dog that'd lost all its teeth and couldn't eat anymore or do anything else anymore and was miserable as hell, well they just took him out behind the barn and shot him.

"How do you shoot a turtle?" someone said.

"Maybe we could cut off their heads," suggested Jamey, reaching a finger down into their glass bowl, giving Henri—or was it Henrietta?—a little nudge. Which got exactly no response.

"Get real," said Beth, her pale face growing paler.

"Ask at the drugstore," said Tree from where she was setting plates around the table. "Ask at the drugstore if they've got something to do in them turtles, maybe some chloroform or something. You'd think the rate they sell them things there must be some way of doing them in."

"Too much trouble," said Paquette. "Just chuck 'em in the garbage. They'll die quick without water."

"That's murder," said the Corset Lady, pulling the dark thread through her teeth and winking it into her poised needle.

Then everybody started talking at once and Popi got all mad at Jamey for buying the turtles in the first place and Jamey said how in hell was he supposed to know they were gonna last forever and how he never heard of them turtles lasting more than a couple of months with any of his friends. And Popi said, don't you swear at me, I'm still your father. And Paquette said how we got the whole thing screwed up already, like in nature them turtles wouldn't last two minutes, something would've ate them by now.

"That's what's supposed to happen," he said, leaning his elbows on the table and seeking the truth in the foam of his beer. "I tell you, the rabbit don't mind getting et by the coyote. He figures it's on'y natural."

"That's it," said the Corset Lady, and all heads turned to her holding up one bent finger, as though testing the wind. "The river," she said. "That way they have a choice."

"What kind of choice is that?" said someone.

"They can bury themselves in the mud," said the Corset Lady.

"They can sit on a rock and get fried by the sun.

"They can sit on the sand and let a magpie eat them.

"They can try their luck in the river."

"They wouldn't have a chance in that river," said Jamey.

"Still, they will have had a choice," said the Corset Lady. "As for chances, that's not your problem. You'll have fixed it so they have a choice. Here, take this shoebox."

So that's how Jamey and me, one May evening at dusk, snuck down to the Saskatchewan with Henri and Henrietta scuttling around in this cardboard box sounding like a dog's toenails on linoleum.

Jamey carried the box in two hands. I squeezed the metal gate latch and slowly lifted it out of its slot. Still, the screech of the hinges sounded loud and we held our breath. But the street was empty and the windows up and down blank squares of light. Feeling like hitmen out on a midnight job, we scurried beneath the streetlights, through the poplar leaf lace shadows. We went down the one hundred and thirty-seven steps to the golf course and across the green and down to the mud flats. We knelt in the silt, dry and still warm from the day's sun, we turned the shoebox on its side and opened the lid.

Henri and Henrietta just stood there, kind of stunned. It must have seemed strange to them, all that space. It must've seemed without end, since all their lives so far they had lived in a bowl.

"We can't sit here all night," said Jamey. So that's when I had to dump them out. Jamey didn't have the heart.

Immediately, they scurried under a piece of driftwood. What told them to hide from the sky and all the things flying around up there ready to swoop, I don't know. But that's what they did.

And Jamey and me left them there and walked back across the dry mud and through the brush fringe and across the green, its shaved circle glistening like a monk's dome in the moonlight. We didn't talk. We felt awful, somehow. But what else could we do? I kept saying to Jamey. "What more could anybody do," I said, not touching him. "You changed their water every day. You fed them raw hamburger."

"I did feed them raw hamburger, didn't I?" said Jamey, his voice perking up a bit. "I did change their water every day. So why did they go and get soft shell on me?"

"If they got soft shell," I said, "what can they expect? If you're a turtle, you can't survive with soft shell. You can't expect anyone to keep you."

"You know what?" said Jamey.

"What?" I said.

"I feel kind of relieved."

"I know what you mean," I said. "Kind of free like."

"Come on, Lilah Delilah," he said, grabbing my hand.

I felt his touch all up my arm and travelling into my body and lifting me clean up off the earth. I felt the spirit flowing from his body to mine, his body that I'd liked right from the time I first saw it, hard and coiled like a spring, swinging on that gate. We ran across the grass and up and up the one hundred and thirty-seven steps, up to our street, up from the cold weight of the river to the lightness of spring leaves. And, through the lace, the windows of our house threw their yellow light out into the darkness like bricks of a road showing us the way back.

JUST SEVENTEEN

Jamey's first recording session started out as one of those days in spring that shouts *split*! No way you can sit one more minute in a stinky droning stuffy classroom watching a mouth opening and closing and going on forever about parallel construction. So at the break when I looked up from my locker and there was Jamey large as life, my heart levitated.

"C'mon."

He didn't have to say it twice.

"What're you doin' here?" I said, grabbing up my jacket. "I thought you were at work."

"I felt like gettin' outa there," he said. "Pat'll cover for me."

We turned so quick, we bumped into a couple of teachers. We turned again and bumped into a couple more coming from the other direction. Like Batman and Boy Wonder escaping evil forces, we found an opening and swung out of there as fast as we could. We were busing it since Jamey's car was up on a hoist. He had a Pontiac then, an old one, as usual, because that's all he could afford, but I remember it clearly because that's the one he taught me to drive on, an automatic transmission, thank God, although later when he got a van, I had to learn the manual. But, anyway, that day we ran across the street, dodging cars and hopping onto a bus just as it was pulling out of the stop.

We lurched down the aisle and dropped into the seat closest to the rear door, since Jamey didn't like to be anyplace he couldn't get out of quick if he had to. Because of his car situation being so unreliable, we actually took the bus a lot, but I never minded. Especially in sunshine, like that day. We sat there, mellow yellow, two blobs in a warm sea, bobbing up and down, swaying back and forth.

Every time the doors swooshed open and closed they let in a dry mud smell mixed with the promise of green starting. They let in the people, clinking their change into the glass box and turning and weaving along the aisle, eyeing the seats but not the other people. I played that game where you stare at a person's face until you get them to look at you. Then I started doing a survey of how many people look at other people and how many keep their eyes to themselves.

That was when I noticed this babe sitting on the bench at the front with her thin legs crossed and her skirt up to here and this hair sticking out a foot all around her head. Through eye makeup so thick you could've scraped it off, she was staring at Jamey as if she knew him. He was looking out the window. But maybe she was playing the game too, because as she kept staring, his head turned toward her like it was on a chain. I just about dislocated my eyes out of their sockets trying to catch the expression on his face. I could see the pulse that sometimes beat in his forehead.

"Who's she?" I said.

"I dunno," he said.

"You do, too."

"I don't!"

"She wouldn't be looking at you like that."

"If I do, what's it to you?"

What could I say? He didn't know that for months already I'd been writing down Lilah Cellini and Jamey Popilowski on scraps of paper and crossing off the letters and counting out Love, Hate, Friendship, Courtship, Marriage. And when it didn't work out with Lilah, I tried my real name, Delilah. I even tried my father's name, Turner.

"She looks like a floozy, that's all," I said.

"Yeah, floozy. How'd you know how a floozy looks?"

"I know."

"So," he shrugged. "Maybe I like how floozies look."

At that moment, I would have given anything to be a floozy. This one had long legs and a short skirt, she had red high heels and red toenails, she wore tons of makeup and smacked chewing gum and had a certain bold flair. Even at age fifteen, I knew that the way Jamey and that girl looked at each other had to do with sex. She oozed sex appeal from every pore, while I was totally ignorant in that area, except, of course, what I'd learned from the movies. All I knew, I wanted Jamey to look at me the way he was looking at her and not the way he looked at Beth. I felt myself plunge into despair. I felt my heart break. But, when we got off at the next stop, I recovered. After all, I was with him and she wasn't.

We wandered around in the stores for a while and tried on women's hats in the Bay and looked at ourselves in the mirror. Jamey with his thin face and mop of curly hair looked better in the hats than me with my broad face and flat hair. I stuck out my tongue and crossed my eyes, which improved my looks a little. Then Jamey made a zany face and I made another and then we started laughing and acting up and then we caught this saleswoman looking at us like we had lice in our jeans. So we went over to the electronics department and Jamey looked at this calculator and stuck it in his pocket. Then he said, "Whaddaya wanta do now?" and I said, "I dunno. We could go to a movie if you have some money."

"I thought you had some," he said.

"I don't have none," I said.

We passed by McDonald's and raided our pockets for enough change for a small order of fries, which Jamey put in front of him on the table. I shouldn't have been eating them anyway because of my face.

"Your face is okay," said Jamey, flicking fries into his mouth. "What's wrong with your face?"

"Everything," I said.

"At least you don't have small piggy eyes like Muriel Dushinsky," he said. "You can't do nothing about small piggy eyes."

"I guess you're right," I said.

"At least you don't have scars like me," he said, chewing.

"You can't even see your scars," I said, reaching across the table and taking a fry. "Only when you're cold. Then they come out a bit. On your forehead there," I said, looking at the left side of his face where there was a curl of hair I wanted to circle with my finger so bad I had to clench my fists to keep my hands to myself. All my desire must have been in my eyes, but Jamey didn't notice, which I was thankful for, actually, because I wouldn't have known what to do if he had. "You can't see them today," I said. "And you only got two."

"I guess it could be worse," he said. "Some people got them all over their face, with pus coming out. You want some more?"

"No thanks."

"Let's face it," he said, scowling and chewing, "there's nothing to do in this fuckin' hole without money. I'm getting out."

I stopped breathing. That meant he'd be taking off again like he'd been doing since the age of thirteen. That meant my life would stop until he came back. "Where're you going this time?" I said.

"North. I want to see," he looked at the floor then quickly up into my eyes, "if it's true it's light all the time up there."

We walked around some more and that's when we spotted MAKE A TAPE OF YOUR VOICE in giant letters you couldn't miss a mile away. Jamey went up and peered closer. *Backup tape or instrument included. Spcl. Promo. Price $29.95.*

It seems strange to me now, with all the technology around, that Jamey hadn't yet heard his voice on tape. He'd already wandered in and out of a dozen loose music groups. Along with band work, he did solo stuff, one-nighters and weekenders as singer or backup guitar for groups. He worked coffee houses and small cafés afternoons or evenings. He hung around anything or anybody he thought might get him a chance to play and sing. He even entered every talent show that came along. He said the competition was good for him. Between gigs, he'd get it together with his friends to jam Sunday afternoons or play for beer and tokes at Saturday night parties. Sometimes, he and his friends got themselves a paying birthday party or, incredibly, an evening in an old folks' home, where they'd play country or folk and Jamey'd sing something like "Hey, Mr. Tambourine Man," which the old folks loved. They'd sit in their chairs, tapping their feet on the floor and their hands on their knees and smiling. But he'd never taped himself.

"It costs money," I said, reading around his arm.

Jamey didn't say anything for a minute but I could hear the wheels clicking. "Not that much," he finally came up with. "How about your mom?"

"You know my mom," I said. "El Cheapo. I have to buy everything out of my babysitting money."

"How about if you need something for school?"

"Anyway, she wouldn't have that much on her."

"How about the plastic?"

"Well . . ."

"C'mon." His face looked pained, his desire was so strong.

Was I trying to hold him, to keep him from leaving? Or was it just that I couldn't deny him anything he wanted. I don't know. We walked the couple blocks to Giuseppe's and went around into the alley and in the back door and there was Tree in white uniform and apron and kerchief, looking like a surgeon holding up somebody's dangling innards, which in her case was a fist full of fettuccine. Tree always looked so strange to me without her hair. With that white kerchief tied close around her forehead, her bones showed so clearly. The bags around her eyes bulged, the lines around her mouth cut into her soft skin. I went close up behind her where her plastic-skin hands were supervising fettuccine dropping from a cutter into rectangular trays, which then moved another notch along the belt.

She looked up. When she saw who it was she frowned even deeper. She looked back down. "Whatcha doing here? Why aren't you in school?" She tossed some fettuccine scraps into a basin and kept her eyes on the cutter.

"Teachers meeting," I said. "They let us out early."

"So whatcha want?" She jiggled a tray.

"I need some things for school."

"Yeah? What now?"

"A book," I said.

"Hmmm," she said.

"If I don't get this book, I fail the course."

"They gotcha comin and goin." She sounded tired. I closed my ears. "How much it cost?" She caught some more scraps.

"Thirty-four ninety-five," I said, quickly calculating a total that included a Big Mac, fries and Coke and rounding it off to an even number.

"I'll give it to you tonight," she said.

"I need it right away."

I thought I had her, but I could never be sure with Tree. Her temper could flare so easily and she could wash her hands of the whole thing. I stood a tense moment, waiting, thinking of Jamey leaning and smoking against the wall in the alley. "So I can go home and study," I said.

She sighed. "Get my card. It's in my purse. The key to my locker's in my pocket." She stuck out her hip and kept her eyes on the fettuccine.

When I returned the key to her pocket she said. "Don't you dare use it for anything but that book."

"Mom, whaddaya think I am?" I said.

"I know you," she said.

I went out the steel door into the alley, into the bright sunshine where I knew Jamey was waiting. "She'll kill me when she finds out," I said handing over the card.

"Just tell her that Reno Enterprises is the name of the bookstore."

"She won't fall for it."

"I'll pay you back before she gets the bill." He was walking fast. I forgot about Tree.

At the studio, this guy snapped the card into metal, zip zip. He pointed to a wall of tapes and instruments, mostly guitars but some accordions and drums. Jamey chose an electric. "What d'ya wanta hear?" he said.

"How about *baby you're all that I want*," I said. "I could do backup vocals."

"Get real on both counts," he said.

"I could do backup guitar," I said. "I've been practising."

He didn't even answer that one. Instead, he played a few chords of "Born to Run." Jamey loved to get off on that song. He'd go wild with it. The guy left us to practise for a few minutes and Jamey flung himself around in the booth, eyes closed, beating that guitar with his lean fingers. He forgot that I was there, he was having such a good time by himself. Then the guy came back and adjusted some knobs and dials. "You ready?" he said.

"Ready as I'll ever be."

When Jamey was finished, the guy played the tape back to us. I have to say it sounded good, the reverb making his voice sound more mature, more finished. As for attitude, if anything he sounded even more rebellious than Bruce Springsteen. A look of delight crossed his face. Like when he brought home his first guitar, like when he got his Sunbeam, like when he was a kid and really believed he was Batman.

"Hey," he said. "Do I sound like that?"

"That's it," said the guy.

"How about that?" said Jamey.

He couldn't get over it. All the way to the door and out onto the street, he kept saying, "Didja hear that? That's what I need. I've gotta get me the right conditions. I gotta get me a real band and some equipment."

By then it must have been about five o'clock, the way the sun was low in the sky and streaming into the canyon between the tall buildings, filling it like a river we had to wade through. And all the people were streaming out of the buildings and into the river.

Jamey didn't like crowds, so he walked fast. His long legs floated him through to a corner where he had to stop for the light. Full in the sun, he shrugged back his shoulders as if getting rid of something. "All the buses that stop along this street," he said when I caught up. "You can get a bus here and it'll take you anyplace you want to go. You can catch a bus here for the bus depot or the airport, and from there you can go anyplace in the world." His head was high and his face was looking up at the patch of blue between the buildings.

And that was when I had the sudden thought that Jamey could go places with his music. He sounded so good on that tape, so professional. It hit me that he *could* be a star.

When the light changed, he set out like a bat out of hell, dodging people right and left, like a halfback going for the touchdown, dodging anything that might stop him or get in his way.

I ran after him. "Hey," I said to his legs. "Where's the fire?"

He slowed down a bit but not much. The wind gusted from behind. My hair was all over my face and in my eyes and I couldn't see Jamey's feet or which way he was going to turn. All of a sudden I lost my balance. Maybe because I hadn't eaten anything that day except for a chocolate bar and a Slurpee, but the world moved before my eyes. Then I had a sensation that was so awful it couldn't have lasted for more than a few seconds because I couldn't have stood it any longer. Like, there I was, completely naked, like I didn't have skin and all my insides were exposed, like those little soft shells we dumped on the riverbank a few years before or maybe like a person with third degree burns whose skin is all burned off so that even the air is painful. And all the people and the cars and everything just kept rushing past.

Then the wind whirled a dust devil and caught me from the opposite direction and my hair whipped back from my face and I could see Jamey's feet again, the heels of his runners lifting like they were attached to springs.

"Hey," I called to the back of Jamey's jean jacket. It stopped and he looked back across his shoulder, scowling into the low sun. When I caught up with him, he whisked me into a doorway and pushed the hair back from my face, back behind my ears. He was laughing, holding the laugh in his mouth, the way he did. He raised his arms and braced his hands on the brick wall above my head.

"What exactly do you want?" he said.

"I want someone to love me," I said.

"I love you," he said.

We left the doorway and went on a little way until we got to the bus stop and when the bus came we hopped on, only now it was rush hour and we couldn't get a seat. We swung and swayed from the ceiling strap, our bodies rhythming together and feeling good against each other. But Jamey did go north that summer, in spite of me wanting to hold him, and the winter after he went to Mexico. While I returned to Terrabain Street because my leave-taking required some years yet of preparation.

SATURDAY NIGHT'S ALL RIGHT FOR FIGHTIN'

After that, every Saturday night Jamey and me broke up, usually after a gig or a party, mainly because he wanted to do *it* and I didn't. Well to be honest, I wanted to do *it* too, but I wasn't exactly sure how and I didn't want to look stupid compared to his other girlfriends. Jamey'd had a lot of girlfriends who did it. I just knew they did, by their attitude and movement and talk more than their hair and makeup and ringed belly buttons.

Why we reserved breaking up for Saturday nights, I don't know, since we saw each other most other nights too, as well as days. But if you stop and think about it, there is something about Saturday night. People gear themselves up all week for it. All through a dull, boring, or otherwise awful week, they dream about Saturday night. They want to finally have a good time. They want excitement, maybe go a little out of control. They want something different to happen. Then if Saturday night doesn't live up to all that, they get a let-down feeling. Maybe that's why a lot of people try to rescue Saturday night by making out.

In our early teens, Beth and me rescued Saturday night by eating ourselves silly. By then Jamey was already out jamming and partying with his friends or, later, playing gigs. He started asking me sometimes if I wanted to go along and then I would, fixing myself up to look older, doing a whole lot of things I shouldn't've been doing at that tender age. But one thing that was legitimate was the singing, at parties that is. Everybody seemed to like the way Jamey and me sang harmony. I'd even sing on my own if I was a little high. His friends all wanted me back, even if I was just a kid. Jamey even wanted me to get up with him at gigs, but I was too shy for that.

But if Beth and me were hanging out around the house, we'd cook up a batch of fudge or brownies or Nanaimo bars and eat the whole thing and roll on the floor groaning in agony, saying things like "I'm gonna puke." On the Saturday night I'll never forget as long as I live, it was popcorn. Tree had gone over to the Popilowskis' where she and Rita could listen to Julio to their heart's content leaving Beth and me at our place to crank up the volume on Bryan Adams and sing and dance up a storm. After a while we got tired of that and decided on the popcorn. I was doing the popping, sliding the pan back and forth on the burner so the popcorn wouldn't burn. At that crucial moment, with eruptions coming from under the lid like a hailstorm was going on in there, in swaggered Jamey, large as life and twice as sassy. "Why are you home?" said Beth. "Nothing happening," he said and walked over to the stove and stood behind me, touching my back with his front, which freaked me out.

For some time and at certain times, him being so close drove me crazy. It was something growing inside me, which I didn't recognize at the time, although of course now I know all about it, that gnawing hunger in your body for another body. That night, his closeness alone was enough to make me jittery but then he jabbed me under the arms and I yelled, "Grow up!" and then his hands were all over me and I yelled, "You want this in the face?" So then he got all mad and flung himself out of the kitchen, out of the apartment and out of the house. So then I said to Beth, "I gotta go," and ran out after him.

"You'll be sorry." Beth's light trill followed me out, but whether she meant about the popcorn or Jamey I didn't know and I didn't wait to find out.

I ran down the stairs and out the front door and out onto the verandah, but I couldn't see him. I ran down the front steps and out to the gate and looked up Terrabain Street to the bus route and the other way toward the river. Jamey's jacket was disappearing over the hill that went down to the river valley. I ran along the street and down the hill steps until I got close to him, then I slowed down. When I got about five feet behind, I stayed there. At a time like that the direct approach didn't work. He'd shrug off my hand and say something rude. That's the way he was when his feelings were hurt. But I had to stay with him because I'd made him feel bad and that's the one thing I could never do in my life was make Jamey feel bad. I just didn't have the heart for it.

Along the bottom of the hill, across the grass and alongside the trees that lined the riverbank, we walked. Jamey was moving his body lightly the way he did, moving his shoulders the way he did, as if he didn't care, but I knew he was scowling.

It was nearly dark, and the light was strange, reddish purple through the clouds. The air was heavy, close like a blanket. Then there came this big clap of thunder and the rain started coming down like crazy, and still the strange light stayed in the sky and the rain came down across the light. Jamey turned into a shed that said Public Works Department in big yellow letters on the side. The door was locked but there was a big overhang of the roof where it joined the top of a partition.

Like two cats left out in the rain, we stood there shivering and watching it come down. Still, Jamey was by himself, refusing to give himself over. I moved in closer until I could smell his smell, of grass and earth and wind and metal. Maybe he could smell mine, too, which he told me later he liked, deep flesh and vanilla. Then I could feel him looking at me instead of the rain. He turned and unzipped our jackets, first mine, then his, to our dry shirts underneath, and he put his arms around me, pressing our warm parts together. Then he stared at me with his face all serious and full, his eyes looking at me but also through me. Then he took off my wet jacket and curled me inside his. We stood together like that for what seemed a long time, which time I wanted to never end. And then he started kissing me on the mouth with long and slow kisses and unbuttoning my shirt. Then his mouth moved down and his tongue nuzzled around and found the tips of my breasts and that was the strangest feeling I had felt up to that time in my life, I swear. All tingly and warm it made me feel and somehow there seemed to be a direct line from there down to that other place. And I closed my eyes and concentrated on the tingle and down went Jamey's mouth and tongue, lower and still lower and all over. And then there was nothing but the warm and the tingle, not even the rain. And he put me down on my jacket and he kissed me lower still. Then he took my hand and put it on his thing, which was hot and hard, hard like a rock and yet the skin surprisingly soft, too, but I didn't know what to do with it but he put it inside me and then it was like something exploded electric in there lifting me even higher than music, settling me down into the warmest feeling yet.

That was when I learned that *it* isn't something you have to know anything about in order to know how to do. It's like breathing, I guess, when you first pop out of your mom, or knowing how to suck milk from her. That was when I learned it's easy to be happy.

The thought made me feel so good, I laughed out loud.

"Hey," said Jamey, "what you laughing at? What's so funny all of a sudden?" But I was laughing so hard I couldn't answer, looking up into his face with his grin curling up the corners of his mouth and even then making those little lines just under his nose. Then he started to laugh, too. I could feel him laughing inside me and he said he could feel my laugh hugging him with short tight hugs. And, holding onto each other like that in our warm sea we laughed and laughed. We couldn't stop laughing.

AFTERNOON DELIGHT

. . . comfort me true/comfort me blue/i walked alone/before i met you//i saw the stars/i saw the moon/but i never felt warmth/before i touched you//so come take my hand/I'll take your hand too/together we'll make/a new space for two . . . Jamey handed me the piece of paper, shyly at first, then after I'd read it, "I'll sing it for you," he said and jumped out of bed and into his pants and sprinted across the hall for his guitar. He was back in a flash. I made him sing it again and again. I didn't want him ever to stop, such a simple song, such a great song, not only the song itself but the way he played and sang it, the way he looked at me.

For a long time Jamey and me were in the dark in more ways than one. Evenings at home, there was always someone older around, and we had no place else to go, except cramped car seats or prickly grass. Then we discovered love in the afternoon. Popi and Paquettte were around even then, but one was so deep into his epic he didn't know what was happening in the real world and the other was tuned in to his quiz shows and wrestling reruns. The important thing was, our moms were away at their jobs. They were the ones who thought they had to keep some kind of control or everything would fly apart into disaster.

It was a hot June that year, made hotter those afternoons when Jamey and me would get our whirly electric going. Holiday time, like kids at Christmas, each package we opened was bigger and better than the last, all the discoveries we made, all the ways we found to make each other smile and laugh out loud, a million times more creative than if I'd been at school. All we were doing at school was rehashing old stuff, prepping for finals, which I couldn't have cared less about, whether or not I passed. I had, what they say, my priorities straight.

Then one afternoon when we were doing our spiralling to dizzy heights, we heard the click of a key in a lock. We froze, right there in the middle of everything, and I opened my eyes and saw the stains on the ceiling, brown and jagged, as if the rain had leaked through. I heard Paquette's television downstairs, voices coming from a distance like they were spookily detached from reality.

Then we heard the creak of hinges and a door opening and on the cracked ceiling I saw an image of Tree without her teeth. I saw the way she looked the time she got her bottom plate, and she came home from the dentist without teeth because he couldn't put her new teeth in right away and her face was all sunken in and she looked about a million years old and I could see the future and it was horrible.

Then we heard a door closing and then silence and that's when we moved, fast.

Jamey sprung into the air like a wired cat. I grabbed my shirt and jeans and was out in the living room like a shot.

"What're you doing home from school?" said Tree from where she was leaning on the door and slipping off the heel of one shoe with the toe of the other. Her face turned to me was a map of suspicion and pain, but that didn't mean anything because it always was, even when she was having a good time.

"What're you doing home from work?" I said, buttoning my shirt and standing in the bedroom doorway.

"Never you mind what I'm doing home from work. Why aren't you at school?" Her voice was getting louder.

"I'm sick," I answered, taking a step toward her, hoping to keep her in the living room.

She gave me one of her tell-me-another-one looks.

"I just started my period," I said.

"Well," she said, blindly shoving past me. "I got one of my migraines

40

and I don't wanta hafta deal with anything and I mean anything, so just stay out of my way and don't you dare play any of that music." She did look pretty bad, too, her eyes closed to slits and groping her way into the bedroom. "It's the heat," she gasped. "I gotta get outa this girdle. Before I die."

She staggered into the bedroom and I stood there and waited for the explosion and death. My life didn't pass in front of my eyes the way they say it does. What I remember, clear as clear, is every detail of the doily on the coffee table, one of countless doilies Tree crocheted, an endless series appearing on end tables, shelves, the TV, on any and all flat surfaces, and disappearing when its time had come around—all part of a rotating cycle of time and event, of colour-matched occasions: yellow and green for spring flowers and Easter, orange and brown for fall leaves and Thanksgiving, red and green for Christmas. We even had a special black one for Good Friday.

Plunk in the middle of the one on the coffee table that fateful day was a vase of pink and blue plastic flowers and green leaves. The doily was leaf-green with pink and blue in the trim and little pink and blue puffs standing up perky all around. The lace was very fine and delicate and I saw Tree's large rough fingers holding a tiny straight pin. The sharp point of the pin was pulling taut one tiny loop of lace, still damp from a special sugar-water solution, enlarging the loop until it was the right size before being speared into thick cardboard beneath.

When the explosion didn't come, I turned and looked through the doorway. Tree was sitting on the bed, bent over, reaching for her girdle, which she had rolled down to her puffed-out ankles. Behind her, the chenille bedspread looked a little mussed up but not bad.

"You could make me a cup of tea," she said, "if it isn't too much to ask." She sat up and pulled her dress over her head. She threw it on a chair and began scratching herself through her slip, where her girdle had been. She stood and started limping on her swollen feet toward the closet. "Well," she turned with her scowl and her downturned mouth, "Are you gonna stand there all day, or what?"

I was paralyzed.

"What's wrong with you?" she said.

"Why don't you lie down?" I said.

"I'm going to. I just wanta get my robe."

"I'll get it. You lie down."

She really looked at me then, through her migraine-bleary eyes. She looked me up and down.

I glanced down my front and saw that my shirt was buttoned crooked. My toes were curled up from the linoleum. I tried to relax them back down.

"Why are you so thin?" Tree accused.

"I'm not thin."

"You're thin," she stated.

"Three months ago you were telling me I was fat."

"That was three months ago." She narrowed her eyes. "You're not one of them anorexics, I hope."

I could feel her eyes probing, gouging. Suddenly, I could smell myself, that earthy mushroomy smell of love.

"Whatchoo been up to?" she said.

Then she turned and pulled open the closet door. Jamey was there all right, framed real good, standing at attention like he was on parade. He had got on his socks, but his jeans and T-shirt were still in his hand. He thought he had himself covered but his you-know-what was in full view although, thanks be to God, at the moment hanging loose. "Hi," he said, flashing his curled-up grin.

"Excuse me," Tree said, "I just wanted to take off my girdle."

Jamey sidled out of the closet. Keeping his back to the wall and his front toward Tree, nodding and smiling and saying "excuse me" and "I'm sorry," apologizing for everything, from being born to drinking Tree's last cold beer, stumbling and putting on his jeans and shirt as he went, he got out of there.

Long after we heard two clicks, first our door then the Popilowskis', Tree and I stood staring at each other. I thought all hell was gonna break loose, but it didn't. The only thing that shouted in that small, close hot room was silence. Except for a bluebottle buzzing, hitting itself again and again against the window glass. Except for Tree's face registering pain like it always did when she had a migraine.

THINGS MY MOTHER TOLD ME

After that, Tree never left me alone. Nag nag nag. If I thought it was bad before, it was terrible then. And not just the dishes and the vacuuming and not going to classes and my hair and my clothes and my music but the way I walked and the way I breathed. Now she really had something to bitch about. She was in her glory, let me tell you.

"I know I can't stop you," she yelled at my turned back. "Miss Smarty Know-it-all, you're gonna ruin your life, because you won't listen to the voice of experience."

"What about you?" I yelled right back. "You didn't have me by keeping your legs crossed all of the time."

"And look where it got me!" she yelled.

"So now you're admitting it, finally. You wish you'd never had me."

"Don't be stupid."

"I always knew you hated me."

"I don't hate you."

"I can't do anything good enough for you."

"Why can't you be a good girl like Beth?"

"Beth! How about Gord?"

"Gord's gonna do all right. Gord's got a job."

"In a warehouse."

"So a warehouse is too good for you all of a sudden?"

"I can't think of anything more depressing."

"It's steady. That's more than you can say for Jamey."

"Putting things in a bin, taking them out of a bin, putting them in another bin. All day. Huh! That's steady all right."

"It's a paycheque. Jamey's never gonna have a steady paycheque." She lowered her voice on this last, so Rita wouldn't hear across the hall.

When Tree got worked up about something, her Italian nature really surfaced. She'd pace back and forth in the small ring of that living room, in her spongy work shoes if she hadn't changed, in her slippers if she had. She even shrieked in Italian, except she had to revert back to English or I wouldn'ta known what she was talking about.

"Okay, baby, you wanta fight, I'll fight." Across the faded flowers of the carpet between the saggy-springed couch and the gas fireplace, cold in summer, she'd dance. "You wanta put the gloves on?" she'd say, hands up ready to whack me. "Put 'em on!" And head lowered, she'd come at me with her black hair and olive skin and scowling face.

But I got pretty good at dodging, so we didn't connect too often.

"Tell someone who cares," I'd yell because I knew that really got her.

"You'll care, my girl. Just you wait and see."

"I'll never care about one single solitary thing you'll ever have to say."

"Here," and she'd wave a piece of paper in my face. "Write it down! I wanta get it in writing. Someday, I'll show it to you. Someday, I'll throw it in your face. Someday, I'll make you eat that piece-a paper."

"Someday will never come."

"Never is a long time."

Exhausted, we'd retreat, Tree sinking into her chair, me slamming out of the apartment or into the bedroom.

Only to come out again, another time, gloves off as it were, bare knuckles raised.

"How come you're so smart?" I'd spit. "How come you can see the future? How do you know what Jamey's gonna do?"

"He's too good looking, that one."

"So what?"

"His jeans are too tight. A man walks like that, in those tight jeans, nothing good can come of that."

"You don't know what you're talking about."

"He's too much into that sex music."

"Get real!"

"Ugh." Tree's voice would fall, along with her body, into the worn cushions. "Why do you insist on ruining your life?"

"You should talk. Working at Giuseppe's. You think that's life, you're pitiful."

"Boy, do you got a lot to learn."

"You don't even know what living is."

"You're gonna learn about life the hard way."

"Jamey's my life."

"I never heard such silly talk. You'll meet a dozen others who can just as well be your life and maybe they'll have some future, at least a steady job. Just take my advice, don't be so quick to hop into bed with a man. Get him to marry you first."

"Get into this century."

"You'll find out, some things don't change. Don't worry. I know something. I don't go around with my head in the sand. There's this girl at work, it's the same thing. She shacked up with this guy and she has a kid now and where's he? That's what she'd like to know, too."

"Well, I know this couple and they lived together and they got along fine and then they got married and that busted them up."

"At least if you're married and something happens, you get knocked up or something, you got something, you can go to a lawyer . . ."

"Oh, sure, do you know what lawyers cost? Anyway, if a guy goes, he goes. You can't find him." I just about said, "You should know all about that," but something held me back. Maybe I was afraid of that subject, maybe deep down I felt there were limits to hurting people, even my mother.

"They've got people to track them down."

"Great. Track them down, sounds like they're some animal or something."

"Why you can't settle down like any normal girl and get married I'll never know."

"I thought you didn't want me to marry Jamey."

"I don't mean Jamey. I mean some nice young man with a good steady job."

That was the summer Jamey went up north. Tree really worked on me then. She really laid it on about a man leaving. That was when she told me about my father.

"You don't know nothin' about life and men," she said. "Your father . . ."

She had me there. One up, for sure. I didn't know anything about my father. For a long time I had thought he was dead. For a long time I had believed he was an astronaut way out in space so no wonder I hadn't heard from him.

"Sean Connery," said Tree, sitting on the edge of a low chair, feet firmly planted on the carpet. "When he was double oh seven." Her slippers with the little cutouts across the instep lay in a heap like dog's ears. It was hot, hot summer, and all she had on was her slip. "Gin and tonic," she said, staring down at her feet. All swollen the way they were, in little bumps where the cutouts had been, they looked like spilled popcorn. "The only person I ever knew who drank gin and tonic," she said.

It was funny. All my life I had wanted her to tell me about my father, but then when it was coming, I didn't want to hear. There was something shameful about being dumped by a man. There was something wrong with me or he wouldn't have left. His leaving was because of something I'd done, like be born. I went and hid in the kitchen and stood by our old gas stove. But you couldn't get very far away from another person in that apartment. "There's something I never told you," came Tree's voice.

I held my breath, the same way I had when she told me he didn't die after all. "He left," she had said then. "He just left. He went to work one day and never came home."

"Your father and me," her voice came at me now around the door frame to where I was watching the precisely placed jet holes in the gas ring of the right front burner of the stove.

"Your father and me were never suited," she said. "Cellini and Turner. He was educated. He liked all those thick books. He liked the symphony. And the ballet. Even though he always said our ballet here was grossly inadequate. I'll never forget his words. Grossly inadequate. He meant it was the pits. But he always talked like that. Funny, like. He was English, straight from England. He said things like, what are the natives up to today? And, what say? And cottage instead of house and chaps, he called everybody chaps. And he wanted everything to be lovely. He couldn't stand things that weren't lovely. Blood and water breaking, which happened with you, you came so quick like, almost at home, we barely got to the hospital. Water all over everything, him and the sheets. He didn't like that. In the beginning was the flesh, he used to say, especially when he was two sheets to the wind, he'd talk stupid like that, and then he'd laugh, but not happy like. A man's reach must be beyond his grasp, he used to say, but for the life of me I didn't know what he was talking about. And then he drank like a fish and then, later, he stayed away, at first all night, then a few days and a week at a time and coming home smelling . . . smelling like . . . women."

It took a long time for Tree to say all that. She told it in stops and starts. I was afraid to interrupt her, afraid she wouldn't get it all out, or as much as she would or could.

"Maybe I did become a nag," she said another time. "Who wouldn't?"

And another—"When it happened, it was like the hand of God. The way I said we needed more money, the way he took that summer job at the Exhibition, the way he went on to the next town with it and never came back and never sent word."

Those few sessions of Tree telling me about my father are all that I have, so I remember them pretty clearly. One time it was raining. I can see the rain on the window even today, rain like tears streaming down the window. I was sitting on the couch, Tree in her chair. We were both looking at the window. "I had you to think about," she said. "To keep me busy, to give me a reason for living."

"Don't put that on me," I said. "I don't want to be anybody's reason for living."

"Maybe you are whether you want to be or not."

"I just want out," I said. "I just want to get going."

"You've got so much to learn," she said.

"You can't stop me," I said.

"I wash my hands," said Tree. "You'll do it anyway. You always were that way. I can tell you till I'm blue in the face how something can't be done and then you just turn around and do it anyways. I remember you playing with matches. It's a wonder you didn't burn the house down. I kept hiding those matches, all the time in a different place, higher and higher. I spanked you every time. Still, you'd get into those matches. I was at my wit's end. How come you can't be a nice girl like Beth, I'll never know. How come you can't sometimes consider others?" She paused and thought a moment. "He told me not to say how come," she continued. "'Why,' he said. The word is 'why'. He was educated and I wasn't. But I was willing to learn. If he'd been willing to teach me. But maybe I couldn't learn. Maybe I was too stupid to learn."

And I thought yes, you were, you stupid old hag. God as my witness, that's what I thought.

"I don't think he ever felt married seriously," said Tree. "Because I wasn't English. He called us Wops."

The room was quiet.

In between and after these sessions, I'd go out with Jamey and Tree would fall into her cups and finally sleep. I'd come home and find her sprawled in her chair, her breath smelling stale of beer, her mouth sagged open, her head back, reminding me of all the things I wanted to get away from, that I was misbegotten and alone in this world. I'd stand a moment and watch the breath go in and out of her and think how we all depend on that air going in and out of us and how it could stop so easily, poof, just like that. And I knew that before I died, I wanted to live.

And the next time, we'd go at it again, our voices rising so the whole house could hear. It's only Tree and Lilah, so what else is new? And somebody in another room would turn the page of a newspaper and somebody would put on a kettle for tea.

"You slut!"

"You stupid old bitch!"

"Coming home in the middle of the night."

"Try and stop me!"

"Where you been?"

"If I thought it was any of your business I'd tell you."

"You're a disgrace, talking to your mother that way."

"You're the disgrace!"

"What a scandal."

"You're the scandal!"

"He'll ruin your life."

"You've already ruined my life."

Once she was waiting for me when I'd been with Jamey and her hand was raised and she turned and I turned right into her hand and it must've been the way the blow fell because it wasn't that strong but she broke my nose.

TEXAS

"There's this guy." Jamey's voice comes, soft and quiet, telling me the story, lulling me with his voice. "This man, this frontiersman. He's a real man. And he's with this wagon train, which is heading for Texas where they've just opened up this new territory, where everything is free and clean and you can start fresh. But there're these guys, see, who want to sabotage the wagon train because they don't want settlers in Texas, they want everything for themselves. This big Texas rancher is behind it all, and he has his henchmen join the wagon train and try and stop it. So they do these different things, like stampeding the livestock, which they blame on the Indians. And there's this big fight with the Indians, but finally this frontiersman gets things all figured out. And there's this big fight with the main henchman, not guns though, just bare fists. The frontiersman cleans everything up with his fists and then the wagon train can continue on to Texas home free.

"And there's these two women, one's a schoolteacher and one's a dancehall girl, although reformed, or at least she's trying to be, except the main henchman is giving her a hard time, having known her someplace once. And she has the hots for this frontiersman but he falls for the schoolteacher even though the dancehall girl saves his life when he gets shot with a poisoned arrow. She sucks the wound clean and spits out the poison.

"And the schoolteacher tries to get the frontiersman to give up his dream of Texas. She's gonna stay in this town where it's more civilized and she wants him to stay, too. And he's attracted to that idea. It's a nice town. But then he decides that that isn't the life for him. Like . . . a frontiersman goes for the frontier. That's what he does. And at the end, when this dancehall girl starts to turn away, he says 'wait.' 'Wait,' he says, 'come on to Texas with me,' he says, and she's standing there all proud and breathing hard. She's a Texas kind of woman. 'We're gonna live it bold,' he says. 'We're gonna live it bold.'"

And there I'd be, kneeling over Jamey, my fingers rippling across the muscles of his back, the tears streaming down my face. I couldn't help it. Anything to do with dogs or kids or people coming together, like at the end where everybody is saved and going to live happily ever after and everybody's hugging everybody else, at a time like that, I couldn't help myself. I'd just bawl, my tears making little salty splashes on Jamey's bare skin.

Jamey told me that story a lot. It was from a movie he saw on the late show. I especially remember him telling it one morning after an out-of-town gig when we were still warm and cozy from our sleep and hadn't yet thought about the day, when the air scarcely stirred and the sun beamed its steady golden stream through our motel room window.

It started with me drumming a rhythm with my fingers on his back, and he had to guess the song. Then I wrote things like I love you, and he had to guess what I'd written. After we got tired of that, I just trickled my fingers lightly along and over his back and played with his hair. I loved the feel of it, thick and strong and curling on his neck. Then I gave him a massage. "Ummmm," he said. "Yeah. There . . . do that again, right there, ummmm that feels good, yeah do that again." Then he told me again about Texas.

Jamey was always attracted to the frontier. He watched the old *Davey Crockett* and *Rawhide* series on video, and when he was in high school he read James Fennimore Cooper's *The Deerslayer* for a book report. He loved western movies and was disgusted that they weren't making many of them any more.

His need to escape what he called the cage of civilization, which translated meant Popi's nagging, set him out on the highway early. The first time he left Terrabain Street, he was thirteen. He borrowed twenty bucks from Beth's babysitting money and hitched into the Rockies, saying he was gonna live it bold. He must have seen that movie by then. He got himself a sixteen-gauge shotgun from a friend or, more accurately, a friend's father, only the father didn't know about it. He was back a week later, a week of frantic worry for Rita, although he phoned once collect to say he was okay. It must have occurred to him that Rita would be worrying. He'd know that she'd never phone the police. He knew that she'd never rat on her son. Besides, cops were not held in high regard by the folks of Terrabain Street. As it happened, with hair all matted and clothes filthy and tattered, he was shipped home by the park warden.

I was in the kitchen when I heard a motor stop at the curb. I looked out the window and there was Jamey being herded along the sidewalk by a man in grey shirt and pants who had *official* stamped all over him. I ran across the hall and told Popi, the only one home. We waited, not saying anything.

After the man made his delivery and gave Popi a lecture on raising kids, he left. Jamey was unapologetic. "There's nothing left for a person who wants to be free," he said, not looking at Popi. "I wish I lived a hundred years ago." He tried to hightail it through the kitchen into his bedroom.

But Popi caught him with the rasp of his voice, dragging him back. "People weren't free then, either," he said.

"Whaddaya mean?" said Jamey, thumping down into a chair at the kitchen table. "In those days, at least you could have a dog without having it tied up. And there was something to do in those days, not like now where there's nothing to do. You could have a gun and go out and shoot meat for supper in those days."

"Yeah," said Popi, sitting himself down across from Jamey, "and what if you couldn't find meat for supper? What then? No Safeway then."

"You'd always find something," said Jamey. But he didn't look like he had. Skinny in the first place, he was really down to bone that time, eye sockets whittled to sharp edges, leaving his eyes like craters you could fall into. And he was quiet, which was different. Later, he said there was nothing like being alone with yourself to make a person look deep inside.

"What did you see when you looked in there?" I said.

"I dunno," he said. "Just . . . somethin'."

Walking along the street to the strange rhythm of our gaits, my busy short-legged melody and his loping long-legged backup chords, our lips clamped around our Big Gulp straws, I tried it. Right then and there, I looked into myself, but I couldn't see nothing, nothing at all. I stood stock still and closed my eyes, but that didn't help. My mind just went blank. I opened my eyes and there bang in front of me was Jamey, his feet leaving footprints in black tar where the city was fixing the sidewalk.

"Your feet are going to be all black," I said.

"So what," he said.

"So you'll never get it off," I said. "Your mom'll have a fit."

"Moms are always having fits," he said.

Rita really had a fit the time she got the call from the border guard saying they had her son and what was she gonna do about it. I was there when she picked up the phone and when she gasped and her face went white. I knew it must be something about Jamey who'd been away a few days. When she breathed out, so did I.

"It's Jamey," she said, turning to look at Popi who was perched at the counter with his green eyeshade like a crest of feathers sticking out from his forehead. "He's not dead," she said. "They got him at Coutts."

That was when Jamey had his Sunbeam but no licence except for his learner's and Rita had to take sixty-three dollars and thirty-four cents of her hard-earned cash and buy a bus ticket and go and get him or they would've impounded the car and sent him home COD.

When the Sunbeam chug-chugged into the backyard, Popi was watching from his window and waiting with his tongue. But when Jamey arrived in the doorway, the two only looked at each other and Popi turned away. And that was the first time I saw how they looked the same, Popi and Jamey, one at the kitchen table leaning forward in a crouch and one leaning on the doorknob doing the same, both with their arched beaks and just the way they stood, perched like, not settled on this earth.

It was amazing that Jamey'd gotten one way across the border without getting caught, but he had. He told me about Montana, the bars open around the clock, the gambling, the video arcades, the free-wheeling non-rated life where anything goes and they don't care about your age as long as you've got money, and the music—the Hank Williams honky-tonking, the rhythm and blues, the rock bars, every kind of music you can imagine. "Next time," I said, "take me with you."

"Sometime . . . maybe," he said.

When Jamey had legitimate wheels, then nothing or nobody could hold him back. He'd quit a job just like that and with a buddy or by himself, and his guitar of course, it goes without saying, he'd take off, especially in summer, sleeping in the car, on a beach someplace, or by the side of the road. Each time he came home, Rita would get him cleaned up and fattened up, he'd get another job at another garage until he got some money together, and then he'd take off again.

A couple of months after making the "Born to Run" tape, he hitched north to the land of the midnight sun. When he left, our eyes met in a different way, but he didn't ask my permission. He never did. He always did what he wanted or what he felt he had to do, and it was up to me whether or not I went along. Except for once. But that was years later.

When he staggered back covered with mosquito and blackfly welts and, according to Rita, spider mites in his beard, he stared with eyes pale and bleached out, like he'd been blinded or seen too much. His hair and his skin, too, seemed bleached, like he was too long in the sun or coming out of a long winter. Or maybe space itself can bleach a person out.

"Those Eskimo girls . . . whooee," he said after a few days, when he'd loosened up and was getting back to normal, looking at me with his eyes gleaming and his grin teasing.

The last time he took off like that, without me, he was eighteen. He was heading for Mexico. It was late November. The poplars along Terrabain Street were bare and grey against the white sky. We stood on the sidewalk and Rita gave Jamey another Saint Christopher medal because he always lost the last one she gave him. She tried to smile and kissed him and let him go. He was hitching again, since he'd sold his latest vehicle to get up the dough for the journey. We watched his backpack, his and this other guy's he was going with, all the way down the street getting smaller. We watched the guitar slung over his shoulder.

"He looks so big and grown-up from when he was a baby," Rita said, sniffling now Jamey couldn't see.

"Of course, whaddaya expect," said Popi, wheeling on his foot to go back into the house. "He's gonna stay a baby forever?"

"I dunno," said Rita, her eyes and nose getting red. "It's too soon, that's all. It went too soon."

"A fart in a windstorm," said Popi, with his one crutch, hopping through the gate. "That's life. We only change from little farts to big farts."

I played our old game where you stare and stare until a person stares back. Sure enough, at the end of the street Jamey turned and waved. And he looked straight at me, into my eyes. I knew he did, because I knew Jamey like myself, even better. He'd told me the week before how he had to go. "I gotta get outta here," he'd said. "This dead-end existence, it'll kill me if I don't get out." We were lying in my mother's bed. He hugged me close. "But I'll come back," he said into the warm crook of my neck. "I'll come back for you." I said okay. I mean, what else could I say? I was thinking, though, how Tree'd have a field day with this one. But she didn't. She didn't say anything to me about it. Maybe she was tired of nagging me, maybe she was afraid I'd go, too. I don't know, but she kept her mouth shut, which wasn't like her.

So we all waved back and then Jamey turned the corner and Rita said, "Sometimes I wonder. I don't know . . ." Her eyes were straight ahead.

"What?" said Tree.

"If I did right by him."

"Whaddaya mean?" said Tree. "No mother could have done more."

"But did I give him the right learning?" said Rita. "I mean, to face the world like. Like, when he was small we used to play this zoo game, him and me. We played this game where you take a card like in Bingo only instead of filling it with numbers you have to fill it with pictures of different animals and the first one to fill their card wins. I used to let Jamey win, but that didn't satisfy him. I win the game! he'd shout all excited and throw up his hands. Now you have to win, he'd say and he'd help me take cards until I had my card filled too. He never could understand how only one person could be the winner. I tried to explain it to him once. But you have to win, too, he'd say, just like that, flipping those pictures over quick as a wink, helping me find the ones I needed. And then he went to school but he never could seem to get that straight, about winning. I don't know . . ."

We stared at the spot where Jamey had disappeared, all us women standing on the cracked sidewalk, Rita's thin ankles in backless satin, Beth's turned-in ballerinas, Tree's thick stumps in plunkety wedgies, my fuzzy boots. Dry autumn leaves blew up in a little swirl around our feet and then it started to snow.

The spring Jamey returned from Mexico, the way it happened, Beth and me were coming home from school, loaded with homework for the weekend. "What're y' gonna do tonight?" I said.

"Babysit," she said. "What about you?"

"I dunno," I said. "Maybe I'll wash my hair."

We slouched around the corner onto Terrabain Street. There it was, our house, near the end, but come to life. Maybe Paquette had done some spring painting. Maybe it was the poplar tree at the front just coming into leaf. But somehow it looked different. Then it came to me. I started running.

"Jamey's home," I called across my shoulder at Beth. Don't ask me how I knew, but I did. I ran all the way down the long block. The heavy books didn't seem heavy anymore because I knew I wouldn't be opening them.

I ran through the gate, up the verandah steps, in the door and up the stairs, heart pounding to the rhythm of my feet. I burst through the Popilowskis' door and there he was with his wild hair and his long legs stretched out into the middle of the room. There he was, his mouth full of laughter but different somehow. It took me a moment to realize that what I saw before me was no longer a boy.

"Hey," he said, letting the laugh out into a deep chuckle and standing up and coming over close to me. "You're looking good," he said.

He looked good, too, brown and hard, but somehow I couldn't tell him. Instead, I said, "No, I'm not. I'm fat. I got pimples." Then, I could have eaten my lips, which in fact I did, turning them inside and clamping down with my teeth, a habit I'd got into and that I particularly hated.

"Hey, you're not fat," he said. "Who's been telling my girl that?" He touched my cheek with his knuckles. "I can't see no pimples." And he really looked, too, at my eyes, down my nose to my mouth, like my face was under a microscope.

Everybody always knew when Jamey was home. The phone started ringing off the wall. People came to the door. Guys came with their guitars and their girls. Girls came with their white lipstick and purple hair. A year earlier, Jamey would have had a girl and I would have been plunged into the role alongside Beth of little sister. But when he came back from Mexico, I was his girl.

It seemed like something life-changing must have happened in Mexico. I asked him about it. He said he went up to a mountain village with some locals and smoked some really great dope and had a vision of how great he could be. But it seemed to me it was more the playing a lot of bars and other venues, too, that really gave him the vision. The audience ate it up, he said. "Like, there I was in another country and the audience really liked me. I think I can do it," he said. "Play on a larger stage. But I have to get myself ready."

After Mexico, Jamey staked himself for a couple of years. He got up his first band that rehearsed regularly and went after gigs and had bookings ahead. Popi yelled at him to get a job. Jamey snapped back. "I got a job. No way I'm gonna be one of them dumb fucks who think listening to music and getting laid Saturday night is living." For a change, he'd come home with money. He'd been gigging all the way up through the States for pretty good payola, as he put it. And that was how he was able to buy his first van.

The Grislies didn't last long because people thought it was about bears and half expected to see the band in teddy costumes. The name confused the point, which was protest against the arms race and

Armageddon and all like that. The sound was heavy metal, sizzling electric and insistent escalation to some crazy height. The colour was black, T-shirts and tight pants. Tattoos were definitely in. Shaved heads, Mohawks or coloured spikes were the hairstyles. The props were skeletons and bombs and stuff. But Jamey got disgusted when people thought they were the Grizzlies. His reaction was to go more abrasive.

That's when Lucifer was born. He got a deal on a paint job on the van because he knew this guy at a paint shop. He got flames and devils and "Lucifer" in black against red. Jamey was Lucifer. He made up the costume himself and got Rita to sew it. He got up all these stage sets with chains and manacles and cobwebby nets and instruments of torture, "all the things," Jamey said, "that keep man in the underworld." He got up strobe lights that flashed red like lightning when he jumped onto the stage in a poof of smoke. Figuring the band needed a female presence, in a gothic burlesque move he got me up to look like Morticia Addams. He taught me about monitors and amps and how to use a mike. As for the music, it was strictly head-banging stuff. I gotta admit, for a guy who'd been raised pretty much on country pop and soft-core radio rock, it was different.

As Paquette said after hearing us rehearse in the cellar, "Jesus wept." No wonder. Paquette liked Wilf Carter. I can still hear him singing "I'm in the jailhouse now" and "Blue Canadian Rockies" or, when his cronies came over, French Canadian songs that, judging from the jokes and laughter, were pretty gross. Rita and Popi were down-home country fans, not your country rock or pop but more leaning to bluegrass, although Rita liked all kinds of music except maybe opera. Tree actually liked opera and especially Mario Lanza, maybe because of her Italian heritage. She had an old record player and some old records that she'd get out once in a while. I can still hear the sound of the needle as the record went around and around and the voice behind it, tragic and heartbroken. Tree wasn't much for contemporary hits but when she and Rita would get into their cups on Saturday night, they'd have a great time with some Emmylou Harris and Loretta Lynn. Rita could really belt out "Don't Come Home A-drinkin' with Lovin' on Your Mind."

Jamey was like Rita in that he liked all kinds of music, which maybe is why he had to try different things and take a while to find his own sound. Early on during his man-in- the-wilderness stage, he even wrote some country songs: *in the bunk house is darkness/outside is snow/the cattle are lost/there's no bunch grass for show/my lariat's wasted/frozen on the wire/i'm not in the saddle/i've lost all desire*, but I think there wasn't enough thumping and bumping in country to satisfy his soul. Not enough screaming . . . *i want to scream/a nightmare not a dream* . . .

"I'm making a statement," he said to Popi during his screaming period, but nobody could understand what it was because they couldn't hear the words.

"You're not supposed to hear the words," said Marie who, since she had left Terrabain Street and was a married woman, knew everything. "You're supposed to hear a primal scream."

"Wait'll they've lived awhile longer," said Tree. "Then they'll have something to scream about."

"That's when you get quiet," said Popi. "That's when you realize it ain't no use to scream."

To Jamey the words were clear. . . . *the river moves faster than it did yesterday/and suburbs are growing where buffalo once grazed* . . . "Urban alienation," he said. "Jesus, you guys are right in the middle of it and you don't even know it."

"De-ball" was a word he was big on at the time. "They not gonna de-ball me," he said. "Turn me into mishmash teeny-bopper mainstream porridge." "They" was popular culture. "They want to keep it safe," Jamey said. "Sanitized. That's why we have to try and make it unsafe."

He listened to a lot of early Rolling Stones and AC/DC and Zeppelin. And night after night he'd get up there, thrusting it with all he had in him, saying fuck you, try'n stop me, try'n put me down, kill me but I won't stop fuckin the world.

After a while maybe he felt defined. Or maybe he got tired of the sharp sound of nothingness, the electric guitar string slicing into the amp like a razor blade. Whatever. Next, he got quiet with The Grunge, which started out as The Glorious Grunge but soon got shortened. The Grunge was into a sort of sweaty rock. That was a couple of years before Nirvana but Jamey must've heard about the movement.

Anyway, after all that garage Gothic, it was some relief and a lot easier on my voice. The Grunge guys didn't have hairstyles, they just had hair and lots of it. They looked like they slept in their clothes. Jamey sold the van to some kids just starting up and bought a new one that was old and dented and rusted and forever breaking down and brought us to our knees more times than I like to remember.

"It goes with the territory," he said once when I asked him if he was having a good time. We were in the dark at the side of a gravel road, coming back from nowhere. He was fixing a flat.

I was huddled into my jacket because it was cold and pacing back and forth because I had to pee.

"For Chrissake, go in the ditch," Jamey said.

"There isn't a ditch," I said, looking around at the landscape, flat as far as the eye could see in any direction. We were near the Saskatchewan border.

"Go in the middle of the road," said Jamey. "Who cares?"

"I care," I said, looking at the other guys in the band all standing around Jamey giving out with the advice on changing tires. I looked up and down the highway. "What if a car comes along?" I said.

"No one's gonna come along," said Jamey. "Not out here, not in the middle of the night."

"Don't any of you guys dare look," I shouted and tottered a distance along the gravel in my high heel boots, in my skin-tight one-piece jumpsuit that was going to turn a simple thing like peeing into a major undertaking. At that moment, I was thinking a lot of things, one of them being was I in my right mind. Maybe I even said it out loud.

I went along with all those bands, at first so there'd be at least one person in the audience and later because I was part of the show. And, always, I wanted to be around Jamey. But it wasn't only Jamey; it was the music, too, or maybe you couldn't separate them. All I know, music filled that lonely space that always threatened inside of me. It filled my head so lonely thoughts couldn't get in. Music and Jamey. And there was the fascination of Jamey's performance, too. The way his noise belted out of his mouth, those first years trying to make up in volume what it lacked in melody.

I got into the whole scene. By that time I was working part time at Zellers and I got me some black leather, not real of course, but the black went with my hair, which I tried to get like Cher's, not entirely successful but not bad, either. And in that leather I could feel my body taking a different shape, curving in here and out there, and not just a square blob.

In the beginning, before she got engaged to Gord, Beth came along, too. We'd listen to the band and get up and dance. I was crazy for dancing, like the girl in the Bryan Adams song. Beth was too, but she was never cut out for the life like I was. She didn't smoke even ordinary cigarettes or try any of the new hairstyles or wear much makeup. She was totally grossed out by one of the guys in the band who had snake tattoos all up his arms and rings in his nose and lips and eyebrows, although she said she didn't mind my one tattoo, a butterfly on my shoulder. I was going to get more, to bug Tree, but tattoos freaked out Jamey. "There're enough scars in this family," he said.

Beth and me would help set up the scenario for whoever Jamey was at the moment, she always staying slightly behind me like a shadow, only a bright one, she was so blonde, like a rim of light around my dark edge. During the show I'd get up and do my thing, harmonizing with Jamey or doing some backup vocals or maybe a warmup number. One solo was about all I could manage because I wasn't comfortable out on that stage all by myself. Unlike Jamey, I couldn't do theatrics. I couldn't get myself to jump around and bang my head. No matter how wild the band got, my thing was to simply walk out there, guitar in hand, stand there and sing my song, then walk off again. But the audience seemed to like it, at least they didn't boo me off the stage. Actually, it was a miracle I got up there at all. But I forced myself because I loved to sing. It's a funny thing, Beth was as good as me, maybe better, but she couldn't force herself to get up there, so she ended up marrying Gord, which is what she wanted to do I guess.

After the show, we'd help take things down. When Jamey did warm-ups for bigger names, creating all that atmosphere might have seemed like a lot of work for a short opening spot. But Beth and me didn't mind helping, it was fun, and the props made Jamey's act different than some of the others around town. Like the man says, you gotta have a gimmick.

Right after a performance, Jamey would be on an adrenalin high, not to mention other kinds, but later he'd start to have doubts. On the way home, he'd mumble, soft-voiced and quick, more to himself than anyone, "Jeez, we did so many things wrong."

"Whaddaya mean, wrong?" I'd say, my body swinging hard into his as he turned a corner. "You didn't do nothin wrong,"

"Don't say that," he'd say. "You know very well we did everything wrong."

"So, nobody noticed but you." My body swerved the other way into the soft cushion of Beth.

Or, munching down his third hamburger, for he was always starving after a show, "We need to get in more practice," he'd say. And he did. Any time he wasn't performing, he was practising.

I watched a lot of shows, and I got so I knew the routine, not only the work routine but the emotional routine, the excitement of setting up, the tension rising to performance. Jamey would jump onto the stage in a flash of lights or walk on slowly under a spot. He'd writhe and thrash or twist and shout or dig himself in with maybe only his heel hammering a tense beat. But whoever he was, in whatever phase, he gave it all away to the audience, and sometimes it was fine because they appreciated it, and sometimes it was sad because they just stared into their drinks or kept on talking or sat there stoned. That was when Jamey cranked up the sound.

The Grunge did okay. They got a lot of out-of-town gigs, which Jamey liked because he could try his material on different audiences. To get away from covers, he wrote new material as fast as he could, and although he still wrote protest songs, he also wrote about being young and rockin'. Young audiences liked that because they could get up and dance. We got more and more offers to headline. Jamey became a local name. He got busy. At times, he was going and coming so much, half the time he didn't know if he was coming or going. "And happier'n a pig in shit," as Rita said.

"What a life," he'd complain cheerfully. "Up all night, sleep all day. But you gotta live it. You gotta act like a musician," he said, "if you want to be one."

Part of living like a musician was the partying. Not that Jamey ever needed encouragement in that area. But in a musician's life, it's part of the routine. I sometimes wondered if the music was just an excuse to party. And maybe sometimes it was. But, also, after being on such a high, you need to unwind. And, after the music ends, after the adrenalin rush, when you pick up your toys and go home, there's always a letdown, an emptiness that can only be filled by carrying on the party. So after a show we always went someplace, a bar, someone's pad, and we'd party until dawn. Then we'd crash where we found an empty mattress or even a place on the floor.

Tree hated me living that life. At first she flatly forbade it, and since I was not quite seventeen at the time, she had some leverage. She screamed that she'd lock me in and throw away the key. I screamed that I'd jump out the window. She screamed that she'd put me in a convent. I screamed that I'd slit my wrists. She screamed slut, whore, bitch. I screamed that I'd cover my body with tattoos. She screamed, "You sing stupid! You look stupid. In those stupid clothes! You look like a clown!" I screamed, "No wonder my father left you. You're so fat and stupid and ugly." After a while, we stopped screaming. Maybe Tree was tired, maybe she gave up, maybe she didn't want to alienate Rita, although she told Rita right from the beginning that she had nothing against Jamey. Jamey wasn't doing nothing wrong, except being a musician was a crazy thing to want to be. Strangely, it was all right for boys to sleep with girls, but not for girls to sleep with boys. I was the one who was bad, a bad girl, who wasn't being a good daughter. Rita nodded sympathetically and got her another beer from the fridge.

So I kept on helping Jamey pack everything into the van. We'd throw in the guitars and the sound equipment. We'd pick up Greg and Jeff or Mike and Bruce and Kevin or whoever was part of us at the time, and away we'd go, a-hootin' and a-hollerin' and having the time of our lives. There were other things I should've been doing, like homework, like passing exams, like learning life skills. But music let me off the hook. Because the great thing about music is, when you're listening to it, you don't think about nothing else. It just takes you and carries you and you don't worry. It's a great way of getting through life.

It seemed to me things were going real good, but one night, lying in the warmth of our bodies, Jamey said, "Trouble is there's too many groups going now for this town. I'm thinking of heading for the coast."

"There's even more at the coast," I said, sitting up on the bed in yet another less-than-ritzy motel room after yet another out-of-town gig we'd played the night before.

"But there's more venues, too. And more chances to make it big." Jamey was lying on his stomach, chin propped on his fists.

"I don't know," I said. "Music's such a big chance. And then sometimes you try'n do something, you know, something different maybe and people laugh at you. Everybody has a ball, laughing their guts out and sneering."

"I tell y' my girl there's them as ud sneer/When y' fall flat with yer face in yer beer . . ."

"Get serious. You'll be making up a song on your death bed."

"That's the time you need a song all right. That's the time to be singing. That's what the Indians did, sang themselves across the finish line, into the Happy Hunting Grounds."

"What if you don't make it?" I said. "Big, I mean."

"Hey!" He turned over. "Don't you say things like that. You're not supposed to say things like that."

"What am I supposed to say?"

"You're supposed to say, *hey Jamey you're the big man, you're wonderful, you can do anything*. Now," he looked up at me with his blue eyes so clear. "Repeat after me . . ."

So I did.

PACKING IT IN

first thing momma told me/i was born to drive/when she pushed down on the gas/it felt good to be alive/then i picked up my own old pickup truck/ and headed for west coast sun/going for a deep sea dive/i was going to have some fun . . .

The next week I left with Jamey, early in the morning with the sun coming up at our backs. We left right after a gig, not even stopping to sleep, throwing the guitars and amps into the back of a souped-up Corvette Jamey had just got on a trade-in. He said he didn't want to leave rattling and clanking down the street in a van. He said he wanted to leave clean and free and not dragging baggage. He wanted to take off in a zoom. And he did. No other cars were on the highway and he drove very fast. I think he was trying to hit the speed of light.

We drove and drove, at first through the dark, then with the rising sun behind us. . . . *first thing i remember/a woman flagged me down/ dressed in boots cowboy style/jet black and brown/she looked at me i looked at her/our eyeballs caught on fire/i remember thinking to myself/ we were doubles twisted on a wire . . .*

I tried to stay awake so I could talk to Jamey and keep him awake, but the fields before my eyes, and then the forests, all blurred and spun and lulled me into a sort of sleep.

. . . making time on a two-lane line/we were feeling late/so i punched

a roar from the four-five-four . . . My eyes kept popping open as pictures from the depths of my brain surfaced and appeared on the landscape, so real that for a moment I would be back in the three-room suite above Paquette's with my mother coming through the door with her wide hips and her shopping bag. Then I'd realize that I was there in the car with Jamey with the dash all lit up green and red and the stereo on low and Jamey's smoke curling around us like grey cozy fur. Then I'd close my eyes again.

. . . *their third sight was the mountains/a prehistoric stone spine* . . . And that's how I first travelled through the Rocky Mountains, the first time I ever went anywhere in my life, my brain drifting between sleep and awake so I couldn't tell what was really happening and what wasn't.

When I woke up for real, Jamey was turning the car off the highway into this restaurant parking lot, and I was suddenly ravenously hungry, besides which I had to pee like a racehorse.

Then I remembered. "I have to phone Tree," I said through a mouth that felt like brown cotton batting.

"What for?" said Jamey, stretching up his arms and shaking his mop.

"I have to tell her I'm gone." I sat up and pressed my hands between my knees.

"You don't think she'll figure it out?" His hand came down and massaged the back of my neck and that felt good.

"I should've phoned already. What time is it?"

Jamey looked at his wrist. "Nearly nine. Soon it'll be eight here. We go through a time zone. We're getting younger by the second." He started fiddling with his watch.

"I never passed through a time zone before." I thought it then said it.

Jamey yawned.

I thought some more. "Imagine," I said. "All over the world, people, right this moment, in different times, doing different things, right this very moment that we're sitting here thinking about it."

"What weird place you beamed me into?" Jamey said, cutting up in his Querulous King waver, opening the car door and stepping out and stretching again and looking around him and changing his tone of voice to the Wizard's and saying, "Earth, oh sire."

"Mom'll be at work," I said, getting out, too.

"To the dungeon with him, men," Jamey quavered. "Hang him by the heels."

"Giuseppe will have a bird."

In the clear mountain air, our shoes echoed on the gravel. Jamey put his arm around my shoulders. I hooked my thumb into his back pocket. "I never could phone her when the belt was on," I said. "Phone at coffee or lunch, she always said. Not when the belt's on." We went in the door of the restaurant. "Still, I have to phone," I said.

"We're both gone, she'll figure it out on her own," said Jamey.

"She'll be upset."

"They get used to it."

"She's not used to it yet."

"After a while they're glad you're gone."

"Not Tree."

"One less worry."

"Not Rita, either."

"You hafta train them to do without you, be independent."

"I have to phone."

"I thought you hated her."

"I do, but . . ." Into my head popped a picture of Tree, red-eyed and pink-nosed, from crying. "I don't want her to worry."

Figuring it'd be better to get Tree on her coffee break, I could put it off for a while longer. In the meantime, like a murderer with the last meal, I ordered the breakfast lumberjack special.

"Whoa," said Jamey. "This mountain air's giving my girl an appetite."

"I know you," I said. "You'll eat yours and mine too."

"Man, man, don't it feel good to be on the road?" Jamey threw back his shoulders. "Doesn't it feel great? And with this weather," he looked at the window. "It's an omen." He grinned across at me. "Hey, Mary, hold your hat on tight, cause we're headin for a whirlwind flight." He grabbed a napkin. "Hey, you gotta pen?" And he started scribbling. And he started talking fast. "Goin down the road, goin on down the line, leaving cold and dark behind, heading for the sunshine beaches . . . no . . . not sunshine, just beaches, we reach up and pick, pluck, whaddaya think about peaches? too predictable, I agree, pluck the blue, the sun, pluck the stars . . ."

Our lumberjack specials came. Jamey made a ball of the napkin in his hand and tossed it across at me and I caught it.

Finally, our stomachs fat and full as lazy cats, sitting in the sunny window with our third cups of coffee, looking out to where the mountains hit the blue blue sky, "It's time," I said and stood up. I sat back down. "WhadoIdo?"

"You got quarters?" said Jamey. "You'll need lots of quarters." And he gave me what he had. "All you do is dial zero and this voice comes on and you say how you want to make a call to Edmonton and you give them Giuseppe's number. The voice takes it from there."

"I'll get Janet. What if I get Giuseppe?" The thought made me break out into a cold sweat.

"Phone person-to-person if it'll make you feel better."

"You do it for me."

"I don't wanna talk to your mother."

"No, I mean just the number part. Then I'll take the phone."

"Look, it's not that hard. Honest to Gawd. Would I lie to you?" He smiled his lopsided smile. "You give it a try. You have any trouble, I'll come."

I closed my fist hard around Jamey's song, which I was still clutching in my hand. I stood up and went to the front counter. Coming in, I'd cased the pay phone in a glass bubble near the door. I lined up my change in neat little piles and took the plunge.

I heard the phone ringing at the other end, across all those miles. Then Janet, Giuseppe's secretary, came on and it seemed like another miracle, the way she was sitting there in that office so far away and I could hear her voice.

"I have a long distance call," said the operator, "for a Teresa Turner."

Dead silence. I could see in my mind Janet trying to put it together. Tree had worked at Giuseppe's for as long as I could remember. Never before had she been called long distance.

It must've been only ten seconds before Janet said, "Just a minute, I'll get her." But ten seconds is a long time when you're waiting for somebody to say something across a thin wire.

I could hear a clatter of the phone being put down and muffled footsteps and then, nothing. I could imagine, though, Janet standing at the door of the lunchroom, her brassy voice announcing long distance, the excitement of the women with this piece of news.

I should've given Janet my name, I thought. Unless I was actually in the same room with Tree, she lived in terror of phone calls. To Tree, the phone was the enemy, the instrument of disaster. And especially at work. Why would anyone phone her long distance at work unless it was bad news? She'll think it's the police or the hospital or the morgue, I thought. All the way from the lunchroom to the phone she'll be seeing my body mangled in the remains of crushed metal.

There was such a sound of silence on the line, like no humming or background noises or nothing, I thought I'd lost the connection. But then the operator came on and asked for more quarters and then another voice, high and thin and out of breath, which I scarcely recognized as Tree's, came on. "Hello," it said.

"Hi," I said. "This is Lilah."

"What's wrong?" I saw her face, full of fear and waiting for the worst.

"Nothing. Nothing's wrong." I said. "I'm okay." I paused. "I'm here," I said, "here in . . .," I looked around for a name and couldn't find one. "I'm in BC," I said. "With Jamey. We're going to Vancouver."

"You can't," she said. "Your toothbrush is here."

"I know," I said. "I'll have to buy another."

"Your clothes are here," she said. "They're in the closet."

"I know," I said. "I'll have to get some others. It was a spur-of-the-moment decision."

"How can you do this to me?" she said.

"We finished this gig and it was such a beautiful morning," I said. "The sun was just coming up. The birds were just starting to sing."

"You'll be sorry," she said.

"Just think of it like I'm away on a holiday," I said. "I'll be back."

"When?"

"Someday."

"Maybe I won't be here." Anger and hostility were entering her voice. I started feeling better.

"Where will you be?" I said.

"In the beyond," she said. "Dead. Killed by my own daughter. My own flesh and blood."

"Oh, Mom. What do you expect? Me to stay with you forever?"

"No." Pause. "Not in the same house."

I looked up and saw Jamey at the cash register, counting out some money. I saw his neck, at the back, where I liked to kiss it.

"I gotta go," I said.

"You'll be sorry," she said.

Jamey was picking up a toothpick from the little barrel. "I gotta go," I said.

"You'll come back on your hands and knees. See if I take you back then!"

Jamey turned and looked around for me. When he caught my eye he jerked his head toward the door.

"I don't have any more quarters," I said, which was just about true.

She changed her tactics. "Last evening I put a new zipper in those jeans for you. I didn't sleep. I kept waking up and seeing those jeans and wondering where you were."

Jamey's jean jacket was going out the door. "Look . . . Mom . . ." I said.

"All night, I kept seeing those jeans, but you weren't in them."

Jamey was now separated from me by three panes of glass. "I gotta go, Mom," I said. "I'll write. As soon as I know what I'm doing. Where I'm gonna be."

She was still talking when I hung up the phone. I ran out through all the doors. "Hey, wait up," I called. "Wait for me. Hey, where's the fire?" I said, hooking on to Jamey's arm.

"So, whadid she say?" asked Jamey, looking down at me. I looked up and the morning was so bright and clear, I could see myself reflected in his eyes.

"Nothing," I said. I looked away, across the highway. My eyes travelled up, up to the mountains, up to the sky. "What's the name of this town?" I said.

"Golden," he said.

He broke away from my arm and started miming guitar. I still had his napkin in my hand. All the time I'd been talking to Tree, I'd been balling it in my sweaty palm so now it was like a bullet. "Here," I said, throwing it at Jamey and laughing. "You and your songs."

So then he started singing. "Lilah, trying her freedom wings, having herself a fling, put away alla her toys, tryin to be one of the boys, with ass and boobs like that who she tryin to kid."

"Ha ha ha," I said, scooping up Jamey's song and putting it in my pocket. "Here's one for you," and I did my own mime and strutted my stuff, too. "oooooo Jamey with your nice tight bum, why you all on the run? and that bump on the front of your jeans, man you gonna split your seams."

And we played and danced all the way to the car. When we got there, we were laughing so hard we could barely stand up.

PART TWO

SHOOTING STAR

I never did write Tree. Dancing across the earth as we did, moving so fast, never staying long enough in one spot to have a forwarding address, I didn't have time. Being in love is a full-time job. You have to have fights, you have to make up. When you're together, you have to talk for hours on end about every detail. When you're apart, you have to think constantly about what he said and then what you said and then what he said. It takes a lot of dedication.

Driving out to Vancouver for the first time is one thing I'll never forget. Through the Fraser Valley, the long corridor out to Hope, through the lush green rising up either side to the forested hills. And then the city itself, which I could scarcely believe it struck me so with wonder, so different from what I'd come from, so varied before us with the tall buildings in the distance beckoning us out still farther. And crossing the Port Mann, I had never seen a bridge like that before, so long and wide, arching and glinting silver in the sunshine across the river we travelled so eager for the experience of our lives. The steamships, the barges, the factories, and in the midst of all that, a temple of gold.

Jamey drove as though he knew where he was going. East Hastings, or what I later got to know as such. All the shops and colourful storefronts, all the strange words and languages printed above butchers, bakers and candlestick makers. Every kind of café, restaurant and deli you could imagine, flower shops with blooms spilling onto the sidewalk, and garden fresh vegetables, so the signs said, strange vegetables too, prickly and barbarous, I'd never seen before. And the people! Crowds of people making the place electric. Like rock concert Saturday night only it was the middle of the day and people were carrying shopping bags. But the way they walked! Not loose and sauntering or even striding the way I was used to seeing prairie people move, but more like rats running a maze with quick, small steps. And the people dressed so strange in colours and costumes, they didn't seem to care what they looked like or if anybody saw them or not. Black people and white people and those in between, with pigtails and ponytails and thick braids and thin braids and hair to their bums and hair shaved off. And one man so fat he could scarcely walk and another so thin he could scarcely do the same.

I'm really living, I thought then, sitting beside Jamey, our shoulders touching, my hand on his thigh, just to always know he was there.

Jamey took us right through it, through traffic I never saw the likes of. Horns honking and cars zipping in and out. He'd get in the left lane only to find everybody trying to make a turn out of it, so quick and sharp he'd get in the right only to find it blocked by a street repair, and back and forth and back and forth, he moved us like a corkscrew working its way to the centre. And all the time I was holding my breath, wondering what sights we'd see next.

Granville, the music all around, a girl my age with long dark silky hair, sitting on a bench, the notes of her sad flute wafting across the street. And, beside her on the bench, her kid playing with a paper lantern. And a guy in a doorway with a guitar singing about how we gotta save the sea, another with an accordion, and then later, on the beach, a group of folk singers and dancers, and guys mostly with guitars but some with a mouth organ or a banjo, everybody with the guitar case open, or the hat.

Oh, and the sea when we got there! I had never seen the sea. So open before us, the fresh breeze coming off. I never could make up my mind whether I liked it better in the mist or the clear. In the mist so mysterious sending thrills up my spine, but in the clear and blue sky such a sense of freedom and like going forever. And so different from the bog I came out of, where you always feel something is going to pull you down and close over your face, like the ground itself is going to swallow you in, or maybe it was Tree or, who knows, maybe it was me, smothering myself. All I know is, I felt good in Vancouver, there with Jamey, doing our own thing together.

And one day on the street, I saw a man walking toward me through the crowd, shouldering his way through this way and that. It was hot and he had on a sleeveless shirt and his arms were brown and you could see the muscles and his chest was wide with a patch of hair showing at the top of the shirt, and just the way his snaky hips moved through the crowd, I thought Wow! there's a real man. And it was Jamey. And it struck me for the first time how he could be another person apart from me, a person I would not know.

Jamey was in his glory. He sold his car and bought a van that had space for equipment. That's when I knew he was serious about the music business because he was still in love with that Corvette. The way cars worked with Jamey, right from the time he was fifteen, he'd cruise used car lots going from car to car appraising bodies and lifting hoods. I'd be admiring a new paint job in fire engine red or stroking down the nap of white shag seat covers, when I'd hear a quick slam bang and know whatever that one was it didn't stand a chance. But if things got quiet, I'd turn around. He'd be standing before an open hood, just looking, as though wanting the anticipation to last, or maybe not wanting to be disappointed. Then, moving real slow, he'd put out his hand and touch. He'd touch everything, liking the feel of cool metal on his fingers. And he'd hold his fingers on each part awhile. And he'd turn to me with that gleam in his eye. After a few months, he'd start saying things like, "she's sure a gas eater," or "she's flooding the carburator," or "didja hear that knock in the engine?" and I'd know the bloom of love had worn off and that it wouldn't be long before I'd find myself in yet another used car lot. But that Corvette, he'd only had it a month, not even that, because he'd traded in the van the day before we headed west.

Jamey knew about a hundred guys in Vancouver, who had all been in and out of about a hundred bands, so it wasn't hard to find a place to crash. Nearly every night we went out to hear a band, blues, jazz, folk, most of them with a solid rock edge. Jamey couldn't get away from that thumping rhythm Rita said he was born with. He did a lot of jamming at late night open stages after hours to make himself familiar in the music scene. From that and from knowing people, he got gigs filling in with bands. Then, through those contacts and his persistence in making calls and trying out, it wasn't long before he started getting solo gigs, one night in this bar, one in that. He got pretty excited the first time he was headlined for a whole weekend.

He wrote a lot of songs that summer. "The blood is in my brain," he said. "Gotta get it down while it's fresh, while it's clear." What he wrote was different, more personal. In Edmonton, he wrote about war and the environment and how we're all doomed. . . . *night will come and some will die/but through it all man must try/now's the time to kiss the bride/man and nature side by side* . . . In Vancouver he wrote about people—restless spirits and misfits of one kind or another and how relationships were like two railroad tracks never coming together. I was the only one who knew he was writing about the people of Terrabain Street, especially Popi and Rita. Even the one that later became popular as a love song . . . *and i want to know will we ever feel the same/it has been such a long long time/i want to know do we need to feel the pain* . . . he was thinking of Popi. He wasn't into writing love songs yet. Maybe love, like Terrabain Street, needed distance between himself and it before he could write about it. But for the time being I had *comfort me true/comfort me blue* . . . , which I held close to my heart.

Those weeks of mostly working by himself gave him a clearer picture of who he was, or who he wanted to be, as a musician, that is. I'm not sure Jamey ever took the time to know who he was apart from his music. And maybe they were one and the same. Like in the Eagles song, how can you tell the dancer from the dance? Maybe he felt he wasn't anybody without his music. Maybe he couldn't ever let himself think of the Adam West side of his character when he had to be Batman. But he hadn't yet decided what the Batman costume would be. He didn't yet have his finger on the pulse of his own music, but he was working on it, nightly exploring possibilities. He replaced the total hair and torn jacket and laceless runners of his former self with a kind of early Springsteen working-class look—a three-day growth and sleeveless T-shirt and faded jeans, but clean and in one piece. For a while he wore a tam onstage to control the wild look of his naturally curly hair.

His sound became less abrasive. Part of the baggage he left behind on the prairies was the head banging and heavy metal. Maybe, on the coast, he didn't feel the need to be rebellious, at least in the same way. Maybe he'd got something out of his system. He was still a rocker, though, he was always a rocker. One of his favourites was Neil Young's *hey hey, my my, rock and roll can never die*. But instead of just going for a loud sound and rhythm, he seemed to be exploring himself more and expressing what he found through his music. He could still howl and snarl about a ruined life or a love that went wrong and sometimes he'd crank up the sound but in the smaller venues it didn't work that well, so mostly he didn't. Same with the writhe and thrash. And while he still had his eye on the arena—Jamey was a performer who needed a big stage and a big audience—for the time being he was having a blast, sometimes playing with someone he didn't know and getting off on reacting quick on his feet, or sometimes leaning into a long improvisational solo. Coffeehouses were good places for him to try things because they seemed friendlier than bars. They gave him a chance to draw out moods or feelings, to mash down on lyrics. Once, in one of those cellars, when he was doing a bluesy number, lazy as smoke, the smell of grass floating lazy, too, from table to table, I looked around and saw how we were all drifting on a calm sea where we were all mingled together.

He was having such a good time, even audience reaction, or lack thereof, didn't get him down. Even bars where nobody listened, they were so busy clinking glasses and shooting the shit, as Paquette always used to say. Even the PNE where he did a gig as a booth musician at the BC Tel display. It was good money, but in the middle of a song he'd get people asking him where the washroom was, even when it was a song he'd poured his guts into, like the one about those late-night sessions with Popi after he'd run away and was brought back home by the police.

Between gigs and in the afternoons, he was busy on the street, making contacts, keeping the ones he had, getting his name around. Zip, zip, he didn't want to even stop to eat. He'd meet me at a restaurant, slide into the booth across from me, eat two bites, jump up to talk to somebody at the next table.

"For God's sake, sit down," I said, knowing I was sounding like Rita or even Tree. I had to admit it gave me pleasure, bossing him around, taking care of him. "Enjoy your meal," I ordered.

"I am enjoying it," he said. "This is the way I like to eat."

"You never eat a full meal any more," I accused.

"Full meals fill me up too full," he answered. "Full meals are boring."

"Your gut has to be filled or you'll starve to death," I said.

"I don't like the feel of all that garbage swishing around in me," he said. "All that garbage slows me down."

Jamey didn't think of those Vancouver days as a period of experimentation and growth and development. That's my spin on it now, looking back. He was just happy doing what he was doing at the moment, landing on his feet and getting his bearings before becoming dissatisfied with that and then having to move on. While fame and fortune were in the back of his mind, that was a hazy picture of the future, which he knew would arrive someday. So even when he had a slow week, he didn't get discouraged. So what if he was only one of hundreds doing the music scene around town? So what if he wasn't in the big time? He would be someday. In the meantime, he was taking pleasure, like in lovemaking when you're just fooling around before the big showdown. He was relaxed, knowing he was holding the winning hand, his secret power.

As he put it once, "If you start sweating winning, you're already losing."

I was happy, too, that summer, not wanting anything more than what I had or to be anything more than what I was, the girl who was loved by Jamey. I swear I fairly floated through each day, just being there with him. A couple of times, I made a half-assed attempt to get a job, but I really didn't have time for one. Jamey liked me to go to his gigs. "Why don't you do some songs with me?" he said more than once, but the thought of getting up on a stage in Vancouver really freaked me out. I'd get all breathless just thinking about it and, let's face it, a singer needs breath.

Then, because of being up half the night, we slept late. Then I'd wash my hair and go to the laundromat and look at all the wondrous and strange things in stores and read magazines at newsstands that had signs up saying this is not a library. By then we had a place of our own and I'd play cards with Carmen, who lived across the hall and wasn't very busy in the daytime either since most of her business was in the evening. We'd listen to the transistor or one of the zillion tapes Jamey had brought with him from home. We'd drink coffee and smoke cigarettes or a joint. She was always giving me advice. "The difference between sex for money and sex for free is that sex for money costs less," she said one day when we were having a conversation about Jamey taking advantage of me, which I wanted to say was total bullshit but didn't want to be rude.

I'd go to the library, which I loved, so hushed it was, and all those books in order on the shelves. I loved choosing books. They all seemed so interesting and exciting. I'd take home a big stack of them and settle myself on the couch with the books beside me and I'd pick up one and read the back cover: Chantel O'Hara, breathtaking aristocratic beauty of imperial will crashes in the far north where she meets virile sardonic doctor who infuriates her and threatens to melt her icy exterior. I'd read inside the back and front covers. I'd study the picture of the author and read the title page and the page across from that with all that publishing information. I'd read a page of chapter one and then I'd put the book down because I was suddenly and completely exhausted. Then I'd pick up another. But I could only ever get as far as page three or four at the most.

I loved Denman Street on a washed-street morning. I saw a lot of men, sitting on benches, sleeping on the sand. Where do the women go? I wondered. I'd get a coffee at Starbuck's and walk along the seawall. Once, I saw a man silhouetted against the setting sun. He was dancing across a log jam, his feet nimble and quick, trying to keep himself from slipping between the rolling logs. He seemed like such a tiny dancer against all that sky and sea, and yet he was managing to stay on top, balancing himself all the time. How long he was able to do it I don't know, because I didn't stop. Wherever I was walking, I could hardly wait to get home to Jamey and, by the end of the summer, my guitar, or, more accurately, Jamey's guitar.

Since arriving in Vancouver, I hadn't even touched the guitar. Maybe I didn't want to get pulled in, I don't know. Maybe I was too busy being happy. But one day while Jamey was out doing his thing and I was waiting for him to come home and I had read the first few pages of all of my current stack of books and I was listening to the radio and on came Emmylou Harris, my eyes went to Jamey's acoustic guitar propped in a corner. I looked at it for a long moment before I stood up. It was another long moment before I just sort of drifted in its direction, not having a plan, not knowing what I'd do when I got there. I put out my hand and my hand hovered over it, just hung awhile in the air. Maybe something was trying to tell me that if I picked up that guitar my life would change forever and I might not like the change. I picked it up anyway.

I sat on the bed and played and played and did it ever feel good, like stretching muscles that had been in a cast for a long time. So after that, while Jamey was focussed on finding his focus, I spent hours playing and singing to myself or Carmen who was totally noncritical. No matter what I played it was met with a "Jeez was that ever good, that was great, I didn't know you could play like that. Jeez." Maybe I got off on the awe and admiration in her voice, maybe I was just satisfying my own soul, whatever the case, I played and played to my heart's content

And so the summer went, but of course it had to change. Paradise can't last forever because human beings become bored with perfection, then, like children with a perfect toy, they have to break it.

Even though Jamey was having a good time, he wanted his own band. But, "It takes time to line up the right guys," he said. "You gotta explore possibilities. You gotta let things happen." What happened was that Jamey kept losing band members to someone else who could get better gigs so could pay better. Also, because of the spontaneity thing, Jamey wasn't easy to play with. You had to second-guess what he might do. The guys at home knew him well enough to do that and, since they were his friends, cut him some slack, but Vancouver was a bigger playground.

To me, letting things happen was like Sunday driving where you go around and around and around not knowing where you're going and maybe getting nowhere. Sunday driving gave me a headache and made me feel more tired than eight hours steady on my feet back at Zellers. But Jamey liked it. He'd be pacing up and down the room, coming smack up against a window where he'd look out at a furniture factory or railway tracks disappearing into the ground or neon flashing through grey rain and he'd say, "C'mon, let's go for a drive."

My job was to keep us from getting lost. "Where are we?" Jamey'd say.

"How'm I supposed to know?" I'd say.

"You're supposed to be watching," he'd say.

"This doesn't look familiar," I'd say. "Let's find a Dairy Queen."

To Jamey, letting things happen had to do with destiny, which everybody in the music scene talked about endlessly, destiny being some big-name producer who would discover you in some obscure dive. We loved to swap stories of A&R men and talent scouts prowling coffeehouses and cellars looking for material. Some said they could tell a scout right away. I wouldn't have known one from a hole in the ground. Still, I kept an eye out. I figured a scout would act different somehow, sort of skulking and pretending not to listen or notice. And one night, sure enough, when I was watching Jamey perform, I turned my head and saw before me, large as life, destiny in black leather. He also had black hair, a black beard and, as far as I could tell, black eyes. And that was the first time I set eyes on Zeke, who turned out to be not a scout or a big-name producer but a sound man. Zeke, who changed my life, I never did figure out whether for better or worse.

EZEKIEL

I was afraid of Zeke for a lot of reasons and one of them was his eyes. Dark, probing, like he was looking into the deep of me and seeing all the squiggly stuff there. He made me conscious for the first time that I didn't know how to act, or talk, or do any damn thing. When he was looking at someone or something else, I'd take a chance and look at him, but I never did when I knew he was looking at me, like when he said, "What do you want?"

"I want what Jamey wants," I started to answer, but didn't. It was too personal a thing to say to Zeke.

Zeke didn't want to get personal, either. What we were talking about was music. What kind of music did I want to play and sing? which was a strictly hypothetical question since I didn't do either, publicly that is. What he really meant was what kind of music would I want to play if I played music.

He had said, "We need a few slow numbers, with melodic focus."

Then I had said, "Jamey wants a strong thumping beat."

We were sitting in the backyard of this house the band was renting near a tobacco factory, tiny brown flakes sifting down on us as we talked. It must've been Monday since that was the day they did the filtering.

It was already autumn, a beautiful autumn day. I thought things were progressing amazingly. We had a band, thanks to Zeke who knew a million musicians. We started doing gigs right away, even though we were pretty rough. But Zeke said we'd get better, meantime we needed the money. And there were a lot of bars and clubs that needed a band for Friday and Saturday nights. I loved to watch Zeke working a room, the way he'd walk to one end of it, listen so intently then go back to his board and adjust a fader, then try another spot in the room, then adjust another fader. He never stopped listening and fine-tuning a performance or even a rehearsal. Already, we were starting to build a reputation around town and up and down the coast, thanks again to Zeke and to the guys in the band who had been around awhile and knew lots of people and people knew their names and came to hear them play. The group worked well together, except for Jamey. Rehearsals were going good, except for Jamey. It was the old problem of spontaneity versus working with other people.

"Tell me about Jamey," Zeke said, taking a long pull on his beer can. We had found some rusty old lawn chairs in the basement by the furnace and had dragged them out and braced them into the stubbly grass and were busy soaking up some last-of-the-season rays.

I looked above Zeke's head at a giant man's mouth smiling and breathing out smoke, floating in the haze. "Rita's got this scrapbook of everything Jamey ever did," I said. "She would've bronzed his turds if she could've. She used to go to Jamey's gigs, and after a set she'd run around to people she didn't even know and say things like 'isn't he great?' and all but force them to say yes.

"Popi," I said, "lost his foot in Vietnam even before Jamey was born. So now he's on the pension but he's not much good around the house. At least, according to Rita. All he does is sit there all day looking at what Rita calls his pickled pecker. Which is really a woodpecker. In a glass cage. Stuffed, of course." I thought a moment. "Why do you want to know about Jamey?"

"He's got what it takes to front a band," Zeke narrowed his eyes, seeming to look through the brassy atmosphere, which gave me a chance to look at him, his tidy head—sideburns connecting with a neatly clipped beard. It was like someone had taken a black pencil and drawn definite lines. He had an amazing nose, not set on his face like most people's seem to be but part of a straight line down from his forehead. It had an exceptionally thin high bridge that made me shiver, it looked like it could snap so easily. And he had these real neat ears, not wobbly flobbly like some men's, but small and compact with no extra flesh on the lobes. One of them had a curled edge. Later, when I got up the nerve to ask him about it, he told me he'd been born with that ear. Just the way he'd been lying on it inside his mother, it had curled around like a little cabbage.

I could see why women were attracted to him. At gigs, they'd manoeuver themselves close wanting to check out his equipment. At parties, they'd edge in his direction and twine themselves around him. Over six feet, in great shape, in black leather he was an imposing figure even before you got to his face, which was dark and brooding, which raised their curiosity. They wanted to penetrate his darkness, get under his skin. They wanted to break something in him; maybe it was that thin bridge of nose that made their fingers itch. A lot of women approached me to find out more about him, but I didn't know much more than they did. I could've told them though to be careful. I'd seen women throw themselves against him like against a steel wall, bruising themselves and not making the least impression on him.

"But the band doesn't always know what he's going to do next." Zeke swung his head toward me and I quickly looked away but not before I turned red. He knows what I was thinking about him, I thought, and turned even redder.

"He's always been like that," I said. "He won't change."

"He'll change," said Zeke. "He has to if he wants to go where he wants to go. Creative outbursts, that's all very well. That's good. But you need to learn control to play with a group. So you're all on the same page. So you're consistent from session to session. We've got a lot of work to do."

I wanted to say, *if you feel like that why did you take on the job*, but didn't.

"He's got a good voice, good tone, good range, not bad accuracy," Zeke went on. "It'll be even better when he learns control. But mainly he's got charisma. Audience appeal."

"He sounds so good the way he is," I ventured to say. "Maybe taking away his spontaneity would spoil what he has."

"Controlled spontaneity," said Zeke, "is what we're aiming for. A defined vision, rather than an exercise in creative energy. Acting instead of reacting."

For some strange reason I felt a chill even though we were roasting ourselves in the sun. Would a nonspontaneous Jamey still be Jamey?

"I never knew singing was so complicated," I said, looking at him, since he was busy swatting a long brown leg where a mosquito was grazing in the black hairs it must have thought was a forest. "I always thought you just opened your mouth and sang."

"This is a tough business. The casualty rate is high. You need more than raw talent. Raw talent is the private person. To survive you have to structure yourself into a public performer. You have to put on the costume, and when you're out on that stage, you have to believe in the role you're playing."

"I think Jamey can do that," I said, remembering his Batman days, how when he put on the costume, he *was* Batman, not Jamey Popilowski playing Batman.

"I think so, too," Zeke said. He looked across the lane into the distance, which wasn't very far before your eye came smack up against old brick walls and iron fire escapes zigzagging down. I knew, though, that any walls Zeke was seeing were in his mind, and he intended tearing them down.

I kicked a beer can into the grass. I tried to think about what Zeke had said about controlled spontaneity and becoming a rock star. For both of them, Jamey would have to give up something of who he was, inside like. I opened my mouth to say, you'll never get Jamey under control but, suddenly, I knew that Zeke could do it. Zeke could change Jamey because he would do what he had to do to become what he wanted to be. Which was another reason I was afraid of Zeke.

I got to know Zeke pretty well that fall, on the surface like. You can't help getting to know something about a person when you sleep in the next room. Before going to bed, it didn't matter what time it was, like four in the morning after a gig, he'd put on something like Dylan's "Tangled Up in Blue" or Zeppelin's "I'm Gonna Crawl." It made me wonder what he was feeling bad about but I wouldn't dare to ask him. And in the morning, usually long before I wanted to get up,

I could hear this sound like somebody practising piano scales. Even before he got out of bed, I'd hear the creak of springs and a button click and on it would come.

"What is that?" I asked one day. "That weird stuff you play every morning?"

"Bach," he said. "Straightens out my brain first thing when I wake up."

No beat, no rhythm, I thought. Just on and on. But I actually got to like it. It was soothing, like, like praying or meditating, but I didn't say that to Zeke.

I was very self-conscious about sounding stupid around Zeke. We got off to such a bad start. In fact, we just about didn't get off to any kind of start, because something happened between us so terrible that, even now, after all these years, I can't think about it without squirming with embarrassment.

Right after we moved into that house in late August, one afternoon we were in his van, which he had parked in the driveway. If Zeke was a magician, his van where he kept his equipment was the magician's trunk. I loved being in it and he didn't seem to mind my being there, watching him clean and fix the equipment. It reminded me of those hot, dusty, fly-buzzing summer afternoons at home, the way I used to sit on a rusty fender in the backyard, watching different parts of Jamey's lower half and talking to a car chassis, which sometimes answered but mostly only grunted.

I was watching Zeke wrap electrical cords. Apparently it has to be done right. "You have to be fastidious about your equipment," he said. I had never heard "fastidious" before. "Otherwise," he said, "it won't be there for you when you need it in a hurry."

I don't know what caused me to do it. Maybe I was bored and looking around—I was always fascinated by those lights and levers. All I remember is me saying, "what's this button for?" and flicking on a switch real quick and hearing this terrible voice, this terrible girl's voice, sort of throaty and breathy and coily and too soft and stuttering and uncontrolled and awful, saying ". . . there's one thing, though, I don't know if everybody's like this but after drinking two gulps of Coke I get the hiccups but I musta drank about ten glasses of Coke today though, it's so hot, but if I'm thirsty boy, hiccups or no hiccups I drink it down."

And that was when I realized how dumb I sounded, dumb and immature and naive, and like straight off the farm.

I switched off the button as quick as I could. I didn't want to hear any more of that voice. I turned to Zeke who had no remorse, only quietness and waiting and figuring with his smartness how he could best get out of what he had done, which, figuratively speaking (another phrase I later learned from him) was to take a picture of me naked.

I honestly don't know where I got up the nerve to say anything but I did. "I didn't know you kept your machine on," I said, "spying on people like that."

His eyes in the dim light were hooded. "Look," he said, "if it bothers you, we can erase it." And he did, right before my eyes. But that didn't make it any better. Because once you hear something you can't forget you heard it. I would never be able to forget my stupid-sounding hick voice. And I could never forget that, by recording it, Zeke was making fun of me.

After that, I stayed away from him. I didn't touch my guitar for a week. I couldn't face my speaking voice let alone my singing voice. Carmen asked me about it and when I told her, she said I had to get over it, the alternative being to never speak again. "Are you going to let an asshole have control of your life?" was the way she put it. "You sound great. You have to like your own voice," she said, "no matter who else does or doesn't."

Zeke and I couldn't help but run into each other. Not only was he Jamey's sound man and manager, we lived together. So one evening when Zeke came into the kitchen where I was eating leftover cold pizza and sat down at the table and opened a newspaper and read it for a while and then said, "How about a movie?" I didn't get up in a huff and strut out of the room like I'd been doing. Instead, I continued chewing my mouthful of pizza and thought about Carmen's words and thought how Jamey was out someplace and I didn't know when he'd be home. *Whaddaya gonna do*, I heard Tree's voice. Sit at home by yourself and be lonely? A movie will at least be something to do and you won't have to talk to him. "Okay," I said and sometimes I wonder what my life would have been if I'd said "Get lost, turd head."

Zeke said he wanted to see something with a little artistic integrity, so we went to this art film theatre and saw this real weird movie all about this guy who zooms around on his motorcycle wearing a snakeskin jacket and playing his guitar and gets the hots for this old Italian babe who looks like my mother and in the end they all get burned up.

"What a dumb movie," I said after, when we stopped for a Coke. Or at least I was going to have a Coke. But then I remembered the tape and ordered camomile tea, which was what Zeke was having, which turned out to taste like swamp water.

"You have to think of it in terms of allusion and symbolism," Zeke said. "The story alludes to the Orpheus myth. Orpheus was a musician who went to the underworld to bring back his love, Eurydice. Hades, the ruler of the underworld, gave her up on the one condition that Orpheus would not look back at her until they reached the upperworld."

He took a drink of his tea.

"So?" I said, not taking another drink of mine.

"So he looked back," Zeke said. "And Eurydice vanished forever. In his remorse, Orpheus became a hermit and wandered in the wilds, playing his lyre for the rocks and trees and rivers. Finally, he was torn limb from limb by a band of fierce women who were followers of Dionysus.

"Dionysus," Zeke continued even though I didn't ask, "is the god of vegetation and wine and fertility. Hence, the phallic symbol."

We sat a moment in silence. I had vowed to never again speak to Zeke and here I was having a conversation with him. What was I? Some kind of wimp to give in that easily? But it wasn't his fault I had a stupid voice, I reasoned for a change. Maybe Zeke's rationality was already starting to rub off on me. All he'd done was reveal the truth to me. Maybe he'd done me a favour. If I didn't want to have a stupid voice it was up to me to do something about it, to work on it and make it better. Still, it seemed like a mean thing he'd done. But, I continued reasoning, are you going to let his meanness affect you? Are you going to lower yourself to his level? He's going to come and go in your life and in Jamey's. You're going to leave him behind in the dust.

Besides, I was curious. "What's that phallic?" I had to ask.

He seemed to give my question serious consideration. "In mythology, the phallus is a symbol of the creative power of nature. The snakeskin jacket in the film represents that symbol."

"And the guitar that guy carried around is supposed to let us know he's like this Orpheus guy?"

"You got it. And what happened to him is a statement of what society does to creative power. If it can't tame it, it destroys it."

I was trying to understand, because the guy in the movie reminded me of Jamey, although he didn't look like Jamey. For one thing he was heavier, but still there was something about him, maybe the way he walked and slouched around.

"So," I said, "phallus is another name for a snakeskin jacket?"

"Not exactly," said Zeke. "Rather, both the phallus and the snakeskin jacket represent the penis. "

I could feel my face going red, as usual.

But Zeke's voice kept coming at me. "Clitoris, too," he said. "The phallic symbol can represent that, too."

I didn't know what that clitoris was, but I had a feeling it was something that would embarrass me even more. No way was I going to dig myself in deeper. "It's all Greek to me," I said, but I don't know if Zeke got my joke because I wasn't looking at his face.

When we got back to the house, Jamey was already in bed sleeping. I shook him and said, "Hey, have you ever heard about phallic symbols?"

"No," he said. "What's that?"

"Nothing," I said and jumped in beside him and he turned to me and we curled into each other like newborn pups blindly reaching.

Zeke was the only sound man Jamey ever had who had the papers to prove it. Even I could see that there was a big difference between someone fiddling with a bunch of dials and faders and someone who knows what they're doing. The way he could manipulate that sound board was pure poetry—the way he could chop off Jamey's voice so tight or extend it and make it echo back on itself or bring up the bass or push it back and make the melody slice across clear and clean and sharp. The first time I heard Zeke in action I could scarcely believe my ears. Jamey was having trouble with a new song, his voice searching out a key that would handle both the high and low ranges. He had himself pitched high so he could get the lows, but then on the high notes his voice got thin. Then, lo and behold, abracadabra, with the flick of some buttons, Zeke gave Jamey's voice a whole new dimension. Deeper, richer. It was as if one minute you heard a boy singing and the next a man.

And his equipment was something else. He had his own system, the largest board we'd ever worked with (which wasn't saying a heck of a lot), mikes, monitors, huge speakers, and he took it everywhere with him in his van, like a turtle carries his house on his back. He had studied audio engineering at a college, plus he had three university degrees, all with a B in front, which, he said, meant he couldn't make up his mind what he wanted to be when he grew up. Maybe it also explained why he knew everything, which made me realize that I knew nothing. But one thing about Zeke, he loved to tell me what I didn't know.

By late fall Zeke and me had moved inside but we still carried on these conversations or, more accurately, question and answer periods, which were the beginning of my education and understanding of anything that wasn't centred on Jamey, which was another reason I was afraid of Zeke. He was so different from anyone I'd ever known, so unlike the people of Terrabain Street who lived by their reactions to situations, mostly emotional. Zeke was foreign territory.

"I never met a Mennonite before." I let my smoke out slowly to drift and mingle with the thick air of the late afternoon lounge. I stretched my legs out under the table and leaned back, comfortable and mellow. I always liked the bars in the afternoon, the way they were so different than at night, the way they smelled of stale beer and smoke that hazed up the unnatural light of day streaming in a window. "I never even heard of one."

"Mennonites are an evangelical sect, originating in Switzerland in the sixteenth century," he said, taking a long drink from his beer glass.

Along to one side, someone was making a soft swishing sound with one of those wide push brooms. I could tell Zeke was listening, just the way his head was down but still, somehow, alert. It blew my mind, the way Zeke heard things, like, I swear, hair raising zap, electric, on a cat's back. Or the hum of an escalator and the little clicks of metal sieving through its teeth. The way he could scarcely stand being in a supermarket because of Muzak, which everyone else could ignore. The way he was almost afraid of bees, not for their sting but for their hum or buzz, which, he said, got in his head. "You don't want that buzz in your head," he said, "that buzz'll do terrible things to your brain."

At first I wondered if him being a Mennonite explained why he talked so funny, always with an underlying meaning that I couldn't make head nor tail out of at the time. Then I decided it was because he read a lot, but finally I concluded it was because he could see and hear better than most people and he could put the two together and come up with a concept, a word I didn't know then, but which was like a sixth sense to Zeke. This talent was a big help with his music, like when he saw a piece of music as a cool blue halo, he could try and produce the sound that way. Or when he saw a love song as being stark, he could produce it so it would evoke the feeling of being emotionally stripped.

"Evangelical." I put my glass of Diet Coke on the table and burped softly, whether he liked it or not. "What's that like? Holy Rollers?"

"No. Holy Rollers are a Pentecostal sect."

Blankness must've been smeared clean across my face, because Zeke took a look at me, set down his glass of beer, put his elbows on the table and hunkered down for one of his teaching sessions. "Pentecostal refers to the Pentecost, which was a Christian festival celebrated on the seventh Sunday after Easter commemorating the descent of the Holy Ghost upon the apostles . . ."

I took a deep drag.

I was fascinated with his voice and mouth, the way his lips shaped each word, the way his tongue danced in his mouth and his words danced off his tongue. I was fascinated with the way he seemed to be creating something with his words, the same way he did with his knobs and levers. Is that why I kept him talking?

"Speaking in tongues," I pulled it out of the smoke haze where it was hovering with all the other Zeke words. "What's that like?"

I watched him take a drink from his glass, watched him thinking about the right way to answer. He answered anything I cared to ask.

He loved giving out with the information. I guess you'd say he was a born teacher.

"It's a prayer," he said, "characterized by incomprehensible speech. It originated in primitive Christianity . . ."

Maybe what gets those women is his voice, I thought. Maybe they wanted to be made love to by someone with that voice—soft and deep, smooth and dark, like velvet, black velvet. He would've made a good disc jockey to soothe the hopeless and desperate in the middle of the night.

"Do you speak in tongues?"

"No," he said. "Mennonites don't do that. Mennonites are extremely rational. That's what they wanted to get away from. Mindless emotion . . ."

"Hey," a voice came from above. "You guys coming for something to eat?" Jamey was standing behind my shoulder. I quickly reached up for his hand.

Out on the sidewalk, I watched the toes of my shoes, the way they avoided the cracks. "How come . . . why do you know so much?" I said, lifting my head and watching the back of Jamey's jacket swinging ahead of us through the crowd of people.

"I'm a preacher," he answered.

"You serious?"

"Anybody can be a preacher. That is, if you're elected by the other members of the congregation."

"What're you doing here then?" I said. "Why aren't you watching your flock?"

That was one question he didn't answer. Maybe he didn't hear it. But that was when he told me his name was Ezekiel. "A major Hebrew prophet," he said. "exiled in Babylonia."

Jamey's jacket was getting away from me, going farther and farther into the crowd, almost disappearing. I started walking faster.

"Ezekiel became the lawmaker," Zeke's voice followed me. "The codifier." We swung into the restaurant and there in the back sitting around a table were the guys in the band. As I made my way toward them and especially toward Jamey, it was like going from smoky haze into a clear focus of my life. I nestled in beside Jamey and was home.

MADE IN CANADA

The first of anything is the best of wonder and discovery, although not the most perfect because, as I learned from Zeke, you have to work at perfection. But even though it had its flaws, of all the albums that Jamey did, I like the first one best, because we were striving for something, we didn't even know what, and because we did it together.

Cellar sessions in the dim February light from small high windows, Jamey leaning into the mike, on his left Clinton, a shadowy hulk, one with his bass, on his right Hector, bent over his guitar, then behind them Geoff perched in his cage of drums. Facing them, at the control panel, Zeke, with me on a stool beside him. That's the photograph my brain snaps. When it turns into a video, Jamey rocks back onto his heel, Hector's strumming hand becomes a blur of motion, Geoff goes wild on his drums. Zeke leaps up from his board, grabs an instrument to demonstrate what he wants or to add another dimension to the mix. The studio had an in-house keyboard that Zeke used on some of the numbers. On one song, Hector did keyboard while Zeke did backup guitar. A communal effort for sure; I even ended up on there doing a duet with Jamey as well as backing vocals.

The way it happened, one night about midnight Zeke said what this number needs is some backup vocals to give it more of a layered texture and somebody said we could place an ad and somebody else said we could go to an agency and someone else said how about that chick who was on with Big Richard and the Overtones down at the Truck Stop last week and someone else said it'd be good to try the idea now while it's fresh and they all looked at me. I started to squirm. I thought about the sound of my voice on Zeke's tape.

But even without that, I would have been scared silly. Sitting on the bed, playing and singing to myself or Carmen was one thing. These guys had been around the block. They were seasoned rockers. They were professional musicians. To them I was Jamey's cute chick who was fun at parties. And then there was Zeke, always the critical parent. I'd feel too self-conscious in front of him.

"No you don't," I said.

"Hey," said Clinton. "Great idea. You have a great voice."

"You've only heard me after I've had a few drinks."

"Give her a few drinks," Geoff said.

Jamey just grinned, since he'd been trying to get me to sing with him for months.

"No way." I might have raised my voice.

"Okay," Zeke said. "Calm down. You don't have to. Nobody's going to make you do anything you don't want to do. Tomorrow we'll make some phone calls. I would point out, however," and he gave me one of his most sincere looks, "this is only a rehearsal. If you fill in, it'll give us an idea of whether or not we want to use backup vocals and also some idea of the timing."

You smooth-talking son-of-a-bitch, I thought, and looked around at the others. There was Jamey with his need on his face and there was the rest of them, too. I'd been around them every day for more than five months. We lived together. They were my family—Hector with his twitchy nerves needing to sink himself into a woman's softness was always telling me the smart things his month-old kid was doing. Clinton was always asking my advice about women. Geoff was always telling me his crazy schemes to get rich. They all had their eyes on me and I thought *what the hell* and stood up.

"Just don't anybody say *anything*," I said, making my way to a mike.

"Just close your eyes and pretend we're back at Terrabain Street," said Jamey.

So I did. And when Zeke played it back it didn't sound half bad. To me, at least. Zeke said the backup vocal was a good idea but it needed work. I said it was a good thing, then, I was only filling in. The others all said no one would be as good as me because I knew Jamey's moves. In the end, I let them talk me into it.

Food breaks were usually at Hurley's, just down the street from the studio. I see Zeke's submarine held high like a conductor's stick, swinging up and out, yellow mustard airborne with his pronouncement. "Each time an Eden. You have to come again each time new for each other. Make it better each time for each other. Inspire each other."

The guys seemed to take him seriously. Maybe because they took themselves seriously. They showed up in the studio when they were supposed to and showed up pretty clean. Even though Jamey was the youngest of the group, he fronted it because he could sing and, although at first they did mostly covers, he could write songs. No one was originally from Vancouver. Like birds wintering it out, they had all migrated from other parts of Canada. Hector was from Saskatchewan, Geoff from somewhere in the east, and Clinton from the Maritimes.

"A band needs to be like a relationship." Zeke held his head like he was listening to his spatter of mustard slide down the window.

Sitting in that yellow-lighted circular booth, around that round table with the guys of the band, my left shoulder and arm inside Jamey's right arm and shoulder, all of us on the verge of taking that big step into perfection, while the voices of the others became dim in my ear, a thought came to me—Eden didn't last forever. Adam and Eve spoiled it for themselves. And I wondered, after they were thrown out into the world, were their hearts still there where they had known such perfect happiness and were they always looking back with a terrible longing?

Back in the studio, we carried on, Zeke saying for the hundredth time, "Remember your audience," and Jamey answering, "Audience is one thing. Mike is another," and Zeke looking up from his board, shouting, "Fuck that mike!"

"I love live performance," Jamey said with feeling. "With an audience you get response."

"We're getting stale," someone said.

"You keep it fresh by trying different things," said Zeke. "Always testing yourself. Always going one step further than you thought you could. Always pushing your limits a little more each time. And you've got the group. The group is very important."

As part of a group, Jamey and me found ourselves doing a lot of sitting around with other people, which was different than just the two of us sitting around together. Letting people into your life means making space for them, whether you always feel like it or not. Between takes, between sets, between gigs, we spent a lot of time with the band. It was one of these times that the idea had come up for making that first recording.

It was the Christmas before those cellar sessions. Christmas is a downtime workwise for rock musicians because everyone is into "Hark the Herald Angels Sing," which was definitely not our schtick. So there we were in our little house with Clinton, Geoff, Hector and his wife Diana, who must've been nearly full term because Andrew was born in early January. Zeke was with his current friend Dorothy, a spazzed out druggie chick he'd picked up at a gig, or more accurately, who'd picked him up.

"Whadid you get your mother for Christmas?" someone said.

"Jeez, I forgot all about it."

"I didn't even send my folks a card."

"That's terrible. That's really terrible. When you stop and think about it. When you think of all the trouble they had having you," Diana said.

"So when did you write yours?"

"I've never written mine."

"I never got the paper and pencil together."

"We got paper."

"Where's the pencil?"

"You got a pencil?"

"Have I got a pencil for you, baby."

"Dear Mom."

Dear Mom. A flash of Christmas on Terrabain Street. Mom in the kitchen Christmas morning whomping up panettoni. Kneading in the bitter peel. Ruining everything. The loaf looked so good, high and round and brown and bursting. You took a big bite and looked for a place to spit it out, what with the peel and the brandy and the raisins too, which made me think of juicy bugs. Maybe that's why I always drank too much eggnog and got sick.

But before that the stockings. Jamey and me, Beth and Marie, 4 AM, stomachs feeling sick and hollow from excitement and lack of sleep, stuffing ourselves with all the candy we could grab before having to sit down to poached eggs. The Corset Lady always slept late but at nine we were finally let off the leash to go down and wake her. "Where's me specs?" she'd call. "Where's my cuppa tea? We'd take her a big bowl of it, shouting "Christmas" into her good ear. "Where's my bran?" she'd call back. "Where's my prune juice?"

"It's right in front of you."

"Where's my paper?" she'd call in a snit.

"There's no paper today. It's Christmas." We always hoped that would make her hurry, but it didn't.

"Where's my wrapper?" she'd finally say, setting down her empty cup and pushing a straggle of grey hair behind her ear.

We helped her pull her nightgown over her head, trying not to look at the folds of collapsed flesh. We helped her wrap herself in her wrapper. We brought her another cup of tea. We pushed and shoved and dragged her up the stairs and into the Popilowskis', which was where we always had Christmas. We plunked her into a chair, a big soft one she couldn't get out of. And then Paquette came bouncing in. And then Popi handed around the presents, one at a time. "Thank you Great Aunt Velma in Vegreville," Jamey shouted to the ceiling, because you always had to thank the giver whether that person was there or not.

Beth got a Barbie dream house, Jamey got a Meccano truck, Marie got a junior makeup kit, I got a second-hand doll that had been in the church crèche. Beth got Barbie outfits, Jamey got a Mickey Mouse wristwatch, Marie got Evening in Paris, I got flannelette pyjamas. Beth got a silver hair brush, Jamey got a guitar case, Marie got fire engine red lipstick, I got more pyjamas. Popi always got a carton of smokes from us kids and he always pretended it was a big surprise.

Fade out to present reality. "I can't write letters," Jamey said. "What would I write?"

"Tell her about the Nanaimo ferry," I said.

"That old hunk of junk," Hector said. "You gotta be kidding."

"They've never seen that much water," I said. "Tree and Rita. All they've ever seen are those little muddy sloughs on the prairie. It'd blow their minds to see that."

So Jamey bent to it just like he was writing a song. We all did except for Zeke, who watched us with narrow eyes through his smoke as though studying us, maybe because he'd been a social worker. But the rest of us were like little kids at school—Clinton who you'd swear was a fugitive from a chain gang with his shaved head and pierced body parts, his shirttail hanging out from his motorcycle jacket and his laced-up big boots; Geoff, the closest in age to Jamey but already showing the effects of drugs in his hollowed-out face; Dorothy, with her long blonde hair and bangs, always sounding like a spoiled brat and looking like one, too, with her pouty lips and her round cheeks in spite of being rail thin; Hector who had the curliest hair and the craziest eyes; Diana with her long braid and her large flesh moving with such slow comfort just the opposite of Hector.

We read our letters to one another. "That's poetry. Pure poetry," someone said.

"That is, that really is, the most beautiful letter I've ever heard," Diana said when she heard Hector's, tears streaming from her eyes as she passed along the communal joint.

We folded our letters, squaring the corners of the paper, running our thumbs along to sharpen the creases. We fit them into envelopes.

We danced out the door and out onto the sidewalk and down the street like in Debbie Reynolds and Gene Kelly, singing and dancing in the rain all the way down to the mailbox and standing in the pouring rain pushing our letters through this slot and dancing back again to our little rattletrap house beneath the man with the huge smiling mouth, smoke curling out of it in the hanging mist. It was only later that we remembered we had forgotten the stamps. But it didn't matter because the next day we discovered that, in the dark, what we'd thought was a mailbox was a garbage container, one of those plastic ones with a push-through slot. It was the slot that confused us.

But we didn't know that that night. We were happy thinking our letters were winging it back to our cozy homes. That was the closest I came to writing Tree and I do wonder sometimes about fate and what might have happened between me and my mom if that letter had made it. One thing might have led to another, we might have stopped blaming each other for our lives. But she couldn't have written me back since I didn't put on a return address. Anyway, she wouldn't have gotten paper and pen together and actually written a letter and got it mailed. It would have all seemed too much for her.

Meanwhile, in Vancouver, "What're we gonna do now," someone said from the depths of the couch so saggy-springed the voice came up from the floor like out of a pit.

"We're going to make an album," Zeke said. "Happy New Year."

And that was the beginning of the cellar project except it took us a while to get organized. In late January, I was with Jamey and Zeke coming out from a gig, into a back alley, carrying their equipment to the parking lot in a sleet storm.

"I think you're ready," Zeke said.

"You think so?" said Jamey.

"The way I calculate it, you've worked through your evolutionary phase. These last few months we're working well together. The band has a following, which means you have a market. What we need now is a distinctive sound. It'll take a lot of work but I think we can do it."

"Okay. Tell me what I have to do."

By the dim light of a bar after an evening performance, they signed a contract.

Jamey signed for the band and Zeke signed as manager/producer as well as sound man. We all drank a toast to our success. It was a true case of ignorance is bliss. The band and Jamey had never cut a record and Zeke had never been a producer. "We'll learn as we go," he said. "It'll turn out fine."

That was the beginning of seriously refining Jamey's rawness and shaping the band's rough edges into a performance that was smooth and cool and knew where it was going right from the get go, a performance that strutted right out with sureness and style. But it wasn't easy. Things you don't notice in a live gig become glaringly evident on tape.

Things you let go on a live gig, you can't let go on an album.

Each of the guys was strong on his own and each played his own music. The trick was to bring them together. Zeke aimed them toward making a particular sound together, the concept he'd put together in his head. He didn't change them so much as develop them as a team. But to start with, he let them try anything to see what would happen. He said he wanted them to discover what their strengths and weaknesses were, to discover themselves by trying different directions. Some of the directions were a mistake, some seemed unpromising at first but after more work sounded okay. Sometimes, they'd all be going off in different directions. That was when Zeke would shout, "Masturbation! The idea is not to please only yourself. The idea is to please someone else. The idea is to make love."

At first, it seemed like every song was a different style. But it was amazing how their sound changed from week to week, getting more integrated. You could really see this in the live gigs they did a couple of times a week, for the cash and to keep their names out there. Still, they kept discarding things and trying other things. But they were honing in and getting their focus and sometimes it all came together and when it did it sounded real nice and everyone was happy. Like finding the erotic zone, Zeke said.

At first, Jamey, who throughout the fall had been progressively working better with the band, regressed. There's something about being recorded. Until you get used to it, it throws you off. Jamey's rhythm came out strong but erratic and the rest of them sounded either lost or desperately hanging on. Then came the versions when Jamey tried to suppress himself but the result came out flat and uninspired. Then the group tried to fit itself to Jamey's crazy inspiration but sometimes Jamey himself didn't know what it was going to be. When he sang *i want to scream/a nightmare not a dream . . .* he went for several bars on the scream part, in a high pitch, probably because that's what he felt like doing at that moment, but the rest of the band didn't know he was going there. Then Zeke stepped in and explained it again to Jamey, how he had to let everybody know beforehand his intention. "What is your intention?" I remember those Zeke words so well, because neither Jamey or me were used to thinking about being in control of direction, in life or in music. Me, I'd always just stumbled along from one thing to another or else hung on to Jamey's whirling shirttail.

From the sidelines, I figured out that Zeke had a vision but Jamey wasn't sure what it was. Jamey had the talent to make that vision real, but he didn't know how to use it to produce what Zeke wanted. It wasn't ego with Jamey the way it is with some musicians. He was trying to cooperate, but his music was a part of his primitive physical self and it was hard for him to change that self. I was surprised he took it as well as he did. But he knew that Zeke could help him become what he wanted to be. So he put up with Zeke most of the time. Only once did he say, "Fuck it!" and storm out of the studio. Zeke and I looked at each other. Which one of us was going to go after him? Zeke headed out the door. It was the right decision. We were doing a job, we needed to be professionals. When they came back nobody said anything. We all just got back to work.

Jamey came out of those sessions needing to bash himself against something or run wild like a horse that's been hobbled and finally gets loose. He loved it if there was some weather. He'd scrunch his neck into his collar and hit himself against the rain and wind or occasional snow. He'd go down to the sea and hope for a storm. He'd sit on a big rock on the sand and play his acoustic as loud as he could and yell out his songs as offbeat as he wanted. It was a true wrestling match between him and himself, between what he was and what he wanted to be, between what he had to leave behind and what he had to take on, between his heart and his determination. I could feel his struggle and I felt bad for him, but it was something he had to do—fit himself to a bigger world, grow up as a musician—and he had to do it alone. All I could do was hold his hand.

The band had its struggle, too, groping for the sound in Zeke's head, working with Jamey as best they could. Everybody had to admit, when Jamey got off on a boom boom thing that really rocked the joint, he was simply exhilarating. Zeke wanted to keep that quality, but he also talked about coordination and phrasing and pacing. I always thought that performance was just getting up there and performing, but I learned during those sessions that there's at least a hundred different ways to do any number and to get the one you want takes endless thinking the project through and talking about various aspects of it until you want to scream.

It seemed like we'd been in the studio forever, not seeing the light of day or any other kind of light, everyone getting totally bombed out with the whole thing when Zeke finally announced it was time to start doing takes. "Enough thrashing around between the sheets," was the way he put it. "Let's get down to business." The first take kind of trailed off into nothing. The second one came to what Zeke termed a tentative resolution. The third one, they lost the resolution completely. The fourth and fifth takes no one could get started on the same note. And so it went. What seems amazing now, is that they kept up their energy. In fact, it actually gathered momentum, and the credit for that goes to Zeke. "All right boys," I can still hear him say. "Do it again. Do it one more time."

"Control," said Zeke, "is knowing you've got a long way to go but not rushing things so you do a half-assed job."

We couldn't have done it without Zeke being friends with the guy who owned the studio. That way we didn't have to pay for time, at least not the going rate. Since the studio was in the guy's basement and he was just getting started in the business, he didn't have that many bookings. As he explained, "This way I'm making something out of it." With the deal on the studio, we were somewhat free of the time element, which left us free to make mistakes and to work things out.

We couldn't have done it without Zeke. Period. There was the space and the producing and, also, he had strict rules about drugs and booze in the studio. He made a rule about coming into the studio stoned or drunk. That was because Geoff arrived one afternoon so high he could hardly find his drum kit and then he kept dropping his sticks. The boys argued that drugs gave them an edge, gave their performance energy and excitement. Zeke said there was a better way. "Let yourself get carried away by your music," he said.

Drugs weren't a big issue then, anyway. That happened later when we were more of a success. Music was the issue. When we were sixteen and eighteen, music was an excuse to party, kids out whooping it up in the night. But the guys in this band for the most part were more serious about their music than about partying. They were all a little older and generally the feeling was that it was now or never for fame and fortune. They were in agreement with Zeke's, "We'll celebrate when it's done." Of course, they could do what they wanted after Zeke said "we've had enough for now," or "let's leave it for tomorrow," which was usually in the small hours of the morning. Even then they'd stay on, except for Hector who sometimes left to go home to Di and the new baby. They'd sit back and roll up a joint and relax and listen to takes. They'd fool around and try things. Some of the things they tried when they weren't trying ended up on the tape.

That the boys were challenged, I think helped keep them clean and sober, too. "I try things I know I can't do," Hector said once. "And then I have to work my way out of it."

"That's exactly it," said Zeke. "It's the working through, that's where the creation is. Working toward the solution."

All I can say is, working your way out and through took time and patience. And Zeke gave the group those things. "Don't rush it," he'd say. "Take the time you need."

"Are we ever gonna get it?" someone said, after we'd done so many takes on a number we'd lost count.

And Zeke, "It'll come. It'll come."

"That's terrible," someone else said after another number.

And Zeke, "That's great. We're in discovery mode, anything can happen."

Some days, though, in spite of Zeke, the mood was less than hilarious. Geoff tended to be on a downbeat a lot of the time, maybe because he was usually on the low side of a high. He'd say things like, "what do we think we're doing anyway? We don't have a chance. A mouse against a giant. What makes us think anything significant can come out of this jerkwater town? With the States such a big influence. We can only follow the trends of the music industry there."

"We can do anything," Zeke would respond. "We have nothing to lose. If we can't compete, then we're free to do our own. If we're not going to make it anyway, then it doesn't matter a damn. Let's just do what we want."

As I got to know Zeke, I got to know that he was always competing inside himself and he had no intention of not making it. He intended working at his craft until he was the best he could be in what he wanted to do. He formed his own terms with his own distinctive sound and went on to produce some big names in country, folk and blues, as well as rock. When he took on a project he put his stamp on it and the music world liked his stamp. And maybe another reason for his success was that when he took on a project and a band, he gave everything he had in him to give, working hard for them, trying to win for them, supporting them to do the best that was in them. And it all started in that little basement studio where he had his eye on everybody, calculating what they were capable of and then pushing them to that limit.

Watching Zeke, I could see the way he'd be with his congregation, inspiring the Ladies' Aid with their quilting bees, the Men's Club with their raffles, the young people with their Christian Life. He'd be good at that. And I started thinking about church singing, choirs and the gospel tradition in the southern States and how those people love singing, and I got an insight into why so much great music comes out of the church. Those people aren't singing for themselves so much as for the glory of God, so they forget about themselves and aren't self-conscious. And gradually I was able to do that too, think about the music instead of myself, just feel good about singing, just open my mouth and let it come out. The way Zeke put it once, "Some day your desire to sing will be greater than your being afraid."

But I was still at the stage of trying to do a good job for other people, especially Zeke. After the success of the backup vocal, Zeke said Jamey and me should try a harmony duet, it would add a little variety to the album. He thought we should try a love song, but Jamey hadn't written many love songs. Sex, yes . . . *come over to my house/I've got something to show to you/rub it once or twice/it ain't gonna spit on you* . . .

We did have *comfort me true*, but I wasn't ready to share that with the public and Jamey didn't mention it either.

"How about a hurtin' song," said Zeke. "You got any hurtin' songs?"

Jamey's hurtin' songs were mostly about the hurt between him and Popi. But no one knew that except him and me, so he did have one. Zeke wanted me to sing the song by myself, from the female perspective. So I'd get the feeling for it, he said. So I'd totally understand my part, he said. Later, I understood why Zeke did those things. But, then, I wondered why he was being so mean to me. Still, I did it, knees knocking, heart thumping so bad it all but drowned out my voice, which wasn't very loud anyway, maybe because I couldn't breathe. . . . *and i want to know will we ever feel the same/it has been such a long long time/i want to know do we need to feel the pain* . . . so pitiful it was embarrassing, and then it got this terrible quaver, which Zeke called a tremolo.

About which he was enthusiastic. "That's great," he said. "Of course we'll have to work on it, but that's the quality we want. Here, we have a woman whose existence depends on this man, this other person, and you've caught that exactly right. Now, listen to Jamey." And he played back Jamey's version and I could hear how Jamey's character felt bad but he wasn't left bleeding on the sidewalk like my character was. So then the whole business got scary in more ways than one.

"I'm going to take a walk," I said. "I need some fresh air."

"Okay," Zeke said. "But could we do it just one more time?" After we did that, he said, "Why don't we just work on the harmonies?" Then he said, "If we could just get this one part here." Then, "If we could just get that one part there." And on and on and on until I was totally exhausted and ran out of that cellar, one more time or not.

It was only a few blocks down to the beach. I walked along the sand in the moonlight. After a while, a shadow joined me. I thought it might be Jamey, but it was Zeke. We walked a ways in silence.

"That movie, *Superman*," I said after a few minutes. "The part where Lois Lane is flying, too. Up there across the night sky amongst the stars. And she isn't scared at all because Superman is holding her hand. But what if she comes to," I said, "and realizes that she can't fly and there's no such person as Superman. Like, there they are, flying way up high, and suddenly he becomes Clark Kent."

"He can't do that," Zeke said. "He can't ever let himself think that he's Clark Kent. Not when he's flying. When he's flying, he has to be Superman. The minute he looks down and thinks he's Clark Kent, he's a goner. He has to control his mind so he doesn't let himself think about things that he shouldn't think about when he's up there."

That was one of the few times Zeke didn't understand what I was talking about. Still, the message was the same. Lois Lane has to control her mind, too. She has to believe in Superman's magic powers. She has to trust totally that he won't let go of her hand.

So I went back into that cellar and tried again. I tried different things because of Jamey, because Zeke said it would make a better album, because the student in me wanted to please the teacher in Zeke. Later, I'd give my all because the music wanted the best out of me, but I wouldn't be there for a long time to come. It took a lot of pushing and pulling from life to get me to do what it wanted me to do. I was stubborn that way, always had been. As Tree said, "You'd cut off your nose to spite your face."

To steady myself, I tried shouting, remembering Jamey's punk period when his voice was changing and unsure of itself and his solution was to bellow into the mike. . . . *i want to know do we need to feel the pain/of knowing what is yours and what is mine* . . . But the Janis Joplin schtick didn't work for me. I felt self-conscious and uncomfortable and it hurt my throat. So I just used the voice I had and put myself into the song, like an actor must put herself into a part. Zeke said it was fine, it gave the number an emotional context that fit it perfectly. The trouble was, that was really me and, according to Zeke, that was dangerous. According to Zeke, you have to wear a mask when you're up on that stage, otherwise your own vulnerability will defeat you.

It was a long hard haul. It seemed like each cut we had to go back to square one and work things through again. But Zeke said we were making progress. "That's close," he'd say. "That's real close. We've got the technical part pretty good on that one. This time let's go for the magic. Make the vocals communicate more of the essence of the song."

"We've lost our spontaneity," someone said. "That's what happens when you rehash something too much."

"Spontaneity on the first take is the amateur," Zeke said. "Working through to spontaneity on the last take is the sign of the professional."

And the day did come when, true to Zeke's prediction, it all came together, the last take on the last cut, what Hector called an accident but what Zeke said was inevitable success acquired through effort.

I remember the look of delight on Jamey's face when Zeke pronounced thumbs up, his, "Is that it?" and Zeke's, "That's it," and Jamey's deep laugh and everybody cutting up and hugging. Except me and Zeke. I kept myself busy hugging everybody else and Zeke pretended not to notice. I don't know why I couldn't hug him. I just couldn't.

No one went home. Zeke would work all night mixing it down, and the guys seemed reluctant to leave the studio, as if they didn't want to let it go. Someone went out and got a case of beer and a bottle of scotch, and Zeke played some of the cuts while we all listened in a haze of sweetish smoke. I remember that tape so well, the way you remember every first time. It was definitely a testosterone-laced rocker, which made my work all the better in contrast. In fact, I thought I didn't sound too bad on there. I thought the numbers where I did backup had a fuller sound, a groovy sound. I thought I fit in with the group pretty good with my sound and my timing and rhythm.

"Jamey really gets going on that one," Hector said about "The Contender," the one Jamey had written so long ago for Popi. "It's like one of them Hollywood westerns where they come out guns blazing."

"You're a wild child, Jamey boy," said Geoff. "A wild child."

"You done gone wild," added Clinton.

"That's it," said Zeke.

"What?" the turning of five heads to Zeke still bent over his sound board.

"Gun Wylde." He raised his head as though listening. "That's who we are."

STONY ROAD

Another gig, another toilet. I tried not to touch my bum to the seat because Tree told me I might catch something that way. It wasn't easy, especially if you were trying to read something. That always struck me, the way some people leave those little messages, their phone numbers or verses or their names, or sometimes their whole life story in the toilet: *My name is Jessie Pritchard and I'm here on my honeymoon and I'm having a real good time.*

I washed my hands, religiously, again Tree's nagging voice in my ear. I looked in the mirror and perked up some strands of hair that were drooping on the top of my head, but I didn't look at my eyes because they didn't match the rest of me, which meant that one or the other was lying, and I wasn't sure which. Maybe the rock scene person was the real Lilah, lying dormant inside for all those years.

I fixed my lipstick, thinking how I didn't hate my lips anymore for being Italian. In fact, I thought I looked shit-hot. That's progress for you.

I went back out through the doors. The music hit me like a blast of heat from a furnace. The band was really grooving, responding to the audience, gaining momentum with the adulation, the whole an upward spiralling of electric energy. . . . *screaming/i wanna be i wanna/i wanna be i wanna be/a contender* . . . Gun Wylde in black leather and rhinestones was snaking it across the stage, holding his guitar low in front, swinging it around to the side like a gun, greased arm and shoulder muscles glistening in the strobe lights.

Maybe that's the real Jamey, I thought. And what's wrong with it? It's no worse than me putting all that gook on my eyes. How about those politicians on TV? They're supposed to be grown men, running the country, running the world. They put makeup on their faces before going on TV or even giving a speech or a press conference.

Not long before, though, I said to Zeke, "Does he hafta dress like that? It isn't Jamey up there."

"It isn't supposed to be," said Zeke. "It's supposed to be Gun Wylde."

"Why can't he wear jeans? He looks good in jeans." I almost added, he has a cute ass.

"People come to see a rock star. He's a professional. He does his job. His job is to please all those people. And he's happy in that job."

"He really believes he's Gun Wylde," I said.

"He has to," said Zeke. "And he can make the crowd believe it. He has that ability. It's a great talent."

"Like the flimflam man."

"Not at all. He delivers the goods, all right. He more than delivers the goods. He can be a star. He wants to be a star, so why not use what comes natural to him?"

"I don't know, being a rock star seems so . . . silly. Like kids playing dress-up."

"What's wrong with dressing up and putting on a show and making people happy? All musicians do that. All actors do that."

"He's not living in the real world. He's so focussed on himself."

"He has to be focussed on himself," said Zeke. "Otherwise, he couldn't get out there and do what he has to do."

"He's so full of himself," I said, "there's no room for anyone else."

Zeke was quiet for a minute, during which I could feel his eyes on me. "Out on that stage," he finally said in a quiet voice, "you start thinking about something or somebody else, you're dead meat."

I'd run out of arguments, so Zeke finished it off. "The getup is only as important as you make it. And the audience eats it up."

Sometimes I tried to save Jamey by trying to bring him back to reality. "Mr. Big Rock 'n' Roll Star," I accused once when at a party the night before I could see how he was lapping up the attention of some female groupie who was sitting at his feet, salivating. "With your tight pants and your open vest and your gelled chest hairs."

"Hey," said Jamey. "You're jealous. I don't believe it."

"I'm not jealous. It's just that I have no intention of being part of a communal prick."

"Whoeee. Them are strong words." And he did look surprised.

"It's just so . . ." I searched and came up with a Zeke word. "Self-involved. You're just so wound up in yourself."

"Aw, c'mon. Ain'tcha bein a little cruel?"

"It's unhealthy. And you're always playing this stupid role."

"So what?" he said.

"So I know who you really are," I said. Maybe I was shouting by then.

"So maybe I need someone who doesn't know who I am," he shouted back. "Someone who doesn't drag me down. Someone who thinks I'm great." And he stomped out.

A man can't do anything worse to a woman than leave her when she still has a lot of things she wants to shout. It makes you want to destroy something of his, so I picked up Jamey's guitar and was about to bash it on the back of a chair when in he came, back in the door, and grabbed it from me. "What in hell you think you're doing?" he said.

"I'm smashing your guitar," I said. "What's it look like I'm doing?"

"That's smart," he said. "That's real smart. You think that's gonna teach me something? The only thing that's gonna teach me is to be madder'n hell at you."

"How can I teach you anything then?"

"By being nice t'me and letting me do what I want."

"Yeah?"

"Yeah."

So I thought, what the hell. Why not give it a try? If Jamey wants to be a rock star, let him be one for Christ's sake. Give the guy a break. If he enjoys doing what he's doing, that's the main thing. Right? Just so long as he remembers the difference between play acting and real life.

By late spring, we were on a tour, down and up the west coast, promoting the cellar sessions album. They got good drugs in California, someone said as a joke, which turned out to be true. At one rehearsal, our promoter turned up with a grocery bag full of a variety of stuff. But along with the partying, or maybe because of it, a tour is hard work. If we had a long way to go to the next town and had to be there the next night, we'd hit the road right away after the show. The guys took turns sleeping and driving. We threw some sleeping bags into the back and it wasn't too bad with five of us. Diana had stayed in Vancouver because of Andrew, only three months old. Sometimes we'd get a motel to stay the night, sometimes we wouldn't. There wasn't a lot of time, and we still weren't making a lot of money. Sometimes we stayed with friends or relatives of the guys in the band, Hector's aunt in Portland or some people Geoff knew in Washington.

As for Zeke, he had his own van with all his equipment in the back. The grey damp typical early Vancouver morning we left, when I came out of the house with my new backpack bought for the occasion, which they called an expedition pack, there was Dorothy with her long legs in tight jeans standing alongside Zeke's van. Something must have showed on my face and Zeke, who was loading in a heavy speaker, must have caught it. Not that he said anything, he wasn't about to defend his actions to anybody, let alone me, but he knew that I wasn't all that crazy about Dorothy. Actually, I was fairly neutral about her. It was just that she was bad news, dragging around her drug problem and putting it on other people's shoulders. I felt that she was bad luck, but maybe I was just responding to my discomfort about being around people who were spaced out. I'd learned that you never knew what they might do. They could turn crazy in a split second.

Zeke gave me a quick look, told Dorothy to get in the van and went on lifting the speaker. Maybe they deserve each other, I decided, getting into Jamey's van. He could play Mr. Social Worker to his heart's content and she could lie and manipulate him like all druggies will anyone who tries to help them when they don't really want to be helped.

Life on the road was crazy—people freely wandering in and out of motel rooms at all hours, borrowing stuff, sharing dope and booze and guitar strings and bags of snack stuff. It was like the communal life of Terrabain Street. It was a lot of fun, but I never did think that was what I wanted to do for the rest of my life. Then, again, I didn't think a whole lot about the future. I just went along from day to day happy being with Jamey.

If we didn't have to get on the road right away, we'd go someplace to unwind. So many groupies, friends of promoters, people who knew people, hangers-out and hangers-on came in and out of our lives then, people you meet along the way, chance encounters that sometimes affect your life more than those you've known forever. These were people who lived on our edge, peripheral people, but one thing I learned about myself, I naturally focus on each person who comes in and out of my life, like, they're important to me for the short time they're there. And this is great for writing songs. Maybe Jamey was like that, too, because a lot of those people showed up in his songs, certain faces, names, voices that clamor for attention:

— Hey, here's Rubin.

— Find him a chair.

— There's some sort of rule about chairs. We gotta find him a chair.

— Hey, way to go. Nice shot.

— Where's the cloth. Get that waiter.

— You'll notice I'm not with Jerry. I told him to get lost. . . . *I'm gonna take some action/I'm gonna travel light* . . . That's it as far as I'm concerned. We're finished.

— Yeah?

— Yeah. After that party last night he was out prancing in the pansies with one of Leona's girlfriends, Cindy, Sylvy, or something, do you know her? Anyways, there we are sitting around and Hank says Jesus Jerry lookit your feet, how wet they are and someone else says yeah Jerry what'd you do, piss on your shoes? So Jerry says it's the dew, there's this heavy dew, I just went out to sober up, it's a nice night out there.

— Whose knee's that under the table?

— It's pretty bony.

— That ain't no knee.

"Rock is our shared mythology. Our common language." Zeke's voice so strong and clear cut through the smoke haze, the dim lighting, the mumble jumble, bringing sense to the scene with his tongue like quicksilver.

— What're you doing out in the dew for Chrissakes says Hank and Jerry could of passed it off, I wouldn'ta thought anything about it, you know how I trusted him, God when I think of it, how dumb could I be? But he and that Sylvy or whatever the hell her name is look at each other real quick, so I know something's going on . . .

— Jeez.

— I think I'll take off my shoes Jerry says and I says don't bother buster, you can leave 'em right on because you're gonna need 'em when you're walking down the road talking to yourself, . . . *she's taking action/a riot scene* . . . and Leona, she says Jeez Roxanne don't be so hard on him, it could've bin worse, at least his knees aren't wet.

"You ask yourself what are the musical components of your style," Zeke's voice intertwined with Roxanne's. "Country, blues, jazz, rock, all these elements combined with the mercurial quality of creativity . . ."

— Where is he, though? D'y'think he's back at the motel? I dunno. D'y'think I should give him a call? maybe he's sitting there in that motel room lonely with nothing to do, one call wouldn't hurt. He's probably out though, with that Sylvy maybe. Jeez, if he's out with her I'll kill him . . . *he never saw it coming/he did not feel a thing* . . .

I looked up across the table to where Zeke was sitting, his face turned to Jamey. As usual, I was struck by his profile, the straight line of nose, the neat angles of hairline, sideburns and beard. Who are you? I thought. He turned his head suddenly. I turned my head away real quick, but he was still in my mind. The devil, I thought, is known for his silver tongue, for being able to talk people into doing things. The devil can take human form, I knew. I'd seen enough movies on the subject. I knew about *Phantom of the Opera* and how the devil can be very convincing. My mind started having weird thoughts. Maybe Zeke is the devil in disguise. Maybe he has the mind of a devil. Maybe from taking all that mind-expanding shit.

"I knew what I was doing," he'd said when he told me about his experimenting. "I wanted to see what would happen."

"What did happen?" I said.

"I saw a lot of things," he said.

I was in the passenger seat of his van, keeping an eye on Jamey's van in the side-view mirror. "You've got to have a precedent for happiness," he said while I watched the highway disappearing behind us, faster and faster into what we had left—Dorothy, lying on the bathroom floor, full of pills and other things, I didn't know what all. Dorothy, her face almost as white as her hospital gown, her hair almost as pale as the pillow.

I'd just said, "She doesn't seem to know how to be happy."

"Being happy," said Zeke, "is a learned skill like everything else."

I kept flipping my eyes back and forward, left and right, two sides of the pavement, one going, one coming and a line going straight down the middle.

I was thinking about all the times I'd been mean to Dorothy, like when she wanted to go to a movie and I wouldn't go with her. "Going to the movies," I said, "was the one thing she liked, was the one thing, maybe the only thing, that cheered her up some. I never knew anyone could get so depressed, like all the time, not just once in a while like most people." Zeke was silent so I kept on. "All those pills she took. I think they actually made her worse, even though they were prescribed by the doctor." Zeke still wasn't saying anything. Suddenly, I got the urge to make him respond. "Sometimes she seemed happy with you." I slid my eyes across and up to his unmoving face.

"Don't nail me to that cross," he said, keeping his eyes on where we were going. "People are the way they are. You can't change them. You try and change people, you can do them more harm than good. And you can end up just as fucked up as they are. And they can fool you. They change for a day, or a week, even a month, maybe even ten years, but in the end, they revert. That's why I got out of social work."

"She'd got off pills. With you. She was off everything except a joint."

"It couldn't last. I knew that at the time. Dorothy wants to be a child all her life. Some people are like that. They want to have someone take care of them and give them love and affection and admiration without them having to do anything to earn it. In fact, some people do a reverse. They act as miserable as possible to test the other person, and then they get all upset when that person has had enough. The reality of life," said Zeke, "is that you have to earn love by loving. But some people find loving too painful."

Is Jamey one of those? The fleeting thought was like a blur across my mind.

"Or they never learned how to love as a child," Zeke was going on, not giving me time to pursue the Jamey thought. "Dorothy can't love," he said. "She can't give, so even if the other person gives a hundred per cent, it's not enough."

"It sounds hopeless," I said.

"It is," he said.

"I still think I should've been nicer to her"

"People like that will drag you down with them. You have to turn your back."

That was the most Zeke had ever said to me about himself, about his personal life, which revealed his deep-down nature. I didn't like his nature. I watched his long fingers smoothly manipulate the wheel. "You have a sliver of ice in your heart," I said.

"You have to have," he said. "To survive."

"You mean in the music business?"

"In any business."

The vans stopped along a lonely beach with the ocean all before us. We opened the doors and stepped out. It'd been raining and I took deep breaths, dragging that good clean moist air down inside me.

"Is this Oregon?" someone said.

"Yeah," someone else said.

"This is great," someone else said. "I think I'll stay."

Jamey came and stood by me and I could feel him, not only his body but something else, like his spirit, there beside me. He put his arm around my shoulders. I was so happy that what had happened between Dorothy and Zeke could never happen between Jamey and me. I was happy that I knew about love from the first time I saw him swinging on that gate. I was happy that we were kids together and made music together and that Jamey was not Zeke with his cold cold heart.

116

What triggered Dorothy's final fit was Zeke telling her he didn't know where he'd be two months from now. "You don't love me," she accused.

"I like you," he said.

When Dorothy told me that, she was safe in her hospital bed with her stomach pumped. She'd be there for a while and we had to leave. Zeke had given her a wad of money to get back to Vancouver if she wanted. At least he'd done that much.

"What a thing to say," I said to Zeke that day in the van.

"I was being honest," he said.

"Couldn't you lie a little?" I said.

"No," he said. "I've never said that to anybody."

"You sound like you're proud of it," I couldn't help but say. And then my mouth opened and words came out and I didn't know where they were coming from, but I didn't want to stop them. "Like some people say they've never told a lie. And they're all proud of it. But telling lies isn't the only way of lying. Sliding out from under the truth is also lying. And sometimes when I ask you a direct question, you don't say yes or no, you throw it back at me as another question or say something that isn't a lie but isn't the truth either. And sometimes," I added for good measure, "saying nothing is a lie."

Zeke seemed to be giving that some thought.

"It's not that I have strict rules about lying," I tried to explain. "Personally, I don't give a shit. It's just that people who say they never lie when they do, that's what gets me."

Like most people, I lied a little when necessary. Except to Jamey. Lying to him would've been stupid, like lying to myself. So I remember very clearly the first time I lied to him, about anything significant that is. It felt so strange, like a ripping sensation inside of me. And it wasn't even an outright lie. It was more the keeping-your-mouth-shut variety. It was a hot August night in Seattle when we opened for Guns N' Roses. We had another great audience. They were lapping up the performance, caught up in the excitement, hopping around in their seats, whether high on drugs or the music I don't know, but they were a lively bunch. It was one big whirl of lights, movement and music. It's times like that you live for, it's times like that some of them die for.

I was standing in the dressing room doorway watching Jamey get ready when I saw him shove something into his mouth. "What's that?" I said.

"They pep you up," he said. "It's no worse than caffeine." I don't know what my face showed, but he went on. "I didn't sleep last night. I drove all day to get here in time. A hundred and twenty clicks all the way. I need to have energy for the performance." He popped another one. "That's the priority at the moment." He turned to me, his eyes bright and shiny. "Fire," he said and struck his chest. "Fire on the nerve ends. Fire in the balls. Fire, fire, fire." He flung himself across the room and gave me a hug.

I have to admit that, whatever spurred him on, he was a wild man on that stage that night and the rest of the band responded. They gave out with all the stuff that Zeke had taught them and more. The crowd loved it. They wanted an encore. Backstage, Jamey said to me, "come on, lets slay 'em," and pulled me out onto the stage with him. It all happened very fast and out of my control. Jamey and the band started in on the duet from our CD. I hadn't even done that number live on stage in Vancouver and here we were in Seattle not only with a huge audience but with Guns N' Roses waiting in the wings. During the tour I'd helped with backup vocals, which wasn't too bad because Hector and Clinton were also there. But to sing harmony alone with Jamey or with anybody, that's quite demanding. If you fuck up in the studio you can do a retake. Out there on the stage there's no retake. You're totally exposed. I'd told Zeke and Jamey right at the beginning that I didn't want to do that number on the tour. But revved-up Jamey, taken up with the crowd and the night, wasn't thinking. There was nothing I could do but open my mouth and sing.

I don't remember the first notes since I was all but fainting. But then Jamey turned himself to me so that he was looking into my eyes with his intense blue that raised the hair on the back of my neck and all I had to do was follow the message I couldn't help but read. I forgot about being nervous and scared, I forgot about the audience. There was only Jamey and me in the world. *I want to know do we need to feel the pain/of knowing what is yours and what is mine.* And then a strange thing happened. Each moment of the song, I could feel myself getting stronger and stronger. It wasn't until it was over, though, that I knew what had happened to me, and nothing in my entire life up to then had ever scared me so much. The singing live and the different scene and a larger audience were peanuts compared to the other. What it was, for one horrible moment up there, I knew I could do it without Jamey, that maybe if I tried I could be better than him. Not *better* because you couldn't beat Jamey for energy and charisma and sheer force in performance brass. But a better musician. I had a better ability to bear down and work, to do something over and over and over until I got it right. It was later I figured this out. But up there on the stage, for a split second, I could see the crack in Jamey's surface. I could see the fragility of his brilliance. He was like the guy on the logs tripping across, who could fall so easy if he wasn't careful. Where with me, it was like I was standing on two feet, braced, on the solid shore.

I didn't want to lose Jamey as my hero. I didn't want to compete with him and do better. It didn't matter to me. I just liked singing and music. I didn't have to be a star. I didn't want to be a star. I wasn't comfortable in the spotlight. It would be too ironic (a Zeke word)— Jamey who first showed me the G chord, who showed me how to use a mike, who showed me how to do harmony—if I shot above him. No way. He'd be hurt if I did that to him. So when I saw what I saw that night, I stepped back quick, because our lives depended on it. Me being stronger could kill Jamey, like with twins, when the stronger one takes the life from the weaker one. And I could live with being the weaker one, but he couldn't.

ROCKET MAN

"Where are we?"

"Over the mountains."

"We're not supposed to be in the mountains."

"In the clouds."

"That's mist. I think we're in a valley."

"That's fog. We're near the ocean."

"What was that?"

"Maybe it was a whale."

"If we went down here, no one would ever find us."

"All you can see are mountains."

. . . see the mountains in the sky/high above the waves of the sea . . .

"And valleys."

. . . castles in the air/never looked so good to me/getting tangled in my hair . . .

"Those are waves and foam, and fog. Jeez, lookit the size of those waves"

. . . don't try to understand/you're naked, alone/with company

"Hey, we're going down. Hang on. Hang oooon . . ."

"It looks like Mars."

"It's cold as hell."

"Ahoy there!"

"Who that?"

"That's the guy's meetin' us."

"Jack Ferguson's the name. We had it planned, a reception committee, a speech . . . but the storm . . ."

"That's okay."

"This fog . . ."

"No problem."

"It didn't seem any use."

"Just tell us . . ."

"Sorry about this weather . . ."

"Could you tell us a direct route to the nearest steak house?"

When the fog lifted we found ourselves in an old seaside hotel, abandoned for the winter, on a lonely ocean stretch, with only a boardwalk and the sea beating on the sand, beating, beating, with no promise of ever stopping. Gun Wylde had been booked for a New Year's Eve gig and TV show at a resort town up the coast. The PR thing behind it was the idea of a known band or fairly known one flying in to this isolated place for a down-home New Year's Eve shindig. If it had happened, the coverage and exposure would have been good publicity. Apparently, everyone up and down the west coast tuned in to this station for the big countdown. As it happened, the TV crew didn't make it out of Vancouver.

The morning after the gig, I was standing at the window with Zeke, looking out at our hotel sign, *Pink Flam*, a top-heavy body of feathers balanced on one incredibly skinny leg. As the hinged board billowed and slammed with the wind, I saw the *ingo* and curved neck lying in shatters on the wasteland of beach before us. The surf seemed carved like a furl of grey stone with no way around it or over it and no way you could ever stop it.

Zeke kept his face straight ahead. He seemed to be staring at a fixed spot somewhere out there in the grey distance. For the first time, I noticed wrinkles at the corners of his eyes. And his eyes looked puffy and tired. He'd had a bad night. That gig was the closest I'd ever seen him to losing his cool. He'd had to use the community hall's sound system and it had been the shits. *Antiquated* was the word he'd used. All evening he'd been fighting feedback. And the room itself sounded lousy. As Zeke put it, the acoustical possibilities were zilch.

Staring out the window into that expanse of water and sky, I tried not to think about Jamey and this bimbo Clinton had brought. It crossed my mind that Clinton had done it to get back at Jamey because he was pissed off at him for always hogging the spotlight. Gawd, I thought, are you paranoid or what? This life is fucking up your mind, too. The real reason Clinton had brought her was because she had a bag full of dope.

She'd been coming on to Jamey ever since we'd left Vancouver, rubbing herself all over him every chance she got. At the dance the night before, she seemed to be trying to prove she could out-drink and out-asshole everyone, which was some trick, the way everyone was drinking and acting in response to the situation we were in. Then an hour ago, I had opened a door to find her and Jamey under the blankets all boozed up and dropping acid. . . . *sleepy eyed/swollen glands/eights and aces/dead man's hand/whiskey bottles/no phones/on my own/don't need a home* . . . She was starkers and I knew for a fact Jamey didn't have his pants on. I didn't even scream or throw things. Happy New Year, I thought, standing in that bedroom doorway wondering what I was doing in a joint like that with a person like that. Jamey and Bimbo stopped what they were doing long enough to turn their heads toward me. We all stared at each other for a minute, then Jamey grinned and waved a bottle at me. I shut the door and went downstairs to where everybody else was wrapped in blankets and huddled around the hot plate engaged in substance abuse, a term I learned in California where they have fancy names for everything.

He's on a downward spin and he's not going to pull himself out of it, I was telling myself. . . . *you got your finger on my pulse but what's the use/if there's no cure I'll just have to go on down this road until I crash* . . . Why do I keep believing he will? Because I want to believe, I answered myself. Looking outside at the storm and inside to the last dance of the night before, I saw Jamey and me dancing against the destruction. *Everything I do, I do it for you.* Jamey told the band to play it, I knew for me. It was the love song I wished he'd written, but that kind of song wasn't in Jamey then. It was like he couldn't say *comfort me true* anymore. His love songs were the breaking up kind, the love hurts kind. Somebody was always leaving or in pain. . . . *it has been such a long long time/i want to know do we need to feel the pain* . . .

But New Year's Eve Jamey set down his guitar, letting the rest of the band carry the rhythm, jumped off the stage and grabbed my hand. One thing I'll say, Jamey and me always did dance good together, the way you do with maybe only one person in your entire life, fitting into each other's grooves. Another thing I'll say, Jamey could really dance, even the old-fashioned ones where you have to know where you're putting your feet. Maybe it was his Ukrainian background, all those country dances, all those family parties. And he swept me away, around and around, circling the outside ring of the dance floor, before he settled down slow and held me close and we hardly moved at all but moved the right parts still.

But that was last night, and this morning was the first day of a brand spanking new year. I hoped it wasn't an omen of things to come.

"Whose idea was this anyway?" One of the bodies in one of the blankets behind me yanked me back to cruel reality.

"That Jack guy."

"Who?"

"Jack Somebody. The guy that met us yesterday. He's with the Chamber of Commerce. They wanted to bring attention to the town. Drum up some business in the winter. So they proposed this TV special."

"New Year's at the Last Resort," someone said.

"Up Your Arse as the Last Resort."

"Actually, it was my idea," Zeke said. "I got it together with Jack and the TV station. It would've been great publicity for us. Wide exposure."

"No use talkin', since it didn't happen."

"Who knew it wouldn't?" Zeke had left my side and joined the others. The hot plate rings were fiery red and actually did throw off some heat. "It seemed like a good idea at the time. ACTRA rates."

"That's another thing. No TV crew, no ACTRA rates."

"We'll get some compensation. And we'll get extra for the dance band, Jack said last night. For filling in for the dance band."

"Whaddaya suppose happened to them?"

"They're probably still digging themselves out of a snowdrift somewhere. What a fuckup all around."

"You have to try things," said Zeke. "No one knew they were going to have the worst storm in history."

"You mean they didn't see it coming?"

"Apparently not. All they said was some rain."

"Andrew, come back here. Andrew stop that. Andrew!"

"Somebody keep that kid away from that cord."

"Andrew come back here!"

"Somebody keep that kid away from the stairs."

"Andrew!"

"Somebody control that kid!"

Andrew, who had been inside Diana this time last year when we wrote our letters home, was only ten months old, but man, could he move. A devil on wheels, emptying full ashtrays onto the floor, pushing open a door and bouncing down some steps, being hauled back by Hector only to go for the hot plate cord. Di tried to keep him on her lap, but then he squealed worse than last night's sound system, which hit everyone's nerves.

Before that gig, I hadn't seen Diana for a few months because Hector had cut himself out of the band. He'd got back from the west coast tour to find that he'd impregnated Diana before leaving. As he explained it, Di was expecting again and they needed some steady cash, although the band was doing real good that fall, steady gigs locally, some touring around the province and in Washington and Oregon. The album was getting airplay and selling. There was even talk about doing another. But Hector said he needed to be more of a family man. And maybe he didn't like what was happening in the band. Maybe we were working too hard, maybe there was too much dope. I don't know, but people were definitely edgy.

Maybe it had something to do with what Zeke called the mercurial quality of creativity, the way every time before a show the band had to go back to the beginning and work themselves up and build up momentum to the extreme of performance and when they were into the role not let anything else get into their minds until the performance was over. So there was always a lot of tension around, like, *can we do it again?* each time, *can we get back to where our strength is? can we build? can we get the right momentum? can we pitch it all to just the right moment?* It's very hard on people doing that. It's hard being around people like that. In spite of Zeke, who was an expert at talking people back from the edge, there were a lot of blowups and people stomping off in disgust, especially Clinton and Jamey, the two hotheads. Geoff just got more quiet and did more dope. Hector didn't blow up but he got so twitchy and fidgety, it made everybody else twitchy.

They were also getting tired of Zeke's constant harping on things. "You feel that maybe you've got it but you have to keep searching, keep letting new things in. Don't close up too soon. You have to be flying and targeting at the same time. You have to sound free but really be focussed. You have to leave yourself open to all influences up to a certain point, then you have to shut it down and focus."

"Just cut the fucking sermons and let us play," Clinton shouted.

"Why does it have to be so fucking complicated?" Geoff growled. "Where I come from we just get up and play."

That was the state of things in late fall when Hector left. But then just before Christmas, Jamey and me walked into a bistro on Davie and there was Hector, in front of the mike, singing like the wrath of God from behind the burning bush of his hair. He was solo including sound, a small board set up at the side that he adjusted from time to time. It wasn't great.

"Whaddaya think?" he said to Jamey when we were having a beer between sets. Hector was buying. "It's on the house," he said. He looked around. "At least I got a good crowd tonight."

"You got a good act," Jamey said.

"Sometimes it's hard to get the time to rehearse." Hector took a long swallow of beer like a man with a terrible thirst. "So you wonder how it's gonna come off." He set his mug down and looked at the table.

"You working construction every day?" asked Jamey.

"I was until last week." While he spoke, Hector darted glances at Jamey's face, at mine, around the room, as if he wasn't sure who to call on for help. "Things're slow in construction this time of year. So I got more time to rehearse. I made a demo tape, on my own. Just a couple of days ago. I rented some studio time. I think it's good. I'm going to take it around. It might get me work." He pounded the table lightly with his fist. "I need a break, just one fuckin' break." His voice was quiet, but the bitterness in it caused me to really look at his face. I saw that it had deep cuts of pain and I thought, *why do they do it?*

"I'm not hoping too much," he said. "I'm trying not to hope. You know, I've had so many near hits in the last ten years. Either by myself or with different bands. Only to have things fall through. Each day I say to myself, maybe this will be the day my break will come. But not hoping too much."

Why not just give up and go home? I thought. *Why not just enjoy life? Why put yourself through this all the time?*

"Sometimes I think 'why not pack it in,'" Hector said, as if reading my thoughts. "But giving up on music would be like giving up on life, wouldn't it?" It wasn't a question.

"How about doing this gig up the coast New Year's Eve?" said Jamey. "It's good money. Union rates, because of the TV."

"Would it be all right if I bring Di and the kid?" Hector said, and now he was able to look into Jamey's eyes. "Di has this thing about New Year's Eve. Spending it together."

"Sure," said Jamey. "Sure." The way he spoke so quickly made me wonder if he felt guilty about the time he said to Hector, "You'll never make it with them," meaning Diana and Andrew, and then turned around and found her standing right behind him.

"Jamey didn't mean anything by it," I said to Diana at the time.

"I know," she said. "He was just being honest. I know that."

As it turned out, Diana was a good person to have along on an ill-fated gig. In the first place, she was the only one besides me not getting high, she because she was pregnant and me because I was too damn mad and disgusted. So I had someone to relate to. Also, she always saw the bright side of a situation, like when she said in her soft husky voice, "Still, the gig last night wasn't bad. The people who got there really seemed to enjoy themselves."

What let Diana be so nice was, like my friend Carmen, she had no critical ability. Everything Hector did was great. As for Andrew, he was another Einstein about to happen.

126

I thought how I used to be like that, but Zeke was teaching me different. "All you ever do is criticize everything," I said to him once. "You do it in a nice way, so it seems like you're not, but you are. You never say something is great and leave it at that. There's always a but."

"That's my job," Zeke said. "That's my role in the group. You've got to keep filing off the edges," he said. "Polishing, trying to do better."

The trouble with that way of thinking, it spoils something for you. You start seeing people in a different way. Like Diana. Moon goddess, Zeke called her. When he said that, I saw the moon at the full, casting her magic spell, turning us all into fairy creatures darting through the trees. She looked like the full moon, too, with her large slow comfort. But I was starting to see how she was too slow moving and too patient and sometimes I wanted to get behind her and push.

"When're we gonna get outa here?" someone's voice broke into my thoughts.

"When the weather lets up," said the pilot. I think his name was Hugh.

"When's that gonna be?"

"There must be a radio around here."

"Don't we have a radio?" Geoff got up to look for one and scraped his chair on the wooden floor.

"Do you have to do that?" Zeke had a pained look on his face.

If Zeke was strung out, there wasn't much hope for the rest of us. We should've all been still sleeping. It wasn't even noon and we hadn't got to bed until six. Then, even though we raided other rooms for extra blankets, it was too cold to sleep, and the beds were not only cold but damp. It seemed like I'd just laid myself down when a spook-like creature appeared beside our bed, which turned out to be Clinton, clutching a blanket around him. "Can't we turn the heat up in this place?" he said.

Jamey, curled around me, didn't budge. I hated the idea of pulling myself away from his heat, but I hauled myself up. It had been too cold to undress, so I was still in my New Year's Eve outfit, specially bought for the occasion and definitely not for comfort or warmth. I grabbed up my winter jacket, which, thank God, I'd thought to bring, and the two of us went off to investigate. After much searching, we found an empty propane tank in the basement. We concluded that the hotel people must have emptied it in the fall before closing up the place.

When I got back to the room, Miss Fancy Tits, maybe feeling the absence of Clinton in her bed, had moved into mine. I woke up and smelled the coffee in more ways than one. In the kitchen, someone had found a coffeemaker and the coffee was brewing. Zeke and Hector had returned from a scouting mission with coffee and milk, bread and peanut butter. As they told it, the one restaurant that was open in winter was closed because of New Year's. They found a general store, which was also closed, but the owner lived upstairs and he came down and sold them the stuff, which was being ravenously consumed by all.

Diana was eight months gone, and she kept making cracks about the baby getting more heat than anyone else, since it was closest to the hot plate. The first few times she said this everybody laughed, but after a while no one laughed. They all just sat and stared at the red coils as if hypnotized.

"I happen to be very sensitive to heat and cold," said Clinton, coiled like a sinister-looking bald-headed fetus on his chair. He seemed to have totally forgotten about Bimbo, or care where she was or what she was doing. "This place smells like a dump."

"Do you smell something?" Di said, suddenly alert and sniffing.

"No. I don't think so," said Hector. "What?"

"I don't know. Maybe gas. Oh Gawd," she said clutching her stomach and Andrew. "Do you think maybe we're gonna blow up."

So the guys trooped off down into the basement to investigate, while Di and me huddled deeper into ourselves and waited.

"It seems to be that propane tank," Zeke said coming back through the door. "Even though it's almost empty, I think we better get out of here."

That brought up the sixty-four million dollar question of *where to?* But thanks be to God, while we were sitting around trying to answer it, we heard the same voice we had heard coming out of the fog the day before when we arrived.

Jack Ferguson stood in the doorway. I could see now that he was a tall, thin, dark man. "Came over to see how you're doin'," he said. "It don't look like the answer is good."

"It is a little chilly in here," said Zeke.

"Freeze the balls off a brass monkey," said Hector.

"You better pack up and come home with me," said Jack.

We were all jammed like sardines into the latest model of this huge American van, when someone mentioned Jamey and Bimbo. "Someone go wake them up," said Jack. So Hector did, although me and Clinton were all for leaving them to freeze to death.

On the drive across town we didn't see one person out on the streets, or even any other vehicles. All we heard was the wind like ghosts looking for lost souls.

"You should see it in summer," Jack shouted so all could hear. "You wouldn't know it was the same town. You can't find a parking space on these same streets." It turned out he was the head of the Chamber of Commerce, which was why he had the lucky job of greeting us the day before and more or less looking out for us. He also ran the garage on the edge of town.

"We never had an ice blizzard like this before," he shouted again. "Coldest New Year's Eve on record."

I believed him. Even going from the hotel to his car and from there to his house I all but perished. A short skirt and spike heels was not exactly right for the occasion.

Then the miracle happened. One step separated hell and heaven. One step across the Ferguson doorstep, from the coldest New Year's Eve in history to a clean, warm, lighted kitchen, to the smells of roasting turkey and dressing and baking pies. You never saw such a hustle and bustle as Irene Ferguson and her six daughters put out. They took our coats, showed us into the living room, grabbed up Andrew and whisked him off, brought us warm drinks and put Diana's feet up on a stool. "Jesus," Jamey said. I had to agree, even though I hadn't looked at him once, not once, on the drive, and going into the house I had stayed as far away from him as possible.

At first, I was nervous about our group being around nice people, but apart from Clinton who had a silly grin on his face and Bimbo who had a vacant look on hers, everyone acted more or less normal if you didn't know better.

At the centre of the activity was Irene, short and broad and strong, but not fat. She had black hair and eyebrows and snapping dark eyes. Her long mouth took everybody into her smile, even when you were a stranger who didn't smell good because where you came from the showers weren't working. I saw how Jack was quiet and gentle with his family and with strangers, too. And I saw how Jack and Irene weren't afraid to give everything away, in their generosity offering us all they had, because we were travellers without shelter and food.

I saw the daughters, how they didn't argue about who was going to set the table and do the dishes, how each one had a job and did her job, the younger ones setting the table, the older ones helping with the cooking, and all of them babysitting Andrew. The girls had friends over and neighbours kept dropping in, and all the time Irene and her daughters kept serving up food and Jack kept serving up drink. And they never seemed to run out. And there was enough for everybody. And Irene was the best cook I'd ever seen. Everything she did, she did special, putting a little something extra in here and there, like walnuts in her stuffing and pineapple in her carrot salad.

After supper we sat and visited in the big comfortable cluttered living room. The furniture wasn't much. Things were pretty shabby from the wear and tear of living. This is nice, I thought. Everyone here has a purpose, what Zeke would say, a role. Everyone gets into the act. Someone here is in control. And I felt a terrible longing inside me, but I didn't know yet what it was for.

COLDWATER MORNING

Surfacing, I came up into the light of day, my eyes stuck shut with white grainy sleep. I got my lids apart and found myself staring at a male nipple and a patch of curly chest hair. I lifted Jamey's limp wrist. The hour showed eleven, the minute twenty-four. The seconds flashed thirty-six, thirty-seven. I dropped the wrist like a hot potato and thought, shit.

My New Year's resolution was a job. A real job, a steady job, that paid money, maybe not a lot but regular. On the way back from that less-than-terrific New Year's Eve gig, it struck me what a stupid life I was living. It was like I wasn't living in the real world, even when I was wide awake in the middle of the day I was confused about where I was and who I was. While bouncing around in that single-engine aircraft trying to hold my stomach down, I'd decided that I had to get back to some kind of reality and that my whole life I'd been too dependent on Jamey, especially emotionally. I needed some friends or at least someone to talk to who wasn't in the music business, someone who was into real life. I needed a real job. I vowed and declared to myself that I'd get up bright and early every single morning and get out job hunting until I found one.

But it was like that New Year's Eve gig was an omen. At the end of February we were stuck in a cheap room on lower Main where you couldn't tell if it was morning. No wonder I don't get up, I thought, lying back on my back. In this room, it looks like night all the time. Why doesn't somebody pull up the blind? Why doesn't somebody let in some air? This must be what Purgatory is like, floating and hazy and not going anywhere. Maybe I'll be stuck here forever. There's nothing to get up for. If I get up then I'll have to do something, wash and dress and eat and get through the day until bed again and sleep.

Where is everybody? I asked myself. *Gone, gone, gone,* I answered myself. Things had been dicey for a few months, even before New Year's. First there was the spotlight thing with Clinton and Jamey snipping at each other. Then there was the money thing—they all thought they should be making more but, as Zeke explained, even though you get the crowds and sell the CD, it's hard to make much profit by the time you pay off everybody—the venue, the promoter, the travel costs. "With a first CD, you're lucky if you break even," he said.

Then New Year's Eve was the last straw. Back in Vancouver, when Clinton came out of his drug fog he was pissed off at Jamey over the Bimbo thing, even though Jamey tried to explain—what's a guy gonna do when a chick shows up in your bed without any clothes on? Geoff didn't get involved, he never said much at the best of times. It was like banging on those drums drained all the hostile energy out of him. And maybe he'd been in so many bands that broke up that when he saw and heard Jamey and Clinton going at it, he saw the writing on the wall. He just drifted off and headed on down the road without even saying goodbye. As for Hector, he'd just joined us for New Year's anyway. He was over on the Island working for his brother-in-law.

Zeke took off for California, said he wanted to find someplace where it wasn't cold and where they had decent acoustics and state-of-the-art technology.

"That's crazy, man," Jamey said. "We've got just as good here. We can find some other guys."

"No," Zeke said. "It's best I move on." I wondered if he was disappointed about the band falling apart. It was his band as much as Jamey's. But if he was disappointed, he didn't say anything.

The last time we talked to Zeke, we were between sets in a bar where Jamey had a week-long solo contract. Zeke was drinking his beer and not looking at me. He hadn't looked at me since the New Year's gig. It had started on the plane home, he hadn't looked at me once. It was like I'd done something wrong but I didn't know what. Did he blame me for the disgusting Bimbo situation? For the band falling apart? But it didn't have to fall apart. Zeke had such force of will, he could have straightened us all out and gotten things back on track. And no one was mad at Zeke. Even though the guys were disgruntled about the gig, which had been Zeke's idea, they were familiar with the ups and downs of the business and agreed that there was no way he could have predicted the blizzard. The fact that Zeke didn't pull things together meant he didn't want to, but whether it was because of the business, the band or himself I didn't know. I did know he was always hard on himself, maybe because of the Mennonite thing and the sense of responsibility that came with that baggage.

Maybe I should have asked right out, "Why are you mad at me?" But he wouldn't have told me anyway. And he wouldn't have said anything against Jamey, especially to me. He wouldn't have talked about personal things, about feelings. And because he didn't, I didn't. There was that reserve between us. So, although I knew there was something about the New Year's Eve gig that had totally disgusted Zeke, I didn't know what it was until a long time after. I only knew my heart took a fall when he said he was leaving. I hadn't realized until then that he'd become my friend. But I didn't say anything. What could I say?

I had to admit, I kind of missed Zeke. As I said to Jamey, "He was interesting to talk to."

"He thinks too much," Jamey said. "That's his problem."

Well, that was six weeks ago and here we were still in this room where, on the other side of the blind, a train rattled past and blew its whistle. I had to get up because I had to pee. Besides, being in that bed was like death warmed over. Slowly, I threw back the blanket, sat up and put my feet on the cold floor. What day is it? I thought. What month?

Tree always told me the worst thing you can do is rub your eyes. I rubbed mine hard. I scratched my eyebrows. White flaked down. I'm probably the only person in the world with a dandruff problem in their eyebrows, I thought. I lifted my head and saw empty bottles, overflowing ashtrays, a greasy couch, gouged wallboard. I started to lie back down but then the pee call came again strong.

If a person stays in bed forever, I thought, what do they do about peeing? A baby just pees and lies in it and hollers for someone to come and make everything nice again.

I put on a shirt and jeans because the bathroom was communal and you never knew who you were going to run into in the hall. The bathroom was cold. I washed off the toilet seat with wet toilet paper. There was no soap. The seat was cold. I sat hunched over staring at the vinyl, trying to figure out the pattern. Whoever made up those crazy patterns must've got a good laugh when they thought about people trying to figure out the pattern when there really was no pattern. A huge cockroach ran out from under the baseboard. I pulled my feet up off the floor and watched as it scuttled across the pattern and disappeared under the sink where the vinyl was damp and brown and curling up.

I had to put my feet back down on that floor because it was the only way out of there. I stood and flushed the toilet, thinking, there I go, down through the drain, down through the rusty pipes of this flea-bitten firetrap, down to the main pipe, and on and on down to the ocean, to the world.

The water from the sink tap was ice in my cupped hands, on my splashed face, but it woke me up.

Letting my face drip-dry, I made my way back down the hall. I tried to avoid the floorboards that creaked the loudest. No way I wanted to draw attention to myself. In a place like this, invisible is the operative, I thought, and, as so often, was struck by how I was thinking a Zeke word or expression. I went into the room and looked at Jamey sprawled on the striped mattress clutching the wadded pillow. His mouth was sagged open. Dried white drool at the bottom corner made him look about twelve years old. I saw Batman in his sister's leotards, his mother's long black gloves, his towel cape, his homemade mask.

But he wasn't twelve. He was a twenty-two-year-old man who'd been knocking at the music industry door for the last couple of years, whose band had fallen apart, and who was taking a sabbatical. He was a guitar player who was satisfied jamming Saturday afternoons at the Commercial where he was just another name on the roster. He said he didn't mind not being the main attraction. He said he preferred it at this particular point in his life. He said things had gotten out of hand . . . *stir crazy/star fire/on stage/desire/black hat/bent out of shape/pretending to be/what i ain't* . . . He was doing what he called freelancing, working a lot of bars and clubs, one- or two-night gigs over a weekend. "The end of the night," he said. "I take my pay. We call it square. No hassle. No paying everybody off. No crawling into the van dogged out and having to drive like hell eight hours to the next town to get there in time. Touring, you start feeling like you're in a prison of your own making, like you've pulled the cage down on yourself and locked the door. You step into the big time, you're not your own person anymore. You belong to other people's expectations of you. I never wanted to belong to anybody but myself."

I wondered how being booked solid in the future, having your own band, getting to travel to warm places could be worse than scrounging for solos in Vancouver in the winter. Although he didn't have trouble getting jobs, thanks to the CD, which was still getting airplay on local stations, he still had to get out there and find them. But what was I complaining about? His ambition to become a star had flown out the window but so had his reliance on uppers and downers. He'd taken off the costume and was back into grungy jeans and cut-off T-shirts. It might have been like the old days when we started out, except, then, he'd been aiming for something. Then, his eyes had flash and fire without drugs.

So what's wrong? I asked myself. Jamey has taken off his mask and you're still not satisfied. What does it take to satisfy you? I didn't know. But into my head popped a picture of Jack and Irene and their house and girls.

Looking down at Jamey's face so turned inward on his dreams, I thought of how we had danced the last dance. For about twenty-four hours there, I had myself convinced that it really was our last dance. Then on the return flight he swung into the seat beside me and swore that he and Bimbo hadn't done anything much under that blanket. "We were too high to do anything," he said. "Besides, how could you even think I'd be attracted to someone like her when I have you? Come on, honey. I'm your boy and always will be, you know that." And on and on like that.

I thought about it for the rest of the flight but, as always with something like that, it isn't thought that decides you. It was when he walked ahead of me off the plane and I saw his back, lean and a nice shape along the rib cage and up to his neck. I saw his neck. It made me think of the time when he was about eight years old and Rita sent him off to a summer picnic at the community hall and he didn't know where he was going but he went anyway.

"Why didn't you tell us you didn't know where the community hall was?" Rita asked.

"I didn't know until I got out there that I didn't know," he answered.

So many memories of Jamey, so many of us. You don't give up on a person when you have that together. And then you find yourself in a grungy room on Main with a train going past outside the window.

Looking down at Jamey's sleeping face, I saw scoops of darkness beneath his eyes. His cheekbones and nose showed more clearly now, and his chin, too, was sharper than it used to be. I tried not to see the stains on the mattress or think about all the other people who had slept on it. I tried not to smell the stale air of bodies and beds all glazed over with a film of pot smoke. The guys in the TV ads with their spray cans would have a ball with this one, I thought. We got odours you ain't even heard of. Stale beer, stale cigarette smoke, stale socks, stale underwear, stale wallpaper, stale McDonald's cartons, stale people.

Pieces of newspaper were lying all over the room where Jamey had flung them the night before looking for mention of his gig. I picked up a section and glanced at the front page. It spoke about some fellow up north who went berserk and murdered his family. I let it fall back on the floor. I looked at Jamey's face, so totally unaware.

There was no way to take a bath or shower in that place, so I just finished dressing as quick as I could, before I changed my mind. I gathered up my stuff and plunked it into my expedition backpack and grabbed up the strap and went out the door. Halfway down the stairs I realized that I couldn't just leave him like that. We'd been kids together. So I sat down on the step, got some paper and pencil out of my bag and wrote, 'I'm leaving.' I crossed that out and wrote, 'I have to leave.' I climbed back up the steps and put it under the door. I didn't want to go back into that room. I knew I'd have to look once more at Jamey's sleeping face. I knew I'd give in to the bit of dry dribble at the corner of his mouth.

The very same day I got a job waitressing in a place with two signs in the window—*meal tickets accepted here* and *help wanted*. The neighbourhood wasn't the greatest and the clientele wasn't too classy, but since I didn't have a red cent, I couldn't afford to be fussy. That first day, this guy came in waving a knife and saying how he'd slit everybody's throat if we didn't give him all our money. But this little scrawny woman who ran the place wasn't having none of that, so when us girls all ran screaming into the kitchen, she marched right out there into the restaurant and gave this guy what for and told him he should be ashamed of himself scaring people like that. "And do up your pants, your dick's hanging out, a fine example for these young girls," she said and took away his knife and gave him a bowl of soup. "Now behave yourself," she said and he did.

As for me, I was so nervous not to mention shaky with hunger that when I was carrying four bowls of clam chowder one on top of the other through the swinging doors, I bumped right into one of the other girls coming the other way. You guessed it, clam chowder from hell to breakfast. I cleaned it up as quick as I could. "I'm sorry, I'm sorry," I kept saying to the woman, all the time thinking, I've really blown it now, and wishing I'd at least had the sense to cram some food into my uniform to eat later when I'd be walking down the road talking to myself. On my final mop-up, two sparrow legs planted themselves in front of my eyes and I thought, this is it, but Mammy Yokum turned out to be real nice and asked me if I had a place to stay.

"Lois," she said, jerking a thumb at this girl with a haystack for hair, "is looking for a roommate, aintcha Lois?"

Lois smiled with large teeth and said yes and I said thanks.

It was a week to the day later that Jamey came in. That week wasn't pretty. I missed Jamey, I missed music. Lois didn't mind me playing the radio, but I didn't want to be a pain. After all, it was her apartment.

Luckily, I got a lot of shifts, after which I dropped like a stone into bed.

I was just setting down two Denvers with fries in front of two customers when I looked up and there he was. "Here," he said and handed me a piece of paper. I looked at it and read what it had to say. . . . *i'm trying i'm flying/but i can't stand losing you/I'm flying well I'm lying/but i can't stand losing you/they say it's just a phase/lost in this soulless cage/but i can't stand losing you/so where is your hand/as i walk through this no-man's land/i can't stand losing you . . .*

He caught my eyes with his. "I thought you liked singing," he said. He looked around at the booths and the counter. "How can you live like this, without singing?"

"I just don't want to live that kind of life anymore," I said, folding the song and putting it in my pocket.

"I'm a guitar player," he said. "How am I supposed to live?"

"I don't know," I said. "All I know, I have to get my shit together." I paused. "You never ask me what I want."

"Well, what do you want?"

"To live like a normal human being."

"Guitar players aren't normal human beings," he said. "They're musicians."

"Why can't they be both?" I said.

"No man can serve two masters," he said.

I didn't know what to say to that, so then he shifted from one foot to the other and looked at the floor. Then he looked up, around the restaurant, as though looking for a way out. When there didn't seem to be one, he settled down some. "I've been thinking," he said, "of maybe getting out of the music business. For a while, anyway."

"Don't do me any favours," I said.

"What's that supposed to mean? Of course I'm doin' you a favour. Why else would I be giving up music? Isn't that what you want? What in hell *do* you want." His voice was going up and up.

"Shhh," I said. "I don't want you to do anything, unless you want to, that is."

"Maybe I need to get a little different perspective," he said. "On my life."

"Don't do anything you'll be sorry for," I said. "Unless you think it's a good idea."

"All I'm saying, I could give it a try."

"There must be someplace a person can live like other people," I said .

"On the Island," he said. "I've always liked the Island."

"Yeah?"

"Yeah."

We looked straight into each other's eyes. His were like swords of blue glass piercing my heart, making my toes curl up in my shoes.

"Me too," I said.

"Okay." He turned his head quick and stood up straighter, relieved that he had the female hassle thing finished with. "That's that then," he said.

PART THREE

GETTING IT TOGETHER IN CROFTON

When you plant a seed, you're responsible for the way it grows. When you have a house, you're responsible for making it into a home, and that doesn't just happen without someone making it happen. That's what I learned in Crofton. But not right away.

Right away, my thoughts went like this: "Here you are, a whole house to yourself. You can do anything you want. All day. So what do you want to do today?" There was music, of course, but music was strictly off limits. I was the one who wanted to quit the music business, so it wouldn't be fair for me to be having fun singing and playing when Jamey was at his nine to five. I had to keep my hands too busy to pick up that guitar. I thought hard about other possibilities but I couldn't think of anything I wanted to do that didn't include Jamey and he wouldn't be back for eight hours.

I was looking out the window at the place where his latest vehicle, a green Chev with a rust problem, had disappeared around a corner. It struck me that because of the music, we'd spent more time together than most couples. It struck me how all my life I'd been watching him, but now thanks to me he was gone for a lot of hours to a place where I couldn't watch him. I was left watching myself, which, quite frankly, made me feel downright uncomfortable. It was worse than uncomfortable. It was impossible. Because there was nothing to watch.

So whaddaya gonna do about it, eh? came Tree's voice, and even my feeble brain could see that the solution was to do *something*. But I'd never done anything except hang out with Jamey. Even school and jobs were just time I put in until I could be with him. So I didn't know how to do something. I didn't have what Zeke called a precedent. I'd worked at Zellers but they didn't have a Zellers here or anything even close. All they had here was a family-run corner store and gas station, a few houses, and a shut-up motel. I couldn't even go to a library or cruise magazine counters like I did in Vancouver.

I remembered how Zeke used to talk about motivation for a project. I thought about how the group would start to prepare themselves by freefalling and letting everything in but at some point they'd get a focus and start to rehearse in a different way and things would get more serious as they started working toward a goal.

It seemed to me, looking out the window that day, my whole life so far I'd been freefalling and if I was ever going to get into the next stage of my life I'd better make a move.

"My life," I said it slowly and out loud. It sounded strange to my ears. "My life. I have a life apart from other people. I am a person," I said. "Who am I?"

"Figure that one out." This time I heard Paquette's voice plain as plain in my ear.

What do I even look like? I wondered. I went into the bedroom and stood in front of the mirror. Too short, I thought, but Jamey likes me this way. Hair too long and bushy but Jamey likes to put his hands in it—he definitely didn't like it the time I went for the spiked look. Too many curves so clothes made for those fashion models don't hang right. Boobs a little big. But that's what Jamey likes.

What do *you* like? I wondered. I bent closer and looked into my eyes. I couldn't see anything in the brown. Brown's a hard colour to work with. But at least they matched my hair and skin. I was all together, one person, but who the hell was that?

Nothing, I thought. You're not even shit, because shit is something. Shit is something that somebody sees. Shit is actually studied very carefully at times, by the medical profession, by the shitter. The trouble is, I said to myself, nobody sees you. Nobody sees *you*. That thought took away all my energy so all I wanted to do was crawl back into bed and stay there forever. But, thanks to Zeke, I now had words like motivation and goal. And thanks to Jamey, I had a situation that was my idea, and if I couldn't do it, how could I expect him to?

I looked at my watch. Jamey would be home at four o'clock.

I ran into the bedroom and snapped up the blind and threw up the window. Fresh cool morning air. I let it all in. I ran into the bathroom. I brushed my hair one hundred strokes. I brushed my teeth, being careful not to slobber toothpaste down my chin. I splashed my face with cold water and patted it dry. I stepped into my jeans. I found a clean shirt. I put an elastic around my hair. I made the bed and fluffed and tubed the pillows and tucked the chenille bedspread up under them. I thought how Tree would be proud of me. I couldn't hang up the clothes that were heaped on the floor because we didn't have hangers. Making a mental note to get some, I folded everything up neatly into little piles on our backpacks. Jamey's socks and shorts gathering fluffs of dust, I put into a brown paper bag for laundry.

At the kitchen sink, I twisted the hot water tap on full force and jetted a spurt of soap in and watched the way it all foamed up. I washed all the dishes from last night, then the others, every single dish in the place, which wasn't a lot. I shook cleanser into the sink and scrubbed everything up and hung the dishcloth on the little three-armed thing that came out of the wall.

And as I was doing these things, I started to feel like somebody. I started to know who I was or, at least, who I wanted to be. I wanted to have a home and family like Tree never had. I wanted to have a husband who'd never leave me like Tree never had. I wanted to have a stable secure existence like Tree never had.

While I swept and mopped the floor, I thought how I'd talk Jamey into buying a vacuum, secondhand would do, as long as it slurped up the dust. In the living room I straightened the plastic doilies and flowers from the last tenant and wondered did she forget them? Or, maybe she left them as a sort of little message to the next woman who came along, which, I suddenly realized, was me.

I am a woman, I thought and stood up straight and stuck out my chest. I've got to get a schedule. I rummaged around until I found paper and pencil and cardboard for a ruler. I sat down at the kitchen table and smoothed out the paper and drew eight straight lines down. I turned the paper and drew more lines, measuring them out as evenly as I could. Across the top, in the first column I printed TIME and in the next seven columns the days of the week starting with MON.

That was when things got complicated. I stopped and chewed the end of the pencil. In the first place was Jamey's shifts. Right then he was on days, so I figured to go for days for the time being. Below TIME I wrote 7:30 but then I remembered how Jamey had to be at work at 7:30 so I looked for an eraser but the only one I could find was on the end of the pencil where I'd been chewing and when I erased with that it left a smudge. Rats, there went my nice clean sheet of paper. But I put 6:30 in the smudged place thinking, God, how will I ever get up that early. I thought how Jamey needed to sit down to a good hot breakfast instead of grabbing taco chips as he passed through the kitchen, and already I could hardly wait for 6:30 tomorrow morning.

Jamey's days off were Wednesday and Thursday. I found them on the top of the sheet, found 9:00 along the side, ran my finger across and wrote BKFST, wondering if he'd go for that. But if I got up and made pancakes and bacon, maybe the smell'd do it. My pencil hovered. Wednesday and Thursday, two wonderful days when we would . . . do what? Go to the beach? Once back home we went to the beach but after about an hour Jamey said, let's go. He never could stand sitting around doing nothing. Go for drives? I hated aimless driving. Shopping? We didn't have any money. Maybe nine o'clock was extreme. Well, I could decide on that later. Anyway, Jamey should have some input. After all, it was his life, too.

Something I could do, though, every day, right across the week, at 6:00 PM I put SUPR. Then I thought how Jamey was always grabbing at the snacks the minute he got in from work, so at 4:00 I put SNCK. Then I looked at the paper. I'd never realized before that a day has so many blank spaces. What am I going to do with the rest of my life? I thought.

I raised my head to the window where a spring fly was caught between the layers of glass. The sound of its buzzing made me think of prairie summer days with everything hanging hot and heavy and droning and going nowhere. It made me think of Terrabain Street. It made me think of the letter from Popi we'd got the day before. He must have written it right after Jamey phoned him and Rita, which he did after we got a postal address. We'd never had a postal address before, but Jamey wanted to get a weekly that listed what was happening in Vancouver plus brochures and such from equipment stores. He didn't say that was the reason, but I knew.

My eyes went to Popi's letter, which was on the kitchen table where Jamey had been reading it before he left for work. I picked it up. Popi had composed it on his word processor and printed it on his printer, but he hadn't edited it like he did his epic.

[Just writing to say yor mom is fine, everybody here is fine, I'm fine too, cant complain, dont do me any good if I do. I manage. I get up early every morning just like always. Funny thing, when I was a young guy on the farm I used to dream of the day when Id be able to sleep in but now I don't want to any more. you got to keep moving or you go into paralysis. So I still get up bright an early an Paquette an me still have our morning coffee and still go down to the Frosty Bar on a good day. Remember that pretty little waitress? Well, she's still there. as I tell yor mom, I may have only one foot, but I aint dead yet. Good morning, I say, howre my girls this morning and you should see them blush. Well, they know me, they know I dont mean nothin by it. I think they even look forward to me an Paquette coming, well, theyre not too busy down there. The other morning, it was there last week I had a bit of the flu you know so I didn't go down. That was one day I couldnt get out of bed, yor mom had the doctor an every damn thing, so he gives me some little yellow pills an he tells me to stay in bed for the day an all the next to an to keep warm so I stays in bed like he say fr that day but that was about all I could take, I got up the nex mornin, well hell a fella could die in bed y know an I goes down to the Frosty Bar as usual y see an well were them girls in a flap, where have y bin they says, we were some worried about yous, it threw them all into a flap but I still get around, I keep going, yor mom takes good care of me too, of course Beth is married now, too bad you didn't make it home for your sisters wedding, yor mom said you were in California. What was that like, Ill bet good, we had it in the backyard and it didnt rain, I cant believe youve been gone two years, well its a different life now with the house so quiet, one thing for sure, life is a strange beast, one minute the house so full an all the voices and then its empty and so quiet, thats what gets me, the quiet, so I put on the television just to have voices but were doing all right too, don t you worry about your mom an me with her working and I just got a rise on my pension and yor mom tells me that now yous kids have settled down and forgot all about that music a lot of foolishness but thats the way of youth, you got to get it out of your system . . .]

"The old bastard," Jamey said, his voice soft when he read it to me.

. . . *but i always did and will love you/for all the things that we went through/yea, i remember/the cuts so deep and the scars so long/but they're the notes of our love song/that i remember/and i'll never trade that song away/and in my heart it will always play/cause i remember/well, i'm gonna be gonna be gonna be gonna be/yeah, i'm gonna be a contender* . . . And he was a contender and I'd taken that away from him. He was going to kill himself being a contender, I told myself. You saved him.

Looking at our window, I saw Popi sitting in front of Rita's white-frilled curtains, and hanging down the wood between the windows, pots of green ivies that she was so careful to water and trim the dead leaves from. I saw him bent over the table, his thin twitchy hands sorting his clippings from the newspaper. A pedestrian hit by a car and killed while crossing a street and the car was going only fifteen miles an hour. The obituary of a woman immigrant from Hong Kong. How cockatiels left for long periods of time may become neurotic and illness and even death can result. No rhyme or reason to those clippings, but he always said they were for his Vegreville epic.

Sitting there at the kitchen table in Crofton, I thought how Popi had been sitting at his kitchen table for twenty years thinking about his epic and never giving a thought to Rita who'd been standing all day in her three-inch heels in Rosa's Beauty Salon giving perms and rinses, all the time wondering what she'd buy for Popi for supper on the way home, and then in the evenings standing ironing his shirts so he'd have them fresh to wear while he sat at that table.

I thought how I'd read in magazines that relationships should be fifty-fifty and how that didn't work in real life. I thought about the relationships I knew that, to make them work, were eighty-twenty or ninety-ten. I thought of how my mom gave ninety and still it didn't work. But maybe she didn't give ninety, I only had her side of the story, I'd never know the other side. I thought how Tree would never write a letter like Popi because she didn't know how.

Why do I hate my mom? I tried to think it through. Maybe not hate. Despise.

Because she had not been able to hold my father? Because she was stupid and didn't try to be anything else? Because she hadn't been able to lift herself up from the shit in her life?

I thought how people can drag you down, one way or another, through love as well as hate, and that includes the ones in your mind, the ones you left behind because you didn't want to get dragged down. I looked around our little house and for one terrible panicky dark moment I knew it wasn't going to work. Like mother like daughter, I couldn't do it. I couldn't lift all the shit of our lives up on my shoulders and run with it. I thought of Tree and how she'd tell me I couldn't do it.

I bent to the table until I had every single solitary blank on the paper filled in, right down to which TV programs we would watch over at Barb and Bill's, a real couple who'd been married twenty-five years and ran the motel next door. They'd sold out a dirt farm near Moosejaw, Saskatchewan and bought the Stardust with its neon sign in the front—a tipped moon and twinkling stars. But they wouldn't have many customers for a couple of months yet, which was why Bill was working at the mill with Jamey.

After I finished, I felt a lot better. I looked at the clock and saw 11:10. I looked at my schedule to see what I was supposed to be doing and found that it was housework. "Ugh." I even said it out loud. But, then, "Get cracking," I told myself, shoving the paper and pencil into a kitchen drawer.

I decided to attack the living room. I made a quick trip to the store for Windex and Mr. Clean and I scrubbed every inch of that room and polished all the windows. I even found an old ladder out back so I could reach the high ones and the ceiling, although I did have to be careful because the paint flaked so bad I thought the whole thing was going to come down on my head. I thought of waxing the floor and put Aerowax, which Tree used, on my mental shopping list. I thought of cedar-oiling the furniture but there wasn't any to oil. We rented the place unfurnished except for stove and curtains and fridge, which was one of those half-size ones. I had to do some fast talking to get Jamey to take the house, because he didn't want to have any part of owning furniture. But it was such a cute little place, a square with a verandah and a white picket fence like in the movies, all freshly painted on the outside, so someone would want to rent it. They'd cut the lawn and everything. And we could see the ocean from the back step. I begged Jamey, saying we could get a few pieces of furniture cheap at an auction.

"Furniture's easy to resell," I promised. "Everyone's looking for bargains with prices on new being so high. Or we can just ditch it, just take off and leave it. Since we won't be paying much." So he agreed to the bed, a couch, a couple of chairs, a coffee table and a chrome set for eating on.

As I stood and looked at the results of my hard work, I felt so good, like for the first time in my life I'd really accomplished something. To hold everything in place, I sprayed air freshener all over like hair spray.

I still had a couple of hours left before Jamey was due home, and I thought how he'd like it if he walked in the house to the smell of fresh baking. I ran next door to the motel, hopping, skipping and jumping over the little hedge between us and it. "Hey," I said, bursting in through the door where Barb was sitting at her kitchen table having a cup of coffee and a smoke.

"Wanta coffee?" she said. I was tempted, but I knew if I sat down at that table I'd never get up.

"Thanks," I said, "but I'm in the middle of baking. You got a cookbook?"

Again, I ran to the store, this time for ingredients. Like, I didn't have one basic—flour, baking powder, etc. As I put things into my basket, I noticed how everything was so expensive. I made a mental note to organize it so I could do my shopping at the supermarket in Nanaimo and buy the specials, which would save tons of money and Jamey would be so proud of me and that would help with the furniture. In the meantime, though, we had to have something for supper. So I bought pork chops, being careful in that I only bought two, but I figured Jamey could have half of mine, too. I bought a whole bunch of lettuce, which was on sale and a very good buy and which I figured both Jamey and me needed since we hadn't had lettuce for about a year.

First thing, I got all that lettuce washed and into the fridge. I had to jam the last head in because what with all those groceries that little fridge was busting at the seams. Then I only had time to bake a loaf of cheese bread, a batch of blueberry muffins, and a double batch of brownies, singing along with CDs as I went—me and Sting sang real good together. I glanced at the clock, thinking how Jamey would be home any minute now, which he was. Only he had three other guys with him and a couple of cases of beer so he didn't notice anything different about the house. He took the plastic bags of lettuce out of the fridge to make room for the beer.

All four of them headed for my cheese bread and blueberry muffins with a sort of glazed look in their eyes. I felt like flinging my body in front of my baking to save it but it probably wouldn't've done much good. I would've just got trampled in the rush. Anyway, the look on their faces eating, like they'd died and gone to heaven, was almost worth it.

Then they all clomped into the living room, layering everything with pulp and paper dust as they went and tracking crumbs with their heavy boots. Jamey got out his guitar and a spare because one of the guys played, too, so they took turns showing each other some riffs. The other two listened, sang, told jokes and smoked up a storm. I recognized the familiar sweetish smell of pot. I went into the bedroom and lay down on the bed and stared at the ceiling and listened to the fridge door open and slam shut. I could've gone out and joined them I guess, but I wasn't in the mood.

I listened to Jamey being happy. The way those guys were rocking it up, that little house was jumping up and down on its foundation and the walls were popping. The other guitar player was more into country rock. I must say my fingers itched at that. Country and old-time rock 'n' roll were hard for me to resist, but I clenched my fists and stayed where I was. Then they switched to some Neil Young tunes and then Jamey put some backup on the ghetto blaster and the live guitars sounded real good against it, the whole scene getting off on some really fast numbers and Jamey's voice tripping across the top register like an eel on stilts with its improvised voice riffs and bigabigabigas he used to like to get off on imitating Elvis.

I was glad he was happy. I felt sad that he couldn't be that happy all the time. I wished I could make him that happy. But I honestly don't think I was ever jealous of his music. I honestly don't think I was the jealous type when it came to Jamey. I wanted his happiness too much for that. I think what it was, I was worried about his happiness and whether or not we could make it in Crofton.

After a while I heard the front door open and close. Jamey came into the bedroom and said how about supper. When I made my way out, I saw that one of the guys, the one who played guitar, was still there. I cooked up our two pork chops and gave the guitar player mine. I wasn't hungry anyway. I drank a cup of coffee and sat and watched Jamey, the way his body was bent forward in a curve and the way his hair curled on his neck. I watched his hands, his thin quick fingers, brown and cracked and already marked with mill work, and thought how they knew exactly where to go, the exact right spot along the frets. He was playing the only song he ever wrote in Crofton, right after we went there. . . . *cowgirl wrangled pups/for another man/never made big bucks/living out his plans//cowgirl paid her dues/cowgirl has deep scars/spending many lonely nights/watching other stars//then cowgirl found some brushes/and some pots of paint/no more pretending for cowgirl/to be what she ain't* . . . The other guy joined in with a backup. It sounded good.

Jamey was bent over with his ear close to the strings listening for a sound he couldn't explain even if he tried. It reminded me of Zeke bent over his board, earphones on. It struck me how close two people must be when they're working for the same sound. How close Brian Eno and Roxy Music must have been or U2 and Lanois. How close Jamey and Zeke must have been. How their relationship must have gone beyond a working one. How it must have been hard on Jamey to break up with Zeke. And vice versa. They're professionals, I told myself. Professionals can let things go and move on.

After the last guy left, Jamey looked at me straight on with his clear eyes and said, "Hey, how are ya?" and started fooling with my clothes.

"It's the wrong time," I said and pushed his hand away.

"Whaddaya mean it's the wrong time?" he said, putting his hand back there. "It's never the wrong time."

I hadn't been organized enough during all the upheaval of the past couple months to get to the drugstore and get my pills, so I'd been using the Russian roulette system, which works okay as long as you keep track. I'd read articles about how one way you can tell if it's the wrong time is by your temperature going high and I could feel mine was pretty high right then.

"Stop that," I said.

"What? That?" he said, making me squirm. "Or that."

By then he was kissing and nibbling me all over.

"Hey," he said. "You mad? What're you mad about?"

"I'm not mad," I said. "It really is the wrong time."

"Aw, what the hell, let's make a baby," he said. "C'mon."

So we did.

It seemed like a good idea at the time.

I WANNA PLAY HOUSE WITH YOU

. . . i am going to have a baby/beneath the west coast sun/swimming plashless beneath the waves/baby we were born to run . . .

Crofton was the happiest time of my life. Oh, I enjoyed the music part and the different bands and being on the road, at first, anyway. It was fun before it got too much into drugs and personalities. But in Crofton I got up in the morning with a song in my heart and happy music running through my head all day. In Crofton I learned that having someone to love is more important than being loved. In Crofton I had Jamey to myself. I was living the dream of most women—living happily ever after in a little house with the man I loved.

That corner store in Crofton had everything from soup to nuts including row upon row of seeds from asparagus to zucchini. People here must be big on gardens, I thought that first day of May standing in front of the rack, not yet knowing that my life was in for a big change, not yet knowing about the seed Jamey had planted inside of me. Maybe his seed explains my obsession with those other seeds, because that's what it was, an obsession, like seed calling to seed.

I knew what a garden was. In my childhood I had some vague notion of the Corset Lady's garden, a whole lot of green leaves and things growing up chicken wire and vines creeping and twining around the backyard. She had the vegetables and Paquette had the flowers. Into my head popped the memory of the summer the Corset Lady hexed Paquette's garden because he had taken a broom and mashed her cat, Willie, who she thought of as her dead husband reincarnated. Memories like that of Terrabain Street came back to me a lot in Crofton, maybe because I had time to think, maybe because the place and the people took me back to a simpler life.

But children don't pay a lot of attention to what the adults around them are doing. They have more important things on their agenda. Gardens for me then were something that grown-ups had, but now I was going to have my own, and that's what made all the difference.

I felt Jamey at my shoulder. "Look," I said and pointed. The pictures on those packages were something else. Tomatoes like you wouldn't believe, so fat and red and juicy. Peas, dewy green and plump in their pods. Radishes like bright red nail polish. I picked up a little envelope of lettuce that said on the back how you could get a hundred plants from the seeds inside. In that moment, in my hands a hundred crisp leafy lettuces exploded.

I watched my fingers walk, starting at one end of the rack and working their way to the other. I couldn't control them.

"What're y'doing?" said Jamey.

"We're gonna have a garden," I said.

"That's gonna be one helluva garden," he said. "Who's gonna dig it?"

"You," I said, and quickly, "I'll do everything else. Like, the weeding and watering. All you have to do is dig up that little patch of dirt in the back. It won't be that bad. Somebody else had a garden there once."

The next day was Jamey's day off so I got him up bright and early and after feeding him pancakes and gobs of butter and syrup, headed him in the right direction. Watching him through the kitchen window while I was doing the dishes, I felt real good. It just seemed right somehow, the two of us together in our little house and him doing something like digging and me doing something like washing dishes. I mean, it seemed so real and important somehow, like we were pioneers or something, a man and a woman together facing the new world. I swear, looking out that window, I saw Jamey strapped to the horse and plow, the sweat streaming down his face, his arm muscles bulging as he built a country.

"This is crap," he said when I went out and stood by him. The furrows of the scowl on his face were deeper than the ones in the dirt he was digging. "What you wanna do this for is beyond me," he said.

"We'll save loads of money," I said, thinking how he always did frown like that, pouting and grumpy, when things weren't going his way.

"Just don't expect me to eat it," he said. "I don't like vegetables."

I resisted the impulse to pat his back and say there, there, poor baby.

I remembered the Corset Lady keeping track of everything, writing it all down in her planting diary, so I started one too:

May 3. J. and me start digging garden.

4. We dig more garden.

5. J. finished digging small garden patch.

6. J. started evening shift. I planted rad., lettuce, spinach, parsley, onions.

7. Sun. We had a nice Sunday. Barb and Bill over. Planted beans.

8. Didn't get much done, planted potatoes.

9. I planted carrots, turnips, and parsnips.

10. Rained about noon, good for garden.

11. Garden all planted.

12. Nothing much to do in garden.

14. Weather's perfect, rain off and on with the sun shining in between. Nothing much for me to do. I can't even weed until I know what's a weed and what's a vegetable. Meanwhile, Barb has a sewing machine and I remember how I used to sew in home ec and I think having a dress might be nice. I haven't had a dress since I was a kid, so I don't know what's got into me. When I told Jamey about my new dress, he just grunted and turned over another page of the paper where he was sitting, elbows leaning on the kitchen table, exactly the way Popi used to sit. It's funny the way Jamey's taken to reading the newspaper and not hearing a word I say.

16. The dress is coming along good. The material is green with some yellow, very cheerful. I don't like black any more. Black's the colour of old Italian women. Today I found myself telling Barb about the last time mom ever sewed me anything, a hundred years ago for the junior

high graduation dance. I chose a pattern full of gathers and puckers and material that was red and crackly. Mom said the material was all wrong for the pattern plus being very hard to sew, and I said well don't bother if it's too much trouble and slammed into the bedroom, so she sat for three nights sewing this dress, then when I put it on and saw how awful I looked, like a brick house only twice as wide, I hated mom for sewing it and I never wore it, not even once, not even to the dance. I don't know. Sometimes I think I should finally write that letter to mom.

17th. Shoots up in my garden! I was just about percolating out of my skin and I ran in and told Jamey and pulled him by the hand out there with me and he looked and looked and said where's the magnifying glass and I hit him and he hugged me.

20. I sing all the time these days. In the garden, in the kitchen when I'm cooking for Jamey. I can't help it. I open my mouth and a song comes out. I think I'm singing to someone inside of me. I can't remember Tree ever singing to me. I'm going to sing to my baby every day of its life.

22. Lots more shoots up. The garden is growing fast. I keep saying to Jamey how I wish Paquette could see it. When I think of how back home you have to pamper some scrawny plant that grows wild here without even trying, it makes me feel like crying for them back there on the prairie.

June 5th. A good day. For supper we had lettuce, radishes, and green onions from our garden. I washed everything real good and arranged it all attractively on a plate and set it on the table before Jamey. I watched him pour half a bottle of creamy cucumber dressing on. I watched him pick up his fork and taste it. "Ummm," he said. I wore my new dress for the occasion. Putting it on, it was funny. I mean how I saw myself in the mirror. I actually liked the way I looked. In my bra and panties, I was smooth and brown and firm and with everything in the right places and not too much or too little of anything. I saw in the light of the lamp my belly so golden it looked air-brushed, I swear, and I thought of what was in there. Although I didn't know for sure yet, but putting two and two together. And that was one of those moments when I was happy and I slipped my dress over my head. "Hey," said

Jamey, his eyes bright when he saw. "That's nice," he said. Although later he took it off and threw it in a heap onto a chair.

15th. Things are fine. Weather is good. Jamey's playing his guitar, something he doesn't do much of lately, sitting on the couch, giving me the twinkling eye, doing his Elvis routine, come back little baba, I wanna play house with you. Life is wonderful when he's here like this. Life is wonderful, period. I get a little lonely in the evenings when he's working. I can't always be at Barb's or her here. She's got Bill to think about and now that it's summer she's busy with the motel. But there's a rack of romance novels at the corner store and it's amazing how I can really get into a book now and can't put it down until it's finished. I'll read a whole book in an evening. And I pick up a scrap of paper and pencil and fool around with some of Jamey's songs . . . *pacific ocean rising/in front of me/four on the floor engine roar/familiar company/i am going to have a baby/beneath the west coast sun* . . . writing another verse to the song Jamey started on the way out here to the sea . . . *i punched a roar from the four-five-four/ our heads snapped back in the seat/your boots were off, the window down/ wind rushing through your feet* . . .

June 21. It's amazing how being pregnant changes you into a totally different person. Like Guns N' Roses gives me a headache now and one day when I was flipping the radio dial I heard this great music and the announcer came on and said it was a guy by the name of Beethoven. Another time, they played Patsy Cline, who I didn't pay much attention to at home when Rita played her records. But now I really dig her and got her *Greatest Hits* last time I was in Nanaimo. Man, what a voice! The way it strides right out there and doesn't hide behind anything and doesn't have to. The CD booklet says she first auditioned when she was only fourteen! I'd like to play our Gun Wylde CD just to see how my voice compares, but that CD is taboo around here. Once when I wanted to play it, Jamey got real snappy. I thought you wanted to get away from all that, he said. I do, I said, but we can still listen to the CD. No we can't, he said. And I have the feeling if I played it when he isn't here, he'd know. He'd catch the vibes in the air.

Anyway, the outside world isn't important, but only what's inside and that's changing so fast on me I can scarcely keep up. And I have seven months to go, seven months of changing. When I talk about these things to Jamey he can't understand. How can I expect him to, when I don't even understand myself? But I still wait for the sound of him coming in the door, the only person I don't mind interrupting me from myself.

Sometimes I ask myself why I remember with such clarity what Jamey called the pot caper. It was later he called it that. At the time he was plenty pissed off, although he still stood behind me on it. And maybe that's why I remember. Sometimes when I'm blaming Jamey for everything that happened, then the way he dug the garden for me and the way he would have taken those pots reminds me how hard he tried to make Crofton work.

The way it happened, one evening when Jamey was working the evening shift, I was over at Barb and Bill's and she invited me to a pot party. I was surprised, but she laughed and said it wasn't a bunch of people sitting around smoking up. It was this guy, this demonstrator they called him, who comes to your house and cooks up a storm in these waterless pots, even a cake for dessert. "You don't have to buy anything," she said, blowing out cigarette smoke and taking a drink from her coffee cup. I haven't said yet how I loved Barb's face and voice, the first like a dried-out prairie slough, all cracks and dun-coloured, the second like smoked lake trout. "You'll get to meet some people and you'll get a great meal," she said.

Well, that set of pots was so new and shiny and it was so neat the way they all fit together, before I knew what I was doing I found myself signing on the dotted line. It'll be worth it, I was thinking. Those pots guaranteed I'd be the world's greatest cook plus Jamey would be healthier because I wouldn't be pouring out all the vitamins. When the demonstrator told us about all those vitamins I'd been pouring down the drain all my life I got thoroughly depressed. It wasn't until I was on the way home, stepping across the little hedge, that I started to wonder how I was going to tell Jamey I'd just spent nine hundred of his hard-earned dollars that he hadn't even earned yet. Furniture was bad enough, and all of it only came to three hundred and thirty dollars.

I went to bed right away, which was unusual not to say unheard of because I always waited up for Jamey and made him something to eat. Then I couldn't get to sleep because I was listening for his sound at the door. When I heard it and then him coming into the bedroom, I opened my mouth but I knew if I said anything I'd start bawling hysterically, so I closed it and turned to the wall. Next morning, Jamey said, "How come you went to bed so early last night?" and I mumbled something about being tired and shoved that tried-and-true solution of food, this time a pan full of hot muffins, under his nose, which stopped him asking questions for a few minutes at least. Then I said why don't we go up to Nanaimo and look at some used cars. Jamey looked at me quick-like but he didn't say anything, maybe because he didn't want me to change my mind. By the time we fooled around up there it was time for Jamey to head off to work and I got through the first day.

Even I wasn't dumb enough to think that could last forever. My brain was percolating. Maybe if I could get a job to help pay for the pots . . . I asked at the store but they had enough family to cover and couldn't afford to take on an outsider. I thought about getting a job in Nanaimo or Duncan but then we'd need two vehicles. I thought about asking Barb if she needed any help in the motel but I knew she'd say yes and it would be too much like charity. Then I thought maybe if I could make it to payday, with all that money in his fist, Jamey wouldn't care so much that I'd just blown a wad of it. So I made a vow with myself that I would tell him June 30th for sure, which was only eight days away.

It was an uncomfortable week. When we were sitting at the table eating, I'd look across at him, the way he was concentrated on his food, completely absorbed and innocent of my scheming. And he seemed to be over there and I was here, we were two people instead of one, because I had put a lie between us. I thought of the time, which now seemed in another life, when I had sort of lied to Jamey by thinking that in some ways I could be a better musician. Was that a wedge and now this a wedge and how many wedges did it take to split a relationship? I thought of all the people who lie to each other all the time and it doesn't bother them a bit. But they weren't me and Jamey and that wouldn't work for us.

At the beginning, eight days seemed like a long blessed time. But eight days never went so fast in my life. I spent a lot of time out in my garden, weeding and hoeing and watering. Finally, I knew what the Corset Lady had gone through. And even Paquette with his flowers. I finally knew it wasn't the work so much but the worrying. Like, if it rained too much I'd be worrying through the window at my little plants being drummed into the ground. If it didn't rain enough, I'd be watering like crazy trying to perk up the droopy little leaves. If it was too hot I'd wilt as they wilted. If it was too cold I got goose bumps for them. If something was growing too fast, I knew it was going to be all top and no bottom, which I didn't want with my carrots. If something was growing too slow, I'd get no top and all bottom, which I didn't want with my spinach. And then there were the cutworms, the slugs and the aphids. And I came to understand that once you have something like a garden you're never again free, you never again have a peaceful moment, because then you have something depending on you for its life.

And yet it was so much fun, too. Like, when I saw those first little shoots coming out of the ground, it was like the beginning of the world all over again.

I kept Jamey busy, too. The landlady said she'd knock some off the rent if we'd fix the fence at the side, so we got boards cheap from some guy Jamey knew at work and we dug some holes and put in some posts and all. Sometimes I felt a little bad about making Jamey do all that work but it seemed to suit him. He was looking superterrific. Not an ounce of fat, but filled out like a man, his arm muscles full and hard, his chest muscles bulging, like Zeke would say, defined. He didn't have that hawk-hungry look to his face any more, either, thanks to my home cooking, which finally made me glad Tree had made me slave away in the kitchen all those years and learn a thing or two.

Other ways, too, I was so good for Jamey. Those days when I was sleeping for two, I was always drowsy, so if he was home he'd join me for a nap. Barb made an appointment for me with her doctor, and he told me to walk, so we went for long walks in the evening or the morning along the beach. The doctor told me to be careful with the booze and pot, so I was and so was Jamey. He said it wasn't much fun to get high by himself. Instead of those parties that used to last for days, we'd maybe go over to Barb and Bill's and watch a little

TV. I loved going over to their place. Barb was always crocheting and knitting and making things nice—frilled curtains and real doilies, and in the bathroom a crocheted cover for the toilet paper roll, an old-fashioned lady in a hoop skirt. And she and Bill seemed to have things settled between them, too, one not having to give more than the other but each willing to give more if they had to. She gave him love and support and made him a nice place to live. Bill, heavy-boned, fully fleshed, not fat, just big, provided strength for her to draw from. It was like if she was the dried up prairie grass, he was the fresh morning dew. Sometimes they'd come over to our place, and we'd play four-handed crib and I'd make a big batch of popcorn. If Jamey wasn't his old hell-raising self, full of beans, well, maybe that wasn't so bad. Maybe people have to grow up sooner or later.

Finally, finally, the big day came. I squared our running bill at the store and dropped in for coffee with Barb and paid her fifteen dollars for something else we owed her for. "The best thing," she said, "is to feed him before you lay it on him." She lent me this cookbook that had ravioli in it made from scratch. I couldn't believe my eyes. Written down like that, in a book, how to make those little dough squares. I thought you bought ravioli at the store and that it came from a place like Giuseppe's where they have special machines. I decided to give it a try. It might take my mind off other things. So I spent the rest of the day making those squares and filling them with meat and spinach. I made dessert, chocolate fudge scotch squares.

I set the table with placemats and lit a candle in a saucer, the way I'd seen at Italian restaurants. I'd bought a bottle of wine because that's what the book said to do, but Jamey said, don't we have any beer? Anyway, the ravioli turned out real good. So, then, since I didn't want to spoil the meal, I didn't tell Jamey after supper, either.

It was a beautiful evening, warm and soft, which made me think of home, coming home late in summer and the lights on in the house and Rita and Tree after a couple of beers singing with Harry Belafonte . . . *day-o, day-ay-ay-ay-o, daylight come everyone go ho-ome* . . .

"What I remember about summers when we were kids," said Jamey. "How you'n Beth were so mean to me. Jesus, you were mean little girls. I don't know how I survived."

161

"Whaddayoumean?" I said. We were sitting on the back porch step. The moon was full and reflected on the water. Next door, *Stardust* held steady in neon along with its moon and stars in soft green and pink, gentle, even fragile, tones. We were listening to the slap slap of waves on the wooden wharf and Sting on the radio, who was always good for a sad song about love and remembering. I snuggled closer to Jamey. "It wasn't that bad."

"It was hell," he said. "Remember that time a bunch of us were playing in the backyard there in that big old poplar tree and us boys wanted to play Tarzan or cowboys and Indians or some damn thing and you girls wanted to play house, but the thing that got me, the thing I remember, is how you girls wouldn't give an inch, it was house or nothing, by God, else you wouldn't play at all, so us boys like a bunch of sheep just go along with you. I'll never forget that," he said.

Somehow, it didn't seem like the right time to tell him about nine hundred dollars worth of pots. Then Barb and Bill came over with a six-pack and we played a little crib. Jamey was feeling so good and having such a good time, I couldn't bear to bring up the subject. And when B and B left, we fell into bed on top of one another, spiralling together the way we did, shooting the dark with our fire.

A couple of days later Barb came over and told me the pots had come. I asked her to keep them just a day or two more until I got up enough nerve to tell Jamey. "Sure," she said, "no problem. I'll just shove them under the bed."

Another couple of days later, Jamey came home from work in a real flap. What happened was, during coffee break, Bill had spilled the beans, making some sort of joke about how he couldn't complain about not having a pot to piss in since he had all ours under his bed.

"Why didn't you tell me?" Jamey said.

"Because I knew you'd act the way you're acting," I said.

"Why did you get goddamned pots anyway," he said. "If there's one thing I don't need it's pots."

"I don't know why I got them," I said.

"I don't want no goddamn pots messing up my life," he said.

"I know it was dumb, " I said.

"Like a goddamn dog with a tin can tied to its tail," he said.

162

Then Barb came over and said how she'd take the pots and it served Bill right for being such a blabbermouth.

"No," said Jamey, "we'll take them. Lilah ordered them, we'll take them."

Then Bill came over, his usually jovial face full of concern, and kept saying over and over how in hell was he supposed to know he wasn't supposed to say anything, if anybody would ever tell him anything, maybe he'd know to keep his mouth shut.

Then Barb said, "I've always wanted those kind of pots, the ones that don't take much water. All my life, at least the last coupla years. My sister has those pots and I've always wanted them."

So, in the end, we did the big generous thing and let Barb have those pots. I sincerely hope that they worked for her in her life. They never would have worked for me in mine.

GREEN APPLES

In August we drove up to Parksville and beyond, way to hell and gone into the bush, because Jamey ran into someone in the Astoria bar who said Hector and Diana were working a grow-op in there.

Bumping along in that unreliable Chev, along two sandy tracks going farther and farther into the dark forest with the trees closing over top of us, I felt like in Hansel and Gretel and thought how we should be leaving a trail of crumbs.

"Maybe we should turn around and go back," I said to Jamey. "Before it gets dark and we're stuck in here."

"There's no place to turn around," he said, busy trying to ease the tires over and around the ruts and fallen brush. "Anyway, we must be just about there."

"Where's there?" I said.

"About thirty kilometres after the turnoff." Jamey looked at the odometer. So did I. Nervously. That Chev had a mean streak like you wouldn't believe. Not only would it not start unless it felt like it, it had a bad habit of stopping without warning right in the middle of going somewhere.

"What if this thing conks out on us?" I said, putting my two hands on my bulge to protect it from the lurching motion.

"One thing you got, you still got me," Jamey sang.

I looked at him quickly. "Why are you in such a good mood all of a sudden?" I said.

"Because I don't hafta smell goddamn pulp and paper for a few days," he said.

Every time Jamey talked about his job these days, his voice got a dangerous edge, an edge I definitely did not want to travel. So I watched the trees and the branches hitting the windshield. If we'd met another vehicle I don't know what we would've done, but there wasn't much chance of that because who but us would be dumb enough to be on that road where things were getting denser and darker and everything was dripping with damp even when it wasn't raining?

"The asshole of Canada," I said. "That's what your dad used to call Vegreville. But this has Vegreville beat by a mile."

"Yeah," said Jamey. "One thing about Pop, he knew how to call 'em."

Next thing we knew, we came slam bang up against a wall of trees. We sat a minute with the motor running. Maybe Jamey was thinking like me how that hum was our last link with civilization, the intravenous to the outside world. Once cut, we might not get anything back except a hollow click.

"This must be it," Jamey finally said, his fingers on the key in the ignition. "Like the man said, when you can't go no further, you know you're there." He turned his wrist quickly. It was one of those decisive actions.

That was when I saw a slithering movement in the trees. Then all hell broke loose in the form of these two great huge hounds of the Baskervilles that came leaping out at us, yelping and foaming at the mouth, tongues lolling and drooling all over the car. Pasted against the windshield was this pink belly, these raw and swollen looking nipples.

I pushed down the lock on my door and listened to the sound of toenails scratching the paint on the car. Through the dogs I could see someone sneaking around in the bush, what looked like a crazy guy with a pulled-down hat across his face, darting from tree to tree with this great big Jesus gun in his hand. That movie *Deliverance* flashed through my brain. "Oh my God," I said and this time threw my arms across my bulge.

"It's only Hector," said Jamey in that tone I recognized from when we were kids, male superiority when dealing with female emotionality, but hiding, or meant to hide, relief. He opened the door a notch and hollered, "Call off the goddamn beasts."

"Oh, it's you," said Hector, stepping out from behind a tree and pushing up his hat. And, changing his tone, "Here, c'mere Sheba. Sol. Shuddup. Hey!"

But those dogs were having so much fun playing man-in-the-wilderness with Hector, they didn't want to settle down, so he had to call them a couple more times. Finally, they slunk over to his knees, curling their bodies like eels and their tails around their bodies.

"You expecting the cops?" said Jamey, putting a leg out the door.

"You can't be too careful," said Hector.

I scrambled out Jamey's side of the car and hid behind him, trying to keep my distance from those dogs, but one of them was taking a special liking to me. It was the female, with the bruised-looking teats.

"What in hell you doin' here?" said Hector who, now I could see him, I scarcely recognized because of the hair all over his face, all curly too, just like on his head, the whole like one big flaming bush.

"They said at the Astoria you were up here," Jamey said. "That you got a little business going."

"Jeez, do they have to advertise it? Something like that can get to the wrong ears."

"You should be fairly safe here," said Jamey looking around. "Someone would have to be real dedicated to find you here."

Back in the trees, a large shadowy shape was slowly moving toward us. It was Diana carrying a kid up high in the crook of her arm. Andrew was hanging on to her knees. When she came up close, I thought how she still looked pregnant, but in her loose dress it was hard to be sure. Then when she wrapped her arms around me, hugging me close, I could feel a firm little mound there.

"Come on, come on in," she said and led us back through the trees to a campsite she had fixed up like a little house, at the centre a camp table covered with boxes and cans and bottles and a dishpan and a Coleman stove. Over it was a tarp for a roof, strung between a tent and their van, a rope from the corner of the tent to a tree for a clothesline and clothes and tea towels drying on it. Off to one side, circled with rocks, was a fire, smoldering, and over it a grill with a big black pot on it. Whether by plan or coincidence, a ray of light shafted down from the sky through an opening in the tree branches.

Hector made a sweep with his arm, like he was ushering us into the best hotel in the country. "It may not be much but it's home," he said.

"Home is where the heart is," said Di, smiling her slow easy wonderful smile.

"Back to Mother Nature," Hector said and beat his chest a little. "Come and see my operation. One thing though, you wouldn't happen to have some beer?"

"Hey, do birds fly or what?" said Jamey, and they headed back to the car.

Diana showed me the new baby, born in February, another boy. She deposited him in a seat contraption and settled Andrew and the dogs down with biscuits that she got out of two different boxes on the table. In her loose billowy clothes with her long hair falling around her like a cape, she floated like a dancer in the spotlight of that ray of light. The sound of water running gave the scene melodic backup. I stepped over to the edge of a small creek just the other side of a wild apple tree. I could imagine Di squatting there on the bank, bashing clothes on a rock. Near the tent, the female dog was lying half on her back with her babies lined up and down her length, like they were plugged into a feeding machine. The femaleness of this place struck me so strong I could almost smell it. I felt a great sense of reassurance. That dog and Diana would know what to do in any situation, I thought, and was proud to be a female, something I'd never thought of much before.

"This is cozy," I said.

"The price is right," Diana said. "So how are *you?*"

"Fine. We're living at Crofton. Jamey quit music."

"I heard," she said. "Is it working out?"

"Oh, yeah," I said. "It's great. A steady pay cheque. Steady hours. Don't you think he's looking good?"

"You're certainly looking good," she said. "Your hair so shiny."

I might've told her then about expecting, but Jamey and Hector came crashing back through the trees.

"Breathe that air," said Hector, raising his head and sniffing.

He was right. Smells of pine and earth and green growth were so strong they overwhelmed the underlying odours of a human family living in the bush.

"What you got there?" said Jamey going up to the fire and peering into the black pot. "After six hours in that car, I'm so hungry I could eat the arsehole of a skunk."

"Barley stew," said Di, stirring it around a bit. It looked like a big pot of porridge.

Jamey's mouth opened, but I caught his eye just in time. "Great," he said. "Let's have a beer."

"I didn't think," I said. "We should've brought food. Especially the way Jamey can eat."

"That's okay," said Di. "We got plenty."

"There's lots of food value in beer," said Jamey, hoisting up a couple of twelve-packs and heading for the creek. The male dog growled and Jamey hesitated. "Jesus," he said, "what've y'got them trained for?"

"They'll get used to you." said Hector. "Just give them time. Meanwhile, don't make any sudden moves."

"They like Lilah," said Di. "Lilah can make any move she wants."

"That's Lilah," said Jamey, grinning at me. "All the dogs love her."

Later, when we were all sitting around watching red and yellow tongues of fire lash the darkness, Jamey was getting more mellow by the minute. He was sprawled under the apple tree, which was heavy with small green apples. One elbow balanced the curve of his body on the earth. The other arm reached up and picked an apple, which he ate in about three bites. He must've been really hungry, he'd passed off his barley stew to me when Di wasn't looking. "This is the life," he said. "Plucking fruit from the trees. Fishing beer outa the creek. One hand reaching up, the other reaching down and me in the middle not even having to move. Freedom," he said. "From the cage of crap." He reached for another cold beer and another green apple.

Watching him chomping away on those apples, one right after the other, I was thinking that, after all, the day was turning out okay, even though things happen in threes. That morning the coffee had run over making a terrible mess on the counter, which had happened because I was out looking at my lettuce, second planting, or I should say looking at where it had been because some animal had nipped off the whole row at ground level neat as you please. Then Jamey had rolled out of bed and said let's go. My first instinct had been to stay home safe and sound. But he was so restless lately, I figured, go with his flow. Same with the joint in my hand, which I could've done without, which actually these days made me feel sick, but if I didn't join him he said, you're no fun anymore, so I did. Lately, Jamey accused me a lot of changing and I had to admit he was right. Used to be, he'd hop in the car and go any damn place and you couldn't hold me back with chains. Now, more often I said, you go without me and have a good time. Used to be, I could listen to Jamey all day and all night. Now, more often I wanted to listen to myself.

I came back from my thoughts and recognized the song on Hector's ghetto blaster was a cover Jamey used to sing a lot. I passed on the joint to Di who passed it on to Hector who said to Jamey, "Where's your guitar?"

Jamey jerked up his knee from prone to a sharp angle. "You still doin' gigs?" he asked.

"Yeah, sometimes. I should be out there doin' one now. But," Hector waved up his arm, "this is a going concern I got here. And the fresh air is good for the kids." We all looked at Andrew who was busily eating out of the dog's dish.

"Get him out of there, will you?" Di who had the baby plugged onto her nipple, looked at Hector.

"Probably better for him than that canned baby food," said Hector, but he jumped up and grabbed Andrew who started screaming until Hector shoved an Oreo into his mouth and jiggled him on his knee.

I found myself wondering about Diana and Hector. Were they actually married? I thought of the fifty-fifty thing. It seemed to me that they gave in to each other about equally. I wondered if that came naturally to them or if they had to work at it and have discussions. I'd never heard them fight or even use harsh words with each other, but maybe they did in private. Maybe they were silent seething types, but I didn't think so.

"I'll get back to it," Hector was saying, still jiggling Andrew. "But I can't hardly believe you going anyplace without your guitar."

"I can't do it part time," said Jamey. "For me it's all or nothing."

"Pick it up sometimes," said Hector. "Fool around a bit. You fool around and who knows? You might find another new sound. Like we did before."

"Naw," said Jamey, flicking his body like a flame, reversing the position of his legs. "There isn't nothing new."

"You don't know that," said Hector. "You don't know until you find it."

"Or not," said Jamey.

"You find it, all right," said Hector. "You fool around long enough and you find it."

"Maybe you don't even have to look," said Diana. "Maybe all you gotta do is stand still. And it will find you."

But no one heard her except me.

"Maybe there's nothing out there to find," said Jamey, scowling.

"Not out," said Diana. "In."

But, again, she spoke too softly.

"There's something," said Hector. "All those bits and pieces. Just waiting for someone to put it together. Then it'll be the new trend. The latest. But you don't know what it's gonna be until you get there. Just like any new frontier."

"There aren't no frontiers no more," said Jamey. "Except maybe on the moon. Or Mars."

"Nothing exists until somebody finds it," said Hector. "And then it's so damned obvious. Take the ballpoint pen, for instance. That happens in music, too."

"It got too serious," said Jamey. "Too much like a job. The simplicity got lost."

"Still, you gotta do something," said Hector. "Or else just curl up and die."

"How about Lilah?" Diana turned to me. "You doing any singing these days?"

"She sings real good around the kitchen," answered Jamey. "And in her garden."

Diana started asking me about my garden and said how she'd like to have a garden and one of these days she would. Then from the sidelines I heard the word "Zeke." It came like a little explosion of brightness out of the dark. My ears perked up.

"I thought he was in California," said Jamey.

"He's here," said Hector, "on the Island. I haven't seen him. But I heard."

"What's he doing here?"

"Sound," said Hector. "What else?"

I could feel Jamey's body from across the fire. I could feel it was like pulled elastic. I was careful not to look at him. "When's your date?" I said to Diana, low, not wanting to interrupt their music talk with my baby talk.

"Late December," said Diana. I must have looked surprised. "I know," she said. Not even a year this time. But this way they'll all be playmates for each other."

"I'm gonna have a baby," I said.

"I wondered," Diana said. "You've got that look, that shiny look. How far along are you?"

"About four months."

"That's exciting. It really is. It's great. To have kids when you're young. You can always go back to music later."

"I can be happy without music," I said. "I can be happy with Jamey and kids. Jamey and kids are enough for me."

"Are you doin' your breathing exercises?" asked Diana. "Are you eating whole grains?"

"Oh, yeah, I'm being real careful. I'm not even smoking these days. At least not much."

"I wondered about that shirt," said Diana. "You don't usually wear that kind of shirt."

"It's Jamey's," I said. "And I can't do up the snap on my jeans. I have to get some looser clothes. I never thought how I'd need some different clothes."

"How about Jamey?" said Diana. We both looked across the fire. "Is he okay with it?"

I just about said, yes, but the word wouldn't come out of my mouth. Instead I said, "How does Hector feel about yours?"

"That's different," she said. "Hector can live with doing music part time."

I looked across at Jamey. "He doesn't believe it yet," I said, and the minute the words were out of my mouth I knew they were true. We had never really talked about it. We hadn't said words like "baby" or "child" to each other. All I said to him one day in between doing something else was how I had missed my period, and he said "mmm" and I said "are you happy" and he said "sure, great."

As though my thoughts stirred up something inside me, that very moment, right while I was thinking those things, I felt a fluttering in my body about where the baby was supposed to be. "Hey," I said. And then everybody, including Jamey who at first didn't want to, took turns feeling the little guy kick.

"That can't be," said Hector. "Not so early. You just got gas from the beer."

"That ain't gas," said Diana. "That ain't the same feelin' as gas at all."

"That's how you felt and it turned out to be gas," said Hector. But then Diana kicked him and he admitted it might be a special case.

I said nothing, because I was staring at Jamey's face. The only time I ever saw him looking that scared was once when he was eighteen and I was sixteen and we were driving home from a party in a condition that never would've passed a breathalyzer test in a million years and a cop stopped us for speeding and shone his flashlight straight into Jamey's face.

"Hey," Jamey said, jumping up. "I just remembered." He headed off through the bush toward the car and came crashing back in a few minutes, holding high a bag full of chocolate bars. "Glove compartment," he said, grinning like he'd just gone out and shot a bull moose and saved the fort from starvation.

"No thanks," I said.

Diana didn't want one either, so the guys chomped down the whole bag. After a while, the talk and the fire died down and Diana got up and lit the lantern and hung it on a tree branch and puttered around the camp like a housewife in her kitchen late at night, tidying up, getting things ready for morning. She took up a bucket and made her way to the creek and dipped up some water and came back with it and poured it on the fire.

"Hector usually takes care of this," she said. "But somehow I don't think he's gonna tonight." I looked toward their tent where Hector's rear end was disappearing.

As for Jamey, he was curled up like a baby inside its mother, hands tucked between his knees, on the cold ground. "We could leave him," I said, "put a pillow under his head, cover him with a blanket."

"It cools off in the night," Diana said, "this time of year."

So we rolled him into a pup tent Hector and Jamey had set up earlier and from there into a sleeping bag that I'd unzipped fully open. Diana handed me a flashlight. "In case you have to get up in the night," she said.

I got Jamey's shoes off him but gave up on the rest. I skinned down my jeans and got in beside him and zipped up the bag. Diana must've snuffed the lantern because it got dark except for the wavering light of her flashlight and then that stopped too. And then it got really black. I had never known such blackness before. Black as the bottom of a mine. Black as the bottom of an ocean. Black as a person's insides. Black as they say some people's souls are.

And such silence. There was a little trickling sound from the creek and the cry of an occasional night critter, but that only intensified the absence of the sounds I was used to. I tried to snuggle up to Jamey but it was like snuggling up to a bag of smelly laundry. I turned onto my back and stared up into the blackness and strained my ears. It was weird. Without sight and sound, I couldn't tell where I was or if I was. It was like, without having something to stake myself to, I couldn't locate myself. I closed my eyes against the blackness and Jamey popped into my head, the new Jamey, sitting on the couch looking lost and naked without his guitar, speaking strangely like he had the wrong script, like he was in the wrong movie, letting himself be strapped to the plow. I saw Jamey playing crib evenings like old men on porches, handing over his paycheque every week. Jamey saying yes'm and no'm and jumping when I said frog. Jamey not even going to the bar much lately because of me.

Then I put my hand on my mound and thought, no, don't think

that way. Think of the baby. How we need Jamey, not to mention the steady job and paycheque. He wasn't all that happy in music, either, I told myself. When it comes down to it, being a musician is one long hell. Remember those times he couldn't get gigs or some promoter left town without paying him. And then when the gigs were coming good, he got strung out from the hours and the pace and the pressure of keeping it up. And how he had to take pills to get him through a show and then he'd be flying so high at the end of the show he had to take more pills to calm him down. Remember how he'd pass out and you'd walk alone along the ocean.

I thought of a song he wrote when we were still on Terrabain Street. . . . *child feels the world so large/grows up and finds the earth too small/to hold his dreams/he needs the stars so he must fly/baby build me another ladder to the moon/the way you did last night* . . . I remembered my seventeen-year-old self sitting at his feet vowing that I would, that as long as he needed me to do that for him I would.

How could I, of all people, have betrayed him?

One night on the States tour popped into my head. The crowd was crazy for Jamey that night. And he was crazy for them. On such a night, things really came together for him. Starting slow and easy, then picking up the pace until he had everyone in the place in a frenzy, including himself. But he took his time and strung it out, enjoying the moment and raising the tension in a sort of pleasurable way. That was the way it came out of him, the way he felt it. He'd hold a note and his voice would groan and sound like he was strangling and then he'd make an electric whip movement. Like a magician, snap snap, now you see it now you don't.

Performance is performance, I thought. It's not reality. It's not learning to live in the real world. It's not growing up.

When finally I drifted off, I dreamt some more about Jamey. His hand on the mike, his fingers running down, curling around, taking hold, gently rocking the mike back and forth, his mouth close to the mouthpiece, his mouth growling a little, his hair a curly mane. And his eyes burning up the front rows of the audience. His body thrusting slow and easy, then his pace quickening, building into a reckless momentum.

I woke up with a start, thinking at first I'd had a wet dream. Then, I could smell something terrible. Then I realized that Jamey was throwing up. Where am I? I asked myself. Then I remembered. I jumped up quick and got all tangled in the sleeping bag and fell back down. Hobbled like that, I still managed to roll Jamey out of the tent and me too, somehow shedding the sleeping bag on the way—it occurred to me only later that I could've unzipped it. At first it was as dark outside as in, but then things started to take shape. I crawled around, reaching and groping for the flashlight. When I found it and switched it on, Jamey was moaning and finishing being sick under the apple tree in the spotlight of my flashlight.

By then Diana was out there. She'd got Hector up, too.

"What're we gonna do with the sleeping bag?" I was whispering but I don't know why. Maybe I didn't want to stir up the dogs who, incredible as it seems, were keeping quiet and still through the whole thing. It was as if they knew that something was terribly wrong with the human condition and they didn't want no part of it.

"We can get it cleaned," mouthed Hector, sitting on a log, looking miserable as hell.

"No way you'll ever get the smell out," said Di. "Green apples, beer and chocolate bars. No way. Best thing is to bury it."

"In the morning," groaned Hector.

"Can't wait until morning," said Diana. "It'll smell up the whole campsite."

It was pretty impressive, the way Diana took charge in her own house. I'd never thought of her that way before, as a person who could take control and get everybody organized.

She found a spade right then and there and handed it to Jamey. My last vision of that night, before I crawled into Diana and Hector's tent, was Jamey hacking away at the ground and Hector sitting on a log shivering and holding a wobbling flashlight, their faces looking pale in the wavering shadows.

In the morning, the sun was shining through the trees. When I peeked out the door flap there was Jamey curled up asleep with the dogs. His hair was matted, his beard was into a two-day growth, his chin was crusted with dried vomit. What jumped into my head was his rebellious bump and grind stage and his declaration, loud and clear, "They not gonna de-ball me."

I crawled back into the tent where Diana and Hector were curled around either side their kids. I lay back down beside them but apart. I lay for a long time on my back watching leaf shadows flickering on the canvas roof. I was thinking how it's not the enemy that defeats you. It's the people you love.

TOUGH ENOUGH FOR LOVE

When Jamey came home from work, or from anywhere, I always ran from where I was, usually doing something in the kitchen. I always gave him a big hug and kiss. "Hi," I'd say. "How goes the battle?"

One day he jerked his body away from me, his face twisting. "I wish you wouldn't say that," he said.

"Why not?" I said, stepping back.

"You said that yesterday. You asked me that yesterday and I told you. You don't have to ask me again today."

Another day, it was his day off and he'd taken the car into the garage for something or other as usual and when he came back, I said, "Hi, how are you?"

"You asked me that an hour ago," he ground out between his teeth. "Nothing's changed in a goddamn hour. Honest to Christ. If it had, you'd be the first to know."

"It's just an expression," I said. "It's just a way of saying hello. Why do you have to make such a big thing out of it?"

"I'm not the one making a big thing out of it. You are. You're the one started it. You're the one said how're you."

"Jamey, this is ridiculous. Can't I even say how are you without you blowing your stack?"

"It doesn't mean anything. What does it mean, anyway? Empty worn-out words."

"It's a kind of communication. I'm trying to communicate. And anyway, I really do want to know how you are."

"Well, maybe you do, but nobody else does. That's what gets me, people going around all day saying how are you and have a good day and no one gives a fuck how anybody is or whether or not they have a crappy day."

"Maybe they don't know what else to say. At least they're trying to make contact."

"That's where you got it wrong. People don't give a shit, so it's better to say nothing. It's better to keep your mouth shut instead of opening it and saying stupid things you don't mean."

I tried to touch his arm but he moved away. "What's wrong with you anyway?" I tried to look into his eyes.

He turned away. "Nothing."

"You're not getting enough sleep."

"I'm getting plenty of sleep. If I get any more I'm gonna turn into a goddamned turnip."

I looked in his lunch bucket and there was the lunch I'd made him that morning all still folded neatly into little wax paper bundles. "No wonder you're cranky," I said. "You never eat your lunch anymore."

I can't describe the look of disgust that crossed Jamey's face. "You should smell that lunch room," he said. "Tuna, egg, peanut butter. It's enough to turn your stomach."

"You're tired and hungry," I said. "Come on and have some supper. I made lasagne . . ."

At that he turned. "Will you stop being my mother! I got a mother. I don't need another one!"

I made sure I counted to ten after that shot. "Why don't we go to a movie," I said.

"No. Wait. We could go to the Astoria." He saw my hesitation. "I forgot," he said, "You don't like drinking beer no more."

It was true I'd cut down on the beer the last couple months because of the baby, but that wasn't why I didn't want to go to the Astoria. I didn't want to go to the Astoria because of Jamey's new friends, one being Martin, who didn't work with Jamey anymore. He used to, but I doubted that he'd kept any job he'd ever had for more than a month. He was short and squat and dark and had dirty fingernails and smelled like he never took a bath and he had a real attitude problem. One night at a party, he leaned over to me and put his beery face into mine and said "Wanta fuck?" but I never told Jamey that.

My hesitation was like waving a red flag in front of a bull. Jamey was sure then that the one thing he wanted to do in this life was go to the Astoria. "C'mon," he said, and when I said why didn't he go without me, I didn't mind, honest, off he went, fairly whistling and jumping like a schoolboy let out of school. I watched him go, swaying his body down the front walk and out the gate and into the car. I watched the Chev move across the sand like a sandpiper, the way it does so light and flickering you wonder if you've seen anything at all. After the car disappeared from my sight I stood a moment longer and thought how he used to coax me, for half an hour if he had to.

I was feeling so lonely I even thought about phoning my mother. Don't all girls phone their mothers when they're going to have a baby? I could hear her voice in my ear criticizing everything I'd ever done in shrill Italian. "I told you so! Now look at the mess you've got yourself in!" I decided against it.

I went to turn to the kitchen to put away the lasagne when through the screen of the door and the pillars of the porch I saw a large shape slide into the place the Chev had been. I went outside, across the porch and onto the step. Through the darkening day, I squinted my eyes. I saw a tall figure get out of a van, slam shut the door and disappear a moment and then come around the back of it and toward where I was standing. What I recognized first was the walk, the slight bounce on the balls of the feet, the sway of the shoulders. Then I knew the leather jacket and then I knew the face. "Zeke!" I yelled and ran down the steps arms wide.

I was so glad to see him, I forgot that I was afraid of him. We hugged and hugged. That was the first time I ever touched Zeke, I mean to really touch him, not just hands or arms briefly passing. He felt strong, large and strong, and I was folded into his strength. It felt good, under the circumstances. He put his arms under mine and lifted me up off my feet in the hug. When he let me down there were tears in my eyes but I couldn't help it. I was that relieved to see him. It was like a weight had suddenly been lifted off my shoulders. Here was somebody who'd know what to do. Somebody who could help me with Jamey.

"Hey," he said, looking down at me, brushing the hollows below my eyes with his thumbs. "Does this mean you missed me?" He said it lightly, helping to keep things casual.

The first thing I noticed, he'd shaved off his beard. "I never thought you'd do that," I said, wiping my nose with the back of my hand. I could see his face better now. I could see his mouth better and his smile, which I'd always liked anyway, the way his lips curved up at the corners, kind of mischievous in an otherwise serious face. I could see that his jawbones were widely set sloping down to a chin that made a statement, which didn't surprise me because that was the way he confronted the world, square on. It didn't surprise me but it was unsettling. His face was unsettling, like I was seeing the unfamiliar where the familiar should be, like for the first time I was seeing someone I thought I knew pretty well but hadn't known at all. It was unsettling to find that Zeke, underneath his mask, might be human. "It's good to see you," I said and really meant it.

While I'd been looking at him, he'd been looking at me, like really looking, not the way most people do, their eyes like ping pong balls. His eyes travelled down and made me squirm. I didn't much dress up those days and the zipper on my jeans was hopeless, and I had on a loose white T-shirt that didn't do much for me but at least I could get into it. Zeke didn't say anything. He just brought his eyes back up to my face.

"You still have your long black hair," he said, and put his fingers into it.

"Come on in," I said turning, feeling a little uncomfortable now, realizing that I'd been too familiar. "You're just in time for lasagne."

He ate half the pan before he asked what he'd come to ask in the first place. "How's Jamey?" he said.

Up to then, I hadn't given him a chance to ask. I'd kept him busy listening to me running off at the mouth about my garden, my house, my neighbours and how much fun I was having. "Great. Just great,"

I gushed. "He's gained about twenty pounds and he's not nearly so twitchy as when he was drinking twenty cups of coffee a day and eating junk food. He gets his eight hours sleep now. Regular."

But Zeke never had let me get away with anything and he didn't then. "Hmmm," was all he said, but it was the way he said it. I realized how phony I sounded and shut up.

He looked around as though expecting Jamey to appear from out of the woodwork.

"He works shifts," I said.

Zeke leaned his chair back, balancing its back legs. He patted his stomach and smiled at me where I was sitting across the table. I noticed the neat little creases either side his mouth. I smiled right back. "You must've been hungry," I said.

"You think that's bad, you should see me when I go home. They cook up a storm back there. My mother and my aunt Gertie and my aunt Sammy. Man, the shoo fly pie and schnitzel and sour cream that comes out of that kitchen. Uh uhn. Someday," he said, "I'll have to go back just so I can taste it again."

I was surprised that Zeke had a mother. I'd never thought of him that way before, I mean, being connected that way to anyone. Or maybe he just seemed too grown up to have a mother. "You never told me about your folks," I said.

"Not much to tell. They're quiet church-going people. They live on a farm. Not much happens."

I watched the way his jaw muscles moved so smoothly beneath his tight brown skin. He always did take a tan well. "Sounds nice," I said.

"A month of that and you'd be climbing the walls to get out."

"Maybe," I looked down at the table. I looked up. "Maybe not. You want some coffee?"

"That'd be nice," he said, softly bringing his chair back down.

When I was up at the counter, I felt his eyes on my back. I felt heavy and awkward and fat and sloppy. I realized how I'd let myself go. No wonder Jamey didn't care whether or not I went out with him.

"Jamey doing any gigs in his spare time?" Zeke asked my back.

"He hasn't picked up the guitar for a month." I put coffee and water in the pot. "Not even to fool around at home. If he really wanted to play, he'd play, the way he used to when we were kids. Don't you think?"

The silence behind me was thick.

"I mean, like just the other day, I got out his guitar and handed it to him and said c'mon play me a tune, but he wouldn't, so I insisted and then he did but it sounded awful. It didn't sound like Jamey at all." I clicked on the red button.

"I guess he has other interests now," Zeke said.

"That's the trouble, he doesn't seem to be interested in anything." I turned and sat back down and waited for the water to drip through the filter.

"What do you want him to be interested in?" Zeke said.

"Why are men and women so different?" I said for an answer.

"Women want love to be real," he said. "They translate it into house and babies. Men want it to be a dream."

"Not all men," I said. "Some want to settle down."

"They're not musicians," he said.

I folded my hands in my lap and bit the soft inner lining of my lower lip. "A million kids across the country buy guitars and think they're Mr. Rock Star himself. Most of them give it up and grow up. Even the ones who get into bands usually only do music for a few years before getting into a normal life."

Zeke was quiet a minute. Maybe there was no answer to what I'd just said. Then, "How about you?" he said. "Are you doing any playing?"

"No." There was a silence it was up to me to fill. "It doesn't seem right to enjoy myself with music if Jamey isn't." Zeke still didn't speak. "The difference between me and Jamey is that I can do it just for fun, but with Jamey, if he picks up that guitar and lets himself get seriously into it, he'll be gone. It's an addiction." Still, Zeke said nothing, while I couldn't seem to shut up. "Maybe I'll sing to my babies," I said. "As for the other, it's no kind of life. I've seen it. Kids raised by nannies. Kids with addictions. Kids with lonely eyes. It's no life for a family. He won't even look at my stomach. He twists up his face and turns away." I couldn't look at Zeke. It seemed like too intimate a detail, both of my body and of our relationship, Jamey's and mine.

"You knew what he was like," said Zeke. "You must have known he wasn't father material."

I certainly didn't want to tell Zeke that in the heat of a moment the concern of making a baby had lost out to headier matters. Again, that was too personal. "I never thought about it before," I said. "Before, it didn't matter."

That talk was making me nervous. I had to stand up. I had to do something. I went over to the sink and started running water for dishes. "What's he afraid of?" I said.

"Maybe that a person can inherit having one foot. Maybe being a crippled bird in a cage, unable to fly."

"You mean, to him being a father is like being in a cage?"

"Maybe he doesn't want to be responsible for another person's happiness."

The red light on the coffee pot went off. I started to get cups but Zeke told me to sit down. "I'll get it," he said. He poured us each a cup. He got some cream out of the fridge. He came back to the table. "What are *you* afraid of?" he said, keeping his eyes on his spoon swirling the coffee in his cup.

"What makes you think I'm afraid of something?" I said.

"Sometimes," he said, still stirring his coffee, slowly raising the cup to his mouth, slowly taking a drink and slowly setting the cup back down. "Sometimes, involving yourself with another person means letting the person be free." He looked up and across the table, right at me. I looked away.

We sat there drinking our coffee for a minute or two and then Zeke sighed and reached across the table and took my hand. "I came here to tell Jamey," he said, "there's talk of regrouping Gun Wylde. Clinton and Geoff. I saw them last week. They were all set to phone Jamey. I said I'd talk to him."

My blood ran ice cold. I looked at Zeke. Is this the devil without his mask? I wondered. Tempting us from Eden?

"We can't be Gun Wylde without him," Zeke said. "But we can be something else. What I'm saying is, he doesn't have to do it. But we have to ask him." After about a minute of my silence, during which I felt myself reeling as if from a blow, Zeke went on. "I was going to stay out of it, but that wouldn't solve anything. And Jamey would wonder why I wasn't the one to phone him." That was about the most defensive I'd ever heard Zeke be. I knew he said it for me.

"I don't think Hector'll go for it," I said, coming to and stalling for time. "He's out in the bush."

"Not any longer," said Zeke. "He was raided."

"Oh no." I thought of Diana and those kids.

"They got out in time. A friend tipped them off. All the cops found was a grow-op. Hector's got a job in Nanaimo. But he's through with the music business. Says he wants to have a half-assed normal life. We'll have to get a new guitar man." Zeke looked at his watch, finished his coffee and stood up.

"I'll leave it up to you to tell him," he said. "I gotta get the ten o'clock ferry back to the mainland."

"You'd do this to me." I stood up, too. "What if I don't tell him?"

"That's up to you." He took my chin in his hand and raised my face. "C'mon," he said, "look me in the eye. Whatever you do, I'm on your side. Yours and Jamey's," he added.

How can he be on both our sides? I wondered and then was struck by the terrible implications of that thought.

"I thought you were mad at us," I said. "After that New Year's fiasco."

"No," he said. His hand on my face was firm and steady. "I was never mad at you."

"Your eyes are hazel," I said. "Why didn't I see that before?"

"You didn't look." And, as usual, he had the last word. "I'm thirty-two years old," he said. "Life gets more and more complicated as you get older."

I stood on the cracked sidewalk and watched the tail lights of the van mingle for a moment with the moon and the stars of the motel and the letters that had been flashing *Stardust* on and off constantly all summer. Zeke's lights grew smaller and smaller, until, at the end of the road, they made a right turn onto the highway. I stared awhile longer into the bright neon.

When Jamey came home, I was asleep, which meant he must've come in mighty late, because I lay awake for a long time thinking about things. I thought about Tree, how she had wanted me to stay at home with her and be happy. I thought about Zeke's words about life getting more complicated as you get older and how all my life it had been easy to put Jamey first and how I still wanted to but I couldn't.

Jamey started going to the Astoria a lot. I figured if I wanted to ever see him, I was going to have to go along. So on a Saturday night I put on my maternity outfit that I'd just bought. I thought it was real cute but Jamey didn't like it, so I put it back in its bag and squeezed into pants that had an elastic waist and a blouse that hung loose over the pants. But I didn't need to worry about what I'd wear because when I came out of the bedroom Jamey didn't even look at me. He was pacing the floor in front of the door. "Let's go," he said.

He drove so fast, hitting the brake, the clutch, jerking the car every time he shifted a gear, it fairly made my stomach go into spasm. And he didn't say nothing all that long way, from our front door right to the parking lot of the Astoria.

Sure enough, we met swarthy sly-eyed Martin just going in the door. Nothing would do but that we sit together. For the next hour Martin ran down all the foremen at the plant who don't do nothing for twice the pay, etc. Finally, Jamey said, "Yeah, I dunno what I'm doin' working there, a goddamn flunky, give me all the shit jobs. That Travis he don't like me . . ." And so on.

Then Jamey wanted to go next door for Chinese food, something that sounded like choo goo gi koo. We'd just got our order, we were at the moment of lifting our forks to dig in when this great huge bruiser came along. I'd noticed him in the bar, spotting him as some guy down from the logging camps, with all his pent-up energy inside, mean as hell and wanting to get it outside of him. Just as he was passing by our booth, he staggered and bumped into our table, jarring Jamey's fork hand just as it was getting near his mouth. "Hey," this guy said, grinning like an idiot. "I never seen anything that looked like that before. How's it taste? Hey, let's have a taste." And he went to put his fingers in Jamey's plate of food.

Jamey held his plate away to one side so the guy couldn't reach it. Then he smiled his crooked friendly grin up at the guy. "You want a taste?" he said.

"Jamey," I said and went to reach for his arm. But I knew already it was too late. Maybe it was too late a few weeks earlier when I first came to the realization that Jamey wanted to hit somebody real bad.

The big guy nodded, taken a little by surprise at Jamey's friendliness, not sure what was going to come down but whatever it was being all for it. At that moment Jamey's plate full of food arched up into the guy's face.

Well, that's all she wrote. Martin jumped in to help Jamey and then some others jumped in, some on this side, some on that. And the women did their part, too, with the screaming, some of them urging the men on. One woman hit this man over the head with the heel of her shoe. He grabbed the shoe from her hand and threw it over his shoulder like it was a toothpick, his face streaming with blood.

I stayed out of it until I saw an opening where I got hold of Jamey's arm and dragged him out of there. He pretended to resist but if he really hadn't wanted to come he wouldn't've. So I figured he'd had enough of hitting something, for a while anyway. I got him into the car and drove like hell away from that place and none too soon, either. Just down the highway we passed two police cars coming the other way, sirens blazing.

After a few miles, I turned off the highway and parked and we walked down through this summer village. We passed a tennis court where two kids were hitting a ball back and forth. They seemed to be brothers, one small, one bigger.

"I can't hit them if you hit them too hard," the small one, maybe about ten, piped like a gull in the clear evening air.

"Was that too hard?" the big one yelled.

"Boy, you're making me run, Eddie," the small one said. "Oh boy, that was a doozer."

"You have a turn," the big one said. "It's your turn. You practise your serve."

Jamey and I stood at the fence, one of those high fences, ten feet maybe. Jamey's thin fingers clutched at the wire. We listened to the thud, thud of the ball, except the boys couldn't keep it going very long at a stretch so usually there was only a couple of thuds before one of them had to give chase. Once the ball came over the fence in our direction. "Hey mister, will you get our ball?" the bigger boy shouted at Jamey.

Jamey ran lightly across the grass, scooped up the lime green ball, ran back a few steps and lofted it up over the fence, smooth and slow so the boy didn't have trouble catching it. Then he came back to where I was standing at the fence. In spite of the blood trickling down in a few places where the Kleenex didn't stop it, his face was happier than I'd seen it in a while.

"Let's just lob it back and forth nice and easy," the big one said. "It's getting dark."

When we were walking back to the car, I thought how I'd turned into one of those women who make homes and how I'd made one and I wanted to keep it. Then I thought, I may as well get it over with. "Zeke was here the other day," I said. Jamey didn't say anything. "Clinton and Geoff want to get up the band." Still Jamey said nothing. "He left a phone number," I finished.

"Do you think I should?" said Jamey. "Call him?"

I thought . . . you're lying in the warmth of the flannelette sheets and quilts, in the coziness you've made for yourself in the night, and the alarm clock rings, and it's cold in the room, and you know that sooner or later you have to get up so you may as well do it now, and the only way to make that cold trip to the bathroom is quick, your feet cold on the tile in the shivering morning.

Quick. Quick. Just say it, I thought. "Why not?" I said.

As soon as the words were out, I knew they were, not the right words, the only words. I could feel that suddenly everything was all right between us again. And it amazed me how something I had not considered an option a few hours before turned out to be the answer.

"Yeah," said Jamey, "maybe I will." And he grabbed my hand and we ran back up the slope to the car, my stomach bouncing like a football as we flew.

PART
FOUR

HUMPTY DUMPTY

"Someday," I said to Jamey, "you're gonna get it."

I'd been saying that for years, every time Jamey snaked through an orange light, which was all the time. And the way one thing leads to another, lots of times he was running reds.

I always figured we'd get it in the middle of the night when the traffic is fast and wild and a lot of people have murder or suicide on their minds and we were in a hurry to get somewhere. Yet when it happened, it was broad daylight and we were Sunday driving even though it wasn't Sunday.

After we got back to Vancouver from Crofton, we were living in this basement that didn't even have a window. When gussied-up Gertie showed us the room, the blind was down and it was night. In the morning, I got out of bed and snapped up the blind and there, staring me in the face, was this blank wall. Not even a picture of a window with ivy and flower pots painted on like we had once in another place.

A month later we were still in that basement, partly because we'd paid in advance and partly because we hadn't got around to moving because Jamey was real busy rebirthing Gun Wylde. And while he would never claim the Expectant Father of the Year award, he seemed to be getting used to the idea. Before we left Crofton, when we knew we were leaving and getting our stuff together and saying goodbye to

Barb and Bill and having a little party, Jamey had picked up his guitar and made up another verse on the spot to *comfort me true*. ... *when dylan arrives/we'll hold him up high/his little round belly/turned to the sky* ... I was over the queasy part of being pregnant and was actually feeling pretty good and going with Jamey to band practices and gigs. The new guitar player, by the name of Joe, seemed an okay guy, and it was fun seeing Clinton and Geoff again. Everybody was making an effort. They had all thought about how the band could be a successful business. And they all wanted to do music.

That day, that particular day it happened, when Jamey dished out his "c'mon, let's go for a drive," I said, "I can't. I just washed my hair," and there hasn't been a day since, in all my life so far, when I haven't wished, oh how I wish, I had stuck to that.

But when he said, "What's that got to do with it?" I didn't have an answer.

That day, sitting beside Jamey in the 280ZX that he'd bought with his last paycheque plus holiday pay and accumulated pension, I was thinking how my hair was going to be frizzy in the wrong places. I felt his foot press the pedal and I looked up into the distance and, sure enough, there was a green light three blocks away. "You're not gonna make it," I said.

"I'll make it," he said.

When it turned orange, we were still a block away. Jamey's foot went heavier still. My arms went across my bulging front. When the light went red, we were just about into the intersection and it was too late to stop. In one flash, I saw the whole thing happen. The car bearing down on my right, one of those giant shark-fin jobs from the fifties. Then the jolt and everything pushed up like a volcano erupting. Flying glass and metal. Sounds of glass shattering and metal crunching and bones breaking. Snap. The smell of blood, which I never realized before is like a copper penny.

That was the day everything went smack, heading on down the track, ain't no way my baby ever gonna come back ...

Surfacing into white. Ceiling, walls, a screen where my life went up and down in a black jagged line that sent out little beeps, and sheets so stiff it was like lying in a cardboard box. A clean place, where I found myself, and everything in order. Like nothing I had ever known before. Except I didn't know if it was me lying there, because I couldn't feel anything. When I lifted my legs, one at a time, it was like they weren't mine, like they were lifting themselves up from the white sheet. One of them was bandaged from ankle to thigh, like one of those pictures of a mummy in a tomb.

And my bottom and between my legs was in a pool of wet. Sticky wet. And then I remembered. I put my hand, which was bandaged, on my stomach, which was flat.

Something's gone, I thought.

After a while a nurse came in and pulled back the sheet and took all the wet bloody stuff away and put on dry stuff, which proceeded to get wet and bloody again. She wasn't one of your smiley nurses but she got the job done. She left me watching the black line going up and down to the rhythm of an old Jamey song. . . . *on a weekend when it rains / doctor can't you give me something for the pain* . . .

Pain, pain, pain, too much pain.

After a while Zeke appeared, like magic, silently and softly, tall, so tall, standing beside the bed.

"Where's Jamey?" I said, watching his face closely. He had his beard again, which hid his face again.

"He's okay," said Zeke. "He's in the hospital."

I felt some relief at that, thinking we were together under the same roof, but then Zeke said, "He's in jail."

"Jail?"

"Infirmary. Because of his foot."

"Foot?" I stared hard at Zeke's face.

Zeke stared back. "His foot got smashed up."

"Which foot?"

"The right one."

I turned my face to the wall and stared at the white.

"He's better off in the infirmary. Otherwise, he'd be in a cell. It seems," Zeke went on, "he had some white powder on him."

"He'd quit all that in Crofton," I said to the wall and myself. "Crofton was good for him."

I turned back to Zeke, who was sitting now, cool and together like always. He looked so neat and whole and unsmashed and unscarred. And then I remembered. "You watched me throw up." The smell and taste and look of horrible green slime against the chrome of a basin came back to me and I was so ashamed that he had seen me in that condition. "I must look a mess," I said.

"You look fine," Zeke said. "You're alive." He stood up. "And then there's the driving charge." He turned to leave. "Dangerous."

After a while, they took me down to physio. When I tried to stand, my legs felt funny, like when they go to sleep and you try to stand or walk on them and they're all prickly and rubbery. A man in a green outfit that looked like pyjamas stuck me in a wheelchair and rolled me down a long corridor and into this huge elevator that was like for cattle and when it opened again delivered me into the arms of the smallest and most cheerful nurse you've ever seen. I admired her, I really did. She had an English accent and every day she said to me, "Hello and how are we today?" all wide-eyed and surprised like I wasn't forty-second on her list.

Then she hung me up on these horizontal bars and how she had the strength to do it I'll never know. She was like a midget darting this way and that. One exercise, I hung from a bar and tried to swing my legs back and forth like the pendulum on a clock. Once, she left me there and darted off to do something for someone else. I went all weak and dizzy and it seemed like the floor was a million miles down, so even though my arms were numb and I couldn't lift my feet back up onto the bar, I couldn't let go, either, or I'd fall like the dream of falling off a high high bridge into nothing. I was sweating and cold and hot at the same time but focussed too because I had to put all my effort into just hanging on. It seemed like a long time I hung there like that, it seemed like years, before the nurse came back, acting like nothing had happened. Nothing. To her it had been a few minutes of a happy busy life, while to me it had been a lifetime of falling.

After another while, they sent me home, which was just great because I didn't have a home. But Zeke had got our stuff from that windowless room, and on the day they let me out he showed up when I was standing in the middle of the ward not knowing what to do. I didn't want to leave the hospital but they said I had to. My body was okay. You're young and strong, they said. Still, it seemed too big a thing to leave that place where life was simple and everything was done for me, to get into the elevator and go out through the lobby and into a vast space without borders.

The world had changed since I'd last seen it. It was colder. The trees were bare.

Zeke's place was half underground and had a bedroom/living room and a small kitchen. He unlocked the door and pushed it open for me and gave me a little nudge. Still, I couldn't seem to take the step. Zeke put his hand on my back. I felt its reach covering the length of my spine. He propelled me in. I stood in the close dusky light smelling Zeke all around me and I felt safe. He set down my suitcase, switched on a light, and said I should take the bed. But a bed didn't matter to me. I couldn't sleep anyway, at least not in any normal way. At first, I'd get really cold all of a sudden and go into what felt like a long coma and always be surprised when I woke up to find out who I was and where I was. Then, I'd just doze off and on all the time anywhere, usually sitting in a chair while watching TV. I kept the curtain closed because there was a lot of glare from the window, which was nearly the length of one wall, and the light spoiled the picture on the screen. I floated in a timeless space, one foot in life and one in some other dimension, maybe death, and I was never sure which place I was in. It wasn't too bad, actually. It was when I woke up that things got bad.

Zeke's hours were totally erratic, but whenever he came in, the first thing he did was fling open the windows to the grey drizzle, which is something about Vancouver in winter, it's always a grey drizzle. But one thing I didn't have to be careful of anymore was smoking. Zeke wasn't a smoke freak the way some people were. He couldn't be because of his job. But he didn't smoke regularly and sometimes it got to him. Right after he moved me in, he appeared with huge ashtrays and set them all around the room. Then he sat down on the bed and took my hands where I was sitting in the one big soft chair and he let go one hand to raise his up and to turn my chin to his face and he put his hand back down to my hand again and looked into my face and said, "Now listen carefully. Try and remember. Between drags put your cigarette in the ashtray. When it gets short, butt it out, make sure it's out. Don't let it get so short it burns your fingers and you drop it. Can you remember that?" he said.

I must have been totally out of it for him to have to talk to me that way, but, strangely enough, I remember so clearly certain details, like his hands, broad across the knuckles and fingers that could reach from c to high g and the nails so clean and square, covering my hands completely where they lay.

If it hadn't been for TV I would have been even more confused. TV gave me some order to my life. First there was the morning interview programs, then the soaps, the afternoon movie, the cartoons, the sitcoms, the detectives, the late movie, the late late movie and the late late late, so I had a general idea what time of day or night it was.

If it hadn't been for TV, I wouldn't have got through. Period. Woody Woodpecker was great, the first time I laughed I was watching it, and they had some creative genius doing the commercials. No way I'd ever get up and go to the bathroom or kitchen when a good commercial was on. I'd wait for the news.

I loved *Love Boat*, of which they were having reruns at the time. It was all about love and romance and nothing bad ever happened. The people were always nice to each other and had nice clothes. Everything was fun and exciting and nobody ever had to worry about money or being sick or alone or having dandruff or underarm wetness.

But my favourites were the old movies. There was one about this woman who falls in love with this man who lies to her all the time about his secret life of killing rich widows but like a dummy she insists on believing him and even when she starts to suspect him she loves him anyway and she trusts him even when you know she shouldn't and he lures her to this lonely spot underneath this lamplight on this lonely corner in the fog and you keep saying don't go don't go but she goes anyway and you're so afraid for her because you know what will happen and you wonder about her, how she knows about him and goes anyway.

But my total favourite of all time was an old Rogers/Astaire dance sequence where she lifts a perfect undamaged leg and all these men in black suits fall over like ducks in a shooting gallery. For some reason, when I watched that the tears streamed down my cheeks. It was unreal.

It was so clean, so precise, so, what you might say, beautiful.

Somewhere in the back of my brain I knew I had to get my own place because Zeke drove me crazy, the way he'd come in without making a sound and say, "Hi, how're y' doin?" right in the middle of the Flintstones. And then he wanted to talk, asking me how was my day and all.

"Shhh!" I'd say.

"What?" he'd say.

"This is a good part here, coming up."

He'd go into the little kitchen and he'd make noise opening the fridge and clattering dishes around. And he'd make crunchy sounds eating toast. And he'd try and get me to eat something he'd cooked up, a tin of soup or maybe even hamburger. I didn't want to hurt his feelings but I had to shake my head no. I would've barfed if I'd eaten anything like that. I could drink coffee and coke, two things I'd cut down on at Crofton, so that's what I did, smoked and caffeined it.

Then Zeke'd want to get some sleep so I had to turn off the TV. At first, anyway. But then I figured out how I could just turn the volume off but still get the picture. So there we'd be, zombie zone, a large dark mound the whole length of the bed and me in that recliner I got to know so well staring unblinking at the screen, the only light in the room its flickering images.

"Did you go out today?" was the second thing Zeke always asked. I always shook my head no and then he'd frown. He said it'd be good for me. Get out and see people, he said. Get away from these four walls. At first I ignored him. But then I thought it wouldn't kill me to go out sometimes to make him happy and to have something to tell him, so I'd walk to the corner store where at first the Chinese lady looked at me suspiciously, probably thinking I was going to lift something, but after a while she smiled at me, and now, looking back, I see as a healing moment the day I was able to smile back at her.

Zeke was foxy, the way he tried to get me to do things, pretending to be casual—like giving me money, saying we needed coffee cream or bread from the store, like leaving his guitar sitting around in plain sight, moving it so it would be in front of my eyes and I couldn't miss it. But I could hardly speak let alone sing. And once Zeke picked up his guitar and started to play, but I had to tell him to stop. Rock or any kind of music shows were the one thing I wouldn't watch on TV. I had to switch to another channel. It was like when you get sick on a food and you can't face it forevermore. I was actually afraid of music, that it'd plunge me into one of my spells.

What would happen, I'd be doing something ordinary, like picking up a bag of corn chips at the grocery, when all of a sudden it would come back on me. A taste bubbled up into the back of my throat and I felt sick to my stomach and I wondered if my brain was rotting like I read about soldiers gassed in the war. And I saw things, too. Wheels, wheels and stretchers, wheels stretching bone and skin. Hurting. I heard things too. It seemed like I was strapped down and I heard so clear the sound of sponge-soled shoes on vinyl and screaming. Then I realized it was me screaming for Jamey. But he wasn't there. So I screamed again, a long scream, and someone was there but it wasn't Jamey. It was Tree with that worried look she always got, but she couldn't do anything to save me either.

But the absolute worst was the power failure. There I was, minding my own business, watching the new *Star Trek*, when all of a sudden the screen went black. I checked all the plug-ins. I switched every button on and off a dozen times. But I couldn't make anything come back on that screen, not even a snow pattern. Total black. I just about snaked out. I mean, how can I explain it? There was nothing. Nothing. Nothing. Nothing. All there was was a big black hole sucking me in. I couldn't breathe. All I could do was turn in a circle and the walls came down.

The next thing I knew Zeke was bending over me where I was in a heap on the floor. "Come on," he said. "Let's get you into bed."

"The TV," I remember saying. "What's on?"

"I don't know. Something," he said.

And sure enough there was a picture flickering on the screen and some words coming out of the picture.

"Do you want me to leave it on?" he said, pulling a blanket up around me.

"No, its okay," I said. And it was. As long as I knew I could turn it on if I wanted, as long as I knew something would be there on the screen if I needed it, I was okay.

"Why don't you come with me?" Zeke said once, stopping as he went out the door.

"What's the gig?" I said for a stall.

"Christmas staff dance," he said. "They'll lay on a spread, lots of food and drink. They won't know you're not part of the band. I can get you in."

"I can't," I said.

"Why not?" he said.

"I have to do my laundry," I said. I didn't want to tell him I didn't want to miss *Wheel of Fortune*.

"The food would be good for you," he said. "You need to eat."

Sometimes I ate. Once, Zeke made me tea and loaded it with milk and sugar, then he made me toast. It reminded me of something. Tea and slops the Corset Lady used to call it, dunking toast in weak sugary milky tea. When I was a kid and sad and lonely and wondering who my father was, she'd give me that when she was rocking me on her lap. So I ate that when Zeke made it for me and, after awhile, I even started making it for myself when Zeke wasn't around.

Zeke made me take showers. I don't know how long it was before the first one, maybe I started to smell. He'd stand outside the shower door, handing me in soap and shampoo and towel and shouting in to me, was I putting shampoo on now? was I washing it off? telling me to shut off the tap, handing me in a towel. Even when I could do it on my own, he kept an eagle eye on me, which I thought extreme, but a long time later he told me about someone he knew who'd slit her wrists in the shower.

The day came when Zeke wet a face cloth with hot water from the tap and washed my face and made me put on some clean clothes. He tried to comb my hair but the tangles made my eyes water. We went out the door and toward the parking lot at the back of the apartment building and past his van. That's when I said, "Where're we going?"

"To see Jamey," he said. I said nothing, but I was worried. I was going to miss *Jeopardy*.

"We'll go on the bus," he said. "I'll show you the way. Then you can go by yourself any time you please."

It was a long journey, from Zeke's apartment to the jail/hospital—

standing on a cold windy street corner waiting for the sad-eyed bus to appear down a long corridor of bare trees, and the gassy smell when it came and its sighing to a stop and Zeke pushing me on ahead of him. He made me deposit the money he'd given me into the glass box. "You have to get a transfer," he said. "Remember that." He herded me down the aisle and onto a dark green vinyl seat and he opened a *Rolling Stone* beside me and hunkered down into concentration mode and then, as though remembering, stuck his hand in his pocket and pulled out a KitKat bar and handed it to me without interrupting his reading. I tore open the red and silver paper, peeling it down carefully, broke off one section of bar, and put the package together again so neat you could scarcely tell it had been opened.

Taking very small bites of my one section, not chewing, more letting it melt in my mouth, and swallowing slowly, I looked out the window at the stores and the café fronts. They were all decorated for Christmas and looked so cheerful. It made me think of the time we wrote letters home. It made me think how we were happy and together then, just starting out with our dreams in our pockets. It made me wonder what happened. Maybe our dreams were too big for our pockets and fell out somewhere along the way.

After a while, we got to a place where Zeke closed his magazine and stood up. We got off the bus and crossed a street and went up some stairs. But first we stopped at a newsstand and Zeke bought another magazine and gave me a five-dollar bill. I bought a *Batman* comic. Then we went up and waited on a platform where a yellow stripe protected us from the trains. Then we got on a train that zipped us through the sky.

When the train came, rushing to a stop, Zeke took my hand and we stepped on. It was crowded and we had to stand. Zeke grabbed a steel pole and I kept tight hold of his arm trying to stay standing as the train went faster and faster. And that's when I learned there was something wrong with my leg. I knew about the scar, and sometimes that leg was stiff and sensitive, but on that swaying train it didn't want to hold me up. It seemed weaker than the other. But, at least I had the other, so I put my weight on that.

At the next stop some people got off and we sat down and Zeke opened his new magazine. I thought about eating another section of my KitKat, which was my favourite, which Zeke knew. But I was saving the rest for Jamey. Still, I thought, he won't mind if I have one more section. That will still leave two for him. But it seemed too much effort to unwrap and rewrap it again. So I just sat there and looked out the window, holding the *Batman* in my hand.

"This is it," Zeke said and stood up. We got off into a cold drizzle. Down on the street I didn't recognize anything, the buildings or anything, and people were rushing around in every direction. I looked up at Zeke's face and he smiled down at me so I stayed beside him. Then we had to take another bus. This time Zeke told me to hand in my transfer. I noticed one corner of it was missing where I'd chewed it right off but the driver took it anyway.

When we got off that bus we walked for a while. Zeke took my hand and shortened his steps. We came to a driveway and went up it and in the door of a large building and got on the elevator. Zeke told me what button to push. "Remember that number," he said. The door closed and nothing happened and I got scared but then when I looked up at the lighted numbers I could see that we were moving. When we stepped off the elevator there was a counter and stainless steel chairs and a low table with magazines. Behind the counter a woman with short curly hair and pale lipstick was writing things on a chart. Her hands and fingernails were very clean. She didn't wear polish. Everything was so quiet and there was a funny smell that reminded me of pickled frogs in biology class.

I wasn't really scared because Zeke was there but I might've been if he hadn't been.

He took my hand again and we went down a long hall and just as we turned to go into one of the rooms, he gave my hand a squeeze. Then we went through a door, which was like a magic door because on the other side of it, ta da! was Jamey, sitting in a chair in front of the window. There was a bad smell in the room, which got worse the closer we got to him. It was a smell like rotting meat. On the way home, Zeke explained that it was Jamey's gangrene but he was on antibiotics and should be okay.

I walked toward him and we held hands. Maybe he looked at me, I don't know, because I couldn't look into his eyes. I would have started bawling uncontrollably. Instead, I looked at his blue plaid bathrobe, sagging open at the neck, and his chest like a boy's it was so thin. I sat down on the edge of his bed, still not looking at his face. "I don't have the baby anymore," I said. I could feel my lips twist. I clamped them tight to control them.

"Zeke told me," he said. "He said you were okay."

We held hands but didn't talk. After a while he said, "What's the comic? Hey, *Batman*. Right on." And he let go one of my hands to pick up the comic that was beside me on the bed. I gave him the KitKat and he said thanks.

Then Zeke started talking about music and bands, which was a good thing. Jamey and me didn't have words deep enough to suit the occasion.

Zeke took me one more time to see Jamey and then I went on my own. I went nearly every day. He was always waiting for me, sitting in the same chair looking out the same window. He was always wearing a blue plaid bathrobe. He was dark around the eyes and his eyes looked anxious, but I'd seen him like that before. What was different was something around his mouth, something pulled in or caved in, so for the first time I could see what he'd look like when he was an old man.

We sat together and held hands and watched this other guy in the ward pack his suitcase and go off and after about half an hour come back. "That's all he does all day," Jamey told me. "Walks to the end of the hall and waits for somebody to come and get him and take him home. Then he comes back and unpacks his suitcase and after a while packs it again. They say glue did a number on his brain."

"He doesn't know how lucky he is," I said to Jamey. "Being in the hospital. Where people take care of him and he doesn't have to do anything."

"What do you mean," he said. "In here, you're not free."

I guess he was right. I was free to come and go on that bus, train, bus. And to see all the things I saw, not just the same thing every day. Like, once I saw a carnival. It appeared in a park, all of a sudden there it was. With all its lights and wheels spinning and calliope music you could hear through the open bus door and even when the driver closed the door you could hear it faintly still. It was just one of those piddly little carnivals, a small Ferris wheel, a merry-go-round, a few lighted tents with games and activities, a couple of trailers where the carnival people lived. I could see it really good because the bus stopped there and waited for another bus to make a connection. I always liked carnivals, maybe because of my father. To me, running away with the carnival seemed a super magic thing to do. I looked forward to seeing it every day. Especially after dark, when I'd be coming home, it looked nice, all those lights and the music.

But about a week later the carnival was stopped, its lights out, its music silent. All that was left were the trailers and a man walking. Through the darkening day, through the bus window, I could see him going from one trailer to another. He walked slowly, weaving a bit, whether from being tired or on something I don't know. He went into the trailer where a woman was and I could see them through the lighted window talking. I thought, for all I know that could be my father. The woman he was talking to looked sleazy and like a Gypsy. Gypsies will sell their kids for a joint, I thought. They'll scar their babies to beg.

All living things try to live. I can't remember where I heard or read that. But I think it's true. All of nature, from the smallest flower to the largest tree, its first priority is to stay alive. Only human beings destroy themselves, but even then, with most people, if the spirit dies, the body keeps making you live. The day came when I felt a surge of something like a stirring of life somewhere deep inside. It was a bright sunny day for a change and I wore my dress, I just felt like it, the dress I made at Crofton in that other lifetime.

"Hey," said Jamey when I walked into the room. "you look great." His eyes were shiny.

Right from the doorway, clear across the room, I could feel the surge in him, too. I could feel something in him springing into life, then pumping sure and steady. It was amazing, the way he looked filled out again, just like that. The caved-in look was gone, and he had some colour in his face. He told me that his foot was getting better. "It doesn't smell anymore," he said, some relieved. I think that smell bothered Jamey more than anything. It reminded him that he was tied to this earth.

"Hey, how are you?" he said, reaching for my hand. And all up through my arm, I could feel the tension in him wanting to be released. I could feel the tension in myself wanting to be released.

"You're looking good," he said, pulling me down on his lap. He started kissing me, pushing up my skirt and opening his robe.

"Be serious," I said, pushing down my skirt.

"Whaddayou mean?" he said.

"You never wanted the baby," I said. "You're glad you're free."

"Aw," he said. "Don't be mean. C'mon." And he straddled my legs across him, pushing up my skirt again. He put his robe around me.

"The other people," I said. "The glue guy."

"He's on one of his trips home," said Jamey. "There aren't any other people." He started to move and move me with him. At first I refused to be moved, but then my body took over. It moved along with him and even became excited on its own. Until we caught together and quickened and finally exhausted each other.

My body sagging against his, I felt disgusted with both of us. How could we forget so easily what we had done? How could we forget about the life we started so unthinkingly in the world and the life we took out of the world?

I've since learned to forgive myself and Jamey for that moment. I've since learned that there are stronger forces in this world keeping us alive than guilt and remorse. And it's a good thing. Otherwise, how many of us would make it? But at the time, I looked down and saw my leg across Jamey, my foot on the floor. I saw my scar as if I was seeing it for the first time. It twisted up my leg, a shiny purplish rope, puckering the soft skin of my inner thigh. I'm not going to look at that scar again, I vowed. But I didn't have to. The sight of it was in my mind forever, branding my guilt on me forever, my betrayal of my child.

I NEVER PROMISED YOU

The day came when I started seeing things again, like Zeke's apartment. The only thing in it that told you about him was the sound equipment, tapes and CDs. In the bathroom, his toilet stuff consisted of a few items lined up with obsessive precision on a shelf. The kitchen counter was bare except for a coffee maker. The contents of the fridge consisted of one carton of coffee cream, a piece of pizza neatly wrapped in plastic, and a few cans of beer. What this place needs, I decided, is a colourful bedspread and some matching curtains and some pictures on the walls. But it was when I thought I should make some banana bread with some browning bananas left on the counter that I knew I had to get the hell out of there.

I got a job at McDonald's, thinking I'd get a place of my own as soon as I got my first paycheque, but when I looked at the amount, I knew I'd have to make different arrangements. But fast. Things were no longer comfortable between Zeke and me. Or maybe it was me— ever since the day when I'd just come back from visiting Jamey, who was out of the hospital by then and finishing off his time, and I was standing by the window looking slightly up because of the window starting at ground level. I was feeling lower than a snake's shadow, as Rita used to say. All the way home on the bus I'd been thinking how things had changed, that I had changed. Always, in going along with Jamey I was going along with myself but, now, in going along with Jamey I was going against myself. It was a very uncomfortable feeling, like I was being divided in two.

Then, in the halo of the parking lot light, which was on a tall pole, through the darkening day, I saw Zeke coming toward me. Suddenly, I swear, he became Clint the Man with No Name, the way in those movies he comes out of nowhere into a town where the people are lost souls and saves the day but also shows them how to save themselves and get back their self-respect.

But the point is, when I saw Zeke, suddenly like that, walking slowly but surely toward me, a large figure with the light at his back, I could hear my heart. I could hear it loud and I could hear it quick. So, when the very next day this Jessie, who was also working at McDonald's, said why don't you get one of them jobs where you live in the person's house and help with the kids and housework and stuff and get a little remuneration on the side, I said to myself, "Yeah, why don't I?"

When Zeke's van slid to a stop in front of a huge red brick house with a lawn like a green plush carpet and trees and bushes growing all coordinated according to height and shades of green and flower beds already in bloom, I thought, *Wow*. I was also scared. Let's face it, I was out of my league. But I couldn't turn and run with Zeke there as a witness, so I took a deep breath and got out of the van. Zeke insisted on walking me to the front door. "How do I know they aren't white slavers luring beautiful young women into their lair?" he said.

I was in no mood for his jokes. I was feeling totally nervous at the thought of being interviewed by someone who lived in a house like that. I wasn't even sure I wanted the job. Everything would be so different from what I was used to. Hoity-toity, is how the folks on Terrabain Street would put it. I'd be cutting myself off. On the other hand, it looked like the perfect place to hole up, to give myself time to think about things, maybe get myself back on track.

"It's like my father taking me the first day of school," I said, scowling and listening to the chimes through the door. "What if they ask who you are?"

But a kid answered, a boy of about ten who gave me the once-over with sober watchful eyes.

I got the job and asked Zeke to phone Jamey. We were driving back to his place to get my things. "I won't be able to go and see him as much because of my hours. And it's harder to get there from here," I said. "Tell him that for me, will you?"

"Why don't you phone him yourself?" Zeke said.

"I'll have to leave the number the way we always do, and then when he phones back, it won't look right. Some guy phoning me first day on the job." I realized it was a lame excuse, but I didn't want to have to tell Jamey I wouldn't be going to see him for a while. Later, I wondered if not phoning him myself was another sort of lie, keeping from him the fact that I had changed, although I didn't know quite how, just that I wanted to draw a sharp line between what I was going to and what I was leaving behind.

I half expected Zeke to give me a lecture on responsibility and facing up to things, but all he said was "Okay." He hadn't lectured me much on anything since the accident. He didn't talk much, period, and only about general things, and never about me and Jamey. One thing, Zeke wouldn't get himself involved in messy emotional stuff. And he'd never speak against Jamey, no matter what he thought. They were friends but they were also business partners, and Zeke never got things mixed up that way. I had the feeling, though, that for every sentence he said, three were in his mind that he didn't say. Maybe he wanted me to figure things out for myself, without influencing me one way or another, although he still, annoyingly, left his guitar sitting around as a subtle hint.

He was watching the road, his head slightly forward of mine, so it was easy for me to look at him without him knowing. I wanted to get him in my mind, since I wouldn't be seeing him for a long time, maybe never. I noticed again the way the bridge of his nose was so thin. I noticed the line of his black hair curving down to his neat clipped beard. I know what his chin looks like beneath his beard, I thought, but I don't really know this person. I've been living with him for four months and I don't know him. And it came to me. If I wanted to know Zeke, I would have to touch him. I would have to trace his hair and beard line with my fingertip. I would have to touch the thin bridge of his nose. I would have to look deep into his eyes with mine without

206

turning away. I would have to hold him and let him hold me. I would have to let him penetrate my body with his. I would have to hold his body inside mine. The thought of doing so made me stop breathing. I'd never thought that way about any man except Jamey. I'd never touched a man other than Jamey. And that had been so easy, like I was born touching him, even before birth touching, like we'd been cuddled together inside the sac.

I turned my eyes away from Zeke and looked straight ahead. I felt really really disturbed, as if I'd cheated on Jamey. Well, I comforted myself, whatever I had just thought was never going to happen. I didn't want it to happen. In the first place, I wouldn't know what to do. In the second place, touching Zeke would be serious business. It would blow apart my whole life. There'd be no turning back.

At Zeke's, it didn't take me long to pack. I threw out everything, including my suitcase, an old one I'd picked up at a garage sale before leaving Crofton, which I needed then because of things I wanted to take with me, my maternity clothes, a petit-point picture I'd done when Jamey was working nights, a little figurine that Barb had given me on my birthday, a package of parsley seeds I hadn't got around to planting. By the time Zeke picked up the suitcase with the rest of our things after the accident, there wasn't anything in it I wanted, and before leaving his apartment, I garbaged the whole thing into the dumpster in the alley. Zeke asked me if I wanted to take a guitar and I said no. "What would that look like," I said, "in a house like that. They'd think some long-haired hippie hipster was moving in."

When I was stuffing the essentials into my trusty backpack, my fingers felt an inside zipper and hesitated. That pocket was where I kept Jamey's notes and songs that I'd picked up during our travels. An enormous thought occurred to me, but then my fingers passed on.

Zeke made me promise to phone him if anything went wrong. Anything. So I said I would just to get him off my back. I didn't look at him when I said it. We were standing beside the van and I was looking at that and at some bare branches of tall trees. But he was looking at me. He was holding my arms with both his hands and then he pulled me in to his chest and then he let me go and turned abruptly and got back into his van and drove away. I looked after him, but I don't think he ever knew it.

Living at the Lieskes' was a real eye-opener for me. I knew ordinary people didn't live like rock bands, but I must've thought, without really thinking about it, that all ordinary people lived the way we had on Terrabain Street. Those communal meals and the way we'd all end up in one room and the way we always looked for each other for company and for someone to talk to, the way we all got involved in each other's lives and problems.

But the Lieske family hardly ever had anything to do with each other, let alone eat a meal together. Their two boys were eight and ten and they always had supper, which they called dinner, in between homework and soccer and swimming and youth club meetings and violin and piano. The violin teacher came to the house where he was driven nuts by the horrible screechy sounds that little Benny managed to get out of that instrument. I could hear him yelling at the kid from where I was down in the kitchen. Then he'd storm down the stairs and out the front door, coattails, scarf and wild white wispy hair flying. The older boy on the piano was just as bad for discord, but a piano can't match a violin for hurting your ears. It was a funny thing, all the pushing of music in that house without music. I mean, no one ever sang or put on a CD or ever seemed to actually enjoy it.

Sometimes, Mrs. Lieske had a bite with the boys, perching stiff-legged in front of the stove with a pot held up to her mouth, scolding at them the whole time in a loud high-pitched cry. That was if she was going off to her church women's group or her creative writing. Sometimes she'd wait and have a bite with Mr. if he was going to be home, which usually he wasn't because he was in business for himself selling furniture, which kept him hopping. If he came home, it was usually about seven or eight. Then he'd eat and go back to work or out someplace.

I ate whichever way Mrs. wanted me to, sometimes with the kids, sometimes with the adults. The first day, or evening, I was eating with Mr. and Mrs. Lieske around the dinette table, which was at one end of the kitchen and looked out over the backyard, which was more plush lawn and flowers already in bloom, so different than at home where everything would be brown for another two months.

That was when I learned that the house that I thought was so great was actually crumbling around us, at least according to Mrs. Lieske.

"The man didn't come today," said Mrs., putting exactly one tablespoon of chicken rice casserole on her plate.

"What man?" said Mr., his tongue flicking out from his round face and zapping up a chunk of chicken.

"The faucet man," said Mrs. "Who else?"

"So," said Mr. "He'll come tomorrow."

"In the meantime I go crazy," she said, gazing forlornly at the walls. "Drip, drip, drip. In case you don't know, they brainwashed people that way during the Second World War."

Mr.'s caterpillar moustache crawled across his upper lip as he chewed.

"And the dishwasher," intoned Mrs. "That's crazy, hauling it over to the sink every time. It's easier to wash the dishes by hand."

"So, get it built-in ," he said, not looking up.

"There's no room and you know it," she said.

"Do you have more of this?" said Mr., picking up his plate. Mrs. Lieske got up and strutted to the stove on her little high heels.

"I was over at Sadie's today," she said. "Her new house." Strut strut strutting back to the table, she tossed him his plate. "Some nice," she said.

"Some nice price, too," he said.

"Everybody's moving out of this neighbourhood," she said from the stove, where she stood and ate the rest of the casserole out of the baking dish. "They're all getting new houses in the suburbs."

"So," he said, "this is a chance for you to express your individuality."

I think that was supposed to be a joke because she said, "Ha ha." Then she plunked the dish into the sink, spurted in a jet of detergent and twisted the drippy faucet to high.

I also learned that the house had once belonged to Mr. Lieske's parents and that his pride and joy was his rose garden, started by his father and kept going by him. He couldn't wait to give me the grand tour. After supper—or dinner—he led me out to the back porch and three steps down into a greenhouse full of the most delicate, fragile roses you ever saw in your life. He showed me the different varieties and explained what he had to do to get each one to grow. It was all so complicated, I immediately forgot. But along the solid house wall he had shelves of trophies and framed diplomas, so other people must've thought his roses were really something, too.

Mrs. Lieske wasn't impressed. "It keeps him out of mischief," was her response to my oohing and aahing when we went back into the kitchen.

I really did like that house. Not brick only on the front, we're talking two whole stories of real red brick. The trim was freshly painted white and nothing was broken or sagging that I could see. A gardener came once a week to tidy everything and cut the grass and dig neat circles around the tree trunks. Inside, the living room was heaven with its satin furniture with curled wooden legs, and these little china figurines on everything and paintings on the walls, like, real paintings, and if I ever thought Tree was a pain with her doilies and dusting under them, I had to take it back when dusting at the Lieske's, there was that much junk to lift and be careful of. But the strange thing was, no one ever went into that room, especially the kids, and everything was always covered in dust covers. I did see it in grand array a couple of times, though, once when Mrs. Lieske hosted her book club and once when it was her turn to have the environmentalists.

It blew my mind, how one family had that huge house all to themselves and then used only about half of it. Mrs. and the boys lived mostly in what they called the TV room, which was really an extension of the kitchen. That was where the boys watched TV while they ate before going off to whatever was on the agenda for the evening. A big part of my job was driving them wherever they had to go or babysitting when they were home. I'd play games with them or we'd watch TV or a video on the weekends. I didn't mind it, they were kind of cute. They spent a lot of time in their rooms with computer games, and from my room or the kitchen I could hear beep beeps like far-off messages from another planet.

The second night, Mrs. Lieske was going out to her Women's Action for the Environment meeting. "I'm not looking forward to it," she said, leaning against a kitchen cupboard with her bowl of dinner.

"I can hear it now, Sadie talking nonstop about her new house." The two of us were eating early with the boys, although we still weren't eating together what with Mrs. Lieske in the kitchen, me at the dinette table, and the boys watching TV. But we were all putting food into our mouths at the same time in the same general area of the house.

The third evening, I ate in the TV room with the boys. By now I was making their meals and I opted to eat one of my juicy hamburgers. I have to say I could make a mean burger. Later I was washing dishes, by hand in the sink because that's what happens when you become an instrument for somebody else to make a statement, when I heard more of the house debate. Mr. was eating some sort of noodle dish he was particularly fond of and Mrs. sat at the table and watched him.

"Have you heard?" she said in her loud piercing voice.

"What?" Mr. hiccuped up from his throat.

"Who's moving in next door?" Silence and me trying not to clink the dishes in the sink. "The mentally retarded that's who," she said.

"I've heard they make nice quiet neighbours," he said.

"It's not that I have anything against the mentally retarded," she said. "It's what they do to house prices."

"It doesn't matter," said Mr. Lieske. "If we don't want to sell."

"You wait too long and you won't get anything," she said. "We'll be designated an inner city slum."

"Here, I don't have to waste an hour getting to my office," he said.

"Sure," she said. "Think only of yourself." You don't have to be stuck in this house all day."

"So when are you stuck in the house?" he said, and I ran up a point for him.

"The boys," she said. "They have a right to a good neighbourhood."

The boys were more attached to the mother than to the father, probably because they hardly ever saw him since he was never home. Even when he was at home, he wasn't really, because he was in his greenhouse transplanting, fertilizing, spraying, potting, pruning, staking, and God knows what all. He was a strange person in a way. You never felt he was really involving himself in anything except his roses. Like, when he said good morning, he was really cheerful but it was like an act. Where, with somebody who's a grump in the morning, at least you feel you're getting the real person.

I couldn't help but wonder what Mrs. ever saw in him. For looks he was as opposite Clint the Man as you'd ever want to see. Short and pear-shaped and on his head a rusty rim of thin hairs. His face always had a surprised look, but maybe that was because of his thick glasses, which made his eyes look bulgy. As for Mrs., she wasn't bad looking for her age. But her face looked brittle and so did her hair, which was a brassy colour. She got it done every week on Friday and then wrapped it in toilet paper for a couple of nights to get it through the weekend.

One time when I was vacuuming between their twin beds, I spotted an empty condom box in the wastebasket. Special cream lubricant, the box said. My mind boggled. I couldn't even picture it. Not because they were old, a lot of musicians on the circuit were even older and they bed-hopped all the time. But with her paper-wrapped head and his pear shape, the Lieskes just weren't suited for that activity, even apart from the fact that most of the time they acted like they didn't even like each other.

Another time, in the living room, I noticed this picture. I'd been dusting it for a couple of weeks without taking much notice because the people were strangers, but then one day I saw it was the Lieskes' wedding picture and you could've knocked me over with a feather, I was that surprised. I didn't recognize them at all at first. The bride was delicate and beautiful like one of those fragile china figurines, and the guy was a handsome prince, slim and trim, with hair, looking as if he owned the world, proud as punch and pleased with himself for winning the prize, her all starry-eyed like he was her sky with all the planets and moons revolving.

What happened? I thought. What terrible thing happened? I stood there a long time with that picture in my hands.

Over the next month, as the house debate got more and more tense, one thing was for sure. Whatever their past, at the moment neither Mr. nor Mrs. trusted the other any farther than he/she could throw her/him. At first I was definitely on his side, because she peck pecked all the time and he said nothing or not much, but then I could see that no matter how hard she tried, she couldn't get through. He was always friendly and joking about it all, he was always ready with the smart crack, but there was no way he was ever going to talk to her seriously. And I could see how she became more and more frustrated. And I could see how living with someone who never listened to you could be a killer, too.

The night Mr. Lieske came home drunk, I was in the kitchen making myself some hot lemonade because I had this terrible cold complete with stuffed nose and running eyes. I was just pouring the boiling water from the kettle into the mug when I heard the back door open and close and I turned and there he was, weaving lightly like a punch-drunk boxer, his tie loose, his hat crooked on his head. I was surprised because I didn't think of him as the drinking type. I said "Hi" and he trickled his fingers in my direction. Then he tried to stand straighter. He looked at me in a puzzled way, blinking his wide eyes.

"I'm Lilah," I said. "Your au pair girl." Which was what Mrs. liked to call me. "Would you like a cup of coffee?" I asked.

"That'd be nishe," he said, sliding down onto a chair.

I was actually quite worried about one of his eyes, which kept rolling to one side away from where he seemed to be looking. I got up the instant coffee, which didn't take long since the water was already boiling. I set it black before him and he grabbed my hand and I thought, "Oh Christ," because I didn't want to have to leave that night what with my cold and all.

"You're a nice girl," he said and patted my hand. "A nishe girl."

"Drink your coffee," I said and took back my hand. He did what he was told and winced.

"Do you want some cold water in it?" I said.

He pointed his finger at me. "I want you to tell me something," he said. His finger went limp and fell to the table. "Tell me, what's wrong with this house?" His eyes floated to the door and to the side of it in the direction of his greenhouse.

My nose was running, over which I had no control, and my box of Kleenex was up in my room and I was getting a splitting headache. I turned to go, but then he started talking, to himself mostly, staring at the table.

"She ushta dance for me," he said. "She was a dancer. She was going to be a ballet dancer. That's what she wanted to be. But, instead, she married me. I'd come home from work and she'd run to meet me at the door and we'd stand there for five minutes saying hello. She'd sit me down in a chair, that one there," he nodded to something in the TV room. "We didn't live here then but we had that chair. We've always had that chair. It was our first piece of furniture. We bought it together, with some money we got for a wedding present. We had a nice little apartment and we had that chair and that's about all we had and we were in love and happy. It was our best chair, our only chair, and she reserved it for me when I came home at night." That was more or less the gist of it, with lots of slurring and pausing and sips of coffee. I thought he was finished, but then he said some more, "And then she'd dance for me, like Salome with the seven veils."

Who's Salome? I thought. "Why did she stop dancing?" I said.

"Tha's th' way it goes," he said. "Th' way . . . it . . . goes."

"Did you ever tell her that you loved her dancing?" I asked.

But by then he was completely out of it. He looked at me like he'd been whacked between the eyes with a blunt instrument, so I went upstairs to bed leaving him sitting at the table with his elbows folded on it staring into the dark depths of his bitter coffee.

I was putting Vicks all under my eyes and around my nose thinking about love and the Lieskes and wondering about life and getting depressed. I wound a warm towel around my head and was about to put the whole mess down on a hot water bottle when I heard glass breaking. Not a cup or a dish, but one great big crash of glass and it came up to me from outside, through the open back window. My God, I thought, he's gone and fallen into the greenhouse.

I jumped up and ran downstairs and out past the kitchen table where just a few minutes ago I had left him. Sure enough, there he was, sitting in the middle of the remains except right away I could see it was no accident. All the roses had been torn out of their pots and a lot of the pots had been thrown through the glass out onto the back lawn.

"Come on," I said, stretching out my hand. He took it and pulled himself up with me helping. He followed me into the house.

Next morning at breakfast, Mrs. Lieske said how vandals had broken into the greenhouse last night. "We've got to get out of this neighbourhood," she said. "This is no place to raise children."

I never did find out what happened in the great house debate, because right after that night Jamey phoned me and said, "Hey, I'm a free man."

I thought about it. Here, I was in a nice house with my own room, cozy and quiet in the evening. Here, I was off the street. Here, I'd made a start in cutting the bonds with my past life. I was thinking of taking an evening course. If I went back to that life, it would be admitting defeat, like an alcoholic who gives in to that one drink that starts him all over again down the dark spiral.

"Hey, are you there?" Jamey's voice called to me across the line, but I was still thinking.

Here, I never sang, not even in the kitchen or doing housework.

Here, I wasn't miserable but I wasn't happy either. Here, I was lonely. Here, where there was no Jamey, there was no love. This was not my place, my home, my people. My life with Jamey was my life, what I was born into, for better or for worse.

"Hey, Lilah, you asleep?"

Don't do it, Lilah, I said to myself. You're gonna hate yourself in the morning.

"Where are you?" I said to Jamey, and all the way up the stairs to pack my things my heart was full of joy making a beeline for him, hardly able to wait to hold him in my arms.

Zeke was right. People don't change. I would always be Lilah Cellini. Whatever path my legs took in my life, my heart would always be at the home place with Jamey. At the top stair, as if to give me fair warning of what I was doing, my scar decided to act up, the way it did sometimes, its length of shiny rope prickling up and down my inner thigh.

HITCH-HIKER

"Is there anyplace to sit down? I need a place to sit down. I can't do that highway tonight. Tomorrow I'll do it, but not tonight. Is there a church? I can sit on the church steps."

On our way back from a gig at Kamloops, we picked up this old woman on the Coquihalla. What she was doing on that godforsaken road I don't know, unless another driver had dumped her before turning off at Merrit. One thing for certain, she wouldn't have survived long out there on a night like that. Even so, when we stopped, she looked at us as if wishing we hadn't. Her eyes travelled backwards along the side of the van, past the flames licking up orange and red and yellow around this bare-chested, leather-legged rocker holding his guitar like a machine gun. That paint job was the reason Jamey had gotten the van so cheap—from a kid whose father was going to throw him out of the house if he didn't give up music and go to university. She looked still farther back, across her shoulder to the cold windy sleety day coming on night, and she must have made a decision.

Climbing into the back, she muttered, "Tomorrow I'm gonna get myself a sleeping bag, then I won't have to ever bother anybody ever again."

Right when Jamey was gearing up, a police car passed, spraying up slush. The way that old woman scrunched down in the seat made me wonder if she wasn't the only one who should be leery what sort she was taking up with.

"You in the electricity business?" she said, sitting up straighter and watching like a hawk that police car disappear into the wall of sleet ahead of us.

"No," I said, looking back. "That's music equipment." Since Jamey hadn't been able to track down Geoff or Clinton and Joe was on the road with another band, he'd been working with pickup bands, various dudes he knew around Vancouver, using whatever sound system was available at the venue. Since the rest of them would be returning to Vancouver tomorrow by car, Jamey was transporting the gear.

"What?" Her voice came from her throat like the growl of an old alley cat.

"Amplifiers," I said. "Amplifiers and instruments. To make music."

"Pianos," she said. "I remember a piano."

"Guitars," I said. "And a bass and drums. Last night we did a gig, show, in Kamloops."

"I left Kamloops this morning," she said, "looking for work. I went into a couple of places but they wouldn't let me stay the night."

Then she stopped talking and when I looked back she was asleep, curled up in a corner of the back seat, her mouth lolling open, her hands like injured paws curved into her front. Her clothes, slacks and sweater, were filthy and smelled of damp and mould and dirt. Her face looked like one of those pictures in a biology book of a living organism under a microscope, cells all in little sections like a beehive. She had no teeth and there were sores all around her mouth.

Why does she remind me of the Corset Lady? I wondered. Two more different old ladies you could never hope to imagine. The Corset Lady would have made two of this one and she wouldn't be caught dead in slacks or on the highway with her thumb out.

"An old woman without a place is a terrible thing," I said, turning back around in my seat and looking at the windshield wipers working like crazy to clear a path. "Somehow it's worse than an old man."

"Something about the house," I said to Jamey who was sulking so bad only the night and the darkness coming down answered. "Somehow an old woman should have a house.

"Or a place." I could feel the creases in my forehead deepen. My scowl. My Italian scowl. Don't scowl, Tree used to say, your face is gonna freeze like that. "At least a place," I said.

Tree's face wouldn't stay out of my head. Her voice was in my ear. ". . . you think too much. That's your trouble. You're gonna ruin your looks." Then the Corset Lady muscled in, her big rear end, her voice, "Lilah's okay. You may not think it to look at her, but Lilah's got a real brain in her head."

"A man comes and goes," I said to the windshield wipers repeating pah dah pah dah to the sleet coming straight for them. "A woman hunkers down.

"To be thrown out into the world without a place. That's death for an old woman.

"I remember the Corset Lady's place. So cozy, her tea kettle steaming up the room on a winter night." I couldn't help but sigh a little. "Sometimes I wish she didn't have to die. I really miss her sometimes.

"Her job, though. It was crazy when you stop and think about it. Sewing those corsets. Keeping everything together, as Paquette liked to say, making a joke of it. But that job made her what she was. Somehow." Again, I felt my creases deepen. I stretched up my forehead, trying to smooth things out. "Do you ever think about things like that?" I said.

It was getting harder and harder to talk to Jamey. Ever since the accident it seemed more and more like we were going in opposite directions, the gap between us getting wider. I figured that was what happened when people weren't saying what they had in them to say, like I really needed to talk about the baby and that was a subject he refused to discuss. I even wrote him a note about it, I was that desperate. I wrote it all down, I poured out my guts, my whole heart and soul, telling him how I felt about things, the baby and all. I handed it right to him, making sure he got it. He tossed it onto the kitchen counter where it lay collecting grease and water spots. I think he meant to read it later and just forgot. He didn't not read the note on purpose. He just had other things on his mind. Maybe he was listening to some music or somebody dropped in or he had to go out right away.

"You don't see many old women on the highway," I said, "I wonder how she got here.

"Why don't you talk to me?" I said.

Just then the top-heavy van winged it this way and that across the road, like it couldn't make contact, like it couldn't set down, so it didn't matter which way Jamey steered or if he braked or clutched or any other damn thing because it had no affect on what was happening between tires and pavement. For a second I thought, this is really it this time. If we fly off the edge of this road, it'll be into a canyon so deep we'll never climb out. But I guess our time wasn't up yet, because those tires settled back down and, once again, we were in business.

"Jeez, Jamey, slow down." My voice, like the rest of me, was all weak and trembly.

"Light me a smoke, willya?" he said.

I reached down for his cigarettes and lighter, to where they'd fallen on the floor, off the dash. "We don't need to drive this fast," I said.

"I like driving fast," he said. "Don't worry. I'm in control."

Yeah, I wanted to say. Just like seven months ago. But I didn't. Somehow, I knew that if I ever said that it would be like crossing a border over which there'd be no returning. Instead, I thought, how can he not have learned something from all that? How can he not have changed? How can I have changed so much and him not at all? But he had changed. That was the thing. Zeke was wrong. Jamey wasn't the sweet boy I used to know. He was irritable a lot of the time, maybe because he was working so hard, maybe because he always had a toke in his hand or some white powder on his hip. Whether it was jail or the accident or his foot, that childlike hope, that boyish bravado had turned hard, with a cynical edge. Maybe it was, like Zeke said, fear of the cage coming down, or threatening to. But maybe that had always been in him, the way he'd fight if he had to. The way he could shrug off things and leave them behind. Like once, years before, after he'd traded in that first love of his boyhood, his Sunbeam, for a jazzed-up '74 Thunderbird, we came across it at a stoplight, pulled up right alongside it. Jamey reconized it right away, even though the paint was all scarred and chipped and it had about five layers of dried mud around the bottom and the engine sounded like an out-of-synch tractor. As it put-putted through the green light, Jamey stayed just behind it in the next lane. His face was twisted in pain. But, then, he shrugged his shoulders, turned his face forward, and stepped on the gas. He had that toughness even then and a good thing, too.

I put a cigarette in my mouth and lit it, being careful not to take a deep drag because ever since smoking so much when I was sick smoke made me sick. "I suppose it was a man," I said, getting back to the old woman. "A woman in misery, there's sure to be a man."

"It's their own fault," said Jamey, taking the cigarette from my fingers. "Women make themselves miserable."

"What do you mean by that?" I said, even though I knew.

"If I could just get a place to stay the night," the voice came out of the back seat. Over and over, fitfully as a child in fever. "I can't go on that highway tonight. Tomorrow I'll do it, but not tonight."

I turned to look at the old woman but she was still asleep. "It's hard to believe," I said, turning again to the sleet and the winding road. "Once she was as young as me. I wonder how old she was when she left home or maybe she never had one." Maybe she took up with a guitar player, I thought but didn't say.

"She got old," Jamey said, flipping the wheel this way and that. "That's one thing you can't do in this life." He danced those wheels across the icy water. "You get old, you've had it."

"You can't stay young forever," I said.

"Maybe not. But you gotta try. In this business, anyway."

I knew last night was on his mind. It had not been a great gig. Ill-conceived, Zeke would have said. Zeke had disappeared a month before, right after Jamey got out of jail. This time he didn't even say goodbye. He was just gone. Still, his words kept popping into my mind, opening a place there like dark fingers in my softest parts. I quickly shut out the thought. "Kamloops don't, doesn't, strike me as a great rocking town anyway," I said.

"Still," said Jamey. "We shoulda had a better audience than that."

"It wasn't your fault," I said. "The kids at the college with exams. The hockey game. It was just one of those situations where things work against you."

I opened my mouth to say more, like, it wasn't our fault if we didn't have all the information and what can you do if you don't have all the information, etc., but then I closed it. For one thing, it was yesterday's news, and for another, the gig wasn't why Jamey was in a bad mood. He'd had enough ill-conceived gigs to give him experience in handling it. No, he was in a bad mood because of me, because when we got out of the motel bed about noon and he pushed aside the curtain and looked out at the threatening sky and said, "You can just go AWOL."

"I don't want to do that," I said. "It's a big sale tomorrow. They need me."

"They'd let you go like that," he snapped his fingers, "if it suited them."

"They made me supervisor of the lunch counter," I said. "They're counting on me."

"They make everybody a supervisor," he said. "They have more supervisors than customers."

"Would you not show up for a gig?" I said.

"That's different," he said. "What's a job at Woolco?"

"I don't know," I said.

"Why would you wanta do that when you can sing?" he'd said to me a few weeks before, when I'd got the job.

"It's steady," I'd said, having at least the decency to squirm at the memory of me sneering at Tree saying that about Gord and his warehouse job. It was true, I needed stability, but maybe I was also hedging my bets. With the singing, I depended on Jamey—I still wasn't into doing solos. But, maybe because of the forced separation of the accident, something had grown in me and I didn't want to depend on Jamey for everything.

"I don't trust life any more," I said to him. "How it can pull the rug out from under you. I want to have some backup."

"Suit yourself," Jamey said. He even wrote a song about it. . . . *Lilah has taken to slinging hash/now ain't that kind of rash/but she don't go for them one night stands/ tagging along behind the band/she says she's gonna take the cure/but what'll I do without her* . . . He was right about the one-night stands. I always liked it better if we were booked for a few nights or booked at the same place the same night every week. But our situation then didn't allow for a lot of that happening.

"I shouldn't've come," I said to the sleet hitting the windshield at a slant.

"Whaddaya mean?"

"Then you could've waited until tomorrow with the rest of the group when the weather's supposed to clear. I'm the only one who has to be at work tomorrow. I should'nt've come."

"You had to come. You're part of the band."

"You could've done the gig without me."

"The audience loves us together. We're a big hit."

It was true. Our harmonizing duets went over big with audiences. And we *were* good together. Even now, when I can bear to listen to that old cellar session CD and some tapes I have of later gigs, I can hear how good we were. Jamey and I always did do well together what came naturally. We were great at lovin' and hurtin', the guts of any song, about which Jamey taught me everything I know.

In a way, Jamey had a day job too, but his hours were flexible. Working the street, making the rounds, checking out leads for gigs, checking out musicians—who was playing where with who, who was at loose ends, who needed a job, who had a job, which groups were starting up, which ones winding down. "I wouldn't've believed how quick you can lose your contacts," he said. He had places to go, people to meet. He was like a revivalist setting up a prayer meeting in the big tent. Gun Wylde is back! Shout it from the rooftops.

If I wanted to find him, all I had to do was drop into the bars or coffee places along his route. The waiters could tell me if he'd been there yet or not. They all knew him, unless a new guy was on. Once, I described him to a new waiter who said, "You mean the guy with the limp?"

I had to think a minute before saying, "Yes." Most of the time I didn't see Jamey's limp. But one day when I was waiting for him on a street corner, through the rain and the wind and my hair in my face, I spotted a different movement, something working against the rhythm and flow of the other people on the sidewalk. A shoulder pushed forward with a jerky beat, the hip of a pair of jeans sliding into a shuddering braking, a foot in a sneaker set down more lightly than its mate. My eyes became glued to that foot.

It's not my fault, I thought. I took care of him the best I could. I made sure he got lots of sleep. I fed him steak and chicken. So how come he got a bunged-up foot? And why now? He could've bunged up his foot anytime during the last twenty-three years. Why now, when it was my fault?

The van slowed as we entered Hope and it felt good to be off that highway and into a place with buildings and lights. We pulled up in front of the Sally Ann. "We're here," Jamey called into the back seat.

"Where?" said the old lady, looking out the window.

"The Sally Ann," said Jamey. "They'll put you up for the night."

"I don't like it in there," she said.

"Well, where d'y'wanta go?" said Jamey. She didn't answer and she didn't budge.

"I'll be back in a minute," Jamey said. He got out of the van and went into the building. About five minutes later, he came back with a woman who was fat and comfortable like somebody's mother. The both of them huddled into their collars as they came up to my side of the van. I slid open the door and they looked in.

The fat woman stepped back and spoke in a low voice.

"Usually," she said, "we put them up, but right now we're closed for renovations. We're using the police station." She stepped forward and spoke louder. "We have a nice warm place for you."

The old lady said nothing.

"We have to use the police station right now," the fat woman called.

"I don't want to go there." The old lady scrunched down further into her corner.

"They'll put you up for the night," the fat lady hollered against the wind and the rain. "It'll be warm there, and comfortable."

"No," said the old lady. "I won't go there. They have no respect for anybody there."

The fat lady straightened up and said in a low voice. "Obviously in some sort of trouble." Then she bent back into the van and yelled, "Come on in and we'll think of something."

"No, I can't. I'm too weak," said the old lady.

The fat woman straightened again. "My husband usually makes these decisions. But right now he's just driven somebody into Vancouver."

Again, she leaned forward. "Come into the office," she said. "We'll talk about it."

"Can I have a drink of water?" said the old lady. "Maybe then I'll be able to walk."

As soon as the fat lady disappeared into the building, the old lady hobbled out from the van and back up the street, drawing the big collar of her sweater up over her head and hunching down into it.

"Can't you stop her?" I said to Jamey.

"What am I supposed to do?" Jamey said. "Wrestle her down? She's doing what she wants to do."

"She'll die out there."

"No she won't. She knows what to do, she's been doing it for years." We both watched her for a moment. "If she does," Jamey added, "she'll be going the way she wants to go."

So there we stood, helpless, looking after, us and the fat woman, glass of water in her hand.

"Do you get a lot of old ladies?" I asked.

"Not as many as old men," she said. "But we get the odd one now and then."

The fat lady went back into her building. Jamey and me climbed back into the van and drove to the corner and turned left. Out my side window, I could see the old lady at the edge of the road, thumb up, going back the way we had come. She's gonna die out there, I thought again. Maybe not today but some day. A person can't live out there in that wind and sleet and cold, just skin and bones against that.

As we hit the junction of lights and turned onto the freeway leading into Vancouver, I was thinking how I had to admire that old lady. At least she didn't have a price. At least she didn't sell herself too cheap.

Still, I didn't want to end up like her. Out in the cold, starving and homeless. On the other hand, I didn't want to end up like the Lieskes, never singing, not remembering what it was like to be young and in love. So are those the options? I asked myself but didn't get it answered partly because Jamey put his hand on my inner thigh and drew me close to him on the seat. I wanted to ask him what he was thinking. Maybe he, too, was considering options. But I kept my mouth shut because I didn't want to spoil the moment.

BIRD ON A WIRE

Jamey's silhouette was outlined against the light of the window, against the full moon, along with a mess of inner-city telephone cables.

"Sometimes I think I should go home," I said.

"Home?" He lifted his head as though listening for a prowler.

"I've been thinking of Tree a lot lately," I said.

"I thought you hated her," he said, turning and rustling around on the TV stand for chips or peanuts.

"I do," I said. "But lately I've been wondering if it's her fault. That she's a lousy mother. Maybe she didn't know any better."

"Ummm," he said.

The time wasn't right for a serious discussion. Jamey was hungry, cruising the dark like a panther for food. I was lazy and mellow from lovemaking and part of me didn't want to spoil it.

Wait until morning, I told myself. Wait until the light of day. You'll be able to see more clearly, then. You'll be able to think. But I knew if I didn't speak up I'd feel sick. I was already feeling a little sick, tight in the chest and stomach. Travelling its silent train of thought, my brain, like the little engine that could, had built up a whole lot of pressure that had to be released.

"Sometimes I think I should go now," I said. "With you and the band starting out new again, maybe it's a good time to take a break. From the singing life."

"Why would you wanta do that?" Jamey's voice was distracted, then it picked up. "Ah," he said, "here's something." I could hear cellophane crackle in the dark and then potato chips being crunched. I could hear chewing and swallowing. I could feel his weight being deposited beside me on the bed.

"Maybe at home I can get on at Woolco. Maybe they'll give me a transfer."

Jamey balled the cellophane and tossed it back on the table.

"Rita and Popi. Don't you ever wanna see them?"

"I'll send for them," said Jamey. "I'm gonna buy them a big house. Out here where it's warm. Where Pop can go for walks even in the winter. Where you have the ocean and the beaches and you don't feel hemmed in." He fixed a pillow behind his shoulders. "This time," he said, "we're gonna make it big. I have a feeling in my bones. Gun Wylde is gonna really roll this time."

His voice turned fast and excited when he got on his subject. All hyped up like he'd been all day, ever since the morning when the knock came on the door and the old man in slippers called him to the phone.

Maybe it was one too many less-than-ritzy rooms. Maybe it was the constant smell of egg rolls and chicken fried steak that wafted up to the open window of our room from the street below. One thing, ever since the first months of being pregnant, the thought of grease made me shudder. Whatever it was, standing at the window waiting for him to come back from the phone, looking down on the street, at the Sunrise Café, I thought to myself, I can't do it anymore.

The sound of his feet on the stairs, in the hall, the upbeat piercing ping, the downbeat thump, the way he burst in through the door, I knew the phone call was good news. As he picked me up and danced me around the room, he was fairly bursting his jeans. But I was braced. Even when he tumbled me onto the bed, rolling on top of me, I was ready. It was when he touched me in a couple of places and said in his honey voice, "Hey, c'mon," that I thought oh well, what the hell.

Then he went out and left me alone with my thoughts and I thought, no. No. Don't let him mix up your brain so you can't think. Don't let him tell you there's nothing wrong. Something not good is happening here. Don't you believe his "water under the bridge" his "you cry over spilled milk, you'll always be crying."

But what do you do when you know something with your heart and your gut and someone you trust keeps telling you you're crazy? Keeps telling you you're imagining things? What do you do when that someone is part of you? I've got to get away from him so I can figure this out, I said to myself. I want my mother. Even if I hate her. Quick as a wink, before I could change my mind, I picked up my backpack from a chair, flung it on the bed and started throwing things in.

When Jamey returned he was totally flying. "This time," he said, "we got our shit together. I just saw Clinton. We got it all planned. Geoff's back on drums. We'll have to get a new sound man."

"Where's Zeke?" I stepped in front of the backpack, but it didn't matter. Jamey was moving too fast between window, chair and bed to notice.

"Rumour has it he's making waves in the big time. And we'll have to get another guitar," Jamey was thinking out loud. "Joe's still on tour. Too bad about Hector. He was a great guitar player. Just goes to show you, family life and rock groups don't combine."

"I heard Superman's getting married," I said. "I read it in the paper."

"He'll be sorry," said Jamey.

I picked up the pack and casually set it on the floor. "Are you making any rules about drugs?"

"You can't," Jamey said, still bouncing around the room. "You wouldn't get anybody."

"But you have to have some kind of discipline too, in a band." I was aware that I was sounding like Zeke. Still I went on. "Otherwise, things fall apart."

"Wild flights, responding to each other," said Jamey. "Those are the most memorable performances."

"How about bad food and exhaustion," I said. "How about people gobbling you up? How about always being in transit and no place to call home?"

"You have to accept those things," he said. "You have no business being in the business if you can't accept those things."

"Maybe I won't go," I said. The minute the words were out, I felt gloom descend.

But he didn't hear me. He was too hyped up.

He's right, I thought. You don't have to put yourself through this. You can go along with him. You can be there for him. You can starch and iron his shirts and believe he's going somewhere, like Rita does with Popi. You can do that. So what's the problem? No problem, I said to myself, unless you make it one. Jamey's right, it's all in your head. I sat down on his lap and I put my arms around him and held him close and rocked him a little back and forth.

It's going to work out, I said to myself with relief while nuzzling my face into his warm neck. We can work it out together. Love can work anything out. You don't have to leave him. You don't have to be lonely for the rest of your life. All the same, I felt uneasy.

That night in bed, I still felt uneasy. Fitted into Jamey's chest, one arm around him, my fingers running up and down his back ribs, it came up on me again, like a bitter taste at the back of my throat. "Do you feel there's something wrong?" I said.

"Wrong?" he said.

"Ever since the accident," I said. "I feel there's . . . something. Do you?"

"No," he said. "It'll take Gun Wylde some time to get things going again. That's to be expected."

So, I said to myself. Whaddayagonnado? For the rest of his life rub his nose in it? Rub his nose in what? I asked myself. And the thought came like a bullet. That he killed our kid. The thought came and I couldn't help it, I swear.

This is too big for me, I thought. Here I am, lying in bed loving up the man who killed my child. I can't handle this. Think it through, I thought. Be rational. The fact is, Jamey did something stupid. That's all it was. He didn't mean to do it. We all do stupid things. Okay, I can live with that, I said to myself. What's the big problem?

The big problem was, he didn't think it was a problem.

"Doesn't it bother you," I said. "I mean, what happened. The accident? Don't you ever think about it?"

"It set me back eight months," said Jamey. "Me and the band."

"I mean, the baby," I said. "Don't you ever think about it?"

"You know something?" said Jamey. "Sometimes you depress me."

"I'm sorry," I said.

"You're never happy."

"Maybe there's more to life than being happy."

"What more could there be?"

"Maybe, somehow, figuring out why we're here."

"We're here to have a good time," said Jamey. "To do that you gotta be free."

"*You say you wanta be free, but maybe you'll find freedom ain't all it's cracked up to be.* You wrote it," I said. "*You sang it.*"

"Hey, don't use my words against me," he said. "Words are only words. Maybe they mean something at the moment, but they're not written in stone. I don't hafta mean them forever. The song changes."

"The meaning's important to me," I said.

"You start worrying about meaning, you get caught in a trap so complicated you can never figure your way out," said Jamey. "Sometimes you get a good gig, sometimes a bad, that's all."

"You didn't always think this way," I said.

"I did ever since I decided to survive," he said.

I thought about it. Maybe he was right. Survival depends on attitude and you have to be able to forget. But, "I don't know," I finally said. "Things must happen for a reason." Why? I asked myself. Because I can't stand it if they don't, I answered myself. "I can't stand all the loss and suffering being meaningless," I said out loud. "Don't you feel that way too?"

But he was breathing deep and regular. Then he gave a little grunt and a snort, and his breath caught a moment, the way it does sometimes with small children and then the grown-ups say, *there's an angel passing.*

No, I thought. You don't feel that way. Because you never felt connected to the baby. While, for me, that was the high point of our lives, the best thing we ever did, something we put together into the cold lonely world. And you erased it, just like that. And you never looked back and thought about what you'd done.

Be reasonable, I said to myself. What's the guy supposed to do? Haul around a truckload of guilt forever? No, I didn't want him to do that either. We could work it out together, things like loss and sadness. But we couldn't work out what he didn't feel. That left me working it out alone. And I could see, lying there talking to the darkness, how that was going to be one tough job.

In the morning, things looked a little brighter. We had it planned. After breakfast, we'd walk the half block down the street to where the van was parked. We'd get in and pick up Clinton and head for Bellingham where the call had come from, Geoff saying it was all set up, the great US tour. Another town, another train, waiting in the midnight rain. Waiting for our order at the Sunrise Café, I was leaning my arms on the table, still trying to make up my mind but feeling it was more clear than the night before.

"Aren't you ever gonna go home?" I said.

"What for?"

"Your roots."

"Roots make you grow old. Man, don't gimme none a them roots." And he started jerking his shoulders up and down and drumming his fingers on the table.

That's not the only thing makes you grow old, I thought, looking closely at Jamey's face, noticing the dark circles underneath his eyes and a burned-out look from too much excess of various types, his boyish innocence now mixed with grown-up decadence. You can talk about freedom all you want, I thought. But you've fought all your life against turning into Popi and you did anyway. "Maybe you're right," I said, taking a drink of my coffee. "Long creepy fingers reaching up out of the ground, catching you, pulling you down."

Jamey looked over his shoulder, uneasily. "Where's that waitress?" he said. "Out gathering the eggs?"

"Snare you into the whole cycle," I said. "The life and death thing. Still, I guess a person has to face it sooner or later."

"Why?" said Jamey, turning back and looking me straight in the eye.

"So you know who you are, of course," I said.

"I know who I am," said Jamey.

"Who?"

"Gun Wylde." Just saying the name filled him with a force, a vigour, that I could feel clean across the table.

"Maybe Gun Wylde is just a passing fancy," I said.

"Whoever, then. Whoever I am when I'm out on that stage. That's when I'm alive. The rest is just waiting. You're only alive when you're reacting to the situation, that hits you pouf! maybe below the belt. That's when you know who you are," he said.

I'm sorry, I'm sorry, I'm sorry. That was what I thought just before the shark fins of that fifties tank struck, lifting me into the air in slow motion and bringing me back down in fast. My reaction to everything was to apologize. But to who? The baby? Jamey? My mother? How about my father? I'm sorry for not being a good girl, for not being a perfect baby, for crying, for pooping my diaper. Please don't leave me, I'm sorry. Why was I apologizing to that asshole, alcoholic, no-good, scum, bottom-of-the barrel bastard? "You're the one who should've been apologizing," I said out loud. "Why was I apologizing?"

"When?" said Jamey.

"The accident," I said.

"Oh, that." The edges of his hands, his thin brown hands, the fingers so shapely, karate-chopped the edge of the table. "Why were you? Apologizing." he said.

I stared at those blades, trying to think. "I don't know," I said. "Maybe I was apologizing for living."

At that moment, the waitress came with Jamey's bacon and eggs and I knew that for the next few minutes I'd be talking to myself. Watching Jamey's toast peck, peck, pecking into the yellow mess on his plate, I thought how I always did love to watch him eat. He did it with such pleasure, such lack of finesse. He was hungry, he put food into his mouth as fast as he could get it there and swallowed it and when he was full he stopped and stretched up his arms and often as not gave one loud loose burp. Anybody else, that might've been crude. But somehow Jamey was beautiful in his crudeness.

He looked at me and gave me an air kiss across the space and smiled his old smile and I thought of his lips on me, kissing all my soft inner parts. We're Siamese twins joined at the heart, I told myself. I can carry my pain by myself if I have to.

Across the table, Jamey's air kiss was forming into words. His forehead puckered. "Why should I apologize?" He seemed genuinely puzzled. "That guy in the Pontiac was doing sixty at least."

My eyelids went down and up across Jamey's face. My head turned to the window.

"Do you remember that guitar player?" Jamey said to my left ear. "Dave Something. Ragoo, I think. That's what it sounds like anyway. I was trying to get him once before. He's really good. We worked real well together before. He's supposed to meet us. Geoff left a message with his sister in Burnaby." He went on some more like that while I looked at the window, not seeing it but then seeing it. And what I saw was that it was covered with a thick smear of grease and, lighted from inside, it became a mirror. In the mirror I saw two people. Me and Jamey. He was on one side of the booth. I was on the other. With the table between. You feel together, you feel as one, I thought. And then you find out you're miles apart, travelling two different roads, going in opposite directions. And you wonder if you were ever as one, or was it just in your mind. We are not the same person, I told myself firmly. I am not part of him. He is there. I am here. I am by myself, on my own, way over here.

And then I felt a terrible pain, like flesh being separated from bone. My flesh being wrenched from my bone, and it seemed to me the bone left was teeny teeny and weak, more like gristle.

"The main thing," Jamey was saying. "To get rolling. This guy in Portland wants us real bad. At his club. He has a partner. He's gotta talk to his partner. But it's almost better not to be strictly logged in. Then we can pick up gigs along the way. Added on to the bookings, wow! It'll be great. We're not too tied down, so if something really good comes along we can take it. Or if someone wants us a couple extra nights . . ."

Jamey was looking at me like I should be saying something but I couldn't speak. I knew my voice would come out funny, harsh and broken and funny.

Danger, danger, I said to myself, outside, standing underneath a lamppost. Full moon last night and what you do this moment will haunt you forever.

232

I caught Jamey's arm. "Jamey," I said. "Wait," I said. "I don't think I'll go after all."

"What do you mean?"

"I don't know," I said. "Just that, I don't think I can do it."

"We need you in the band," he said.

"You'll get someone else."

"You can't do this to me."

"It's not that big a deal," I said. "There's a million singers out there."

"Not like you."

"You'll find another singer."

"Maybe. Okay, don't sing. Take a break from that. Just come along for me."

"I can join you later. I just don't want to hit the road right now."

"You're going to miss a lot of fun," he said.

"I know," I said.

Jamey's eyes swept up to the distance. They looked one way and then the other. His eyes fluttered back to my face and clutched, like a bird on a wire in a prairie windstorm.

Time to help him go, I thought. Time to let him off the hook. "You go and have a good time and I'll see you later. It's not like this is the end or anything."

"How could it be?" he said. "It can never be the end for me and you." He looked at me then, right into my eyes, into me. . . . *and i would like to get inside her head to know what makes her tick/taste the life in her veins where blood is running thick/but i can only touch her and feel her touching me/I'm glad she made the trip/I'm glad she crossed the sea . . .*

"I know what I have to do," he said, "to go where I want to go." For a moment he was my old Jamey, with eyes so clear and honest. Then, his eyes loosened their grip. He grinned his infectious grin. He even chuckled. "Remember, that couple weeks down in . . . Oregon it was, swapping songs, music, nobody cared. Remember that Saturday morning when we played that Uncles-at-Large gig in the park? with the trailer opened up all along the side and the sound coming together so good? Jesus, talk about winging it. Zeke was with us then. But this new sound guy isn't bad. In fact, he's pretty good." He shifted his weight to his good foot. He looked down at the sidewalk. Inside, he was squirming. I could tell because one thing for sure, I would always be able to read Jamey like a book.

"Hey," I said, "write me a letter sometime."

I smiled and he smiled. We both smiled at the memory.

Then I turned so he could turn. We both turned. We turned away from each other. We turned and went in opposite directions. But, like the lady who got turned into salt, I couldn't resist one last look. Neither could he. We waved across the space between us. This time, he turned first. He took a few slow steps, then he started walking faster. I watched his shoes, grey canvas on grey cement. I watched his legs and his lope, the swing of his bony-shouldered, jean-jacketed back, his new rhythm, a slight lurch in the beat that made his walk his own.

He's going to make it this time, I suddenly knew it. He's going to make it because sometime during the past few months he'd made a decision for the mask and for the hardness it took to wear that mask. That had always warred in Jamey. That had always held him back. It wouldn't anymore.

Watching him walk away, watching him get into his van, watching the van disappear, I felt myself shiver and grow cold. I felt myself shrinking. I felt myself disappearing from the earth. I'm nothing without him, I thought. My existence depends on him. Turn quickly, I said to myself. Your life depends on you turning quickly. Still, I couldn't move, not even to save myself. My feet seemed glued to the cement. Then Paquette, of all people, gave me some help. This is going to take one big Jesus wrench, I said to myself the way he'd say it. Do it. Now! Still, I couldn't. But then I did. I turned away from Jamey one last time.

And as I turned, I felt myself grow warm again. I felt myself grow. I felt myself take up some space on the earth's surface. Not a lot of space, maybe not even three-dimensional. Maybe only an outline. But at least an outline.

What'll I do now? I asked myself, being truly on my own for the first time in my life. I could cross the street. I could go up a flight of stairs. I could go into a room. No, I can't, I thought. Not right now. So I started walking and I kept walking right past the rooms-to-rent doorway. My head was down and I saw that I was walking an old sidewalk full of cracks. I remembered how, when I was a child, I stepped on cracks on purpose, defying everybody and everything. I thought of the hurt and grief and death I'd caused.

Then I looked up and saw the trees lining the street. They can't be the same ones as at home, I knew. But they looked the same. I remembered how the ones on Terrabain Street would come into new tender leaf in spring and how in summer the leaves would flutter and fly to Jamey's music bouncing out the windows of our rooming house. I heard Jamey's music, plain as plain, the way I'd heard it for all the days and nights of my life, filling the whole neighbourhood with life, with beautiful noise. Then the music in my head changed to the clear clean notes of "Walking After Midnight." I fit my stride to it and sang along with Patsy Cline.

CASING THE PROMISED LAND

Be a camera, I told myself. Click, click, click. You may never come this way again.

Walking down the highway between Vancouver and Hope, heading east. It was a fine morning for the coast, where the view is rarely clear. A haze in the air made it seem like I was breathing through damp gauze. The sky was blue, but the sky is never as blue there as on the prairies.

I was content inside. Or fairly so. I missed Jamey, that goes without saying, and in retrospect I can't believe I did what I did that Vancouver morning. I must've been in some weird mental state, like out of my mind. But I knew we'd be together again. Maybe I'd join him after I got myself sorted out, after I got my dead child into some sort of perspective that I could live with. Meanwhile, it was morning and I was twenty-one.

The traffic whizzed past. Whoosh. Whoosh. Zoom. Zoom. I hadn't begun to stick out my thumb. I was enjoying the walk and the morning and the fields either side the highway, the rows of green corn, the baby sunflowers with their faces still asleep and dreaming, their eyes still glued shut with sweet sticky nectar. I was enjoying the mountains rising up to the north and the fields stretching into the distant south. I was enjoying the fences and the signs along the road, the cows and horses grazing, the big barn yellow as the sun.

That's when this vehicle pulled over onto the shoulder and sat there, waiting quietly for me.

Wouldn't you know, I thought, just when you don't need a ride, just when you don't care. Let there be a storm, let you be dragging your ass all up and down a lonely road at the end of the day, no one stops then. Not one soul.

Then I saw it was a van, and I thought, *Jamey*, and I started running and stumbling along the edge of the highway, my heart so large and in my mouth, beating there. But almost right away I knew it couldn't be him. I was on a road going east and he was on one going south. Unless he had changed his mind . . . When I got closer, though, something else twigged, and when I got closer yet I could see that the van looked familiar and when I got closer still, I knew who it was.

"Hey," Zeke said to my peeking-in-the-door face.

"This is too much of a coincidence," I said, throwing in my backpack, climbing in after it to the empty passenger seat. "This can't be happening in real life."

"In real life you can have coincidence," Zeke said, checking his rearview mirror and gearing up.

"Real life," I said, settling back and watching the easy way Zeke manipulated us back into the traffic. "I wonder what that's like. It's as though I've always stood outside the door, not knowing how to get in."

"As a matter of fact," said Zeke, "I intended seeing you. I was talking with Diana."

Another coincidence? I wondered. Or did she phone him? I *had* told Diana my plan, phoned her and told her. She was the closest friend I had at the coast. Maybe I didn't want my time there to go entirely unnoticed. Maybe I wanted a witness to my existence. Maybe I didn't want to be invisible.

But would she have had a phone number? Where had Zeke been? "Where've you been?" I said. "We . . . Jamey looked all over for you."

"In the States. Seeing about a job. I'm going back, soon as I tie up loose ends."

"Maybe you'll come across Jamey. Gun Wylde's got it together

237

again. They got a whole tour booked. At least partly. Six weeks up and down the coast. Sunshine beaches."

"Maybe. Since we're in the same business. But I'll be heading for the east coast. Diana said you were going home," Zeke went on.

Home. Was I going home? I thought of Terrabain Street with its poplars and tall, narrow houses, our house, white with green trim. I saw myself going up the steps of the verandah, down the dark cool hallway and up the stairs. I saw my mother and the others. But there was a blank space where Jamey should be. Could home for me ever be anyplace that didn't include Jamey? Could I change the meaning of the word *home*? I didn't think so. "Where're you headed?" I asked, wrenching my thoughts away from that dangerous territory.

"Through the mountains," he said. "Then I'll take a run across the prairie. And then . . . ." For a moment he lifted both hands off the wheel causing me to gasp a little in all that traffic. "The world," he said, "is waiting. But first I have to stop in at Steinbach for a few days to say hello, to fill up on schnitzel and shoo fly pie. Then I'll be moving on."

"Jamey used to say Rita's Ukrainian cooking would be the end of him. He said he's going to stay away from that comfort food."

We drove awhile in silence. Through the passenger window, I watched the distance. South. South, I thought. Jamey is out there somewhere. And I saw his face, large as the sky. The skin had just been shaved and beneath a week's stubble it turned out so pink and clean looking, so smooth and new. The head was covered with wild curly hair. The eyes were the clearest blue, like the sky itself, beyond man's scheming but ready for whatever adventure might cross it. With its sweet smile it was a boyish face. I would always see him that way. He couldn't grow old, because then he wouldn't be Jamey.

The face in the sky turned into a body rocking back from its toes, bouncing around light, holding a guitar down low, aiming it, thrusting it toward an audience.

"That's Jamey," I said. "He's not happy unless he's up on that stage feeling the rush. I knew that. I always knew that. I wonder if he'll pluck the peaches?" I rambled on. I could see his bare arm, perfect like those Greek statues, his fingers strong from all those years of playing, reaching up to the perfect peach, a peach so round, so rosy golden, its fuzz hairs raised, magnified and quivering in the sun's rays coming through the leaves. It was hanging from the tree branch, just waiting for his hand.

The traffic was heavy, which made me realize we were in rush hour. Everybody who lived in Vancouver seemed to have jobs in Langley or Mission or Abbotsford. And everyone who lived in those towns seemed to work in Vancouver. The whole world was moving, shifting and scurrying like an anthill. But it didn't bother Zeke. "At a time like this," he said, leaning back relaxed into his seat, "best thing, settle into the flow."

So I leaned back too and watched the southern sky. I saw Jamey with his first guitar, the first time I ever heard him play, wearing his rubber boots, with his baseball cap turned backwards on his head, me, sitting on a wooden chair beside him. I was looking at him. He was looking at his guitar. Why did I think he was looking at me?

"Real couples," I said, talking to myself out loud, "choose for each other, knowing that when they do, they're also making a choice for themselves. But it got so choosing for Jamey was choosing against myself. I thought we were the same, but we weren't," I prattled on, trying to work it out in my own mind. "Maybe it was my fault for thinking that."

"Why does it have to be anybody's fault," said Zeke, putting on the Gun Wylde CD. The first cut was that impudent *backyard* one ... *I've trained it/not to bite back hard/i can chain it/out in the backyard ... you don't have to be my friend/you don't have to stick to the end/oh no no no ... won't you play/come out today ...* , which always made me laugh out loud, the way he sang it with such sass and brass. I could hardly sit still in my seat.

"Lord, can't he sing!" I said. "Like, oh my God, he can deliver the goods. He makes people smile. He makes people cry. What a crazy guy. His voice can be so wild. His voice can be so sweet and gentle. One thing for sure, nobody can sing like Jamey. He always sounds like he really means it."

Forgetting about Zeke beside me, so taken up with Jamey's voice and music, I sang along with the CD. I sang along with my own voice on the backup vocals and on the duet we did. . . . *and I want to know will we ever feel the same/it has been such a long long time/i want to know do we need to feel the pain/of knowing what is yours and what is mine . . .* I sang along with Jamey on his solos. I hadn't listened to that CD since before the accident. My voice had changed. It wasn't whispery and tentative any more. It came out loud and clear. When did that happen? I wondered. When did that happen?

Singing those songs I thought how it was all written there in Jamey's music.

Like a prophecy. Our story. Even before we left Terrabain Street . . . *and holly she don't live there any more/she would if she could but she can't/because there comes a time/when the young make up their mind/to trade old custom for a chance . . .* Is the end of a story always written in the beginning? I wondered. The first time ever I saw Jamey, swinging on the gate, licking his ice cream up with his tongue, was I saying hello or goodbye?

"That sounds good," Zeke's voice broke into my song and thought.

I stopped singing immediately. Jamey's voice went on.

The CD clicked off, but Jamey's voice continued in my head . . . *cowgirl broke her guitar/cowgirl lost her voice/she still has a lariat/but she is desperate for a choice//thank god for the cowgirl/she makes the room go round/keep the doggies in time/keeps the music sound . . .* We did a good harmony on that one.

"We sang a lot together this past month," I said to Zeke. "The audience liked it. Jamey and me always did sing good together."

"You sing good by yourself," Zeke reached out his long arm and ejected the disk. "Have you ever considered singing?" he went on. "I mean as a career. On your own."

I looked at him quickly. Was he making fun of me? I noticed his ear. His talented ear, already becoming known in the music industry. Curled at the edge from where it had been pressed against the wall of his mother. Listening. To what? To his mother's veins and arteries pumping blood. To her close heartbeat, her ticking out the time of his whole universe. And I suddenly understood Zeke and why he was different and why to some people he might seem strange. He received his life message from a different place than most people did. It was like they say some animals can hear a whole register of sound that isn't available to humans. Zeke always had one ear pressed to another space, a more profound space than of this earth. While Jamey had come into this world a hoppin' and a boppin', Zeke came in with his head throbbing with the sound of those deep layers that his subconscious could never forget. And I understood why Zeke was multilayered and marbled with darkness and always would be. Do you want to get involved with a man with a bent for darkness? I asked myself.

"No," I said, turning my head, looking out the windshield.

"Maybe you should," Zeke said.

"You know how I am about performance," I said, ". . . the spotlight. I can't do it."

"That's because you're thinking of yourself instead of the music," he said. "Once you grow up and stop thinking so much about yourself, you'll be able to do it."

I turned my head sharply toward him.

"You have everything you need to take the lead on stage," he said. "To be able to get up on that stage and hold a room. It's not easy but I think you can do it. You have the voice, but you also have, or could have, the presence."

"Whaddaya mean presence. Like a strand of limp spaghetti has presence?"

"You hide behind disparaging yourself," he said. "But once you have the courage to think you're great, you will be. You have a great talent and once you decide to stop treating it like dirt, once you respect your own talent, you'll be fine."

"Whoeee," I said. "You sound tough."

"I can be," he said.

"How come . . . Why didn't you say these things to me before?" I said.

"I was waiting for you to grow up." He turned and flashed me the black lightning of those scary eyes. "Do you think you've grown up yet?" He turned his face back to the highway. "You walk out onto that stage, beautiful and self-contained, and you open your voice and a great sound comes out. That's your style. You'll have to work on it.

You'll have to work on your guitar. But you can do it." His voice when he said all this was low and reassuring, like that radio announcer in the night. It didn't seem like he was trying to talk me into something, but he was.

Be careful, I said to myself. Remember the women who got burnt when they flew too close to this man, like moths to a flame.

It was so totally out of *Phantom* and *Music of the Night*.

"Music is dangerous," I said.

"It's not the music. It's the people."

"It's not a good way to live."

"It can be. It depends. You have to protect yourself."

"I'm not a rocker." But, then, maybe I didn't want to discourage Zeke too much, because I found myself saying, "I like to rock it up sometimes, I mean, I *can* do it, but it's not my favourite . . ." And so, we headed into the rising sun, me going on and on like that, blabbering and qualifying all over the place and Zeke steadily driving, keeping his eyes on the road ahead of us.

Zeke stayed at Terrabain Street for two weeks that time he gave me a lift on a sunny morning that seems to have happened to other people in another lifetime. "I could take a detour north," he said, face pointed east toward the mountains, "over the Yellowhead, before heading southeast through Saskatchewan." And then when our tires scrunched to a stop in front of the house I remembered so well in my dreams, the long verandah and top windows silent with all their secrets, I asked him if he wanted to stop awhile, "I guess I could," he said. It wasn't until later I realized that he would have detoured to the moon and stayed there forever for me if I'd asked. It wasn't until later I realized that I was one of the loose ends he came back to tie up.

During those two weeks, I saw yet another Zeke and was amazed. He got along with everybody. He talked to Popi about his epic, shot the shit with Paquette, flirted with Rita, agreed with everything Tree said, while I wrote songs. I bought myself a guitar with my holiday pay from Woolco. Strange to relate I had never owned my own guitar but always used Jamey's, which he had several of off and on, in and out of pawn shops in the early days. In fact, over at Rita and Popi's there was an old one he'd left behind, but Zeke said I needed my own and helped me pick one out. It didn't cost a lot of money but it had a good tone. I still have it, my kids play it now.

I wrote songs, mostly about Jamey, using all those balled up napkins and notes that I'd accumulated along the way, that I'd kept in the zippered lining pocket of my trusty backpack. To the sounds of radio and television in the other apartments, with the curtains floating in voices from the verandah below, Tree's and Rita's and Zeke's joining them, I wrote the story of Jamey and me in song, maybe knowing that if I didn't write it then, it would remain forever unwritten, something deep in me knowing that I was moving on.

Maybe, too, that's why I wrote about Terrabain Street, home songs, which I never thought I'd do. Maybe I had to write about Tree, for while we reconciled after a fashion, we never did understand each other. She never did acknowledge my music, never altered her opinion that I looked stupid and sang stupid. When I tried to tell her how I felt about things, she thought I was attacking her and went all defensive—you just try and be a mother to a wild bad girl, see how you like it. She never talked about how she felt about things. It's not that she doesn't have feelings, I'd tell myself, she just can't express them, or as Zeke would say, articulate. Is that why I felt compelled to write songs, to try and articulate some of the things my mother couldn't?

Sitting up late, late into the evening, on the couch by that same window where a light breeze used to waft Jamey's songs out into the street, I wrote about the hitchhiking old woman and the Lieskes, not directly, but about not wanting to grow old alone and not wanting a loveless marriage. . . . *looking west this evening from my mansion/i ask what the hell was I thinking of/you screaming loud behind me something about pain/what more do you want besides parties and cars/we made the grade/we won the game . . .*

I wrote about snatching up the note I wrote to Jamey out of the wet coffee grounds where I'd tossed it and stuffing it into my backpack with all the other notes . . . *backpack filled with grief like stones/carry it with me wherever i go . . .* , before the songwriter in me even then subconsciously knowing that everything is grist for the mill.

I wrote the end to *comfort me true*, adding a verse to Jamey's love song . . . *so much to tell/so much to live/one day we'll be old/so much to give* . . . with the idea that I'd sing it to him when I saw him, but I never did.

Because at the end of the two weeks when Zeke said it was time for him to leave and asked me whether or not I was going with him, I said yes. I could go on about what happened next, which was plenty, but Zeke and I are another story. As for this one, I left Terrabain Street forever, although I didn't realize it at the time. I thought I'd be back so I didn't take the time to look, really look, at everything and everybody. The only picture I have in my mind of leaving is of me waving from the van window and the people of Terrabain Street standing on the sidewalk in a little huddle growing smaller and smaller until the van turned a corner and then they disappeared.

EPILOGUE

It flew sky high, they said, like a meteorite, before it landed and became a charred ruin. I should have been there, I should have been with Jamey when the car crashed into a cement barrier.

That was my first thought, even before opening my eyes.

. . . *she never saw it coming/he did not feel a thing . . . she pushed on to sing her song/into the west coast sun/going for a deep sea dive/she was going to have some fun* . . . was my second thought, words Jamey wrote even before we left Terrabain Street.

Across the hall, the Popilowskis' radio was tuned to country rock. If I kept my eyes closed, I could believe that any minute now Tree would shout at me to get up or Beth would come over and want to go to the malls or Jamey would saunter in with his guitar on his back. I could believe that my mother was clanking things around in the kitchen and then sink cozily back into sleep. I could believe that time had stopped back there twenty years away and that I'd never left. But I had left. I must open my eyes and face it.

9:46. The red numbers glowed. The last ones I saw were 2:58. That was when my eyes closed on the last note of the box of notes I found in the dustballs under Tree's bed. How she would have been horrified that anyone would find so much as a speck of dust in her house at any time and especially after her death. But dust has a way of gathering, and the apartment had been vacant for almost a year.

"Throw everything out," I said on the phone to Rita. "Take what you want and garbage the rest."

There was a long silence. "I'd rather not," she said. "There's a buncha boxes under the bed."

"Okay," I said. "Tell the landlord to keep his shirt on. I'll keep paying the rent until I can make it up to Canada."

I didn't make it for Tree's funeral. The night she was taken to the hospital I was on a stage in Berlin, unaware of what was happening in the little world of Terrabain Street. The day of the funeral I was in Stockholm.

I might never have made it, in spite of Rita's phone calls, if my agent hadn't got me a gig at the Edmonton Folk Festival. She kept pestering me and I kept thinking about it until I decided that I couldn't ignore such coincidence. I gathered my resolve and told her to buy me a plane ticket.

The red six had turned into a nine. Make a move, I commanded myself. You can't stay forever curled in a fetal position on your mother's bed with your jeans pulled up tight in your crotch and your mouth tasting like a sewer. You'll feel better if you stand up, if you go into the bathroom and shower. You must get yourself to the airport. At the other end of the flight, Zeke will be waiting for you, Zeke and the girls. He'll be wanting to hear how the gig went, even though you told him on the phone it went fine. But he'll want to hear all the details. He'll want to know if the sound man was any good.

Straightening my legs and turning onto my back, I felt the stretch and pull of scar tissue down my leg. Shit, I thought. Don't tell me it's going to be one of those days. But, of course, it had to be.

I looked at the paper scattered on the bed beside me. I looked at the shadows on the wall. I stared at the patch of sunny light beneath the half-pulled shade. I should have phoned. I should have phoned at least once from the coast. I'd go crazy if either of my girls took off and I didn't hear from them for three years. She might have been happy about the baby—it had never occurred to me before. She was happy about the other two. She liked babies. She might have been able to put the baby above her hatred of me being a bad girl and the scandal of having an unmarried mother for a daughter.

Such thoughts had me totally agitated. I had to pull myself together. "It is morning." Saying it out loud made it seem more definite. "It must be Sunday. I stayed a day to sort out Tree's things. The gig was Friday."

They all came to hear me sing. It was a fine August night, the grass covered with people of all ages, lots of families with children. Rita and Popi were right down in front, with Paquette and Beth and Gord and two of their older kids. They'd settled themselves down with blankets and folding chairs and a cooler full of beer and snacks.

After the gig we went to the bar. Knowing that red wine would make them think I'd gone hoity toity, I ordered beer. I looked around the table at the circle of faces and realized they were not the ones I visualized when Tree phoned or visited and gave me the lowdown on what everyone was doing. Those were as they used to be, constant as the photographs Tree kept in shoe boxes on the closet shelf. And as long as I didn't go home, they'd stay that way forever.

As long as I didn't go home, I could believe that Jamey was still alive someplace in the world, it was just that I hadn't seen him for a while. After all, I hadn't seen him for a long time before he died, either. And adding to the unreal element was the fact that I didn't hear about the accident right away. That time I was in England. I didn't see the article in the papers, a couple of paragraphs inside the entertainment sections about the lead singer and guitar player of Gun Wylde. I might not have heard about it until music industry gossip got to me, except Zeke had saved the write-up. "Do you want to talk about it?" he said, watching my face closely as I read. "No," I said, and we never have. I've never been able to share Jamey. I've never been able to say the words that would make his death a reality. I've never been able to give up the pain because it is all I have left of him.

The people of Terrabain Street had faced eight years ago what I hadn't yet faced. "There was nothing left," Beth told me. "No body to claim. It was like his life never happened. We didn't have a memorial, only a mass said. Mom couldn't face a memorial." She flicked the ash off her cigarette. Her mouth twisted in a way I remembered, as if she was trying to hold back tears.

We told stories like at a wake. "I'll never forget," said Rita, "the night Jamey's belly button thing came off." It was a story we'd all heard before, but we wanted again the familiar words.

"I'll never forget how Jamey used to like to play Batman," Beth said.

"He really believed he could fly," someone said. Maybe it was me.

"He had black swim trunks," Rita said, "and a towel cape."

"He made a mask out of cardboard," Beth said. "It had slits for eyes and two points at the top corners and elastic bands to hold it on his head."

I wondered if he threw that bundle out before he left. Or did he leave it for Rita to find? If so, my bet is she still has it. She could never bring herself to throw out anything of Jamey. We were the same that way.

Like the box of notes under Tree's bed. Which I found when I got back from having supper over at Rita and Popi's on the Saturday. Beth and Gord were there, too. I wouldn't be seeing them again so I wanted it to last. We all did. It was pretty late when we finally said our goodbyes and I crossed the hall. I was tired, having spent the day going through closets and drawers. But I wanted to get the job done and over with and all that was left were the boxes Rita had mentioned on the phone. "Boots," "clothing," "xmas decorations," each box was labelled with a black marker. Kneeling on the worn linoleum, I said a silent prayer, thanking God for Tree's orderly housekeeping. With any luck, I'd be able to throw everything out without even opening a box. Flattening myself further to reach the second row, I pulled out "games," "wallpaper ends," "wrapping paper." On my stomach, I wiggled myself through the dust to reach the third tier. I hooked a box of old curtains and a brown cardboard box with Aylmer Soup in red letters on the side but nothing marked on top. I pulled up the flaps. At first I didn't recognize anything—the handwriting, a round childish script, the sheets and scraps of paper filled with words, the words themselves. I was like a person with transient amnesia who's blanked out a particular incident.

Full of wonder, I dug in my hand and turned over the contents, like you do compost. There were sheets of scribbled notes for possible songs; there were all the attempts and aborted attempts; there were paper napkins, match folders, brown envelopes, menus, programs of events, posters of gigs. I totally could not believe my eyes. I had totally forgotten all those bits and pieces of Jamey I'd gathered over the years before we left Terrabain Street then, after, collected in the zippered pocket of my backpack.

I glanced at some pages, read a few lines here and there. At the bottom of the box was the scrap of paper about picking up toothpicks, the balled up and flattened napkin from the pancake house in Golden. There was a page torn from a notepad covered with almost indiscernible scratches about peaches and sunshine beaches. Jamey abandoned that one, but there were notes for some of the ones that became hits, too, *West Coast Sun* and *comfort me true*. There were notes for the songs I wrote before leaving, some I still sang. Then it all came back, so strong I could taste it—the summer Zeke and I came through, sitting on the couch writing songs from those notes and match covers and napkins, making more notes of my own and adding them to the box, my notes and Jamey's all scrambled together like the two of us had been all our lives. But I still couldn't remember piling it all into a box and shoving it deep beneath the bed before leaving with Zeke. But I must have. Who else would have? I must have thought I'd be back for it.

Scarcely pausing in my reading, I lifted the box up onto the bed, swung myself onto the bedspread, wadded two pillows behind my neck and settled into the sag of the mattress. And as I read those notes, I relived my whole young life.

Anything is possible in the night, but in the clear sunny light of morning, lying straight on my back on my mother's bed, I couldn't believe I was ever that brash bratty girl who left home with only her hasty heart to go out into the wide world to seek her fortune.

With a movement so quick, I made myself dizzy, I swung myself into a sitting position on the edge of the bed where Tree used to sit to put on her stockings.

I should have come to visit her, I thought, even if the very thought of it caused my stomach to ache. I should have invited her to my house more often. But she didn't feel comfortable there, with a tablecloth and flowers, and people sitting around the table talking about ideas. What's that stupid talk, she once said to me? She didn't understand why we didn't smoke in the house. She could not believe that second-hand smoke was worse for children than first-hand. She didn't understand our food. What's that? she said when I served sushi. You expect me to eat raw fish? She was suspicious of prosciutto, even though I told her it was Italian ham. "I never heard of that," was her reply.

She didn't like the dishwasher. Her big job when she visited was washing the dishes by hand, endlessly. It drove me nuts the way she'd take her stand at the kitchen sink and slowly and methodically wash and rinse and dry each item. It was like she was working Giuseppe's assembly line. When I complained to Zeke, he said, "Give her something else to do, get her to make some homemade pasta and some of that good sauce."

"I don't want girls with a weight problem like I had," I said. "And all that rich food isn't good for your cholesterol."

Why was I so rigid? It was only for a week or two a year. Why was I so sure we'd all go to hell if we had a little Alfredo sauce made with forty per cent cream?

Sitting there on my mother's bedspread, I was starting to feel sick, as if I'd just ingested the cream. All you have to do is get through another few hours, I told myself. My flight was booked for three-thirty. Next week, the bed and mattress would go to the dump. Rita said she could use the dresser and night table. She had already sold the kitchen and living room furniture. The only things left for me to deal with were the boxes under the bed and the few items Tree had gathered over the years, trifles, which is all she ever had in her life. Then I would never come home again

But why did I still refer to Terrabain Street as home? Home was Nashville where I lived with my husband and children. Home was not those walls or Tree's voice in the empty space, both closing in on me like a claustrophobic womb:

". . . whaddaya mean comin in this time a night? where ya bin? you bin in the back seata some car, I can tell, whatcha wanta go and ruin your life for? for a boy who'll never give y' nothin but misery, plain an' simple, misery . . ."

. . . or singing in the kitchen as she mixed up muffin batter after mass or stirred tomato sauce for supper on Sunday. Or mixed with Rita's, as with their beers and smokes they gossiped and told jokes in the porch swing on a summer evening.

The voices were gone. I must get my mind around it, the idea of an abandoned site, a window, grimy from rain and prairie dust. My eyes travelled to the dresser, oak with hinged mirror, a neighbour's discard that Tree appropriated from the back alley. On its top was a runner of wrinkled linen with an edging crocheted by Tree. There was a purple glass bottle of eau de cologne, yellow plastic bottle of hand and body lotion, mauve plastic cup containing a swirl of Q-tips. There was a green plastic vase filled with permanently attached pink and blue plastic flowers and for a moment I couldn't breathe.

I was back to another hot August, an afternoon when those same plastic flowers were a witness to Jamey and me. And then everything in the room spoke of Jamey—the ceiling, the walls, the pictures on the walls, the bed on which I sat, especially the bed. I could feel his presence, I could smell his male sweat smell, slightly salty like the fresh breeze coming in across the ocean.

Control your thoughts, I told myself. I let out my held breath. I took a deep breath in. Think things through, I told myself.

I shouldn't have come. I should've stayed the hell away. For starters, by bringing Jamey back into my life, I was being disloyal to Zeke.

But, then, hadn't I always been? There were the songs I wrote. There were the songs I sang . . . *I'm trying/I'm flying/I can't stand losing you/I'm crying/I'm lying/but I can't stand losing you . . . where is your hand/as I walk through this no man's land/I can't stand losing you/ where is your golden halo/I can't see a thing/I can't stand losing you . . .*

"Comfort Me True" became my signature song. People forgot that Jamey had actually written it. And since I had added a few verses on my own . . . *we'll buy a goat/share a library card/grow some green grass/ in our own backyard* . . . it became a kind of co-written song, which, in a way, our early lives were, co-written and a song.

Jamey's face, like that vision of it in the southern sky, was the backdrop to the stage on which I'd lived my life. After his death, night after night I woke myself up with the thought: I could've saved him. I should have been there for him when he needed someone.

I was addicted to the "what if " game. What if I had not told him about the band getting back together? What if "Jamey is the man who is loved by Lilah" had been enough? And the time we said goodbye on a street corner in Vancouver, when his eyes clutched at my face, what if I had gone with him? What if I hadn't sent him out there alone when he didn't really know where he was going? What if I'd insisted he read my note? I could answer that one—he wouldn't have read it even then, because he didn't want to be stopped. And what if our child had been born? I've answered that, too. He would have felt bad about it, but he wouldn't have, couldn't have, stayed with us.

And then there was the "if" game. If I'd gone with him, I could have saved him from that crazy life, that crazy spinning California music industry life, where every second player is a casualty. If I'd been with him, I wouldn't have let him drive that car when he was stoned. If I'd been driving, the accident wouldn't have happened.

When I got out of the shower, I could smell bacon. I went across the hall where Popi had just made a pot of strong coffee. Paquette was drinking beer. Rita, in a loose wrapper reminiscent of what the Corset Lady used to wear, cigarette clamped between her lips, was flipping eggs. She put a plate in front of me—bacon, eggs, hash browns.

Sitting at the kitchen table where we always used to sit, I noticed that Rita was wearing floppy old slippers. She showed me the sensible nurse's shoes she wore to work now, still at Rosa's. "Got them on sale at the Army & Navy," she said. "Twelve ninety five."

"Jeez," I said. "No kidding." And I felt a little sad for those clickety click heels of my memory. But Rita would be all right. Although Beth and Gord had moved away from Terrabain Street to a new house in the suburbs, she still saw a lot of them. And her grandchildren visited often. "Don't know what I'd do without them," she said. I looked into her brown eyes that would never give up their sorrow. As Tree often intoned, "Something like that, you take it with you to the grave." Life has taught me that my mother was right. I couldn't even imagine Rita's reaction when she heard the news about Jamey. She was just about the grandmother of my child, I thought. But I'd never tell her that. I wouldn't want to cause her that pain. There were lots of things I'd never tell her, that her last St. Christopher medal ended up around the neck of some floozy groupie at one of those post-gig parties, that a fellow musician told me she saw Jamey sitting on a Los Angeles toilet with a needle in his arm. I'm not going to remember those things, either. I'm going to remember the way we held hands and ran through the sun on the California beach, the way we sang so good together.

It was Popi I was worried about. He looked like he lived on air, nothing but knobby bone and swollen purple veins. It was as if the flesh had been siphoned from beneath his skin. His eyes were rheumy and anxious, as though he'd been staring too long at his computer screen, into his lifelong epic, and seeing things there that frightened him. Although he was twenty years younger, he looked older than Paquette.

They had no problem talking about Jamey. It was like he was still part of the family. "Jamey did okay, when you stop to think about it," Popi said, as if in his mind he was constantly mulling over his former opinion on the subject. "And he mighta made it further. He was only thirty."

With the young people gone, the house on Terrabain Street had changed, but some things would never change. Popi was still writing his epic. Paquette still pined for Marie. He told me how she didn't come around much any more. "She got a big Jesus house in the west end, her kids go to them special schools, her husband's a big shot in the bank now. She's at the university and drivin' the kids to every damn thing. She's busy, that one."

"Don't give her the right to break a person's heart," Rita said, blowing out her smoke and plunking herself into a chair.

"Hearts are meant to be broken," he said, staring into his beer the way I always remembered him doing, as if the answers to everything in life were to be found floating in the amber foam. "You don't want your heart to be dented and bashed, put it in the garage and don't ever drive it."

Sitting at that table where we always used to sit, I felt myself once more to be Lilah Cellini. It was like getting back into my own skin after a long time out of it. Still, I didn't want to stay. Being disconnected was what my life was all about. Being disconnected gave me my music.

Quickly, I looked at my watch. There'd be enough time if I hurried, if I didn't sort and sentimentalize. "Do you have some of them green garbage bags," I said to Rita.

She jumped right up and went to a cupboard. "Here, take more," she said, pushing another handful of green plastic at me. She was relieved. She thought I wouldn't get the job done.

Back at Tree's, I stuffed everything that wouldn't burn into those bags. I cleared the closet of clothes. I stripped the bed of its bedding. I hesitated at the green vase and the plastic flowers, the linen runner on top of the dresser. Each loop of Tree's crocheted edging took on monumental proportions. Keeping my eyes wide, daring the tears, with my left hand I held the green bag open, with my right arm I made a clean sweep.

I hauled bags and boxes down the stairs and out back. The bags went to the garbage stand in the lane, the boxes to the trash burning barrel. I started a fire with old newspapers. It really got going when I threw in the prepasted wallpaper ends. Then in went the gift wrap and games. I held in my two hands the two decks of cards that Tree used when she sat at the kitchen table playing endless solitaire. I shook my head to clear it of the picture and tossed them in, along with boxes of recipes clipped from newspapers and magazines.

On a roll now, adrenaline pumping, I ran back upstairs. All that was left were the shoe boxes containing photos and the piles of paper on the bed, those notes that had been waiting for me all those years, waiting for me to find them. Those notes could still yield material for songs about young love, first love, lost love. I'd get some heavy twine from Rita for easier carrying on the plane.

I started stuffing the notes back in the box, catching words and phrases as I went. . . . *maybe i should have heeded him/maybe he was right/but whatever he said I'm alive, he's dead/my morning was his night* . . . chilling words that Jamey wrote about Popi but they spoke to me now like a message from the grave.

"You gotta throw out your own stuff." Now it was the Corset Lady's words coming back on me, her words of all those years ago when Jamey had to get rid of those soft shell turtles. I'd been tough enough for the job back then. Just like I'd been tough enough to say goodbye on a street corner.

I don't have anything more to say about young lost love, I thought, staring into that sea of notes. I've said everything I want to say on the subject. I have to get on to new material. Steeling myself, but quick so I wouldn't change my mind, I crammed the remaining pages and scraps into the box. I picked up the box and raced downstairs.

By this time, the flames were leaping out of the top of the barrel. I was panting from my manic activity and the effort of keeping my sobs in my chest. I didn't let myself think. I gave one mighty toss. Of course, the minute I did it I was sorry, but it was already too late. I made myself look into the barrel until all that was left was embers.

What if I had stayed with Jamey? The question glowed in the fiery remains. Then I wouldn't be with Zeke. Then our daughters would not have been born. I'm going to live in the present with Zeke and our girls, I vowed to myself. I'm going to write new material. I have a different home. I'm a different person. The naive girl and boy who scribbled those notes no longer exist. They were characters in a story, two kids who had such wild hearts and were so crazy in love and left their paradise never to return. But I have other stories to tell, other boxes of notes, and I can't tell them until I let this one go.

I looked at my watch. Time to go. Time to let go. Time to leave it all behind. The only thing I couldn't leave behind was my heart. I'd have to take it with me wherever I went for the rest of my life.

"I thought happiness was a right," I said in the bar the other night when we were reminiscing about the old days. "When I was young that's what I thought."

"That's what everyone thinks when they're young," said Paquette.

I gritted my teeth, stiffened my back, marched into the house and up the stairs. I brushed my teeth, put on makeup, put the last few items into my bag. I'd take the boxes of photos across the hall to Rita. From there I'd phone a taxi. I'd say my goodbyes.

"You're always welcome," I'd say. "Come any time."

But I knew that they never would.

ACKNOWLEDGEMENTS

My sincere thanks go to many people for this book. The musicians: Don and Buzz who first let me sit in, Jeff Kushner and manunkind for later letting me sit in, Doug Frey for information about the music industry, Doug, Chris and Brendan for surrounding me with music always. And the editors: Willie Fitzpatrick and Dixie Baum whose discerning comments were invaluable, Barbara Scott whose perceptive suggestions enhanced the work, and Lee Shedden whose careful reading and insight insured accuracy and coherency. My gratitude to Candas Jane Dorsey who steered me in the right direction. I would also like to thank Ruth Linka and the people at Brindle & Glass who saw me through to the end.

For the title I'm indebted to Bronwen Wallace's wonderful book, *Keep That Candle Burning Bright*, and for lyrics to Topher Gun Wylde.

An early version of "Soft Shell" appeared in *Wee Giant*. "I Never Promised You" was first heard on CBC Anthology, Edmonton, as "The Rose Garden."

CECELIA FREY has written six books of fiction including *The Prisoner of Cage Farm* and *A Fine Mischief*. Her short stories and poetry have been published in dozens of literary journals and anthologies as well as being broadcast on CBC Radio and performed on the Women's Television Network. She has worked as an editor, teacher and freelance writer, is a three-time recipient of the Writer's Guild of Alberta Short Fiction Award, and has also won awards for playwriting.